A titanic exoskeleton rises from the waves, interlocking armor plates a sleek purple.

It unfolds its long arms, each sheathed in an ivory gauntlet, and stands atop a pair of legs. It's humanoid, bilaterally symmetrical. A fission halo encircles its faceless head, spitting plasma sparks in all directions. A pair of silver handles jut from its rib cage like knives buried up to the hilt. It has no eyes, only a smooth purple dome, reflecting all around it.

This titanic disaster could have landed anywhere else on Earth. There was an entire planet of perfectly apocalyptic locations, and a huge pantheon of faiths to satisfy with a melodramatic entrance. But no, it had to show up at the exact spot where Gus was trying to get comfy for his own doom.

Juliette the Vanguard, destroyer of six colonies and two worlds.

Soon three—counting Earth.

Praise for Alex White

"A clever fusion of magic and sci-fi makes this book a total blast. I was hooked from page one."

—V. E. Schwab, *New York Times* bestselling author, on *A Big Ship at the Edge of the Universe*

"Perfectly paced, full of intense, inventive action and refreshingly honest characters. It's the seamless hybrid of fantasy and sci-fi that you didn't know you always needed. Do you miss *Firefly*? Do you want it back? Well, sorry, not gonna happen. But this book is damn close."

—Nicholas Eames, author of *Kings of the Wyld*, on *A Big Ship at the Edge of the Universe*

"Racing! Treasure and smuggling! *A Big Ship at the Edge of the Universe* is a gripping quest for justice among salvage and magic—I really loved it." —Mur Lafferty, author of *Six Wakes*

"To call this book fast-paced or action-packed is underselling it. Buckle up, readers: this is a ride you won't want to get off until the end."

—*B&N Sci-Fi & Fantasy Blog* on *A Big Ship at the Edge of the Universe*

"White's assured debut is an entertaining throwback with some fun worldbuilding and two great lead characters."

—*Publishers Weekly* on *A Big Ship at the Edge of the Universe*

"*A Big Ship at the Edge of the Universe* is a rollicking fun ride. I enjoyed it a lot, and I'm looking forward to the sequel." —*Locus*

"This ambitious start...combines magic and space opera to create a fast-paced adventure with charismatic characters and formidable enemies in a realized universe of greed and power."

—*Booklist* (starred review) on *A Big Ship at the Edge of the Universe*

"Fast, compelling, epic in scope, with stakes that just keep getting higher and tension that mounts and mounts to the breaking-point, *A Bad Deal for the Whole Galaxy* is excellently paced, with engaging characters and worldbuilding that crams as much fun cool shit in as seems remotely possible. It's a deeply enjoyable ride. I recommend it and its predecessor heartily." —*Locus*

"White combines elements of magic and traditional space opera to create an intricate world laced with fascinating characters, expansive spaceships, and compelling settings."

—*Booklist* on *A Bad Deal for the Whole Galaxy*

"[Fans of the TV show *Firefly*] will find a lot to love in this fast, funny, and wickedly smart series."

—*B&N Sci-Fi & Fantasy Blog* on *A Bad Deal for the Whole Galaxy*

"Unputdownable.... White's tale of justice and vengeance sends the series out on a high note with electrifying action sequences, depth, and darkness. This thrilling finale will have readers on the edges of their seats."

—*Publishers Weekly* (starred review) on *The Worst of All Possible Worlds*

"One of the best sci-fi trilogies released in the last several years."

—*BookPage* on *The Worst of All Possible Worlds*

By Alex White

The Starmetal Symphony

August Kitko and the Mechas from Space

The Salvagers

A Big Ship at the Edge of the Universe

A Bad Deal for the Whole Galaxy

The Worst of All Possible Worlds

Every Mountain Made Low

Alien: The Cold Forge

Alien: Into Charybdis

Star Trek DS9: Revenant

The Starmetal Symphony, Movement One

ALEX WHITE

orbitbooks.net

Cover design by Lisa Marie Pompilio
Cover illustration by Ben Zweifel

Author photograph by Renee White

Orbit
Hachette Book Group
1290 Avenue of the Americas
New York, NY 10104
orbitbooks.net

First Edition: July 2022
Simultaneously published in Great Britain by Orbit

Orbit is an imprint of Hachette Book Group.
The Orbit name and logo are trademarks of Little, Brown Book Group Limited.

Library of Congress Cataloging-in-Publication Data
Names: White, Alex (Novelist), author.
Title: August Kitko and the mechas from space / Alex White.
Description: First edition. | New York, NY : Orbit, 2022. | Series: Starmetal symphony ; movement 1
Identifiers: LCCN 2021061175 | ISBN 9780316430579 (trade paperback) | ISBN 9780316430555 (ebook)
Subjects: LCGFT: Novels.
Classification: LCC PS3623.H5687 A94 2022 | DDC 813/.6—dc23/eng/20211216
LC record available at https://lccn.loc.gov/2021061175

ISBNs: 9780316430579 (trade paperback), 9780316430555 (ebook)

Printed in the United States of America

LSC-C

Printing 1, 2022

For Luno.

For Bea.

And for any other hearts that deserve a more loving world.

Part 1

Giant Steps

Chapter One

Our Final Hour

August Kitko doesn't want to see the end of the world—which should be any minute now.

He leans over the stone railing and gauges the distance to the jutting pediment of the cliff face below. A couple of sharp rocks poke up from beneath the choppy surf to say hi.

We're here for you, buddy, comfortable and quick.

Gus grimaces and waves back at them.

He stands at the very edge of Lord Elisa Yamazaki's estate, one of a few dozen lucky guests brought in for this momentous occasion. Behind Gus lies the famed Electric Orchard, full of algae-spliced fruit trees: cherry luxes and pearshines. They waver in the night like old diodes, dropping off in places when the breeze rustles them too much. Over the course of hours, their inner lights will fade, and they'll lie upon the grass, gray as a stone.

The taste is ultimately underwhelming. It's a glowing pear. It doesn't have to be good.

Gus was drawn to this place by the long stone wall with crystal lanterns, the cliffside overlook, and the patch of soft synth grass. This part of the estate has probably stood since the Middle Ages, though the lanterns are obviously new—concentrated vials of the spliced algae *Plantus glowname.*

Gus missed the taxonomy twice when the lord gave everyone the tour, and was too embarrassed to ask for a third repetition.

As final resting places go, this one won't be so bad. The estate has a commanding view from the eastern rise, so he gets the best sunset he's ever experienced. Monaco's slice of the Mediterranean glitters in the moonlight like no other gem. The city is a thousand icicles jutting up from craggy mountainsides, lining the hills all the way down to the artificial land extensions in the harbor. The Nouvelle Causeway stretches seaward, a big tube atop massive struts, its iconic boxy apartments encrusting its underside like ancient pixels. The Casino de Monte Carlo's searchlights are on full blast in La Condamine district by the harbor—because of course there's a type of person who wants to spend this once-in-a-lifetime night gambling. Gus wonders: Why is anyone hanging around to take their money?

SuperPort Hercule, stretching between Monaco's two artificial mountains, is a relic of another era, when single-terrain vehicles were more common. Rich people still hang on to their water-based yachts, and rows of white boats nestle into slips like suckling piglets. Beyond these exotic antiques, a long expanse of water lily landing pads remains dark—the unused starport. Towering craft loom in the evening, engines cold.

The last ship from Earth launched three years prior. No one else dares—not with the Veil across the galaxy.

Gus blinks at the waves. The fall is going to kill him either way, but for some reason, he'd rather hit the water than the rocks. It mostly comes down to a choice of who gets to eat him—the seagulls or the marine life.

And seagulls are assholes.

Gus needs to wrap things up; he doesn't want to be here when *they* arrive. He'd once been a bit more single-minded in his suicidal ideation, and he finds this last-minute attachment to survival annoying.

It seems unfair that life could get so fun right before the end. He'd forgotten the taste of good times, and a dram of happiness has made him too exhausted to complete his morbid task.

If only Gus can make himself climb onto the railing, he knows he can take the next step.

Other "bon" vivants cavort nearby, drinks in hand, some clumsily pawing all over each other. Gus straightens up and stares wistfully at the sea. He can't be seen moping like he's about to jump. They might try to stop him, and then they'd all waste their last few minutes of life trying to calm him down.

Or maybe they'd actually let him do it.

Then he'd spend his final second offended with them.

Perhaps instead, Gus could go to his rock star lover, apologize to them, and pull them in close for the literal kiss to end all kisses—except Ardent Violet is on the veranda, holding court for their adoring public. People and holograms no doubt sit rapt before them, listening to some captivating speech. Ardent isn't about to even talk to Gus, much less peel themself away from a scintillating evening of compliments and basking.

Not after Gus screwed everything up.

The drunken revelers flop down on the nearby grass to step up their make-out game, hands going for buttons and clasps. Another team of horny fools joins the fray, giggling and gasping. Maybe Gus's cold stare will shrivel their resolve.

They don't even slow down.

There must be somewhere Gus can find a blissful moment of peace. He thrusts his hands into his pockets and wanders back up the estate grounds toward the main house. The lonely path winds past botanical oddities and designer plants of all shapes and colors, vibrant like the coral reefs of old. Lord Yamazaki says she takes her inspiration from Dale Chihuly, but to Gus, she just seems like she's really into jellyfish.

La Maison Des Huit Étoiles rises out of the Electric Orchard like an enchanted castle, its eight glossy blue spires a stark contrast to the archaic walls surrounding the grounds. Atop each spire is a bright light, for the Yamazaki family members who . . . something. Again, Gus wasn't paying full attention during the tour of the place. He'd had his mind on other things, like being surrounded by the best musicians on Earth.

The bay breeze this evening is unbelievable, the kind of night best spent at an open window with a piano and a drink. The piano still exists, but the booze is all gone, guzzled by the revelers, the staff, and the talent. The staff can't be blamed; they've got their own partying to accomplish, and it's not like Gus is doing *his* job. Few people are—for any reason. Whole swathes of the world are going unwatched, on the verge of collapse, and it doesn't matter.

Gus Kitko, renowned jazz pianist, was flown here to play during the victory party, but they canceled that two days ago.

More accurately, his job was to play during the victory party after-party. His style doesn't exactly draw the millions required to headline, but he's a musician's musician. Some days, it's like his fans are all more famous than he is.

Gus has almost reached the sprawling manse when he detects Ardent's musical laughter. He doesn't want to look—he knows it'll stop his heart—but he glances out of pure masochism.

The rocker stands resplendent in a flowing robe, textiLEDs luxed up like a bird of paradise. Their hair is an anodized red this evening, cut short with an edge like a knife. They've painted their exquisite face in jewel tones, pale skin traced into captivating shapes. Electric-blue lips remain quirked in a smile—until Ardent claps eyes on Gus in return.

They don't rage or scowl. They simply note him with a neutral expression and move on. Ardent Violet lives in another world of packed arenas and coliseums, of paparazzi and nightly jaunts to the most exclusive clubs out there. Gus will never run in their circle again after Monaco—they're above him.

But there is no "after Monaco." Every last person dies here tonight. Even the beautiful, fabulous Ardent Violet.

Yep. Looking was a bad choice.

As it turns out, Gus won't have to feel bad for much longer. A pale streak bisects the sky—a superluminal brake burn and the crackle of lightning. A flaming comet falls from the heavens, and the SuperPort's harbor erupts into a geyser in the wake of a towering splashdown. All eyes travel to the site of the crash, and even the raw magnetism of Ardent Violet can't continue to hold their attention.

A titanic exoskeleton rises from the waves, interlocking armor plates a sleek purple. It unfolds its long arms, each sheathed in an ivory gauntlet, and stands atop a pair of legs. It's humanoid, bilaterally symmetrical. A fission halo encircles its faceless head, spitting plasma sparks in all directions. A pair of silver handles jut from its rib cage like knives buried up to the hilt. It has no eyes, only a smooth purple dome, reflecting all around it.

This titanic disaster could have landed anywhere else on Earth. There was an entire planet of perfectly apocalyptic locations, and a huge pantheon of faiths to satisfy with a melodramatic entrance. But no, it had to show up at the exact spot where Gus was trying to get comfy for his own doom.

Juliette the Vanguard, destroyer of six colonies and two worlds.

Soon three—counting Earth.

Two days prior, Gus had hope—tangible hope for the first time in five years. The remnants of the Sol Joint Defense Force had just deployed the unfortunately named *Dictum*, the "solution to the Vanguard Doom." It was a big fancy battle cruiser that could drag travelers out of hyperspace, yanking them into its firing line. That seemed to Gus like a meaningless achievement, but there was a sudden surge of hope among the populace.

The United Worlds leadership were eager to tout their coming success. The plan was to intercept any Vanguards and sucker punch them with the most powerful particle cannons in existence. With defense figured out, the Sol system—last bastion of the human species—could finally go on the offensive.

Gus had dropped his toast when he checked the news that first morning: "Ghosts Massing, Vanguard Incoming, *Dictum* Will Destroy in Sol System."

The harbinger of humanity's end was on its way, and the superweapon was going to stop it—foregone conclusion. Nothing in the news articles indicated this was an "attempt," or that it could fail. Every content outlet talked about the *Dictum* like it had already vaporized all fifteen Vanguards. Anything less spelled the destruction of Earth.

Gus reacted to this news in much the same fashion he handled all his problems: He sat down at his piano and began to play. The ivories calmed his nerves like a gentle rain, and he wrestled with the mortality that everyone on Earth faced. Young or old, they were all in the same boat, tomorrows potentially truncated.

Then came the holocall: General Landry and a cadre of USO coordinators, looking to put on a star-studded concert to celebrate their forthcoming first Vanguard kill. They offered Gus immediate passage to Monaco and accommodations at Lord Yamazaki's, asking him to be ready for the big party.

Gus agreed, and when he terminated the call, a swish Brio XR idled in front of his Montreal walk-up. Its swept nanoblack form absorbed all light, coppery windows and lines of chrome the only reflective surfaces on it. A team of smiling assistants hurried Gus from his house, promising to send anything he needed to Monaco. They even gave him a carte with a few thousand unicreds to load into his account, in case he wanted to relax ahead of time.

It was a hell of a lot nicer than government work was supposed to be.

A stratospheric jaunt later, he was brunching on the deck of a yacht with musical luminaries from the top of the charts. He had one piano song that had been sampled and remixed into a hit, so he felt a mild kinship with these gods. They'd all been summoned by their governments to boost morale, and they were excited to meet August Kitko, "the guy behind that one sample."

Everyone talked about the various battle watch parties they'd be attending that night. People spoke to Gus like he'd already been invited to one. He would've been glad to clear his busy schedule of clipping his toenails in his bedroom and staring wistfully out the window.

No invites were forthcoming, however, and Gus was too shy to ask. He could only hope someone would take pity on him so he wouldn't spend the most stressful news broadcast of his life alone. The pundits figured the *Dictum*'s interdiction would come sometime in the next twenty hours, pegging the likelihood at eleven p.m.

Victory event details to follow.

To compensate for Gus's lack of friends, government handlers arranged activities and meetups. Every minute of the day leading up to the night was mind-blowing goodness. Champagne and croissants, wandering the casinos, staring into the seaside sunset from the little park at Point Hamilton.

Even though the greenway was just a couple of statues and a few bushes crammed between two luxury high-rise condos, the place had a peaceful air. Gus's hiking buddies, a pair of rockers from a town named Medicine Hat, said they wanted to call a friend to bring some wine. That friend turned out to be the multi-platinum-record-selling Ardent Violet, who showed up with a block party in tow. Food, liquor, and drugs followed, and Gus found himself ensnared by the wildest rave he'd ever attended in a public park.

When the throng became unbearable, Gus pushed out to the street for some fresh air. He wound down a few side alleys, trying to get a little space from Ardent's many admirers.

Instead, he ran into Ardent Violet themself.

They sported a forest-green pin-striped suit, its edges given careful folds like paper animals. A few fresh flowers bloomed on their wide-brimmed hat. The whole outfit looked like it cost a fortune, which was why Gus was surprised to find Ardent sitting on the old stone curb, flicking through the Ganglion UI on their bracelet.

Gus wasn't a fan, but he knew a member of the pop music royalty when he saw one. He was always wary of speaking to the big leaguers like them; half the time, they turned out to be nightmare humans with disturbing views.

"You okay?" Gus asked.

Ardent rose and brushed the dust from their butt. "Yeah. Just had to come up for air."

Gus glanced back the way he'd come, toward the party in the idyllic park. It was too much for him, a person whose scene was quiet piano bars, but surely Ardent could handle it. The rocker regularly flounced about circus-ring stages with all sorts of holograms, drones, strobes, tractor beams, and earth-shattering bass.

Gus frowned thoughtfully. "You *brought* the party."

"I always do." A bitter note flavored their voice.

"That sounds difficult." Gus sauntered over to a parked CAV and leaned against it. It squawked a warning at him, and Ardent jumped. Thank goodness, they both laughed.

"Uh, sorry about that..." Gus resettled himself against an aging wall near a historical marker dating it all the way back to the 2150s. The building's moneyed architecture bore the hallmarks of the Infinite Expansion—right down to the streamlined, printed flagstones flecked through with precious metals and gem shards.

"Gus Kitko." He raised a hand in a brief wave, then crossed his arms.

"Kitko," they repeated.

He pushed off the wall. "And I should go, because you said you were out here to come up for air."

"Aw, whatever."

"No, no! I shouldn't be taking up your time. Being Ardent Violet looks, uh..."

A raucous roar from the party wafted by on the breeze.

"Exhausting," he finished.

They fixed him with their gaze, and it was like staring into the sun. They'd tinted their irises an inhuman red to complement their dark green suit. What was going through their head? Had his comment crossed the line?

When the silence grew too painful, Gus reached into his pocket and pulled out his battered old mint tin. Its contents jingled softly as he flipped it open. Ardent immediately perked up.

"What do those do?" they asked.

"Taste like mint," Gus replied. "Would you like one?"

"You're probably the only person here who carries candy instead of drugs."

"Then you need me around, for when you'd rather have things sweet and calm."

"Is that what you are?" Ardent asked, red eyes boring into him. They drew close and plucked a mint from the tin. "Sweet and calm?"

"My friends would say so."

Ardent cupped the candy in their gloved hand and keyed their Gang UI. They closed their fingers around it, and the glove flashed inside: a chemical analysis.

"No offense," Ardent said. "I'm a target for kidnappers."

"None taken. Sorry you have to deal with that stuff."

Ardent popped the mint into their mouth, and Gus took one of his own, savoring the evolving fizz of classical molecular gastronomy, the flowing of spearmint tendrils in his mouth.

Ardent let out a happy sigh, resting their hands on their hips to stare down the hill. "Pretty good mint."

"Straight from Old Town Montreal. Local delicacy."

"Really?"

"Nah. Bought them at Trudeau. What kind of a town would have a local delicacy like that?"

Ardent let out a short laugh. "You're proud of poutine."

"Well, where are you from?"

"Atlanta," they said, and he could *almost* pick out the accent.

"Ah, biscuits," Gus said. "So simple, yet so perfect."

Ardent cocked an eyebrow. "You need to get in the kitchen if you think biscuits are simple."

A few of the celebrants from the park made their way around the corner, screaming "Ardent!" the moment they saw their leader. Gus had fans, too, but they mostly held listening teleparties and talked about whether a seventh or a ninth was a more appropriate resolution to the end of Guy Keats's "Too Blue a Bird."

Teleparties were easily escaped. Real parties could hunt one down, as this crowd did to the unfortunate Ardent Violet.

"You're coming, right? To the prince's tonight?" Ardent asked. "Secret military watch party."

"I don't think I've got an invite."

"*I'm* your invite."

"Oh! I would love that. How will I get in if we're separated?"

"You won't. Better hang on to me, Kitty Kitko."

They gestured for Gus to follow, and—though he hated this sort of loud affair—he did.

That night, they gathered in the prince's palace to watch the action unfold. The atrium gardens were a labyrinth of wonders, each turn hiding another botanical curiosity. Torches slow-waltzed over the silent, somber processional, and Gus kept close to Ardent. At last, they came to an expansive amphitheater, like a small stadium for the prince and his friends.

Coats of arms flew from above, hovering in suspension fields. The prince considered it gauche to holoproject his country's flag instead of using the real deal, so he had actuweave banners up everywhere with recordings of wind playing into them.

Gus found all the magical fanfare silly, but wizardry took over the royal aesthetic a few hundred years prior and never quite let go. Perhaps it was their way of explaining their place in the world, which was esoteric at best, borderline arcane. Either way, Gus preferred his tech interactions a bit quieter, with fewer moving paintings and enchanted chandeliers.

A set of crisp, tasteful numbers counted down atop the central dais amid swaying droplets of crystal—a timer on humanity's final trial.

Gus settled into his fluffy polyform chair, happy the prince was a man of comforts. Ardent took the seat beside him, which expanded to fit them both, and wiggled in close.

Very close. Hitting-on-him close.

The place brimmed with dignitaries and important folx.

"I am definitely the least cool person here," Gus whispered.

"Should I move? Are you not good enough?" Ardent pulled a stray hair back behind their ear. "If you could sit beside anyone in this room, who would you pick?"

"Ardent Violet, hands down."

While they all waited, the prince's fountains played a poignant water ballet by Maddie West, *Sins of a Civilization*. Holographic dancers flitted between fountains, seamless illusions immersing Gus into the thesis of the piece. It reflected on the evils that'd shaped their world, and expressed the desire that their reality exist long enough to be fixed. Too many, it argued, will be cheated out of their justice if death takes everyone.

Forty-five tearful minutes later, the ballet ended, and the *Dictum* appeared abruptly in their midst, white hull shining in the light of Sol. Gus figured there ought to at least be a bit of fanfare since the superweapon was their only salvation—maybe a logo or a clever jingle.

Just *boop—starship*.

The *Dictum* certainly didn't look like humanity's only hope. It was mostly cannon, with a little bit of ship appended to the ass-end for control. A couple of engines salvaged from the remains of a wrecked fleet provided propulsion, and it was escorted by Sol Joint Defense Force ships more appropriate for towing and rescue than countermeasures.

But it was humanity's verdict, one way or another, so they all looked on in reverence.

Ardent's fingers found their way into Gus's in the cool night air. They leaned in even more as they rubbed a thumb over his knuckle. Perhaps, after five years of watching humanity crash and burn across the galaxy, this day would be the start of Gus's renaissance.

The *Dictum* worked precisely as promised, drawing Earth's would-be destroyer, Juliette, into the center of the fleet near Jupiter—but they'd only sprung the trap on themselves.

A swarm of golden robots erupted from Juliette's superluminal braking path like glowing dandelion seeds. These choked out the meager starfighters of the Sol Joint Defense Force, murdering the human pilots with superior reflexes, awareness, and maneuverability. Gus couldn't make out any details, just a lot of small pops and the murmur of the crowd.

Juliette blasted out of the kill zone like an avenging angel, slicing up Earth's dreadnoughts with its glowing whips. The *Dictum* didn't even get a shot off.

The Vanguard and its Gilded Ghosts took one minute and thirty-eight seconds to finish everyone, saving the observing ships for last. It would take some time for the Vanguard's folding reactor to recharge, but after that—

—Earth was finished.

When Gus understood, he looked to Ardent. Every other eye in the crowd remained fixed on the holoprojectors, but he was curious. He wanted to know what the most beautiful person he'd ever met looked like in this singular moment.

The whites of their eyes had gone pink as cherry blossoms, and tears spilled over their pale cheeks. The smooth lines of Ardent's otherworldly mask of makeup glowed faintly in the dim light, contorted into an awkward rage. They pulled a handkerchief out of some hidden pocket and dabbed their eyes and nose. It came away with the luminance of their highlighter.

"I'm going to bed," Ardent whispered, gaze falling to the ground.

Gus nodded.

"Will you... will you please take me there?"

Gus nodded again.

They went back to Ardent's room and fucked like there were only two tomorrows.

Gus had expected to be thrown out the next day. He wouldn't have blamed Ardent if they'd had places to be, other people to do. Surely there were folx in the rocker's life who needed them.

But Ardent let Gus hang around, thank heavens. The pair had a natural chemistry that kept them together in one way or another for a blissful thirty-six hours. Ardent was an excellent conversation partner, and let Gus ramble on about pianos whenever it was his turn to talk. Gus felt bad going on about his favorite instruments, but he'd essentially been holed up in his apartment looking at music sites for the past five years. At least Ardent was a good sport about it and tried to ask questions.

They didn't have a single disagreement until it came time to discuss their end-of-life intentions.

Ardent wanted to spend their final hours saying goodbye to fans. Gus wanted to be alone with someone special. It'd started off a hypothetical discussion, but without realizing it, they'd both drifted into actual plans. Gus hadn't meant to get emotional, but these were to be his last moments. He'd be damned if he squandered them.

The whole argument tensed up before the sprain.

"You'll have a front row seat at the fan party," Ardent said. "At least we can be together at the end that way."

It'd been an offer.

The answer came out completely wrong: "But I'm not a fan."

"'Not a fan'?"

"No, like I'm just... I don't want to spend my last few hours playing the game. Doing the celebrity thing."

"And I live for it, so you know where I'll be."

Ardent returned their attentions to the mirror cams, touching up their already flawless makeup.

"Ardent, I feel like we've got a real connection, and besides, I'd be out of place. I'm not like... a pop person."

Ardent's then-emerald eyes narrowed. "Just because you fell in love overnight, my little Kit-ko, does not mean you get to own this."

"I meant I'm not *just* a fan. What we have is more."

Ardent's expression went from bad news to blaring warning sirens.

"More than the people who care about my art and identity? More than my wishes for how I want to spend my life?"

"I didn't mean that—"

"I know what the fuck you meant, and some of these people have devoted *the last five years to my career.* They're my friends now. Even if they do worship me, I worship them right back. So far, we know two things about our relationship: *I'm* a great lay, and *you* like to talk about pianos a little too much."

"I didn't... only talk about..."

But he had.

They prosecuted him with a single question: "What's your favorite Ardent song?"

"I don't normally listen to pop—"

"Mine is 'Get the Hell Out.' Want to hear it?"

"I—"

"Get the hell out."

After he'd been dismissed, Gus looked the song up, just to be sure the godforsaken tune existed. It was catchy, with a great piano solo in the middle. To his surprise, there was a lot going on in the composition.

Gus was allowed to remain on the grounds, but Ardent's people made it clear he needed to stay away. With only a few hours left to live, there was nothing to do except wait to die as Lord Yamazaki's guest.

Juliette, Vanguard giant, hums like a tuning fork, and Gus has regrets.

He should be standing on the veranda with Ardent, hand in hand as they take in the end, not gawking from the garden path. They might be the most captivating person he's ever met, and they stand before him like a phoenix, wreathed in the misty, shattered holograms of SuperPort Hercule. Even with a world-killing giant crashing behind them, he's transfixed. It's profoundly unfair that this is how he met them; he wanted more time.

Ardent is swallowed by the crowd—folx rushing to see Earth's executioner.

Juliette draws up to its full height, vibrating in Gus's vision like ultraviolet light. He has to squint to look directly at it. The robot raises a white gauntlet, and every harmonic overtone seems to fill Gus's mind—possibilities even beyond human hearing. The atoms of his body thrum in time with unseen oscillations. He's aligning to something—attuning.

All around him, activity slows to a halt. Other people's hands drop to their sides, and they stare, wide-eyed, at Juliette's forming energy field. It's a thing of beauty, pulsing and beating with a thousand dancing lights.

This feels amazing. I—

Conscious thought begins to fade.

Another superluminal brake burn splits the air like an elephant's shout, this one close enough to send a colorful borealis of solar particles rippling across Earth's atmosphere. The shock wave throws sailcraft against their slip walls, its force rushing up the hill, flattening every potted plant and partygoer like a ripple of dominoes.

Gus can't do anything about it.

The hit knocks the daylights out of him, and he goes sprawling across Lord Yamazaki's lawn. Others weren't so lucky, and a lot of terrified screams go up all at once. People broke bones, hit their heads and split them like melons. Pained cries join the cacophony as yet others come to grips with new injuries. In all his years playing concerts, Gus has never heard a crowd make a noise like that—but then, he's never been in a bomb's blast radius, either.

A jump that close to Earth's atmosphere is beyond illegal, so that means only one thing: another Vanguard.

A second titan comes streaking out of the sky in a ball of fire, pile-driving Juliette into the dark waters. Some bright soul has the idea to use a holoprojector as a searchlight, filling the bay from the top of a high-rise. The newcomer thrashes in the water with Juliette, forming a maelstrom of whitecaps.

That collision wasn't an accident.

The Vanguards are fighting.

The city booms with joyous voices like an arena. Horns blare. People set off fireworks. They're all happy.

Except Gus recognizes the sleek, jet-black form of Greymalkin—destroyer of seventeen worlds. That bastard has taken even more lives than Juliette, so it's not likely to be helpful when it's done beating its comrade to death.

Greymalkin's body is a symphony of black lacquer and sleek lines. Torrents of water pour down its head, running along a pair of vertical green slits where its eyes should be. Wicked claws tip its fingers, engine nozzles on each knuckle. The jets spit and hiss like a pit full of pissed-off cougars, and Gus has to cover his ears.

Fists ablaze, Greymalkin assails Juliette into the waves, sending pillars of steam up to join the clouds. Juliette uppercuts from beneath the water, knocking its assailant loose. In a flash and flurry of rain, the purple Vanguard is back on its feet. Greymalkin coils and strikes, but this time, the bots are more evenly matched.

Still, more hopeful whoops and gasps go up from the assemblage of people. Gus isn't sure why they're so excited.

They're probably just fighting over who gets to kill us.

The Vanguards' musical ululations fill the city's glassy streets, bending Gus's mind. It's a language, and whatever they're saying to each other, he can almost understand it. The sound resonates in his bones. These are gods, and they speak with infinite choirs.

He quickly picks out the key—F Dorian, a favorite of jazz musicians everywhere.

With a perfect view of Juliette's havoc, the elevated veranda becomes a choked throng. Celebrities, wealthy elites, and ladder climbers—not particularly considerate in the first place—run one another over to get a good look at the two monsters clashing. Gus hangs back, because if he's going to spend his last minutes on something, it's not gawking.

There's always the piano. It's deserted now.

Gus swims upstream against the revelers pouring from the house. It's a gauntlet; they'll trample him if he falls, and they won't even have time to feel bad about it. Gus isn't into going out like gum on some well-heeled heels, so he ducks and weaves until he's through the door into the Maison.

He heads to the Crystal Parlor, its interior holoed over for a performance that will never occur. Jagged patterns throb gently on every wall, awaiting musical cues. The room's many interactive facets and light shows would've made for a fantastic concert venue back in Montreal. Gus knows a bunch of promoters. He could probably scrape together enough venture capital to get a club off the ground and—

Even at the end, he often forgets he has no future.

The abandoned setup of Lord Yamazaki's house quartet sits on the neon stage: a grand piano, an upright bass, an electric guitar, and a drum kit. The ones hired to play the lord's private party already quit, so the instruments sit idle.

Cups and bottles lie strewn across the floor where they'd been dropped in everyone's haste. Some asshole spilled their whiskey across the piano bench, but Gus situates his rump on the leather cushion anyway. No time to tidy up.

He taps the F-zero key, and it's like heaven under his fingertips. The Roland Grand Alpha tunes to the ambient noise of the clashing Vanguards, and Gus lays in a gentle pad of fifths. A light glissando carries him up and down, and he shifts modes to keep in sync with his new playmates.

He doesn't want to dance with these monsters, but they're the only game in town. He can face them and make music where it's possible, take the party to the very end—or he can hang it up and wait to die.

Hit it.

Gus unleashes a flurry of hammer strokes across the board. His sweet music intertwines with the Vanguards' hypnotic melodies, subverting them, patterning their voices into a trio under his command.

The Crystal Parlor comes to life, facets dancing in the lamplight. This is Gus's favorite room in Lord Yamazaki's house—the way it seems to breathe with his song. Surfaces align, creating impossible illusions of expansive spaces unfolding into nothingness. Gus plays a deceptive cadence, and the electropolar glass responds in kind, translating tonality into color. The room becomes a cathedral to craft Gus's remaining opus.

He dances over the Vanguards' sounds with his own, playing for life, attacking the attackers, snapping back at them with triplets made from their own chord progressions. If they want to end the world, fuck them. At least he can make it catchy.

No one else troubles Gus's line of sight. They're all too excited about the robot devils duking it out in the bay. Alone with the ivories, Gus isn't performing for anyone, and it's exactly what he wanted for an ending.

The titans shift musical modes again and again, and it takes everything Gus has to keep up. A smile tugs at the corner of his mouth; this might be the most fun he's had in a jam session since he lost his bandmates in the Gus Kitko Trio.

He plays for them, too.

Lisel and Gerta were his bassist and drummer—a wonderful couple, and the best friends he'd ever had. They'd been killed in an attack on the nomadic preservation cruiser *Paradise*. It was supposed to be safe there, hidden, but the ship hunters found them. The dark behemoths caught every spacefaring vessel, eventually.

Gus pushes the Vanguard chord progression into an accusation. *Fuck you for killing my friends.*

He parts ways in deliberate dissonance, shoving in Lisel's favorite bass lines to the beats Gerta always laid down. They might be dead, but he has them in his head, ready to jam. They've got something to say to these Vanguards, too, and Gus hears them loud and clear. When he shifts key to bring their harmonies back into line with the Vanguards, it's like slamming the accelerator. He shakes his head, smiling like the Trio is playing together again at last.

The mirrored hall gasps in delight as Ardent strides beneath the archway in their glowing robes. It scatters their splendor up its oscillating crystals before bringing itself back into tasteful alignment with the song.

Ardent breezes past the piano without a word, stopping at the guitar. It's a metal-flaked red Strat with scintillating white accents, but against Ardent's wardrobe, it's positively bland. When they wrap their fingers around the instrument's neck, their textiLEDs steal colors from the guitar body, erupting in a bloody display of light.

Far from being a distraction, Ardent's presence completes the need. Gus feels whole, like he can truly cut loose and play humanity off the stage.

Ardent tosses the strap over their head and slips a silver guitar pick out of a hidden pocket at their wrist. They lean back, letting the instrument's body rest against their hips, as if testing it, before squaring up to play. Their electric fingernails arc along the strings, infusing the instrument with a rising drone as they capably run a hand up the fretboard. They nod in time with Gus, keeping a beat with quick palm-muted strums as they wait for the right place to jump in.

Gus digs this improvised jam like he's never felt a song before. If this were a performance, it'd be one of the proudest moments of his life. This should've been at Lincoln Center. It should've been in a big arena, even.

Stay in the moment, man.

His fingers go faster and faster. People are screaming outside. Ardent raises their hand for the first rocking strum; their pick shines like a guillotine blade.

"Here we go!" Ardent's shout is a bolt of lightning into Gus's soul. A jet-black robot fist punches through one side of the room, covered in gore and broken stone. It slams into Ardent, and they go flying toward an open window. The hand stops short of Gus, sweeping aside the baby grand as easily as dollhouse furniture. He staggers backward, trying to get away, but it digs out more of the house and catches him like fleeing vermin.

Unyielding fingers close around Gus, and he beats on Greymalkin's wet armor plates to get loose. He thought he wouldn't panic at the end—he's known he was going to die for a long time—but it's still terrifying. It's crushing him. Breath won't come.

The fist draws Gus out through the smoking remains of La Maison Des Huit Étoiles, revealing only bloody devastation in its wake. The world careens, and Gus's head lolls atop his neck. When his view rights itself, he's face-to-face with Greymalkin.

Its twin vertical slits fill the dripping night with venomous green light. Up close, the Vanguard's hum is all-encompassing, and Gus's hair stands on end. So many lives have been taken by this thing. Why did it come all the way from the darkness of space to terrorize him, specifically?

Greymalkin's armored breastplate opens up, and electric-blue muscles flicker along connective tissue. There's a gap in the middle of Greymalkin's chest, a yawning nest of pumping tubes and the heartbeat of lights. Probes and wires slither about the entrance, and Gus screams in horror as it plunges him forward.

He's encased in goo, and the whole world goes dark and quiet. Every wriggling motion meets with blubbery resistance, and his muscles burn within seconds. It's trying to exhaust him, suffocate him.

It's definitely going to work.

The mucous wall suctions to Gus's body, slurping away the remaining air bubbles, plastering his hair with lubricant, smearing his face. Gus makes fists, trying to grab on to something, but the gelatinous material squishes out between his fingers.

His lungs burn and stars dance in his eyes. He can't take it. Gus's body is about to breathe whether he wants to or not.

This is where you die.

A pair of protrusions slither up his nose, and Gus reaches up to pull them out. Those aren't tubes; they're the goo pressing into his sinuses.

There's a popping noise inside his skull, and air flows into Gus's nostrils, cold and fresh. He shuts his mouth and breathes hungrily, coughing with each exhalation. The whistling hiss of air dies down as the pressure evens out, and he's oddly comfortable.

Gus stops struggling. He doesn't see the point. Maybe this is the afterlife, and he's actually supposed to be super snuggly and fall asleep.

Something tickles Gus's scalp.

That something turns out to be a brain drill.

His pain ratchets from terrifying, to explosive, to personality-skewing. His vision whites out as the drill bit chews skin and bone, and he smells rainbows. A spike of lava burns up his insides, threading along his backbone. Probes stab through his whole body, and he hopes it will end soon: the suffering, his life, everything.

A cool mist trickles from the back of Gus's neck into his form, and all fear vanishes as his extremities pleasantly tingle. Something alien, yet familiar, creeps into his mind. Thoughts are being forced into him.

It's like learning the parameters of a dream, changing the truths of his world. All at once, he understands that his pain is an illusion created by the body to illustrate danger. With the right modulation in perspective, illusions can be destroyed.

Gus's pain vanishes. In fact, he feels great.

Perhaps a little too great—there are definitely some drugs in his system.

"What's happening to me?"

Concepts filter into him, the language of an advanced intelligence. Gus's mind isn't *exclusively* his anymore. Greymalkin and Gus are connected.

Light fills his vision, the water and sailcraft wreckage coming into ultrasharp focus. He's seeing through Greymalkin's optical sensors, and a thousand colors he's never glimpsed come smashing into his nervous system. Radiant heat and gamma rays fluoresce in his sight, rendered in fresh clarity by ultra-powerful sensors across the Vanguard hull. He could count the fish in the sea if he so desired. Monaco is even more beautiful than before, but when Gus looks into space, he's floored.

A million destinations spread before him, clouds of possibility scattered across the sidereal firmament. Even background radiation stands out, remnants of the Big Bang cast into distant nothingness. Nebulae swirl across the cosmos, thickening into a panoramic arm of the Milky Way. Curiously, two other lights stand out in the darkness.

Those are other humans, Greymalkin explains, pushing more thoughts into his mind. Not everyone is dead.

Juliette's fist plows into Gus's view, sending Greymalkin backward into the SuperPort starship pads. He goes stumbling into the dry-docked *Zephyr's Rest*, supposedly the most luxurious starliner in existence. Greymalkin's claw snaps out to catch itself, and Gus's arm follows suit against his will. Nails dig into the silver hull and rip a huge gash down the side. Bundles of wiring, metal, nanocomposites, and a thousand other things tear loose from the *Zephyr's Rest* like whale fat, and Gus seriously doubts it'll ever fly again.

"Oh my god! I'm so sorry!"

His jaw hurts like hell from taking that last punch. Bones clacked together across his face that he didn't even know he had; Greymalkin's armor plates—acutely sensitive to the tiniest vibration—took a hit with the net force of a hypersonic missile. If it weren't for the Vanguard throttling its sensor input, the shock of a full-impact strike would've burned Gus out like a tiny fuse.

Juliette goes down on all fours, scrambling toward Greymalkin. It clambers along the starliner's roof, punching another half dozen holes before leaping onto Gus's Vanguard host. Gus feels Juliette's ivory gauntlets around his neck, and it brings another fist across his face.

Greymalkin wants Gus to know: He will not survive a third hit like that. Its neck has taken too much damage, and needs time to regenerate.

They must work together to create an advantage.

"I'm in control?"

The answer comes through in a flash. Gus is a Conduit, and Greymalkin contains the Fount: the universal database of all harvested human memories.

The bargain: Gus will give Greymalkin access to the knowledge in the Fount. Greymalkin will give itself over to his control.

"You want to put other people's ideas... in my mind?" he asks, flinching as Juliette comes at them.

Gus's arms once again move against his will, blocking blows that could've cratered mountains. Greymalkin rolls and throws Juliette at the fuel storage depot, but it catches itself on the traffic control tower, clambering down the side like a spider.

If Gus consents to be connected with the Fount, he can be of some use to humanity before he dies from his grievous wounds.

"Wait, what?"

In the interest of speed, Greymalkin had to jam everything into him without anesthesia. There's a good chance he'll perish after this; Gus's body has suffered an inordinate amount of trauma.

Panic scratches at Gus's thoughts, but Greymalkin twists his mind—keeping him in the moment. His Vanguard needs his explicit agreement. Perhaps he would rather be dead, Greymalkin suggests. Gus's choice not to help would damn humanity, but it would also be understandable. Most humans do not enjoy having their minds manipulated.

Juliette shoulder-checks Greymalkin, sending it skidding off the coastal shelf, into the depths of the Mediterranean. The Vanguard sinks deeper, beyond the reach of Monaco's lights. Its armored back comes to rest against the seafloor, kicking up a swirl of silt. Radars render the 23,168 fish-sized life-forms nearby.

"Will it hurt?" Gus takes a dry swallow.

He can save humanity. Who cares if it destroys him?

He nods and makes a tight fist. "All right. Do it."

His viewport fills with the words *Deepsync in progress…*

A thin ray of light spreads through his head, scattering across his many nodes and subsystems. Greymalkin's psyche fuses with him, the connection snapping them together like two droplets of water.

Middle C, played on Gus's childhood piano, comes through the connection first. A sparkle of notes form the backbone of a song, and his limitless imagination provides dozens of branching paths.

An illusory drummer follows, a snare in a swing time march, then a horn section hums a tense pad before going sforzando.

The full orchestra builds in Gus's mind: loud, clear, and soul-rattling. Memories spill into him at the crescendo, and he becomes multitudes.

It's electrifying. Countless warriors of all shades, genders, backgrounds, and beliefs fill Gus with a battle cry, and his breath comes in panicked, wide-eyed huffs. They're so loud—every thought he has seems to belong to someone else. He feels their lives and motivations, the core of what taught them to fight. These were the people who laid down everything to stop the advance of the Vanguards, and they only ended up being absorbed by them.

Greymalkin informs Gus: He can only withstand five minutes at a time.

"What happens then?"

His personality will dissolve under the weight of all others. He'll be nothing more than a drooling amalgam, unable to think or speak for himself. In that instance, Greymalkin will do him the favor of termination.

"Aw, thanks, buddy."

When Gus sits up, so does Greymalkin. It crouches on the seafloor, preparing to launch its counterattack.

"Looks like we've only got five minutes to dance."

Gus pounds his fists together and slogs up the shelf. He breaks the surface, and Juliette is waiting, whips at the ready. It draws back to swing and—

Elation as she steps forward to preempt her master, taking him by the wrist and hurling him to the mat.

The memory of another life takes over Gus's being for a split second, and he executes a perfect hip throw. Juliette careens overhead before kicking loose in a tangle of limbs. It lands hard, but not enough to damage it. It rushes at Gus and—

They spread their feet to receive the linebacker, because they're going to teach this motherfucker about inertia.

Greymalkin goes low, grabbing Juliette by the waist and directing its momentum into the sharp cliffs of the land extensions. The purple Vanguard rolls into the water, buying Gus a moment to catch his breath.

Gus looks down at his dark claws, lined with hissing jets. He has become what he must to save the Earth. He has every memory he needs to kick this thing's ass.

Now he just needs to get lucky.

Chapter Two

Front Row Seats

It's like getting punched by a bus.

But for the airbags built into the dress, Ardent would've been shattered into a thousand little pieces against Greymalkin's fist. Ardent's agent always insisted on having Stalker Shields installed, just in case some mouth-breather got handsy.

A giant robot fist is as handsy as it gets.

The guitar breaks against Ardent's torso—taking with it a few of their ribs—and Ardent goes flying out the window like a strobe-lit piece of popcorn. Their whole vocabulary blueshifts in the fall, and they loose a remarkable streak of swears in a single operatic screech.

They're sieved by tree limbs before albatrossing onto the synth grass. Their exploded textiLEDs flash in alarm, automatically trying to call the authorities for help on a dead Net connection.

Ardent hasn't been hit that hard since they botched a flip during their final tour rehearsals. They gasp, lungs quivering as lights dance in their reddened eyes. Trying to sit up is a terrible mistake, and they lie back to catch their breath. Wooziness overtakes them, and the world spins.

Ardent gives a few weak flips of their wrist to get their Ganglion

UI to appear. With shaking fingers, they push through the menus to throw a painkiller on their lower back. A choked sigh escapes their lips as their bodysuit applies soothing electropulses to their spine and ribs.

When Ardent overcomes their violent reorientation, they find themself in the front garden beside a stone fountain. They roll onto their stomach, flipping the hair out of their eyes and blinking the focus back into them. If they'd landed even a little differently, they'd be dead.

Above them, Greymalkin withdraws its fist from the remains of Lord Yamazaki's manor, collapsing the building in upon itself.

There's someone within its black talon, head poking out between thumb and forefinger. A mop of curly black hair shows up briefly in the searchlight.

Gus?

Greymalkin opens its chest plate, probes drawing his body inside like an octopus drags a mussel.

"Don't eat him!" Ardent screams.

It eats him.

"Listen here, you big bastard—"

Looking into the sky is like staring out at an arena crowd—swaying devices glowing and glimmering as celebrants dance—but multiplied by an order of magnitude. Ardent can almost hear the roar, feel the speakers and the stage beneath their feet. The whole of the stars convulse, growing brighter in cycles until they have to squint. Rainbows spill across the heavens, engulfing the planet as countless more brake burns encircle the Earth.

More folds?

But that would be thousands, right at the edge of the Earth's magnetic fields.

The incoming ships carve flaming lines across the sky before breaking apart into more vehicles. Those divide even further, until vast fleets of tiny engines crowd out the stars. They fly in formation, parallel lines deviating from a single branch, barbs in the vane of a feather.

Ardent has seen the holos, knows what the streaks are: the Gilded Ghosts, foot soldiers of annihilation. Every Vanguard comes with a swarm of them, and they're the virus that will destroy the Earth—but not with something as clumsy as raw force. If the Ghosts had wanted, they could've jumped into the atmosphere and fried everyone with solar wash.

Their plan is far worse than radiation poisoning.

This day has ensnared Ardent's imagination for the past five years, infecting their music, relationships, and even the safety of dreams. There's no escape from this fate, no fleeing Earth. Every starship has been chased down. To their knowledge, no bunker on any other world has withstood an onslaught from a Vanguard, or even a Gilded Ghost.

In the harbor, Greymalkin explodes from the depths to smash its rival with rocket-propelled claws. It wraps its arms around the purple Vanguard's waist and suplexes it into the rocky hills of the land extensions.

Ardent whoops, but they lose their view of the action behind the Electric Orchard. They have to get closer if they want to watch the end.

Golden light passes overhead. Ardent looks up to see an entry vehicle streaking along, a starmetal spore pod splitting into thousands. They're getting brighter—closer.

One of the luminous objects shoots out of the clouds, neatly lancing a nearby tower of apartments before burying itself in a park. Screams erupt from the balconies, but there's no time to watch in horror—dozens of other engine streaks stab the city, flames gushing forth from the wounds.

Other guests stumble dazedly from Lord Yamazaki's house,

survivors of Greymalkin's initial hit. They cling to one another, weeping and looking around for safety. It's getting a bit Ragnarok outside, though, so they won't find it anywhere.

Fashion is always intentional, and Ardent has carefully selected their cataclysmic attire for maximum mobility. They tug at the various restraints securing their exploded dress, tearing it away to expose the sleek bodysuit underneath. They'd worn this ultrabright stage display on their *Hellbitch* tour, and had grown to love it for both its breathable layers and sheer goddamned fabulousness. Ardent taps the sides of their recall rubber stilettos, softening their heels before squishing them against the ground. After a second touch, clumsy heels become brisk flats, ready for sprinting.

Ardent waves to the others. Maybe they should group up for this part of the apocalypse. "Hey!"

The pack of survivors heads in Ardent's direction—but a rocket strike craters the ground between them. Clods of dirt rain onto Ardent, and they cover their head to avoid any sharp rocks. After the sand shower settles, everyone straightens to peer at the new hole.

A manipulator emerges from the smoking crater, sharp, robotic fingers gripping the broken earth. The design of the claw is like the Vanguards—smooth, sweeping, and organic. Another one follows, a pair of arms dragging free. The rest of the machine rises from its cradle, a loose congregation of thin palladium plates, lashed together by articulating wires. It's a mesh, a flat surface like a cloak—draped over a nightmare. It unfurls into a feline body, the metallic gesture of a great cat stalking the grounds. A lens assembly forms the "head" of the beast, sweeping its surroundings with cold light. Beneath these unnatural eyes, it bears a pair of white-hot fangs, long as Ardent's forearms, arcing with malice.

It's almost beautiful.

Almost.

One of the men shouts in terror and takes off running—never a good move around predators. The Ghost launches after him, catching him within seconds. Its wired chains of plates tangle around his legs and arms, and he falls, screaming.

"Help me! Hel—"

The robot flows over him, encasing him in its golden mesh before sinking both fangs deep into his skull. There's a flash and a pop, and the rest of the man's body jerks to a halt. The Ghost shakes its head, releasing its prey, and the fellow flops to the ground with eyes and mouth steaming. A pair of large holes along the top of his skull weep blood, and the machine steps over him.

"It's all good!" it says in the dead man's voice. "I'm fine. You guys good?"

Ardent backs up a step.

"Oh, fuck that."

The video is grainy.

There's a titanic purple robot, accompanied by a swarm of gleaming locusts, falling from the sky.

Wind buffets a cityscape, and buildings collapse in the distance.

A man in the foreground screams at someone off camera, "Juliette!"

The robot charges up some kind of field, and the image sensor whites out.

That file, shared far and wide as "The Juliette Video," was Ardent Violet's introduction to the Vanguards—giant robots built from tech far beyond human. All 2.2 million colonists of Persephone were destroyed in under ten minutes, but it took the rest of the galaxy weeks to understand what'd happened.

After nine hours, the feeds came back online. Videos of the attack emerged, depicting moderate carnage with a miraculous recovery. Family members called home, tearful and glad to be alive. They reconciled old grudges. They mourned the confirmed dead. Four of Ardent's biggest fans from the system called, and they were fine.

They were also perfect, real-time fakes.

Every aspect of the victims had been faithfully re-created, from speech patterns and intimate secrets—to their network credentials and knowledge of critical infrastructure.

Persephone asked for help, and the United Worlds sent fifty of their best ships. Those brave rescuers were never seen again, and the loss of those scarce vessels debilitated humanity for the rest of the coming war.

The malicious signals eventually caused every world and outpost to turn inward, walling off their communications for fear of hacking and reliably false information—and of seeing their own beloved dead, beckoning them to the end. This gradual corruption of all interstellar communications came to be called the Veil.

The Gilded Ghosts struck worlds and stations across the cosmos, absorbing their populace's knowledge. Ten more colonies disappeared overnight. Before the Veil smothered the galaxy, new videos of other giant robots emerged—always under a minute long, always terrifying.

Some poor soul got footage of a Ghost Wipe before getting the big bite themself. No one wanted to believe the images were real. After all, the Ghosts had fabricated humanity's dead relatives. Why wouldn't they fake this, too, to demoralize the remaining populace?

Ardent had certainly denied it.

But now they stand horrified on the Yamazaki Estate grounds. This Wipe, this man, his steaming, ruined eyes—they're real enough to smell at a dozen paces.

The robot launches for the remains of the group, and Ardent

sprints in the other direction down the estate drive. They won't die here—not yet. The fight between Juliette and Greymalkin is the last great show, and Ardent refuses to be killed before it's over.

More Ghosts come raining from above, sending up thick columns of debris and rock everywhere they hit. Terrified screams choke the night air from the surrounding villas. Horrors stalk the chaos, spreading in every direction. There is nowhere to run on Earth or in the stars.

People pour into the streets, headed away from the huge mech battle in the water. SportCAVs and exotic aircraft launch from every rooftop, only to be blasted in midair, shot through by Ghosts on the way down. Anywhere the vehicles crash, bots pry them open and drag out the screaming drivers. Classic hovercars fare little better, making easy prey for the shining robots. The road out of the city is choked with a massacre, because no one wants to walk toward the final confrontation of two unstoppable forces in the harbor.

But if the world must end, Ardent wants the best seat: front row, mosh pit.

Down the hillside at the port, Juliette throws a boat at Greymalkin, who knocks it into the city. The point of impact erupts into flames, destroying the block that—until recently—contained Ardent's favorite chocolate shop, along with the good shoe store. It's not like Ardent is ever going back to Monaco, but it's the principle of the thing.

Why isn't Greymalkin "eating" anyone else? There's no way it traveled across space just to devour one man, even if that man was as delicious as August Kitko. Why is it fighting Juliette? No one has ever seen a Vanguard behave this way—jamming pianists into its chest and punching another of its kind.

It's simply not how they do business.

The closer Ardent gets, the thinner the population becomes. The Ghosts are sparse down by the marina, harrowing stragglers, and Ardent has to be a lot more careful. Away from the herd, a lone pop star is easy pickings.

A pod strikes the roadway ahead, and Ardent detours down a side path, over a greenway, and into a high-rise apartment. The security guard is absent, probably off getting killed somewhere with family, like Ardent should be. They still feel guilty about that. Maybe the bunker will save Ardent's siblings, unlike all of the other bunkers in the galaxy—which the Ghosts scraped out as though they were warrens full of soft baby bunnies, and not military-hardened structures.

A sprint to a knee slide takes Ardent behind the lobby desk, where they curl into a tight ball and try not to move or breathe too hard. Eleven years of ballet and seven years of rocking packed arenas have given them fantastic cardiovascular health. Running from Ghosts is way easier than the dance number they had planned for the victory party.

The lobby remains quiet, save for the distant thunder of battling Vanguards and dull shelling of Ghosts outside. The front door chimes, and Ardent balls up even tighter. The tick-tick of metal claws on marble fills the grand foyer—the Ghost that crashed outside has followed them.

Ardent's chest stings like there's a stitch, but it's more likely a broken rib. If they try to get up, the Ghost will catch them for sure. If they don't leave, it'll scan for Ardent and find them instantaneously. Right on time, blue light washes over their body, through the stone desk, through their skin—a multispectral sweep.

Busted. Still a pretty legendary end—got punched by a robot and lived.

But the Ghost doesn't come tearing over the lip of the desk to suck out Ardent's memories. Why not? There's nothing that stands between it and them.

As if in answer, there's a ding.

"Suivez-moi, tranquillement," comes a woman's urgent whisper from the bank of elevators. She's cut short by a chorus of screams as the Ghost goes scrabbling into the elevator car with the occupants.

The monster is busy; now is the best chance to get away.

Ardent uncoils and rushes around the reception desk, past the open elevator. They look inside as they flee. There are only minutes left for the planet. No point in turning away.

The Ghost—now more like a net than a cat—stretches to ensnare anyone in reach. It hooks them between its segments, wrapping cables around their necks and drawing them toward its mass of captive corpses. It takes no time wrapping up their heads for its grotesque probes.

There's a kid in the mix.

Ardent wants to help, but what are they supposed to do? Earth's big plan is to die. Everyone knew this was the last sunrise. Ardent can almost hear their grandfather's voice.

Keep going or that'll be you.

"No."

Ardent flicks their wrist; the Gang UI sends their bodysuit into Stalker Defense mode. They slap the Ghost, and fifty thousand volts and an EMP loop go shooting through the crowd, seizing everyone up and rebooting all their wearables. The Ghost is shielded, but it definitely feels the hit. The creature releases its victims and scrabbles up the wall, screeching alarms and showering everyone with marble dust.

It turns its lenses on Ardent, long fangs still dripping blood. Run or don't run, this beast is coming.

With a quick spin on their heel, Ardent takes off for the far end of the foyer. They shoulder through the revolving door and out into the road. There's a trash can nearby, and Ardent hauls it over into the spinning exit, effectively barring the mechanism.

The Ghost yanks the door leaves once, then gives the whole assembly a shove in the other direction. The revolving door safety frame turns caution yellow, a pattern of black *X*s blossoming across its panes—*not allowed, wait ten seconds.*

"Ardent!" says the Ghost in the familiar voice of a screaming fan. "Don't go! It doesn't hurt!"

That's Narika, the former head of their social team, consumed in the attack on Abode Colony. Ardent had cried for a whole week after she died.

Ardent blanches. "Bad kitty."

They search for some means of escape. There are a few rentable "Ciao!" scooters hovering nearby. The Net is down; it's unlikely they'll take payment, but it's worth a try. When Ardent jumps onto one, they find a message:

There are no more tomorrows. We encourage you to use this vehicle to be with loved ones.

Thanks for the memories, and
Ciao

"Aww, cute," they say, revving the throttle and shooting up the boulevard on their free end-of-days scooter. This might be the first time in Ardent's life they can remember reading a corporate statement that wasn't totally disingenuous bullshit.

The skies above are bedlam, with CAVs dropping out of the air left and right, passengers screaming the whole way down. The House of Grimaldi opens fire from the Rock of Monaco, and a host of golden bots descend upon the palace to choke out the defenses. It's unlikely His Serene Highness is living up to his title at the moment.

A couple of famous hairpin turns bring Ardent out at Portier, taking a hard left to rocket onto the Nouvelle Causeway's Skyline Boulevard. The atrium's rooftop road never fails to amaze, clear aluminum stained cyan like old glass bottles. A hundred meters below Ardent, overpriced neighborhoods whip past—the sorts of people who'd pay more money to live under an expressway because it's in Monaco.

The panoramic battle between Greymalkin and Juliette swells to encompass all sight. Every jab and kick rocks the earth, and the clash of starmetal limbs rings through Ardent's bones.

Salty spray stings their eyes, and they wipe them clear. To miss even a single minute of humanity's final battle would be a crime. If an errant Vanguard fist or foot mashes Ardent into the ocean floor, it will have been worth it.

A glance backward reveals a host of pursuers—three Ghosts closing in with teeth arcing, literally thirsting for knowledge. Ardent hunkers low and twists the accelerator, bobbing and weaving with the drive assist. Sadly, the Ghosts are faster than a rental scooter and gain ground with every second.

Keep going. Stay alive. See everything you can.

The Vanguards' songs fill the whole spectrum of sound with tonal bliss, sizzling against Ardent's nerves. Greymalkin plows a rocket claw through one of Juliette's elbow joints and unleashes a noise like a thousand slot machines jackpotting in glory. Robotic eye slits flash in delight against its shadowed carapace.

"Punch it again!" Ardent shouts up at them, virtually standing atop their scooter seat to try to get a better view. The safety system chirps a horseplay warning: Two more of those and it'll shut down.

"Aw, screw you. I'm in danger! Override!"

"No network activity," the scooter retorts, unable to understand.

Juliette crosses its ivory arms, reaching into its rib cage. It pulls free a pair of glowing whips that slice across the night. When the bot jerks them taut, it's like a bolt of lightning snapping, unleashing a hail of sparks to devastate the surrounding hillsides. Balls of plasma erupt from the impact points, demolishing mansions and toppling high-rises.

Greymalkin contorts out of the way, taking advantage of its inhuman center of gravity for a masterful leap. It ducks and dodges, picking up a mossy boulder from the harbor floor and bashing it across Juliette's face. It's a solid hit, bass rumbling through the city.

A blur of gold comes at the scooter from the side—an attacking Ghost—and Ardent narrowly swerves out of the way. The killer bot lands on the glassy road, claws sparking as it pivots after the scooter, and Ardent ducks another pounce. The Ghost catches on a lane divider, buying them a bit of breathing room.

Another horseplay warning buzzes from the scooter console: strike two.

The Ghost hasn't given up, though, and it flattens out, rolling after Ardent like a saw blade. Its companions undergo a similar transformation, and soon, Ardent is whipping all over the road to get away from the beasts. The Ghosts' assault consumes all of Ardent's attention, and they're missing the end of the world because of it. One of the Ghosts manages to catch Ardent's arm, leaving a nasty cut.

"Get off me!" They trigger the Stalker Defense, and the Ghost lets go before Ardent can shock it.

Another set of Ghosts comes rolling toward Ardent from the front, and it's almost flattering—everyone gets a personal murderer, but Ardent gets several. Instead of netting the scooter and Wiping Ardent's brain, however, these newcomers charge directly into the pack of pursuers. They tussle in a jingling orgy of wires and plates, ripping and shocking one another with teeth and claws. Deadly welding lasers ignite inside the whirling ball of death, smoking scrap flying out of the catfight at high speed.

Just like the Vanguards, the Ghosts have started killing one another. Ardent certainly isn't complaining.

If the Ghosts are in open conflict, what the hell is happening? Throughout the city, green welding beams slice the night—errant shots from more bot fights breaking out everywhere.

Do humans have a chance?

Juliette's fusion whip comes down behind Ardent with a light brighter than any stage beam. Steam surges up from below, and aluminum glass panels go skyward, orange slag glazing where the whip cut through. The causeway bucks into Ardent's scooter, fouling the repulsor's spin—and no safety system will fix that. The vehicle tips forward, giving Ardent just enough time to be sad about what's coming.

"No, no, n—"

Without the popcorn suit, the ground is a lot harder this time. Ardent bounces twice before skidding to a halt. Their face, shoulder, elbow, and knees all ring with debilitating pain, but they're conscious and alive.

The scooter grinds across the pavement, buzzing a third horseplay strike before shutting down.

Ardent looks up just in time to watch Greymalkin grab Juliette's arms and wrench them like a ship's sailing wheel, tangling limbs until they snap free at the elbows. Milky blood sprays at all angles, raining upon Ardent, Monaco, and the surrounding environs in a torrential storm.

The purple Vanguard blares an agonized wail, its resonant harmonic voice growing discordant and detuned. The euphoria Ardent felt at hearing the Vanguard song wilts into dread, and they cover their ears. Juliette's scream passes right through their fingers, into their auditory canals, their teeth, their bones, and the chambers of their heart.

Greymalkin shuts the noise off by hauling a yacht out of the harbor and stabbing its bow into Juliette's head. Purple armor parts beneath the blow, revealing a thunderstorm of broken electronics. Not satisfied, Greymalkin hooks its shiny black claws into Juliette's rib cage and fires reverse jets on maximum. The purple Vanguard looses a rising squeal before its breastplate gives way. Wires slough from its interior, and Greymalkin yanks them free in huge bundles before kicking the dying Vanguard backward into the ocean.

The gentle wave of Juliette's demise brushes beneath the causeway, washing back out to sea. Ardent blinks the robot blood and salt water out of their eyes, staring thunderstruck at the sinking corpse. Any moment, a Gilded Ghost will grab them and core their brains out—but at least Ardent got to see the single greatest fight in the history of humanity.

Except no fatal bite comes. When Ardent turns to look for their pursuers, they find the Ghosts at peace. The creatures pad back toward the city like a pack of lions, and Ardent watches them go with mounting confusion.

"Okay."

Greymalkin bellows an agonized cry before doubling over like it's going to throw up. Its chest opens, and in the scant details of the night, Ardent sees Gus tumble into the water from an open cavity.

"August!"

No further splashes trouble the surface of the sea. He must be unconscious out there.

The scooter isn't operational, but there's no shortage of wrecked boats nearby. Surely one of those is seaworthy. Ardent clambers down the narrow walking path along the side that leads to the water, winding between the smoking remains of boxy apartments. No one else is here. Anyone who has an apartment in Monaco's Nouvelle Causeway is probably rich enough to be trying their luck in a bunker.

As expected, a lot of boats have drifted against the causeway caissons in a big pile, like scum at the edge of a pond. Ardent picks over the various stranded watercraft, desperate to find some way to get out to Greymalkin. They leap onto the raft of flotsam and overturned hulls, trying to ignore the fact that these vehicles probably all had occupants recently. It's slippery work, but Ardent's rubber soles stick down like glue. The obstacle course shifts uncomfortably beneath their feet, and if they fall, they'll probably get squished between two big boats the next time a wave hits.

"Hey! Anyone alive over here?"

Unfortunately, the answer is yes.

The sound of sharp metal on composite hull reaches Ardent too late. A Gilded Ghost languidly climbs over the keel, head stabilized despite the bobbing of the waves. Its twin fang-probes are dim, but they drip with recent blood all the same. It beam-scans straight through Ardent's torso, several boats, and about a hundred meters of harbor. Broken ribs glow beneath Ardent's skin, illuminated by the scan. This creature knows their weaknesses—

—which seems like overkill, really, since all Ardent brings to the fight are some fancy shoes and a glowing bodysuit.

"Nice kitty," they breathe, raising a hand.

The Ghost lunges, entangling Ardent's slender form, plates slapping flat against their body as wires pull taut. It's so strong, beyond anything they've ever felt, squeezing any pretext of resistance out of them. The grip hurts more than they expected, and the top of their head tingles in horrid anticipation of two sizzling tusks. Ardent's personality is narrowed to a single frightened animal thought.

I'm not ready to die!

Something sharp punctures Ardent's rib cage, and they give a little shout. They keep cringing and waiting, but no other wounds come. The only sounds are the hushed waves and Ardent's wracked breaths.

They were planning to get stabbed in the brain, though this hurts a lot, too. Not as much as they were expecting. The Ghost loosens around them and gently disentangles itself before wandering off.

Warm, fuzzy pleasure spreads from their broken ribs. Ardent watches in chemically detached wonder as bones shift and realign beneath the bodysuit. A biolattice?

Installing an organic regrowth structure should be agonizing, but this feels excellent. The Ghost wanders away in a straight line for the city, a webbed blanket of plates slinking over the edge of the boat. Ardent watches it in a shivering daze, patting their wounds in confusion as though checking their pockets. Why did it let them live?

For that matter, why were the Ghosts fighting one another, and why aren't they still?

Gus!

Ardent scrambles over the keel to find a watersweep idling, thrusters tinting the sea an even sweeter blue. A dead man rests in the driver's seat, vacant eyes sunken and bruised. Bright blood flows over the white polycalf headrest, and Ardent tries to control themself. They've seen a lot of disgusting stuff—most of it at the front rows of concerts—but this is a whole other level.

Remember, Gus is drowning.

They gingerly step over the guy and into the passenger's seat.

". . . a collision," the watersweep's computer says, smoky masculine voice firm and reassuring. "Should I alert the authorities?"

"No—"

Ardent reaches over and tugs the steering wheel from its mag plate.

"Remote drive," coos the boat, and some thumb nubs emerge from the soft-textured surface of the wheel. Ardent pulls apart the coupling, watching the quick holotip tutorial. They swipe a gloved finger over the screen to beginner mode—Ardent was never much of a driver, and the scooter only proved it.

The system lights up for them, eager to give a taste of its full potential. Ardent kicks the motor into high gear, spins the boat, and bounces out over the waves. The computer elegantly translates their shitty steering into something resembling actual navigation, and they're racing toward Greymalkin in no time. A jerk of the wingtips sends the craft into the air, wafting over the sea, and Ardent swoops toward the place they saw Gus fall.

"Alert: swimmer ahead," the computer says, automatically throttling down. A few twists of the stick get the watersweep close enough that the proxy sensors refuse to allow Ardent any farther, and it bounces to a halt.

They scramble over the windshield onto the prow. Balancing on tacky, soft soles, they peer into the dark waves. Every second could be Gus's last.

Ardent clenches their fists and takes a deep breath. "August Kitko! You had better explain yourself! So..." Frantic eyes rake the dim churn. "Stop drowning, okay?"

A splash erupts momentarily from the deep, but it's enough to hitch Ardent's breath—it's life.

Don't be a dolphin.

"Hey! Gus! Hey!"

Ardent frantically reaches for the movement, leaning down into the water, but they can't quite grab whatever it is. Their eyes can't pierce the murk, and the watersweep is too sporty to have something useful like beams.

Their bodysuit should still have the last tour program. With a flick of the wrist, Ardent calls the Gang UI to their palm. All their textiLED operas are still in there, including *Grant Me This.*

Third verse, big finale.

Ardent thrusts a fist skyward to kick off the opera, and a

supernova of stage light explodes from their high-powered wearables. The black water turns translucent green under the beams, revealing Gus's unmoving body just beneath the surface.

"No!"

They plunge into the emerald rush, wrapping their arms around him. With some work, they're able to pull him around to the back of the boat, where Ardent hits the ramp control. The craft kneels back into the harbor, unfolding for entry. Between the pull bar and the boarding-assist conveyor belt, Ardent is able to drag Gus onto the dry deck.

"Life harness... life harness..." Ardent casts about for the safety equipment but only sees the one the dead man is wearing—not like it's saving him.

They manage to cringe their way through stripping the vest off. Every jiggling movement of the corpse reminds them that this could be their own body cast off in a boat—their own vacant eyes. It makes them feel disgusting, just a scavenging crow.

But Gus is dying, and he needs that vest.

"Get—the fuck—off!"

It comes free, and Ardent nearly goes over the side in the process. They take their grim prize and rush to Gus's side.

Stab wounds cover Gus's stomach, neck, and arms, yet there's very little blood. When Ardent wrestles him into the life harness, they feel a set of metal ports running up the length of August's spine, along the back of his head. The vest snaps shut over Gus and immediately lights up rescue red with a loud alarm—no pulse. Crimson chevrons travel along its Kevlar textiLEDs toward Gus's heart, a sure sign to any medic that they need to come to Gus's aid.

It hasn't been too long. He can make it.

The vest wrings Gus's chest like a sponge, squeezing the water out of him while Ardent searches for the first aid kit.

"Check airway!" shouts the vest for anyone who will listen.

Ardent sweeps some of Gus's lunch from his mouth, and the vest gives its captive another bear hug. Then another.

And another.

It's not working.

On the fourth rib-crushing vise hug, Gus splutters half upright before looking at Ardent in horror. He's quite alive, though his feelings on the matter are unclear. Hands shaking, Gus touches one of the ports on the side of his neck.

"Okay, baby! Hey!" Ardent says, wrapping their arms around his shoulders to cradle him. They have to shut off their glowing bodysuit so they don't blind the poor guy. Stroking his cheek, they murmur, "You're good. Don't panic. You're safe, and we're going to get you some medical care, okay?"

He relaxes, gratitude in his eyes. He's about to speak when he sees the top of the dead guy's head in the front seat, a pair of bloody holes in the scalp. Gus screams, attempts to panic, and faints. At least his vest dims to stable blue, pulsing in time with a healthy heartbeat. The doctors can take it from there.

Ardent navigates the center well of the watersweep to grab the steering wheel off the floor. It blinks with a connection, holos cycling through all the customary checks.

The Net is back online.

Humanity is talking.

"Well, I'll be damned. Nerds got back to work *quick*," Ardent mutters, swiping the controls. "Let's see if we can get some help."

When the boat finishes connecting, however, it's been reported stolen.

ANTI-THEFT SYSTEM ACTIVATED—DO NOT RESIST.

The craft swings around, and Ardent almost falls out. They pin Gus to the seat and buckle a safety harness over both of them. Gus groans beneath their weight, but he's still in the boat, so Ardent decides his opinion doesn't matter that much.

The craft weaves beneath the struts of the Nouvelle Causeway, shooting out toward one of the slips of SuperPort Hercule. Indicators along the approaching gangplank flash yellow to summon the local constabulary, and Ardent grimaces. There are already a few surly-looking security types gathering at the slip.

The world almost ended. Why are they even nearby to care?

"Hey, um...I'm like...*not* stealing this dead guy's boat," Ardent calls to the assemblage as the craft settles into its charging cradle.

"I'm not worried about the boat," says a French woman with dark skin and silk-interlaced cornrows. "You've got something else I want, Ardent Violet."

She intones Ardent's moniker with some amusement, like she's seen it all now.

"You have something I want, too," Ardent replies. "Your name."

"Elzahia Tazi, United Worlds Intelligence. I'm going to need that drippy fellow right there." She points to Gus, one of her fingernails painting him with a laser designator. Drones detach from her backpack, holos illuminating Gus for all her troops to see. "The one you fished out from beneath Greymalkin."

Ardent isn't sure they can trust this person, and it might be best to confuse the issue until Gus can get a lawyer. They smile sweetly while their mind races for excuses.

"I think you're probably mista—"

"Before you even attempt to deny it," Elzahia says, "you lit up like a firework beneath the giant robot we were all looking at... with every spy satellite on Earth."

"Not denying it," Ardent replies, clearing their throat. "I was just going to ask if you had a towel."

Chapter Three

Back Among the Living

The man once called Gus is forever changed in Greymalkin's breast.

A thunderstorm obliterates his identity: water and light, cannon claps of armor and steel, the howling keen of the Vanguards.

A vision of red. *Ardent Violet?*

For an age, Gus is dead as the soil—a tangle of interconnected ecologies without a consciousness. The thin skein of his mind regains a bit of its shape, and he begins to dream. He's a lone vibration against the cosmos, diminished, but growing brighter with every second.

He has touched a boundless network unlike anything he could've imagined, and it reached into the deepest parts of him in return. A database of souls, end states of a civilization, flooded through Gus. With their help, he smote a Vanguard, then became nothingness.

Gus finally remembers his own body. He'd forgotten it in death.

It grows harder to ignore his corporeal form, with its sweaty back and painful chest. Someone is pushing on his face and being loud. He's nauseated. Dreaming was definitely better.

"—ko," a voice says. His name?

Gus's bones ache; his joints are bruised and swollen. The air smells nice and clean, though. He opens his eyes to regal majesty.

He rests on a lovely four-poster bed within a cherry-walled room, gaudy gold accents proclaiming the reigning house of Monaco. Medical control surfaces and signifiers are holoed to every wall, blinking and breathing in time with Gus's vitals. There's even a baroque convalescence chair in the nearby corner, for those who might want a bunch of nude cherubs to help them recuperate.

A couple of folx in crisp military uniforms have gathered around the foot of his bed like a row of tombstones.

"Soldiers?" Gus says.

"Mister Kitko—" comes a smooth, masculine voice beside him.

Gus turns to find a handsome young doctor—not a hologram, but an actual physician, in person. This beautiful specimen looks like he just walked in off a vites advertisement, with white skin and startling blue eyes.

"Hello, there," Gus says, dreamy from whatever is in his system. "Aren't we all scheduled to be dead?"

The gathered audience visibly deflates, and Gus realizes he's disappointed them. What were they expecting him to say?

Cute Doctor smiles. "Let's start with your name. I'm Doctor Jurgens."

"Gus," he says, then takes a dusty swallow and coughs. "August Kitko."

"Can you tell me where you're from?"

"I live in Montreal. I was born in Wisconsin."

Doctor Jurgens is quite thorough, going through the checks

with the aid of a nurse. If any of the basic stuff was off, the hospital scanners should've caught it, but Jurgens manually takes Gus's heart rate through his glove. After what Gus has been through, the warm hand is nice.

"What's the last thing you remember?" Jurgens asks.

That's a complicated question. Water springs to mind, and before that, the persona-warping experience of connecting to an alien intelligence. But the last thing he properly remembers is a shining figure with red hair.

Gus closes his eyes and smiles. "I was rescued by an angel."

A veritable cackle fills the room. Some of the military types part so Gus can see Ardent Violet lounging in one of the hospital chairs, orange-tinted sunglasses resting on their nose. They're dressed in all-white shinewrap, a glossy pastiche of a doctor. Ardent pops their tangerine-colored bubble gum and gives Gus a finger wave.

"Right answer, baby, right answer," they say.

Gus stares at them with a sleepy smile. "Sorry I was a dick about pop music. I wanted to tell you that, but uh, someone crashed the party."

Ardent laughs even harder and rests their fingers against their chest. "Be still my heart! A man who knows how to apologize."

"Mister Kitko," says Doctor Jurgens, "these people have requested some of your time. Your scans show that you're generally stable, but you can say no."

"Who are they?" Gus asks, and they introduce themselves in turn.

"Sol Joint Defense Force, Colonel Edwin Kelley."

"United Worlds director of security, Yuna Landon."

"UWI, Elzahia Tazi."

On and on the battery of experts goes, until others start arriving by hologram: His Serene Highness Prince Robert III, European

Union Governor Adana Kent, American Alliance President Jennifer Rossuck, Canadian Prime Minister Kate Bryski.

Ardent Violet, rock and roll slayer of coliseums, disappears in the crowd of top people eager to have an audience with Gus.

He sits up straighter in bed, coughing up some chemical gunk. Doctor Jurgens hands him a glass of water, and he takes a grateful swig. Gus is accustomed to minor celebrities, not generals and presidents. Wooziness follows excitement, and he has to tamp down his nausea.

"Doctor, you didn't tell me I'd be meeting the United Worlds leadership," he says, blinking and resting back on his bed.

"We all just wanted to come together and express our gratitude," PM Bryski says, stepping forward. "For... whatever you did to save us. I'm not sure any of us expected to be alive here today."

"Ardent Violet." She turns to the rocker. "Your quick thinking and bravery saved this young man's life, and it appears the world may owe you a debt as well. If you hadn't recovered him..."

Ardent rises with a vibrant smile. "So my watersweep theft isn't going to be a problem?"

"We've taken care of it," Bryski says.

Gus watches the exchange in wonder. *Holy shit. That's the PM you actually voted for.*

She's taller in person, commanding the room. Her embroidered peacock coat tapers to silky tails of copper, turquoise, and violet, and she sweeps aside brown hair with a gray-gloved hand. "It's an honor to meet you, Mister Kitko."

Gus nods, sifting his mind for any possible thing he could say to make a good impression. "Thanks. I, uh, voted for you."

The assembly titters with laughter; they think it's a joke. Lisel, Gus's late bassist, would be proud to see him finally warm up a crowd with a one-liner. Maybe she could have explained what the hell happens next.

"Well," Gus says when no one else talks, "thank you...for coming?"

They wait for him to speak. This is Gus's personal hell.

His pulse monitor speeds up, which worries him, which accelerates his pulse, and he begins to sweat. He kind of stinks. Can the prime minister tell that? She's not particularly close to him, but Gus's odor can fill up a room if he's funky enough. It's not pretty.

She's a hologram, and you need to get a grip.

This is exactly why Gus never told jokes from the bench. He's not a talker or a showman—he's a pianist.

"Swallow, Gus. You look like you're about to throw up over there," Ardent says.

The UWI agent, a Black woman with a high, starched collar and a pile of elegant braids, steps forward. Gus thinks her name is Tazi, but he's not sure. He just woke up, after all. She has her coils all luxed up like they can move, and they slowly coruscate around her scalp. Though her clothing fits with the gathered dignitaries, her expression is far less welcoming.

"Mix Violet." Tazi sighs, powerful voice tinted with a gentle French accent. "We're all so grateful, but as you can imagine, we have urgent business with Mister Kitko. We'll send for you when we need you."

And a pair of interns hurries them from the chamber. The last words Gus hears out of Ardent are "Oh no. Did I talk too much?"

But now Gus is free from his debilitating anxieties, because he can no longer be the most embarrassing person in the room.

"Please, Mister Kitko," Tazi says. "Tell us what happened last night."

"I...I was inside Greymalkin as, uh, not like a passenger, but maybe, uh," Gus says, and all eyes snap onto him, any interest in Ardent's disruption vanishing.

Tazi flips up the Gang on her wrist to launch a camera drone.

A lens sphere rises from her pack, repulsors warbling like a distant songbird. She checks the feed on her wrist and nods.

"For everyone's sake, I'm going to be recording this," she says. "I'll be asking my questions first, and others will be available for follow-ons."

"You're doing an interview like... this second?" Gus asks.

"That shouldn't be a problem for you," she says, pointing to the charts. "You're healthy."

"Okay," Gus says, strongly considering asking them all to leave.

Tazi nods. "Tell me what happened."

"So, you know," Gus says, "it was, like, last night, and I was playing piano. I started hearing this screaming—"

"Any particular song?" Tazi interrupts.

"What? No. Uh, I was just like, jamming. You know that noise the Vanguards make? That singing noise?"

A smile plays at the corner of Tazi's mouth, but she stifles it. "You call that... singing?"

"No. I'm just trying to—I don't call it singing, *per se*. But you know what I'm talking about? The music?"

Tazi nods. "Yes. The Harmonic Carrier Communication Protocol. We've been studying the phenomenon for some time. There's a lot of data embedded in the signal, but teasing it out of the encryption has proven impossible."

"Well, I heard F Dorian mode, so I started jamming to it, and Greymalkin punched the house I was in, grabbed me, and—"

The memory of the brain drill comes tunneling back into his head, and a shiver travels up Gus's spine. His back itches, and he reaches behind himself to scratch. Instead of bare skin, he finds a dermagraft bandage blocking his fingers, with a little metal nubbin no thicker than a pen sticking up through the center. He runs his hand over his lower back, finding a few more bumps along the line of his spine.

"What did it do to me?" Gus asks Doctor Jurgens.

The doctor purses his lips as he puzzles through what to say.

"Mister Kitko, you're physically stable," Jurgens says, "but I'm not sure about the side effects to your person. You've undergone considerable trauma and body modification. I'm concerned that some of this might impact you long term."

Gus laughs, and immediately apologizes. "Wasn't expecting to live past yesterday."

"Take your time, Mister Kitko," Jurgens says. "This is more difficult news than you're giving it credit for."

Gus gingerly pulls up his gown and pushes down his blanket, finding little squares of dermagraft running all around his soft abdominal muscles. Each patch pokes up in the middle, just like the ones on his spine. It hurts to touch them, a deep, stinging ache.

"You were septic when we got you," Jurgens says. "If it weren't for medical intervention, you'd be looking at double pneumonia and dry drowning. You had a lot of open wounds, and then you were dumped into the SuperPort—shouldn't have survived. We're not entirely sure what Greymalkin did. A lot of this is beyond us."

Gus's pulse shoots back up. "What..."

Jurgens pulls up a set of scans on his Gang UI, throwing them to the holos mounted over the bed. Gus's masculine form appears overhead for everyone, including the prime minister, to see. Thankfully, all the sensitive bits have been obscured, but that's still Gus's glowing ass before the leaders of humanity.

He flushes. "Hey, Doctor, can we not show... like, everyone..."

"These people are charged with the survival of our species," Jurgens says. "Most of them invoked galactic security and saw your scans six hours ago. This is a briefing for you." He looks ashamed. "Apologies."

"We're sorry for the invasion of privacy, August," PM Bryski says, "but this is the future of civilization we're talking about. You wouldn't believe what has to be done to preserve that on a daily basis, and most of it isn't peeking at medical charts, you know."

"Yeah, um... of course, Madam Prime Minister," he murmurs, still mortified.

Gus swallows his discomfort and looks up at his own hovering body. Beneath each port is a cluster of spherical modules, like a pearl-encrusted hairpin beneath the surface of his skin. There are dozens of the stab wounds lining his body, but Gus isn't truly disturbed until he looks at his brain.

His skull is spiked inside, jutting needles in the fashion of an ancient iron maiden. Wires pass through every part of his cerebral cortex. Grids of ports line his scalp, spines sunk deep into his gray matter, branching out inside him.

Reaching up to touch one of the ports, he finds his hair is missing, shaved smooth with a few hours of shadow. He runs his fingers along the rows of dermagraft bandages, pressing at the metal structures beneath.

"Let's not touch that, Mister Kitko," Jurgens says, gently taking his hand and guiding it back onto the bed.

"How am I... me?" Gus asks, voice trembling. "With all that shit in my head?"

"We don't know," Jurgens replies, patting his hand. "It's eluded us for the moment, but we're working on it with all speed."

"You said you were inside Greymalkin," Tazi prompts. "What did you experience?"

He tries to conjure the words to embody those tense moments. If she'd asked which keyboard has the best hammer action, Gus could've droned on for hours. When it comes to descriptive language for the mind-bending odyssey of connecting to the Vanguard, he's adrift.

"I—" Gus stammers. "Well, I—okay, so Greymalkin grabbed me and shoved me into it. Then it told me I was a Conduit."

"Can you clarify?" Tazi asks.

Gus searches for the right words. She's looking for a clean answer, but nothing in Gus's life has prepared him for those five minutes. It was all such a blur, and there are too many chemical cocktails in his system now.

"It's like I'm an interpreter. Those fakes the Ghosts make out of us are more than simple bots. They're whole lives captured in amber. Memories and knowledge, collected and collated."

President Rossuck's throat bobs, and she blinks a few times in rapid succession before her dignified smile returns. Gus remembers that her husband got Wiped at Proxima.

"Do they speak to you?" Rossuck asks. "The dead, I mean."

Everyone leans in a little closer at that. The media have always been ablaze with speculation that the fakes were more like the afterlife. They wanted their loved ones to still be around, chatting happily with one another inside a simulation.

"They're not people anymore, Madam President. They're just buckets of data. I felt their instincts, but not their voices. I know that's not the answer you'd like."

"What about Greymalkin?" Tazi directs her humming camera sphere closer. "Does it talk to you?"

Gus wrinkles his nose. "Not in, um, speech. Greymalkin doesn't have a voice. It sounds like reality."

The UWI agent looks up from her Gang, where she's been taking notes. "I don't follow."

"It *makes* me know what it wants me to know. It puts facts into me so seamlessly that my whole perspective shifts. Like if you dreamed you had gills, you wouldn't ask why. You'd just know it was true."

"Can you give me an example of one of Greymalkin's 'facts'?" Tazi asks.

"Like... like..." Gus swallows, because what he's about to say sounds delusional—but he's certain in his heart. "Everyone thinks the other colonies are dead, but two of them are still out there."

A chorus of murmurs goes up from the gathered luminaries, and Tazi's eyes grow stern.

"That's quite the statement, Mister Kitko. No one has heard from anyone outside the system for years."

"New Jalandhar and Fugelsangen are both still there," he says. "Greymalkin pointed them out to me."

"Meaning..."

"People are alive," he says, a smile dawning on his face. His heart leaps as he finishes his thought. "We're not the last ones! Holy shit, we're not the last... buh..."

The blood pressure peak comes with a commensurate plummet, and Gus starts to feel ill. The holos around the room pop up a few caution bubbles, and Doctor Jurgens reaches forward to lay two fingers to his neck.

"This is a lot of stress, Mister Kitko. I think I'm calling it." Jurgens turns to the dignitaries. "Friends, I'm afraid I have to ask you to leave. This young man needs to recover, and I let you have your time."

"He just dropped the most significant piece of intelligence since the start of the war," Rossuck interjects, smile fading. "You can't expect us to just go."

"He has more stab wounds than Caesar," Doctor Jurgens says. "He needs rest, or he won't be dropping any *more* intelligence."

"With all due respect, Doctor Jurgens, we're not the sort of people who can be turned away," the president says.

"Madam President, as a hologram, that's exactly what you are. Farewell, and I'll let you know when he's ready."

Jurgens taps the wall beside Gus's head a few times, pulling up the room connection and severing the protesting elites. Only the military folx remain: mostly shocked, save for Elzahia. She's just disappointed.

"Doctor, I told you I wouldn't be responsible for the behavior of politicians. Not my fault when Americans act like that," she says with a shrug. "Let me stay."

The doctor brings up another panel, cycling through meds. Gus closes his eyes as waves of fatigue threaten to sweep him away from consciousness.

Jurgens's tone is polite but resolute. "You have to give our guest some time. He just woke up. Besides, it's a moot point. I drugged him."

Ah, thank you, Doc.

"We can't sit still here," Tazi says. "Mister Kitko, one last question before you go."

He's already starting to drift, though he hopes to stay in the moment. He genuinely wants to help, but his body won't listen. "Lay it on me."

"Why did it choose you?" she asks. "Why are you special?"

It's funny to him. "I'm not. I'm one in a million. So there are plenty of people like me. Thousands."

"Until five years ago, tens of thousands," Tazi says, and he nods sadly.

"I was in the hot seat at the right time. Greymalkin likes..."

A yawn erupts from him without permission or warning, and Gus has to stretch. He squirms under Tazi's gaze before getting his swooning head back under control. "...likes the way I play piano. Music is a pattern. Sentience...loves patterns..."

He sort of sings the last bit, even though singing isn't his forte. "I'm just kind of Greymalkin's...funny valentine."

His eyes droop.

"And pincushion," he concludes.

"Perfect. Thank you," Tazi replies, and a blanket of darkness muffles all. "Get some rest, Mister Kitko."

* * *

For the seventh day in a row, the subtle movement of air over Ardent's bare skin is the only indication they're not alone. The door swishes open, and Ardent sits up, scrambling back against the headboard. A Gilded Ghost stalks into the room, claws silent as cat's paws, and stops at the foot of the bed.

This Ghost could easily kill Ardent right now. It's two and a half meters of merciless metal, with a pair of knife-sharp probes for coring brains out. Ardent remembers pulling off the dead man's safety vest in the boat, the way his empty head lolled. What would the big bite feel like? The machines can't be resisted—Ardent knows that firsthand.

Don't go! It doesn't hurt!

Narika Tanner's terrifying exhortation still rings in Ardent's ears when they look at the Ghost. She'd been such a sweet fan, and now her captor stands ready to murder Ardent as well. Narika's kids must be locked up inside the Ghosts somewhere, too. They'd all been Wiped last year when Abode went down.

Ardent pulls the bedsheets tighter, swallowing hard. The saber-toothed robot locks its lens upon their form, and its housing splits open to eject a beam scanner barrel. Blue light sweeps over Ardent's body, rendering their organs in gelatinous detail.

But it doesn't Wipe them, and that's what matters most.

Since Juliette's demise, the bots have been acting strangely. Instead of their normal "kill all humans" programming, the walking chain cloaks have been checking up on Ardent, looking after those broken ribs once a day for the past week, dosing Ardent when required. Every morning at 8:08 sharp, a Ghost shows up to scan them, tracking them down no matter where they might hide.

Their leader, Greymalkin, sits idly in the harbor near Monaco, still. It hasn't moved at all or made any demands. Most importantly, it hasn't ordered its swarm to eat everyone. Ardent hasn't seen the Vanguard since they evacuated the city, and truth be told, they prefer it that way.

This scan seems to be going well—there are a lot fewer red glowy bits on Ardent's abdomen and more blue and green glowy bits. They can only assume that's a good thing, because the Ghost doesn't react in any meaningful way. It concludes this morning's scan the same way it has concluded every scan for the past week: The beam projector snaps back into its head, and it pads out the door.

"Okay, bye, then," Ardent says before pressing their lips tightly together. When their shaking subsides, they reach over and page the front desk.

A holo avatar—the illegibly calligraphic hotel name—swirls to life at Ardent's bedside. The Edwardian copperplate logo is ostensibly made up of words, but at a glance, it looks like gibberish. Everyone calls this hotel "the Palms," so Ardent calls it that, too. The brand mark, however, leaves the impression that the name is longer than their attention span and French-er than their tongue.

"Allô!" the ligatures throb in a man's voice.

Ardent squints as the room raises the lights. They slept with their mouth open again, and their throat hurts a little. At least they don't have any concerts booked.

"Hey, why didn't you call and warn me that thing was coming up here again?"

"Sorry, Mix Violet, but the security scanners didn't catch it. Probably came in the third-floor balcony."

He doesn't sound like he cares enough. Ardent will fix that.

"Lock the fucking doors and give the guests manual keys. I shouldn't have to wake up every day to a murder machine wandering into my room."

The calligraphy sighs, and Ardent's room holos spin up, projecting a security feed over the bed. The cheeky desk jockey is sending a video to prove his point.

The third-floor balcony comes into focus, a couple of tall ferns atop a roof garden. The Ghost clambers over the glass railing, skitters across the slate to the door, and places a claw to the lock plate. The door flashes green and opens immediately. The video freezes, and a highlight appears around the Ghost's paw.

"They bypass all our security." The Palms logo goes on to explain, "Even if they can't hack or pick a lock, they can weld it. Maman, who was taken... Wiped on Titan, thought a vault door would stop Ghosts, but—" His voice shakes a little. "Nothing will. Either we let them in, or they cut their way in. We don't want them on the hotel grounds, and we're trying our best, so please be patient... Magdalena, a member of our staff, was injured yesterday trying to keep one of those... things... out of the pool."

Please tell me they aren't attacking people.

"What? What happened?"

"She tripped over it. Just a sprained ankle, and it—the Ghost treated the injury as soon as it occurred."

"They've been doing medical scans on me every morning whether I want them or not."

"Yeah. My supervisor is dead, but her boss has a baby on the way. The Ghosts have been stopping by to check on the baby every hour. After the bots killed so many of us, being touched by one is..."

Ardent dons their favorite polysilk robe, bright white and blue like a jellyfish, with floaty, trailing tendrils of fabric. Tails swim weightlessly in their wake as Ardent strides barefoot across the marble. "Why do you think they're helping us?"

"I think... maybe it's the will of the Heavenly Father. It's the Rapture."

A Rapturist. Great.

"Listen, I've got to go. I'm sorry for being so cross. I know it's not your fault."

"It's okay. I really do think everything is going to be okay."

Ardent waits long enough to make the guy feel heard, then says, "Yep. I tell you what, I'm going to go get a coffee, and you can figure out how to handle your haunted pool."

"Oh, uh...you should also know there's a, um, lady in the lobby who's been asking for you."

For the second time that morning, their heart skips a beat. "Who?"

"Dahlia Faust?" The guy sounds unsure, but Ardent knows exactly who's downstairs—and they're in trouble.

"She's been waiting at the café all morning. Said she called you, but I don't believe her. Between you and me, her name sounds made-up."

"What, like Ardent Violet? Some people find choosing their names empowering, honey."

"Oh, uh—"

"Tell her I'll be right down."

They hastily jump in the blast shower, arms up and singing the whole time, then throw on a charcoal-gray sundress. Ardent grabs their Ganglion bangle and slips it over a wrist, flicking once to activate the UI. At a button press, their Sif circuit braids their hair into tight Viking rows and stains it pearlescent white. It's one of Dahlia's favorite looks, and Ardent needs her amenable after leaving her waiting so long.

Ardent Violet, the person, considers themself a singular individual, fully possessed of their identity. Ardent Violet, the company, career, and legend, is the collaborative brainchild of themself and Dahlia Faust, senior agent at Interlink Artist Management.

Ardent met her at age fifteen, streaming concerts from a rented youth venue. She'd been a hard sell to Ardent's mother; a stranger ten years older offering contracts under the name *Faust* was rightfully dubious. Her skepticism had nearly blown Ardent's blossoming prospects.

So they invited an unwitting Dahlia to family dinner to see how she handled it. Dahlia showed Ardent that an agent understood diplomacy just as well as contracts, capably fending off the pack of older siblings with various motives. When she survived a meal at the Aldridge family home, Dahlia Faust was officially Ardent Violet's agent.

The next nine years brought misadventure and heartache, triumphs and, thankfully, a big break. Ardent made Dahlia a very rich woman, but the agent put in more than her share of work, running down every opportunity, handling PR crises and Ardent's smart mouth alike.

She's the rock upon which Ardent's castle is built, so it's bad to keep her waiting.

After a quick spritz of perfume, they head down the elevator to the lobby. Dahlia is nowhere to be found, and the religious white guy at the front desk points outside to a large CAV parked under the awning. Ardent thanks them and rushes out to their agent.

Dahlia Faust is an imposing height at almost 190 centimeters, a fact she regularly exploits during negotiations. She calls her style "dramatic monochromatic," adopting a drab, severe counterpoint to Ardent's colorful plumage. This day, she wears a cream linen suit, a bloodred silk scarf, and a flat expression behind round, crimson-tinted sunglasses.

When they'd parted ways before the fauxpocalypse, Ardent had made peace with the fact they'd never see her again. They'd both had a few things to do before they died. Upon seeing the agent in the flesh, Ardent is nearly overcome with tears of joy—were it not for the foreboding look in Dahlia's eyes when she takes off her glasses.

She purses her dark-painted lips as they approach. "I got up at three a.m. to fetch *your* pod—"

"I know, I'm sorry." They make sure they look extra-rushed and mortified, arriving in a whirlwind.

It does little to quench the growing anger. "—and fly it to you from Berlin—"

"Yes, and that obviously makes you a saint."

"*Obviously*—" One brown eyebrow shoots up, and Ardent squirms. Dahlia's stony gaze has been crushing them into line for years. "Which is why I want to know why you didn't answer my first three hails. After you rushed me over here, I thought you were dead. It's been going around nowadays, you know."

"What, dying?"

"Yes!"

She seats a snake-shaped actuweave tie between her lips and pulls her long chestnut hair behind her head. She places the snake to the bundle and plays its stored motion. It twists through her long strands, securing them by fashioning itself into a jeweled Celtic knot.

"I promise I'm sorry," Ardent says.

"Marilyn warned me you'd be like this." She looks away, shaking her head, but Ardent catches the flash of a smile.

They drop their hands to their hips. "Uh-huh."

"Totally true."

Ardent can't restrain a laugh as relief washes over them. "I genuinely thought you were mad at me—"

Dahlia looks heavenward, ever the martyr. "All those years ago, your mother said, 'My baby will only bring you trouble.' Why? Why didn't I listen?"

Ardent runs to embrace her, squeezing an "Oof" from the agent and stealing the rest of her monologue. Her familiar scent envelops them, and for a moment, Ardent is sent back to their teenage years.

"I'm so glad you made it," they mumble into her collarbone, and she drapes her arms around them like a blanket.

"You too, kid. It's a lot easier to say goodbye when you're sure you're going to be killed."

Ardent pulls back and dabs an eye. "I'm really glad you came. You could've said no."

"Leaving you a ton of affairs to manage. Who's going to help you with that?"

A couple of gulls cry nearby, and Ardent shields their eyes to watch them coast on the breeze. "I don't know. Does it matter? Aren't we just, like, fiddling while the world burns?"

"Ardent." Dahlia takes them by the shoulders. "You're basically my only job. I can't abandon you."

"Aw, Dahlia—"

"You'll perish," she says. "I don't even think you can feed yourself."

"Oh, hush. I love you, too."

"I talked to your mom this morning," Dahlia says. "You didn't check in last night."

"I'm twenty-five."

"So you're old enough to treat her right. You worried her."

"About what?"

"You told her you were being stalked by a Ghost."

"Dahlia."

"Hail her when we get settled, and I'll drop it."

Ardent bumps her fist on the way past. "Rock on, then."

The TourPod Platinum is Ardent's little slice of heaven anywhere on the Homeworld. From the haptic massage seats to the ChoetteChef, Ardent can't be happier than when they're resting in its comfy environs. As Lord Yamizaki's guest, they hadn't required it, and after the attack in Monaco, global infrastructure had been so badly damaged they hadn't been able to fetch it. When Dahlia had finally gotten in touch, asking if Ardent needed help, they'd begged her to bring the TourPod along and rescue them from the crowded French hotels.

The interior is a bit stale now, a custom royal-blue jacquard by Juniper Foundry, with silver inlays holoed onto the trim. Ardent has always liked the ensemble, but it doesn't match their current clothes, so they pull up the CAV's interior options and throw on the UltraGloss.

The walls flatten to a shiny white, simulated embroidery going mirror-slick in an instant. Holos trim the cabin with Ardent's favorite neon, a classic undulation of cool blue and purple. The primitive polys of the furniture relux from Juniper Foundry's overwrought style to crushed velvet in Ardent Violet's signature brand color.

Now Ardent can match their environs. UltraGloss goes with everything.

They pat the wall as the transformation finishes. "I've missed you, Bess."

Dahlia scoots past, headed for the bar. "Bess is leased. If you don't drop the nickname, it's going to hurt when we give her back."

"No!" They throw themself across one of the chairs, gently nuzzling the soft velvet. "We'll run away together."

Dahlia twists her cocktail stick like a pepper grinder, shooting the contents into the tumbler. "Don't get weird with the TourPod."

"I'm being perfectly natural." They stroke the upholstery and sigh. "She's drawn to me like a unicorn to a virgin."

Dahlia sprays out the first sip of her cocktail, coughing and fanning herself before setting the glass down on the table.

"I'm not that bad!" Ardent flops into the chair, throwing a leg over its arm in a photogenic slouch.

"Ardent, you literally had me call a bunch of generals and diplomats to set up a playdate with your new boy toy."

They blush, trying not to think about Gus's stubble against their neck. "And you did. So you're an enabler."

Dahlia gives her drink a defeated look and downs it in one.

"Dollface," Ardent says. "This will be fun. And you'll like Gus. Maybe you'll even want to represent him."

"Yeah, I'll add him to my roster of obscure jazz pianists."

"He's going to be very popular."

Dahlia snaps together another cocktail while a second tumbler prints. "And when you break his heart in front of the whole galaxy, do I keep representing both of you, or..."

"Fair point."

"Here." Dahlia shoots a gin fizz into a fresh glass and hands it to Ardent before adding another for herself. "To life."

"To us," Ardent says, raising their drink. "Even extinction events can't stop the music."

Dahlia clinks her glass. "Nothing can, superstar. Now let's go break in the new guy."

The flight across town takes fifteen minutes, only because the government-provided approach vectors to Gus's location are so specific. Ardent's vehicle is subjected to a thorough scan, flying past wounded laser cannons. The Ghosts must've been a little frightened of the massive focusing arrays, because most of the lasers bear gashes along the sides from attacks.

The Château DiLorenzo is almost four hundred years old, but its signature "flying box" layout looks like it was designed yesterday. Interlocking chambers form a stacked tower, forever on the verge of toppling, and it boggles the mind up close. Ardent leans to stare out the window as the CAV descends, glassy facets of the château capturing the chunky TourPod.

The house doesn't have a lawn to speak of—just a few meters by a public street—but that hasn't stopped the paparazzi from trampling what little grass exists.

"How did they find us?" Dahlia sighs, taking note of the copious journos swarming the CAV's hospitality cradle.

"How do they always?" Ardent turns to bang on the window. "Hey! You're blocking me in! You have to back up if you want to harass me."

Taking a steadying breath, Ardent emerges from the TourPod into a hailstorm of strobes. They pose and smile, giving the vultures a little bit of meat for their news feeds.

"What are you doing at the château?" calls one of the journos.

"Visiting you, of course," Ardent says, winking for the eager lenses. "What have you heard, my dears?"

"You're here to see your boyfriend!" another guy shouts from the back row.

"Would you like that?" Ardent runs a finger along the soft skin beneath their jaw. "Dahlia, do I have a boyfriend? The press is asking. I think they're into me."

Dahlia emerges from the TourPod cabin, glasses darkening to red in the bright sunlight. "It's hard to imagine you ever leaving the press for another lover."

Titters of laughter.

"We heard you rescued Kitko from under Greymalkin!" a white woman shouts to them, and Ardent blinks.

The government made Ardent promise not to talk about that, and no one had asked so far. But anyone could've had a lens pointed at Greymalkin the night Ardent rescued Gus. The bodysuit was basically an emergency beacon—though the government people argued the intense lights obscured the identities of all concerned.

It's a bit of a shock to Ardent's system, and the one-liner required to dodge the question evaporates from their mind.

Ardent opens their mouth a few times. "I'm not sure what you're insinuating, but—"

"Is that why he's in the hospital? Because of the effects of Juliette's blood? Have you got the nanites, too?"

Ardent recoils. "What are you talking about? Juliette's blood... nanites?"

The reporter pulls up a news story on her wrist Gang and throws it to her holos, projecting an image of an ivory gauntlet emerging from the waters of SuperPort Hercule. Milky fluid stains the sea, diffracting in the sun like mother-of-pearl. A small fleet of spill-abatement ships close in around Juliette's corpse, containing the spread of the opalescent cloud. A few words hover over the image in a big banner.

POSSIBLE EXPOSURE RISKS? NANITE PRIONS IN ROBOT "BLOOD"?

A week ago, Ardent had been absolutely soaked in Juliette's circulatory fluids. The government told everyone to go take a shower and see a doctor every two days. Ardent's doc said the stuff was basically harmless. Body-safe hydraulic fluid, radioactively inert, but it might dry out the skin if left on too long. *Quarantine isn't necessary*, she said. *Everything is under control.*

Unless Ardent has nanite prions eating their brain.

Their eye twitches. "You're not funny, lady."

"Not trying to be. The Monaco evac is permanent," the journo says. "Ten-kilometer Quarantine Exclusion Zone. They're saying the blood is bad, bad stuff."

The holo switches from the drowned Juliette's hand to a map of Monaco and its surrounding territory. A bright red circle demarcates the "QEZ," and a shiver runs up Ardent's spine. Juliette's corpse is poisoning the earth, and they'd been standing at ground zero. If Ardent had run away instead of trying to get close to the fight, would they have been exposed? The journos keep their drones rolling, soaking up Ardent's reaction to the news.

A golden glimmer in the distance tickles Ardent's vision—one of the Ghosts scaling a skyscraper, bound for a mission only it would know.

The planet is still crawling with these killers.

For Ardent, every day since the Vanguard planetfall has been better than the last. Flowers are more vibrant, lights are brighter, music is fresher—new songs torment Ardent every night like a fever. They've spent their waking seconds either eating or playing the guitar, and they're no longer ready to die.

"No one told us about any exposure risks," Dahlia says, voice commanding. She rests a hand on Ardent's shoulder, rock-solid. "This is confirmed by the authorities?"

"Straight off the official principality stream," says the reporter, checking the feed on her drone. "You're looking pretty shook over there, Ardent. You okay?"

It's like their ability to swallow stops working, and Ardent signals that they need a minute, faking a coy smile to mask panic.

"Ardent Violet has seen the very best doctors the area has to offer, including those from the UW," Dahlia says, and Ardent hides behind her like she's a linen-suited shelter. "We have a regular schedule of care, so I think we'd have been told if there was a problem." Her tone is firm, uncompromising.

"I'm just sharing the knowledge," the reporter says, raising her hands in surrender.

"Okay, well, you can see how that's upsetting my client, and I'd like you to stop."

"It's not my job to make you feel good," she says with a sneer. "It's my job to get pictures."

"Hey, fuck you, lady!" One of the paparazzi wheels on her, a little Black guy in a vest overflowing with chargers. "We've got a good thing going with Ardent, and if you're going to jeopardize that, you can—"

The other journos join in, and it turns into a shouting match.

Ardent takes a few steps back, clutching their chest. Their heart aches, and their breath comes in quick bursts.

"Good riddance," Dahlia mutters, turning to face Ardent. Her concerned double take just makes the panic worse. "What's wrong?"

Ardent wants to tell Dahlia that they're scared, that they need to go inside to get away from the press, but they can't stop thinking of the Ghosts screaming at them in the voices of the dead. Ardent's lips tremble uselessly instead of making words.

The agent nods in understanding and turns to the paparazzi. "Okay, we've got appointments to keep, so you all fight among yourselves."

Dahlia doesn't gently lead Ardent away so much as drag them inside like a small child. As soon as they're through the door, the château staff rush to Ardent's side, proffering water and fanning them with their scarves. It's supposed to be calming, but it's like being attacked by peacocks. They corner Ardent into one of the lobby chairs.

"Back up, please," Dahlia says, putting her body between Ardent and the staff. She fixes Ardent with her blue eyes. "Hey, look at me. I want you to imagine licking a brick of salt."

Ardent knows this game. Dahlia has used it plenty of times when they were drugged up and out of it, but never sober.

"What the hell? I don't panic, Dahlia," Ardent mumbles, almost in tears. "I've been on so many arena stages—ran toward a Vanguard fight. I don't panic. I'm not weak."

It's embarrassing, is what it is.

"You don't have control over what makes you panic; now imagine licking a block of salt," Dahlia orders them. "Do you need your inhaler?"

"I haven't needed it... in two years." Ardent huffs, trying to imagine the crystalline burn of sodium saturation on their tongue.

Dahlia pulls an atomizer out of her pocket and gives it a few shakes before priming it. The inhaler case goes green, and the agent hands it off to Ardent. "But you're going to take your meds right now. You remembering salt? Yeah? Good. What does rust feel like?"

Ardent imagines metal crust crumbling under their fingertips, and a touch more of the panic recedes from their mind. They take a hit off the inhaler, holding their breath and counting to ten. More of the panic washes away with the eggy taste of the vapor.

"They're just paparazzi." Ardent hates how whiny their voice sounds, and it makes them want to cry all the more. "I *have* to be able to talk to paps. I *have* to."

"And you can," Dahlia assures them, "after you deal with your shit. Did you see a lot of bad stuff at the end of the world? I was passed-out drunk, but the morgues were all full when I came to."

"One of the Ghosts screamed at me in Narika's voice," Ardent says, eyes stinging. First they lost it in front of the journos, now they're crying in front of their fucking agent. "Dahlia, the Ghosts... they're everywhere now... They're not screaming, but I can hear Narika every time I look at one. I don't know what to do."

"Get an appointment with a therapist," she says. "But for now, finish taking your inhaler before I call your mother."

"You wouldn't," Ardent says, but takes another hit of their medicine before Dahlia can prove it.

"What does wet granite feel like?" the agent says, rubbing Ardent's back while the sniffles subside. "Imagine it cool on your cheek."

The staffers and guards at the château are still staring, and some commotion burbles up behind them. They part, and Gus stands there, looking down at Ardent in bewilderment.

After all of Ardent's careful prep, all their hopes to make a good impression, they've collapsed, weeping in the lobby like some kind of child.

The pianist cuts a striking silhouette in his dark suit. It hugs his slender body, from his mirror-shined oxfords to his silk ascot. After a week, the poor boy still doesn't have much hair, and silvery ports poke out where there'd previously been glorious shaggy curls. The rest of his scalp is covered in an even layer of black fuzz. Ardent hopes to run their fingers over it.

"Ardent?" he asks. "Are you okay? What happened?"

"I don't know." They smile, defeated, raising a palm before flopping it to their lap. "Just got... overwhelmed by the apocalypse, I guess."

"I don't blame you at all," Gus replies. His voice falls into that lovely low register, with a slight stony grind to it. Ardent could listen to him talk all day, but tragically, he doesn't sound like he can carry a tune.

Talented hands, though. Pleasant memories, along with the inhaler, tamp down the last of the panic.

"Hello, Mister Kitko." Dahlia steps in. "I'm sure you can understand that Ardent needs a little space. If you'll direct your people that way, we're parked out front in the blue TourPod."

Gus nods. "Oh, sure. Yeah, absolutely. Let me move along. Just, uh—thanks for coming to get me. So happy to see you."

He gives Ardent a little wave, then departs. An entourage of guards and minders follows in Gus's wake.

Dahlia leans over and rests a hand on Ardent's shoulder. "Figured you'd want me to go distract him while you fix your face."

"Ah, my Faust, what would I do without you?"

She winks. "Sell french fries at a FuelStop in Georgia."

"Please. The mountains can't contain me."

Dahlia's eyes crinkle at the edges when she smiles. "I like Gus. Don't know about the haircut. Now you take some time in the bathroom and sort yourself out. I'm going to go babysit this unfortunate soul you've ensnared."

Chapter Four

Spring Blessing

For the majority of the flight to the safe house, Gus sits alone in the TourPod lounge with Dahlia while Ardent freshens up in the bedroom. He tries to make small talk with the agent, but she keeps getting hails. She isn't trying to ignore him, per se, but she's so important that he feels guilty for talking to her. He eventually gives up, and leaves Dahlia to sign out messages in the corner. From her clipped gestures, it looks like someone is in deep shit.

A military escort falls in behind the TourPod, an ill-fitting parade for a pacifist like Gus. He almost never wants to blow any-one up. An occasional shimmer of multiband stealth is the only clue that the CAV is flanked by a swarm of tactical drones.

"This is a lot of security for someone like me," Gus says, and Dahlia laughs. "What's so funny? Why would someone want to kill me?"

"You did something great," Dahlia says. "Ardent gets death threats all the time. Like one a month at least."

"For what?"

"That's the wrong question, because it makes it sound like

Ardent did something to deserve harassment." Dahlia gives Gus a sunning-cat smile and smacks her lips. "The jerks give a variety of excuses, but it's always some variation of 'for existing.'"

"What do you do about it?"

"Refer them to the local health ward officer," Dahlia says. "These people need care, not direct contact from the subject of their delusions. It's the compassionate thing to do. Oh, and I file a fuck ton of restraining orders, ban them from all events, and have them monitored for any and all activity."

The agent toasts Gus from her chair. "If they violate the orders, I bury them in consequences. No one touches Ardent."

Judging by the look in her eye, Gus believes it.

This part of the French Riviera was devastated the worst by the effects of the Capital Age, the period of industrialization and war leading up to the Infinite Autostate. True desert took most of Italy and half of Spain four hundred years ago, transforming everything from Rome to the equator into a scar for all future generations—a legacy of famine to untold millions. The broken bones of cities like Saint-Tropez lie swept into the sea by floods and superstorms, transformed into playgrounds for rich divers and treasure hunters. Ironic that the divers visiting would've been the inhabitants in another time.

Maybe that's why Gus loves and hates the modern music scene's obsession with that period—it's both appropriate and annoying. Small wonder that when Vanguards started wiping out humanity five years prior, everyone got into the early-millennium style, because that's the closest the species came to vanishing previously. Gus sees the parallels, but it's different. Sure, there were a bunch of people making music like the world was ending, but it was by their own hand. To Gus's reckoning, the year 2657 and its citizens are far more innocent. Their cataclysm is external, not sabotage.

Arcologies dot the sharp brown ridgelines like blackberries, their polarized windows violet and gold in the merciless sun. These cliffs won't support life without severe assistance, but there are always people willing to move into the teeming, self-contained colonies. The buildings' vast entanglement of ecosystems makes them impervious to the deleterious effects of climate change, and there's a certain bleak majesty in their view of the raging sea.

To Gus, however, they look like expensive prisons in the middle of nowhere.

"Les Couteaux," he says, looking out the window. "Not exactly luxury."

" 'The Knives,' " Ardent intones from the door to the bedroom. They emerge from their self-care chrysalis in a brilliant white tunic, its surfaces smoothed featureless, matching snowy hair hanging down to their shoulders.

They walk to the window and press a red-gloved hand to the glass, staring out at the boiling storm clouds on the horizon. "Fuck me, this place is something. Look at those waves."

"It has all the airless joy of an undeveloped world," Gus says, "but I'd imagine we'll find some way to pass the time."

Ardent pulls up the TourPod route on the holos. They're headed past the mass of smaller arcologies for the largest of them all—"Belle et Brutale."

"That's a big egg," Dahlia says when it comes into view.

Gus has seen plenty of holos of this building: an ovoid balanced upon its point, concrete pedestal white in the sunlight.

Iridescent diamond windows gleam in the heat, encircling the massive gray arcology like jewels on a Fabergé masterpiece. Wide horizontal strips of the shell have been cut away, exposing docking pads, climate systems, and the underbelly of the monumental self-contained architectural ecology.

Beyond Belle et Brutale's staggering girth lies the sea, a blanket of waves whitecapped with fury. A smattering of multicolored metallic scales glitters in the rock before the pedestal, a new addition since the last time Gus looked the place up.

He finally figures out what the colorful chips are: shiny CAVs nestled into the crevasses along the dusty cliffs. Solar shelters pockmark the nearby landscape, some of them trailing wisps of smoke from portable kitchens.

"Refugees," Dahlia says. "News reports say the remote arcologies barely got hit when the Ghosts attacked. They're all supplied up while some of the nearby areas are floundering."

"So everyone is coming here," Gus says. "That's not going to go well."

"Why not?" Ardent asks.

"I doubt the people at Belle et Brutale are the sharing sort," he replies.

Gus's grandmother, Doctor Betsy Kitko, hated the arcologists. Called them "arrogant dicks and isolationists at best," and wrote one of the most well-regarded treatises on the subject, *Survivalist Domain and Its Self-Fulfilling Prophecy*, during her residency on Phaeton.

The TourPod flight path takes them under the hip of the egg, and Gus surveys the huge forest of passive air purifiers, carbon crystal stalactites like smoked glass. Instead of going to customs like everyone else, their CAV rises to a secured platform overlooking the docking cradles.

An armed detail awaits them as their vehicle settles onto the charger—three bruisers in matching casual clothes. The tactical drone escort swarms the area, perching in strategic positions like refractive condors. The TourPod door opens, and the ozone stench of repulsors in a high-traffic airway stings Gus's nose.

He offers his hand to Ardent. "After you."

"I do love a gentleman," they say, intertwining their soft-gloved fingers with his before descending the gangway.

A tall white enby waves at them from the entry to the central arcology, a bright smile on their face. Once everyone is safely disembarked, they come striding toward the assembled VIPs.

They're well-dressed, but not enough to upstage the clientele. Their sleek black suit ripples with their movements, dim patterns of textiLEDs revealing the grace of a ballet dancer.

"Ardent Violet! Hi. Such a pleasure to meet you," they say, giving a tiny dip of their head. "I'm Calico. Welcome to Belle et Brutale."

As if finally able to see past Ardent's blinding brilliance, Calico adds, "Mister Kitko, I'm guessing? I was sent to personally give you the tour."

Gus nods, amused that everyone always greets Ardent first. He can't blame Calico; he'd do the same. "You guessed correctly."

"Excellent. Follow me."

The doors to the interior part, and they ascend a long escalator into the atrium. The ceiling curves up and away from Gus, and the hallway traces the circumference of Belle et Brutale's widest point. The main thoroughfare is a dense indoor jungle, ripe with birdsong and vibrant foliage. Shafts of sunlight pour through the huge diamond windows, falling upon hanging gardens to rival Babylon.

After the desolate atmosphere and dust of Le Couteaux, the burst of color inside the atrium is jarring. Gus almost wishes he'd brought his sunglasses—until he remembers those are entombed in the remains of Lord Yamazaki's estate, along with half of her guests. The lord herself escaped unharmed.

"Belle et Brutale is home to the largest collection of biodiversity in any arcology," Calico says, gesturing to the lush waterscapes. "Our scientists have mastered the art of balance, just as our architects have with the *Ovum Inversus*, speaking to a perfection known only in the ancient art of biomimicry."

Arrogant dicks. Gus's grandmother's words tickle his thoughts, and he struggles not to laugh at Calico's artistic statement. The guide clasps their hands before themself as they walk, like a monk, or maybe a museum curator.

"In addition to the engineering marvel of the *Ovum Inversus*, there's an agricultural one. The plants in this structure produce enough oxygen for the residents to live in deep space, and our upper-level farms generate food for three times the current populace."

"That's really great to hear," Gus says. "It looks like you have a lot of people outside who want help."

Calico clears their throat. "We do. That's why Belle et Brutale's outreach missions travel far into the surrounding countryside to install water purification and mentor mini farms."

"Oh, sure," Gus says, "but obviously, the people outside have more immediate needs that aren't solved by, uh, mentorship."

"They won't breach our perimeter, if that's what worries you, Mister Kitko."

"It doesn't," Gus says with a smile, "because that'd be a gross reaction to have to refugees."

Calico's eyebrows jump up. "I'll...send some information about our philanthropic initiatives to your room."

"Great," Gus says, already annoyed with himself, and that means Ardent is probably annoyed, too. He's been looking forward to getting out of the château hospital for a whole week, and now that he's here, he's shooting his mouth off at the hosts.

"Hey, how much touring do we...like...have to do?" Ardent asks.

Calico wrinkles their nose. "I mean, we could just cut it now."

"It's been a day," Ardent says.

"The elevators are over there."

Calico dons a tight mask of a smile, rattles off a quick list of amenities, and takes their leave. Gus then has to wait while the guard detail radios in a change of plan and clears the floor early. He watches with mounting guilt as they hail back and forth, clearly inconvenienced.

"I'm sorry, Ardent, I—"

"No, no. I hated Calico, too. I'm just more patient about it." They're smirking at him. "You look hangry."

"I think you're right. I've been excited about you, not guards and drones in the Knives." He shakes his head. "I tried to keep my mouth shut, but they said the perimeter thing."

Ardent's mischievous laugh is like a feather on Gus's neck. "Oh, you were upset? I hadn't noticed."

He flushes, hoping it's not too apparent. This is supposed to be a date, even if there is a protection detail and neither of them chose the location. Gus's haptic coat taps his shoulder in the message pattern, and he checks his Gang to find one waiting.

Your apartments are ready upstairs. Please give fifteen minutes of advanced notice before requesting a change of plans.

"What are we thinking for lunch?" Ardent asks.

"I can't possibly choose a restaurant," Gus replies.

"Oh god, if you're one of those types, I'm leaving," they say.

"I've already inconvenienced the guards. They had plans and I wasn't...How do I put this?" He waves to the captain of the detail, who has occasionally reminded him that's entirely unnecessary. "Changing plans isn't the classy thing for me to do—to them, or to you."

Gus gives Ardent his "album cover" stare and a smile. His photographer coached him on looking sexy, and he took it to heart.

"I wouldn't want to keep Ardent Violet waiting, either," he says.

Ardent clears their throat and swallows.

Even with his hair shaved after a near-death experience, Gus still has his smolder.

"That's, uh, okay," Ardent says. "I'm as classy as any Hellbitch can be, really."

"FYI," Dahlia says, fiddling with her Gang, "I've seen Ardent eat three hot dogs after a show."

"You didn't have to help, Dahlia. I had that one."

She looks up and smiles. "Perfect. Since I'm not needed and don't require a guard detail, I'm ditching you."

"Where are you going?" Ardent asks.

"The Sundial. Top floor. The stage here is supposed to play some good talent."

Ardent rests their hands on their hips. "I thought you didn't have time for another client!"

"I probably don't," Dahlia says. "Just tell yourself I'm checking out the future competition."

"Which is what you're doing, right?" Ardent asks, but Dahlia is already leaving. Ardent calls their question once more at her back, and she waves goodbye without turning around.

"She said she wasn't taking on any more clients," Ardent says, "so that was just confusing, is all."

"No worries." Gus holds out a hand. "Shall we?"

"We haven't decided where we're eating..."

"Yes, we have," he replies, an idea coming over him. It's romantic, and it doesn't inconvenience the guard detail. "A week ago, you told me to get in the kitchen, so let's hit mine."

Gus drops Ardent off at their room to get their things settled, and they say they'll be along shortly. He's grateful they did—he wants to get a look at the place alone so he can plan his big date.

Gus opens his door, and upon seeing the lodgings, even he must admit:

"I'd kill for a place like this in Montreal."

Two stories of decadently single-use rooms yawn before him,

with ample space to stretch his legs. A full-size Yamaha grand piano sits before a panoramic window. The sea rages outside, a liquid patch of lapis blue on a cloudless day.

There are two bedrooms, one quite a bit smaller than the other. Two beds to try—if he's lucky.

Luggage secured, he's off to the kitchen to see what's on hand. There's a full complement of utensils, along with all the typical appliances for steam, pressure, flame, and radiation. He spots a decent-sized extruder and a multimill. In the cabinets, he finds basic cookware with all the traditional sensors, so he feels certain he can whip something up.

But what on earth is he supposed to cook for Ardent Violet?

Gus signs for the computer's attention and asks for groceries. Ardent is super-famous, so they probably eat fancy gourmet food all the time—or as often as they want. Simply going for lavish or obscure dishes won't do, and he might mess those up anyway. What Gus needs is a personal touch. Something that says, *I have been bored out of my mind having medical tests run on me all week, and I haven't been able to stop thinking about you. Please make out with me.*

Already, he's a little sad he can't look over and see Ardent standing there, reading the feed off their Gang. Gus chides himself for mooning over someone he barely knows. They don't have a relationship; he's been in Ardent's bed. There's a difference, and Gus has no idea what's going to come of their time together.

A meal, hopefully.

Improvise, Curly! He can almost hear Lisel's voice.

Lisel was the tallest of them, a presence that tamed her upright bass. She liked to dress in an orange suit and had an easy smile. Everything about her scarcely fit the room she inhabited.

"No curls, Lise. They shaved them off," Gus remarks to her departed spirit.

Holos render the bounty of Belle et Brutale's produce for Gus's perusal. Heaps of plantains sit beside bushels of apples. Ancient grains spill from barrels, herbs burst forth from gardens, and the heads of cabbages line one wall like an ossuary.

Gus loads up the proteins on offer, and the room shifts. Dark crimson links dangle from the ceiling; steak packs lie strewn across countertops in great red mountains. Mussels, clams, and fruits of the sea tumble from the kitchen sink. Fillets of fish leap through the air, flopping to rest on packs of ice. Everything is exquisitely laid out, as though the food is a prized artwork, and Gus must admit the selection at the arcology is good. The oppressively minimalist architecture makes the perfect canvas for such extravagance.

The store has a sausage blender with a fair variety of sequenced tissues, and Gus is browsing the artisan links when he sees hot dogs. It's literally the only food he knows Ardent likes, but Lisel liked them, too. When he first moved to Canada, the bassist showed him a whole world of cuisine, and the steamé taught him to appreciate dogs. They didn't have to be cheap fare; he could fancy it up. With the right ingredients, he might impress Ardent and show them he knows how to listen instead of just talking about pianos all the time.

He keys in a few custom blends and places the order. He warps to the bakery and grabs a few crusty rolls, too, before heading back to produce to complete the trip.

The room alerts him to a guest at the door, and Gus closes out his order. When he checks the holos, Ardent waits outside, and it only takes him a moment to realize the terrible thing he has done.

He's cooking hot dogs for superstar Ardent Violet.

When his friends ask him where he blew it, he's going to know: It was this decision.

The door chimes again, and Gus has no choice but to face the music. He throws the open sign, and Ardent comes breezing into the commons. "This is—different in here!"

"What about it?"

"Oh, my room is just a lot more, um, alive. They put you in the brutale section."

"There's a belle section?"

"I feel certain you'll have occasion to visit," Ardent says with a wink, short-circuiting any response Gus might have. "What are we having?"

He blinks, trying to get his mind out of Ardent's room and back into the present. Gus has to formulate some kind of replacement for the hot dogs. "Oh, I think you'll like it."

"Do I get a hint?"

"Only if you don't like mystery. I'm terrible at this game."

"Very well, dear. Keep your secrets." Ardent prints a glass and runs a soda from the tap. It's one of the sugary fruit ones, and Gus grows a little more confident about his hot dog decision. They might like gourmet stuff, but they're probably not stuck up. He's about to broach his daring culinary choice when Ardent's Gang gets a hail.

"I'm sorry!" Ardent says. "Can I take this here?"

"Be my guest."

A short woman appears in their midst. Her clothing isn't nearly as loud as Ardent's, but the vibrant jumpsuit is a statement. She beams at Ardent with bright eyes and rosy cheeks, and when she holds her hands together, she reminds Gus of a stoat.

"Mom!" Ardent says. "Hi! We're at the place!"

"Ah! Do you like it?" She squints around. "Can you turn on the background?"

"The soldiers said no," Ardent says.

"Well, I didn't know if that was still a thing. Is it a bunker?" she says. "A safe house?"

Ardent laughs and smooths their snow-white hair behind their ear. "An arcology. I'm at Belle et Brutale with Gus Kitko."

"Oh, right. Is he here? Can I meet him?" She looks around.

When Ardent said they were from Georgia, Gus had wondered. He's only ever heard the barest hint of Southern sweetness in Ardent's voice, but this woman is basically corn syrup.

Ardent looks to Gus and gestures to their Gang. "Jump on and say hi?"

He blinks. "I'm meeting your mom?"

Ardent laughs. "Not if you're going to be weird about it. She knows all my friends."

It's both disappointing and exhilarating to be referred to by Ardent Violet as a friend. Gus flips out his Gang and adds himself to Ardent's hail. The second he loads into the mother's sight, she snaps onto him like a hawk.

"Are you the pianist?" she demands, eyes keen as she comes to check him out. "Oh, I love your piercings!"

Gus backs up a step on reflex. This hologram has managed to invade his personal space. "Piercings?"

She gestures to his scalp.

Oh. You mean my brain piercings.

"Thanks!" A compliment is a compliment.

"I'm Marilyn Aldridge," she says, then jerks a thumb at Ardent. "I made this one." She belts an unapologetic laugh that fills the entire room.

"August Kitko," he says, pressing a palm to hers in greeting, diffracting the hologram, "but my friends call me Gus."

She gives him an exaggerated elbow in the gut. "What do your admirers call you, sweetheart?"

Ardent gasps. "Mom, stop!"

Marilyn looks Gus dead in the eye. "You have a sense of humor, don't you, Gus? My baby can't be around boring people."

Ardent looks like they're about to sever the call. "Gus isn't boring."

"I'll say!" she says, waggling her eyebrows.

"Mom!"

"Where you from, Gus?" she asks, not acknowledging Ardent's protestations.

"Wisconsin, living large in Montreal, ma'am. You?"

"Indianola, Mississippi."

"The Hurricane Belt," he says. "Tough folks."

"Used to be farmland in another era." She points to Gus as she says to Ardent, "He should go into politics. Look at that smile. What's your situation in all this, Gus? How are you doing at the end of humanity?"

"You don't go for the small talk, do you?" he says.

"No time, sweetheart. Things okay nowadays?"

He shakes his head no. "Not really, but I have to say, your child is like a breath of fresh air when you're choking."

Ardent and Marilyn go wild for that one, loud laughter almost bowling him over. He's not sure if they're laughing in delight or at his goofy line, but maybe he ought to improvise more. They seem to think it's sweet, at least.

He chats with Marilyn for the next half hour, and she's such a delight that he forgets all about the order on the way, and the catastrophic Operation Hot Dog. A holo pops up behind Marilyn's head to let him know his doom has arrived at the front door step.

"Mom," Ardent says, "I'm sorry to interrupt, but the groceries are here and I'm famished."

"Maybe you two can keep talking, and I can get it started," Gus says, scouring his brain for something else to cook.

"What are you having?" Marilyn asks, and Gus's head nearly pops. He's about to get vetoed for sure.

"Nothing if you don't let me get off the call!" Ardent says, mock whining. "I'm starving to death. You're killing me, Mother."

"Okay, fine, fine," she says, waving them off. "I'll let you two kids get on with lunch. Need to start breakfast anyway."

"Give everyone my love!"

"You could hail more often and do that yourself," Marilyn says, holo-kissing Ardent's cheek with a silvery shimmer. "But I know I'm your favorite Aldridge."

"Don't tell anyone," Ardent says, kissing her back and finger-waving. "Bye, gorgeous."

After terminating the call, Gus and Ardent fetch the crates of groceries from the front stoop: some produce packs, a steaming-hot baker's cradle, and a little paper package with a cow on it. They take the spoils inside and lay them across the kitchen island.

"How's your onion game?" Gus asks, fetching a knife from the wall magnets. He grabs a big yellow onion, the kind bursting inside with natural sweetness.

"Bad enough to make *you* weep."

"All right," Gus says. "Well, I'll cut up the onions to caramelize them. If you can cut the tops off the garlic, we can roast it for—"

"Gus."

"Hm?"

Ardent drops their hands to their hips. "Onions and garlic? I don't know what you're making, but it doesn't sound like date food."

He sets the onion on the counter, positioning it just so. "I—yes. I can see how that would be the, uh... the case."

"These onions... what were you planning to put them on top of?"

"... Hot dogs."

There's a reaction. It's a strong one, but not a bad one.

"What's our bread situation?" they ask.

Gus cracks the shell of the baker's cradle, tearing open plastarch to get at the warm, steaming buns inside.

"Ooh, they look like lobster rolls," Ardent says.

"It's kind of hard to get bad bread in France."

"Let's do something light on top. You've got a cabbage. Slaw?"

He thinks of a sour burst, crisp and creamy against the meaty snap of sausage. "That does sound good. You cook?"

"Not at all."

"Okay," Gus says. "Well, I think between the two of us, we can still come up with a steamé that'll keep things, um, steamy."

"Come up with a what?"

Gus can almost hear Lisel in his own words. "The greatest hot dog on the planet."

Ardent doesn't agree with Gus's statement, but they keep it to themself. The food is good, and the chef is cute—not much more they could ask for.

Food consumed, Ardent and Gus set out to stretch their legs with the help of their battalion of guards and drones. The many halo-shaped floors of the *Ovum Inversus* link together in a long spiral stretching for several kilometers. The promenade is popular at this time of the late afternoon, with its long windows and outdoor gardens. Squares of orange light slide along every walkway, sun fading to evening.

From this new vantage point, Ardent can show Gus the dichotomy between the "belle" sections, with their floral assaults on the senses, and the "brutale" sections, where the infrastructure and engineering of the arcology are on display in sharp concrete.

"Oh!" Gus says as a couple of piano notes color the air. "I think this is the Shiitake Six. I know these folx."

Ardent strains to listen. "Sounds like the kind of thing you hear in a starport restroom."

"I make about a third of my royalties off public plays," Gus says. "Lot of restrooms."

"It's good money! I didn't mean it like that. I've done way worse."

Gus winces. "'Worse,' huh?"

"Fuck, okay, I'm going to dig out of this hole. In Brazil, they use my song 'Winding Fire' to sell antacids."

"See, that's pretty—"

"The commercials make it look like the song refers to your intestines. Some locals call my anthem about overcoming my ex the 'Hot Shit' song, but I still collect my payment."

"I feel better already."

Ardent savors his sweet cologne as they lean in close. The memories of his powerful arms are still warm on their back, and they idly sigh them away. Ardent kind of wishes the pair could skip all the bullshit and get to a kiss.

Perhaps just an overt reference to the fact they'd slept together at all would be nice.

They want to hit on him. Well, they *want* to tackle him and treat him right after what was clearly a week of hardships. With any other boyfriend, their relationship would've already gone superluminal, slammed into a star, and supernovaed in the gossips.

Problem is, Gus is sporting a brand-new set of neck bolts and about a hundred other piercings. He's been through something deeply invasive, and it doesn't feel right to push him. Ardent is a star—they know people will do strange things at their request, go too far, too fast. Gus wasn't any different when they'd met—entering Ardent's bed simply because they'd asked him to on the first night.

Gus starts in on another architecture speech, and Ardent tries to pay attention to the words more than the bass of his rough voice. They never should've kicked him out the first time. They'd chewed him up on a technicality at the estate when they could've simply been firm with him.

But hey—it was the end of the world. Everyone was getting pretty emotional.

"—and my Nana Kitko basically made the case that survivalists were damaging the ecology to the point that it encouraged the collapse they feared."

I wasn't paying attention.

"Wow, so then, um—"

Gus shakes his head. "I'm sorry. Not everyone wants to jabber about buildings, and—"

"No! No, I was just thinking about you, actually!"

He almost misses a step and smiles. Though he usually looks quite intelligent, his green eyes sparkle like a sleepy puppy. "You were?"

Maybe it was his comment to Marilyn in the kitchen about Ardent being a breath of fresh air, but they're aching to give him something in return.

"You remind me of the rain," they say, immediately able to imagine it in one of their cringeworthy adolescent poems.

Too corny. Now he's staring.

"This is why I don't write my own lyrics half the time, but... I meant that," they add, hoping the moment will pass and they can both forget about it. "Something about you. Quite rainy."

"I'm not sure how I'm supposed to live up to that one. I love the rain."

"Aw, Gus, but you don't love yourself?"

That stuns him. "Well, sure, I'm an accomplished musician, and I like to think I'm a pretty good cook."

"I know lots of musicians and cooks, Gusto, but you're something special."

" 'Gusto'?"

"I'm guessing it's short for Gustopher. I tried a thing, and we can both agree it didn't work," Ardent says. They stop short and turn to him. "Listen, I love this chitchat, but there's something I've been dying to do with you, and if I don't say it, I'm going to lose my mind."

The look on his face is priceless, but Ardent promised themself not to push, so it's time to deflate the joke with the truth.

"Screw all the cynical architecture, and let's jam," they say.

His smile goes wider.

Ardent stops before their door and turns to Gus. He's almost vibrating with excitement, and Ardent hopes they'll actually manage to jam this time. Sex is great, but they've already had plenty of that.

"It's not exactly a concert hall, but..." Ardent's door opens, and they bid him to follow them inside, spreading their red-gloved hands like they're introducing the circus.

His eyes widen as he steps through the door. "Holy cats, this place is..."

"A menagerie!" Ardent finishes.

Botanical life springs from every corner: roses, ferns, soft moss dotted with tiny wildflowers, and dozens of semi-exotic plants. Daylight emerges from hundreds of sunpipes to paint the countless specimens and brighten the space. Butterflies flit through sun-dappled foliage overhead.

"Like twice as large as my apartment," Gus finishes, and Ardent feels a bit silly. "I thought my place was too big, but yours is hilarious."

Good thing you didn't take him to your mansion, babe.

"I like it!" Ardent protests. "Besides, mine has a better balcony."

They take Gus through the enchanted forest halls of their lodgings and up the stairs to the open loft, where he stops before Ardent's silver piano.

"This yours?" he asks.

"Came with the place," Ardent says. "Haven't touched it."

"That's what I'm talking about," Gus says. "A classic right here. You know Elsie Franklin played one of these on her second album."

"I didn't!" That's technically true, because Ardent doesn't know who that is.

Their balcony has a similar view of the sea to Gus's, but with an entertaining space big enough to land a transport shuttle. It's a shame Ardent can't call a thousand of their closest friends up here to bring down the house; the wide-open view of the shattered coast is entirely too moody to be denied.

As if reading Ardent's mind, Gus heads for the piano, turns on the furniture repulsors, and begins pushing it toward the balcony doors. Ardent throws the computer sign and opens the place up. Every window in the apartment pivots to vent, filtering outside air through the plants to freshen it with a mild floral aroma. The apartment seems to sigh, enticing those cooped inside to enjoy the outdoors once again.

Ardent grabs their guitar case and heads back to Gus. He's positioning the piano as close to the edge of the balcony as possible, only separated from a sixty-story drop by a holoflaged barrier. Ardent strides to the edge, reaching out to see if they can feel the cold steel behind the projections. All balconies must have some sort of handrails, after all.

The safety cage exists, but an *uncomfortable* distance past the edge of the balcony.

They hide their slight quiver as they pull their hand back, then lean down to open their guitar case. After pressing their thumbs to the latches, they raise the lid to reveal the treasure within.

"Hello, Baby."

The day Ardent signed with Dahlia, they bought themself this Powers Vitas X six-string, an unreasonable guitar for an unreasonable person. "Baby" was far beyond Ardent's high school wardrobe (and income).

The instrument had been purchased on Marilyn's credit without her knowledge. Ardent believed that Dahlia would sort the income out, get them enough gigs to pay it down before Marilyn got the news about her creds. That turned out to be a pipe dream, as acquiring fame takes years of fishing for a break. Marilyn gave Baby her original moniker: "The guitar you'd betray your mother for."

She'd meant it as an insult, but Baby brings undeniable bliss in Ardent's fingertips. They love their mother, and wish they'd gotten the guitar through honest means, but there's no changing history. Might as well enjoy it.

The translucent body of the instrument rests atop crushed white velvet, deep magenta in the center, going dark violet at the edges like an orchid. Curling neon vines rise through the jet-black fretboard like demonic flames. Pickups blaze beneath glassy strings, carrying black light up the neck. Baby spoke to Ardent's soul from the moment they'd laid eyes on her, and they would carry her cry to the edge of the universe.

When Ardent touches the neck, the Vitas X logo cracks to life above the headstock. Baby's operating system seeks out the balcony audio projectors, reporting them ready for anything Ardent wants to dish out. Holos offer an expansive array of patches and effects, and Ardent gently lifts the instrument from the case to cradle it in their arms.

"That's a hell of a guitar," Gus says.

Ardent slips the hand-embroidered strap over their head. "Yes, she is. Any chance you can play the same song you were playing at Yamazaki's?"

"I don't know if I've ever played like that before," Gus says. "It was ludicrous."

"What do you mean?" Ardent asks.

"It's like... a lot of stuff made sense that normally doesn't. I could do, uh... polyrhythms without thinking, and the whole thing was modal."

"What was the main thrust of the song, darling?"

Gus sits down at the piano bench, smoothing his slacks. "Seven-eight time, starting in F minor, but it flies off the rails after that."

"Starts with seven-eight and gets harder. Why not?"

"Let me try something, and you can see if you like it."

"Bold words."

They take off their red gloves, setting them atop the guitar case. Their nails bear a dark umber polish, and when they activate the mag implants, orange veins light up like lava. Ardent draws out their signature silver pick, flipping it in the air once like an old coin.

Gus's fingers flutter over the keyboard, arpeggiating and climbing to its summit in warm-up. Ardent notices he's playing the "wonder scale," and his intonations conjure thoughts of astronomical phenomena best glimpsed from the bridge of a starship.

Okay. B flat Mixolydian, just like your solo in "All the Way Down."

Ardent plucks a few strings, stretching their thin hand across capable scales before blasting off. Years of practiced muscle memory guide their fingers, and they punctuate their complex phrase with a sassy guitar lick.

Gus halts his warm-up and quirks an eyebrow like he's just been challenged to a duel. "How fast are we going? Full throttle?"

Fingernails arc on strings, infusing them with harmonic resonance. Ardent steals a little of Gus's tone, pushing a thrumming drone into the amp to imitate the keening of the Vanguards.

"I can handle whatever you want."

That might not be true, actually. Ardent has heard what Gus sounds like when his soul is on fire.

"I'd like to take it a little easy at first," Gus says, giving Ardent that awkward sexy face he keeps making.

Bless your heart, Gus.

They're so enamored of Gus's goofy simmer that they miss the count in, and the pianist slingshots into a heady opening barrage of chords. The sound fills the whole spectrum from top to bottom with a booming procession, and it's a hell of an entrance. Gus's harmony doesn't sound that fast at first, and Ardent keeps counting to seven, trying to find the beat.

"This is seven-eight time?" they call to the pianist.

"Yeah!" he says, banging out another chord and shaking his head like he's having a minor seizure.

Oh, no. He's not nodding; he's counting the beat at over three hundred.

Ardent scours the phrases for a point of entry, but it's like searching for the best place to jump into raging rapids. They close their eyes, swaying and trying to feel it.

Gus keeps hitting the same high note at the top of the measure, and Ardent realizes he's trying to help—reaching out a hand. Ardent takes a deep breath.

ONEtwothreefourfivesixGO!

Ardent shreds a few notes, mercifully catching the beat and hanging on for dear life. Musically, they're the total package—proficient on six instruments, an accomplished dancer and award-winning vocalist. By comparison, Gus is a theory-obsessed technician who has diligently devoted himself to a single tool.

Baby wails a sour note, and Ardent swears inwardly. This is only a jam session, but they've still got their pride. They dust themself off with a quick, easy bass line and catch up to the jazz monster, matching harmonies while Gus calls out the chords, each more arcane than the last.

Ardent picks up the pattern, and the frantic struggle to participate eases somewhat. They start predicting his moves, navigating the rapids together in sweeping song.

You've got this!

Ardent gets a decent flow going, and they're feeling pretty good about themself when Gus shouts, "Nice! You ready to get started?"

"*'Started'?*"

The pianist doubles the complexity of his patterns, sprinkling ornamentation over the phrases like he's not even trying. Ardent ducks through his melodies, biting their lip as they desperately ride the wave.

OnetwothreefourfivesixGO!... sixGO!... sixGO!

He flies out of a solo right as the sirens go off.

Gus stops playing and rises from his piano bench to look out over the balcony. "What the hell?"

Ardent follows his gaze and sees CAVs taking to the air in droves, glowing repulsors flitting in the afternoon sun like scarab beetles.

A good distance down the shoreline, Greymalkin drops out of the sky, landing in a cloud of dust.

Its long shadow falls across the Knives, jagged cliffs blurring the edges. Greymalkin strides over ruined shorelines, running toward Belle et Brutale at a frightful speed. A thousand golden glimmers sparkle in its wake: the cohort of Gilded Ghosts that always accompany such monstrosities to every abominable act.

UW guards come bursting into the flat, rushing up the stairs with their rifles drawn. Ardent isn't sure what they're planning to do with bullets, but that's for the pros to worry about. As long as someone is in charge, that's what counts. Except the guards don't whisk everyone away to safety—they take up positions at the perimeter.

Elzahia Tazi, the dark-skinned UWI officer who'd captured Ardent the night of the attack, comes striding in with a small entourage. She heads to the balcony edge with one of her camera drones, and focuses the warbling sphere on the distant Vanguard, routing its vision to her holos. A projection of Greymalkin appears in the air before her, hurtling toward them all with deliberate steps.

"Hi, again. Fancy meeting you here," Ardent says, but she holds up a hand to silence them.

"I'm always near Mister Kitko," Tazi says. "Now, Gus, what should I expect when Greymalkin arrives?"

"I don't know," Gus replies. "I can feel it, though. It's coming for me."

Ardent takes Gus's hand and turns to Tazi. "We've got to get out of here, then."

"And go where?" Tazi asks. "Do you think there's a single part of Belle et Brutale that can stand up to a Vanguard onslaught?"

"We can't just wait around!" Ardent says.

"That's exactly what we're going to do, Mix Violet," Tazi says. "You're welcome to leave whenever you choose, but Mister Kitko stays. Humanity has a vested interest in finding out what this Vanguard wants."

Gus goes to Ardent and takes them by the shoulders. He has such large, capable hands, and his grip is reassuring. He gazes into Ardent with clear green eyes.

"I don't think we're going to die today, but I understand if you want to leave."

"But please decide, because we're busy," Tazi adds.

Ardent bows up at that but holds their tongue. Tazi is probably right that there's nowhere to run, so the choices are likely stay and watch or get kicked out.

"You and I—we called Greymalkin, Ardent," Gus says. "I don't know why I didn't realize..."

Ardent wavers, a bit adrift. "'We'?"

The Vanguard's omnipresent keen reaches them, a galactic pipe organ, and Ardent winces. It's the same chord progression Gus and they were playing before, but folded over upon itself thousands of times.

"Mister Kitko," Tazi says, turning to Gus, "that Vanguard is going to be here in the next two minutes, so I'd like you to step away from Mix Violet for their safety."

"If you're willing to stay," Gus says, "I don't want to be alone."

"Of—of course! Where am I going to go?" Ardent says, unable to meet his gaze.

"I'm going to see what it wants, and hopefully we can get back to the best date of my whole life."

"I'd like that," Ardent says. "Please don't get re-eaten."

He nods, taking their hands and squeezing them before backing away. "Wouldn't dare."

Ardent grabs a place in the corner near the interior door, ready to bolt into the complex if necessary. Gus stands at the infinity edge of the balcony, legs shoulder width apart, fists jammed into his pockets. He's planning to meet it face-to-face.

The land between Belle et Brutale and the sea has become a swarm of fleeing CAVs, and Ardent hopes they'll get out of the way before Greymalkin arrives. The Vanguards don't exactly seem to value human life.

Greymalkin draws closer, crossing the field like a conquering general. No one dares get between the Vanguard and its intended destination. Thunderous steps rock the earth, thumping in the pit of Ardent's stomach.

Its armor has changed from the last time: lacquered white accents offset jet-black plates, almost like piano keys. Vertical arrow-slit eyes still blaze green in the evening sun.

It's briefly out of Ardent's view as it reaches the base of the arcology, and they're pretty sure it's going to try to climb up. The crunching noise of Greymalkin's claws on concrete comes in answer. Ardent measures the Vanguard's ascent in the soles of their feet, and they summon the courage to stand firm.

Greymalkin rises before the congregation like an angry black dragon. Green light consumes all other colors. Gus stands silhouetted in its unearthly glow.

The Vanguard halts, livery blazing in the sunset. Its head

comes just above the balcony, and the air flutters with the wash of a dozen holoflaged drones—unlikely to be effective at all. Ardent swallows hard. Sure, the thing helped humanity before, but no one seems to know why. It might just vaporize everyone on the balcony and call it a night.

It reaches over the edge, grip relaxed. It's not groping around, thank god, because it could absolutely break the entire structure to pieces. The hand stops before Gus, index finger extended ever so slightly.

Everyone else has backed away; all Gus's guardians and minders hold their positions beside Ardent, leaving the pianist to face his fate alone. They're not here to protect him—just the public. The Vanguards can apparently do whatever they want with Gus.

The pianist reaches out, his hand touching Greymalkin's armored finger—man to god.

Gus's knees buckle and he stumbles backward, clutching his head. He can't seem to rise, and every movement drags him closer to the ground. Ardent tries to run toward him, but a bodyguard stops them in the blink of an eye.

"I'm going to need you to step back, Mix Violet," she says, palm out like she's directing traffic. "Let the professionals handle this."

"Whatever it did to Gus wasn't good for him!" Ardent says, gesturing to the groaning man. "You need to pull him back from there before it does something else!"

But no one is moving a muscle. They're just watching him writhe on the ground before Greymalkin's blazing eyes like the village sacrifice. The guards aren't monitoring his vitals or making sure he's safe. They're observing.

Do they expect him to control it?

The Vanguard anchors a hand into the concrete on either side of the balcony. Armor plates snap tight against its body, welding every edge with a glowing seam. Its carapace resonates like a tuning fork, vibrating Ardent's very bones. Then the eyes go red, and the keening stops, leaving only the breeze to fill the vacuum of silence. Gus drunkenly rolls onto his hands and knees, praying to the ground. Greymalkin has become a red-eyed statue holding vigil astride the egg.

Gus looks around, reddened eyes locking onto Ardent's as people finally rush to help.

"Are you okay?" they shout over the others. "What happened?"

But Ardent is ushered from the room, and even from their own apartment. By the time they can get their bearings, they've been gently yet firmly ejected into the hallway.

Dahlia is already there, a fresh drink in one hand and a rosy blush on her cheeks. She must've run.

"I heard the sirens, Ardent!" she says. "Are you all right?"

"I'm fine, but I just got kicked out!"

Dahlia flips out her Gang. "I'll call Calico—"

But the agent stops when she pulls up her UI. She nods to no one in particular, taking a deep breath like someone just gave her tragic news.

"What?" Ardent says, afraid of any headline that could be more important than a giant Vanguard standing watch outside the balcony.

"The public knows you and Gus are involved with Greymalkin now."

Ardent frowns. "What's the reaction?"

"Utter chaos."

Chapter Five

Rhythm Changes

Before Gus, there is only eternity.

The Milky Way spirals into existence, and he traverses its jewels. He doesn't know where he's going, only that Greymalkin is guiding him.

A distant colonized planet, New Jalandhar, orbits a healthy yellow sun, its slow transit almost identical to a Homeworld year. Rings surround the mass, dotted with space stations and outposts.

Two beings await Gus on the surface, and he knows them to be Traitor Vanguards, like Greymalkin. They call to him, the harbingers of Ghosts in the night. Gus can feel their Conduits, too—a strange connection to a pair of human psyches halfway across the galaxy.

They need help soon, or they are lost.

Another presence weeps in the darkness, far from New Jalandhar, at a station called Firenze Habitat. It's scarcely anything more than the remains of a candlewick, a lone spark almost snuffed out. There's fear, agony, and longing—

Another Traitor Vanguard, alone and confused, but growing stronger by the second.

* * *

Gus returns to consciousness in a stretcher on the balcony, the night breeze tickling his nose with sea salt. It should've been late afternoon, but the full moon beams down at him from an open field of stars.

Soft blankets cover his torso, and a warm, fluffy pillow cradles his head. The Vanguard looming over him is an odd addition to the landscape, but not the weirdest thing he's seen this week.

Even dead silent, up close, the Vanguard is still intimidating. It's as solid as a marble bust, visible from the shoulders up to its sleek dome. The swept-back lines of Greymalkin's mouthless, noseless face give it a predatory look, and its vertical slits glow with a deep crimson light. A pair of protrusions lie flat against its scalp on either side, the "cat ears" from which Greymalkin got its name.

Gus runs a hand over his face, pulling on his stubbly chin. His skull is like an overfilled balloon. The connection to Greymalkin has gone tenuous as smoke, but it's still present. When he looks up at the dim red eyes of his quasi-overlord, it's tense. It's not like he can tell from its expression—he's not sure how he knows. Maybe it's the proximity? Being around humans also makes Gus tense, so he can't fault it.

Soldiers and scientists have been busy in the interposing hours, and they've set up a solar outpost's worth of surveying gear, instrumentation, and sensors. The array of antennas, dishes, and projection domes surrounds Greymalkin's head like a sad wall of pikes. Folx of all nationalities fiddle with their various stations. The piano is gone, moved to make room for all the tech.

It looks to Gus like there are a lot of red lights in the tangle of tech. Some of the stuff isn't working right.

"Hi, hi, Gus." Doctor Jurgens gives him a cordial wave, then clasps his hands behind his back. The guy looks dressed up to go on a date, sporting a dark, tasteful tux. "How are you doing?"

"My new best friend showed up," Gus says, and Jurgens laughs.

"I wouldn't call myself that. I'm just here to care for you."

Gus had been joking about *Greymalkin* being his new best friend, but guilt stops him from correcting the nice fellow. "I fainted?"

"Yeah. It wasn't great."

Gus spies Tazi talking to some scientists across the landing, and she makes an unpleasant face upon eye contact. Something has her upset, and she's heading his way.

"Doctor, you were supposed to grab me when he woke," she says.

"This is a recent development, Miss Tazi," Jurgens replies.

Gus sits up a little straighter, and the bed helps him. "How long was I out?"

The doctor clears his throat. "Two hours. It seems the government's experiment on you took quite a toll on your nervous system. I would've preferred to know the precise extent, but I wasn't allowed to move you to the hospital."

"Because we weren't sure what cutting him off would do, Doctor," Tazi says. "To Mister Kitko, or to us."

Gus sits up the rest of the way, leaning forward onto his knees. "Excuse me?"

"Greymalkin flew more than a hundred kilometers to get here," Tazi says. "It took off when you started playing, which means it probably didn't come to the noise. My observers detected a radio signal emanating from your skull."

She looks up at the monstrous being. "The closer it got, the stronger the signal became—more complex, too. Loads of bandwidth. The radio link hit its peak when Greymalkin arrived, and we've been trying to decipher the contents ever since."

"When did it quit?" Gus asks, and Jurgens glares at Tazi.

"It didn't," the doctor says. "I thought you should be moved to a shielded location, and your experimenters disagreed. We don't know what Greymalkin was doing to you."

Tazi huffs through her nose. "Please don't call us 'experimenters.'"

"Oh, what would you call it?"

"Doctor Jurgens, we've been over this," Tazi says. "Moving him could've upset the Vanguard. It's already destroyed seventeen worlds. You wish to add Earth to that list?"

"No, but I wouldn't let it beam strange signals into Gus's head." The doctor's voice sours. "Admit that you wanted to know what would happen."

Tazi snaps, fingernails flashing, and her camera drone zips out of her backpack. "Find phrase 'It thinks of me like a pet,' speaker August Kitko."

A short holovid appears above the drone's projector—Gus nestled into his bed. He recognizes it from the battery of debriefings he had to do at the hospital after that first day. Tazi and her people questioned him endlessly about all aspects of one of the worst days of his life—certainly the most physically traumatic.

"It thinks of me like a pet, I guess," the tiny Gus says. "Like it's a little protective, maybe. Have you ever had a dog?"

Tazi shoos away the camera drone and gives the doctor a foreboding look. "Now I ask you, Greymalkin is here to kill our species, and you wanted me to hide its dog?"

Jurgens struggles for a response, but Gus interrupts him with a hand.

"It's fine, Doctor. Understanding Greymalkin improves everyone's odds of survival. I—I'm fine."

Tazi's stern expression breaks for the briefest moment. "I respect that, Mister Kitko. I really do. You showed a lot of courage."

It's nice to win her approval, even a little bit. She seems like she probably knows some tough people, so it's a decent compliment. It almost breaks Gus's heart to have to tell her what he's learned.

No time like the present.

"So, uh, I have some news," Gus says. "Um, Greymalkin is... going to leave Earth in two days."

Judging from the look on Tazi's face, he needs to work on his bedside manner.

"What?" she says.

Gus sucks his teeth. "Yeah, I wasn't quite sure how to tell you."

"Where is it going?" she demands.

"New Jalandhar. Have you made contact yet?" Gus asks.

Tazi shakes her head. "If Earth were able to reliably talk to a lost colony, that would be classified."

"Don't you think I'm part of your team or whatever? I'm pretty deep in all of this." He taps one of the ports on his scalp to make a point.

"Understood, but you also have a lot of communications gear installed in you by something that was our greatest adversary until last Tuesday. You deserve to know everything, but you'll only be receiving a fraction of my situational awareness. There are enough leaks around here already."

"What do you mean?"

Tazi gestures to the piano. "You and Ardent playing a show drew some attention, but you're musicians on a date. Not galactic news. The robot's arrival—"

"Greymalkin doesn't like being called a robot. When I was linked up, I couldn't even really think it. Which is, uh, weird, right?"

Her silent rebuke says he shouldn't have interrupted her.

"Why not?" she asks.

"It's an unkind word. Means 'forced labor.' Greymalkin doesn't serve us."

"Do you know what Greymalkin's preference is, then?"

"Traitor Vanguard," Gus replies, and she rolls her eyes.

"Oh, mon dieu. Fine. It is a Traitor Vanguard," she says. "Why is it leaving?"

"To link up with the other two Traitor Vanguards at New Jalandhar. They need help."

For someone who looks unpleasantly surprised all the time, Tazi tops even her meanest face. "There are more? How did you leave this out before? Is there anything else important you forgot to tell us?"

"I just found out, when it like... touched my hand, okay?" Gus says. "What do you want from me?"

"I want you to help me keep humanity alive," she says. "We have to make friends with that thing and fast, because it's the only force standing between us and the Gilded Ghosts."

"I'm trying!"

Tazi crosses her arms. "I think you can expect to clear your plans for the evening, Mister Kitko. We need to discuss the most recent developments with the Security Council, and time is of the essence."

Jurgens shakes his head. "Miss Tazi, I must protest. This man has been through enough this evening."

"He might be the last hope of humanity—"

"But he won't be if you kill him," Jurgens says.

Gus is almost flattered by the immediacy of their bickering. The doctor argues for his health. The intelligence officer talks about his bravery and necessity. Gus sees it from both sides, though Tazi's idea of an evening is bleak.

He thinks of Ardent Violet, as he has every ten minutes for the past week. They'd both been enjoying the date when Greymalkin decided to interrupt. What was the etiquette surrounding gargantuan gate-crashers? Surely Gus couldn't be faulted for the way the jam session ended.

It'd be nice to get back to those piercing eyes and soft lips.

He's about to beg for Tazi's mercy when a commotion breaks out: Some of the scientists huddled around a console begin talking excitedly. A white guy waves to Tazi.

"We broke the jamming!" he calls. "We're ready to start scanning."

Gus shivers, unsure if it's a sudden cool shift in the breeze, or a feeling of creeping dread in the pit of his stomach.

"What jamming?" Gus asks.

"Greymalkin has deliberately fouled every sensor we've pointed at it," Tazi says. "Laser blinding, frequency flooding, all of it. But we have our ways of getting information." She gives the scientist the go-ahead. "This... Traitor Vanguard isn't going to sit still forever, and we need to understand what we can."

Panic coils in Gus's gut. "Okay, but I don't think you should do that."

Her opinion of his opinion seems low. "Do what? Understand it?"

"What's wrong, Gus?" Jurgens asks. "Can you explain what's worrying you?"

"Yeah," Gus says. "If Greymalkin was jamming you, it doesn't want you scanning it."

"I know why jammers exist, Mister Kitko," Tazi says. "But we have counter-countermeasures. Doctor Jurgens, if you're ready, I'd like to try moving Mister Kitko inside."

Gus's hackles rise, and he finally catches a clear emotion from Greymalkin—the walking apocalypse is pissed off.

"Okay, Gus," Jurgens says, taking hold of the stretcher and powering up the repulsors.

"Stop. You really need to stop!" He points to Greymalkin. "You're making it angry!"

Jurgens immediately lets go of the stretcher, which locks back down. He holds his hands up in surrender, and Tazi firmly pulls him away from Gus. Behind her, the scientists continue tweaking settings in holo menus and rigging data paths to perfect the scanning pattern.

"I meant stop scanning!" Gus shouts.

The Vanguard's voice fills the air like water, a deafening set of furious fifths ringing out into the night. Three beams erupt from Greymalkin's plated face, converging a few meters overhead to trace a pyramid. Where they intersect, the space seems to wobble and distort.

Gus's stomach registers the queer sensation of falling, like the gravity drive failing on a spaceship. Between the sonic assault and all the commotion, it's not clear what's happening. A point of anti-light forms at the conjunction of Greymalkin's beams, and at first, Gus thinks he has something in his eye. The speck is so powerfully dark that it resembles a black circle stranded in three-dimensional space.

"Shut down the scanners!" Tazi yells, storming toward the scientists. "Stop all of it!"

They try, but the connector cables rise among them in serpentine coils, all dragged toward the point of anti-light. Gus's blanket rustles softly and ascends from his body like a spirit. His arms drift upward, absent the traditional earthly tug of gravity. Jurgens panics and grabs the stretcher, which tilts unsettlingly in the nauseating changes.

The moment gravity disappears altogether is a ticklish one. Dust, snacks, and loose screws go tumbling toward the anti-light. Cables tangle with startled workers. The black dot draws Gus toward it, and he instinctively grabs the sheets. They come loose, and when he flails, they wrap around him like he's underwater. By the time he clears his view of fabric, he's lost contact with any terrestrial surface.

He's falling upward.

"Jurgens!" he cries, reaching out a hand, but the doctor fares no better. It's just one victim clinging to another.

Nearly all personnel have taken flight, screaming and groping for any purchase they can find. Tazi hangs from a wall sconce with all the experience of a seasoned mountain climber, barking orders at anyone with enough coherence to obey.

Then the black speck vanishes, and it all comes crashing down.

Gus and Jurgens fall onto the stretcher, and Gus knocks his head against something metal before rolling onto the unforgiving concrete. His back lights up with pain, and he grits his teeth to get through it. Other terrified shouts ring out, and he sits up to find a cluttered pile of equipment and people. He scans for anyone not moving, but they all seem to be alive. It was a lucky break for everyone—that fall had to be at least two meters.

Jurgens comes to him, checking him for wounds.

"I'm okay," Gus says. "Just bruised, I hope."

The beams snap together again, and the anti-light returns.

"Get inside!" Tazi yells.

Bodyguards come rushing out to Jurgens and Gus, ushering them inside and shielding them. They're rough, and it hurts to be so mistreated, but at least Gus isn't about to float away from a sixty-story drop.

"Stay down, sir!" they shout into his ears. "Stay down!"

Yes, that's the goal.

Inside the apartment, the influence of Greymalkin's gravity distortion falls off sharply. Gus's clothes go heavy on his shoulders, and he almost topples over under his own weight.

The last of the science team staggers into the apartment as the gravity on the balcony reverses at full Earth power. The black point of anti-light rises, refracting the world around. Expensive, calibrated equipment takes to the sky in a chunky flock, falling upward in silence.

Moments later, the balcony is empty like it's just been cleaned. Not a speck of dust, stick of furniture, or transit case interrupts the view of Greymalkin's bulk. Several million unicreds worth of gear is simply missing.

Tazi, Jurgens, the guards, and the science staff all lie on the ground in the apartment, huffing. Relief grows by the second as they sound off, realizing everyone survived. Some of them smile and laugh, hugging one another.

"I told you not to scan it," Gus says as he rises to look out the window.

Tazi works her jaw. "Yes, Mister Kitko, I can—"

Everything comes smashing down from the heavens in a single barrage. The whole balcony structure fractures up to the apartment door as gear shatters against its pavement. The stretcher is last, rolling down the mound of broken trash.

Tazi saves her breath until the last piece of scrap has clattered to the ground.

"I can see that."

Ardent's heart has been a furnace ever since they got situated in their new apartment. Recent events have them riled, and their new environs do little to calm their nerves. After Greymalkin gate-crashed Ardent's previous apartment, the folx at Belle et Brutale put them up with Dahlia in the "Master Architect's Residence." It turns out that the guy who designed the big egg hates color, texture, and fun. Even with a good night's sleep, Ardent can't get over their annoyance, and paces their bland living room.

Dahlia reads her Gang feed, rattling off the state of the world as it reports in for another borrowed day. The markets are all in the toilet. Billions of unicreds' worth of damage to critical infrastructure. Several nations are in turmoil after the deaths of leaders during the Ghosts' initial planetfall.

"Oh, but it says here the Ghosts are building something in

the Scar that officials think is a big farm complex," Dahlia says. "That's good news, right?"

"Nothing grows in the Scar."

"That's exactly the thing," Dahlia says. "The bots started leveling a site and screwing with the ground, and when the science types analyzed the soil, they found arable farmland."

"No microbes."

Dahlia inclines her head, reading aloud. " 'Officials believe the Megafarm is now a growth medium for all the bacteria needed to sustain organic life.' They think the Ghosts are going to perform a transplant somehow."

"Whoop-de-shit."

"What is your problem, Ardent?"

"No one helped Gus last night at all! We need to say something!"

"I hear you—and I need you to keep your voice down." Dahlia stands up from her chair before coming to Ardent and taking them by the shoulders. "It's going to be—"

"Don't say it's going to be okay."

The agent gives them a contrite smile. "Whatever it's going to be. You can't make an enemy of the United Worlds. I love you, Ardent, but you need to recognize that *you* are an entertainer, and *they* are the entire remaining government of humanity. You may be a big deal, but this is all out of your hands."

"I want to talk to that Tazi woman, Dahl. You've been coordinating everything for me. Tell me you can make it happen."

Dahlia starts a few failed responses, but each one is some variation of "That isn't a good idea, Ardent."

Ardent rests their hands on their waist, cocking their hips at a sassy angle. "Well, I'm not going to stand idly by while they abuse him. I'm going to tell Tazi exactly what I think of her program and—"

The room comm chimes, and Ardent gestures to answer. A holo voice panel pops up with the words, "Guard detail."

"Yes?" Ardent asks.

The little waveform on the panel jiggles with each word. "Miss Tazi is here to see you."

They exchange glances with their agent. "Uh, sure. Give us a moment and send her in?"

The second they terminate the connection, Dahlia says, "You had better be careful, Ardent. Tazi doesn't look like she's playing around."

Ardent scoffs. "What's she going to do?"

"Cut off your access to Gus."

"Oh, please. We would raise such a fuss in the press."

"She seems pretty important, babe. Not sure you want to fuck around and—"

The door slides open, and Ardent stiffens. Tazi enters, clad in a formfitting brown silk suit, cornrows luxed forest green like twisting serpents. She clearly knows how to wield fashion like a sword, and Ardent respects that.

They're suddenly feeling underdressed in their old tour shirt and tight leather pants. Their hair is frizzed out from where they've been ruffling it, and their makeup is probably worn off or smeared.

"Miss Tazi," they say icily.

"Mix Violet," Tazi replies, and they can tell from her tone that she's already tired of their crap—and they haven't even started talking.

"What can I do for you?"

"We all had quite an evening, no? I wish to ask you a few questions about it."

Ardent orders a mimosa from the room's bar, giving Tazi the evil eye while the machine preps the concoction. "Okay. I've got a few questions of my own."

The intelligence officer smiles, tucking her hands behind her back and squaring her stance. "Excellent. I would be glad to answer anything you need. Why don't you go first?"

They were expecting a fight, and Tazi's response throws them. They toss their seafoam hair to cover their fumble. "Uh, okay then. Why aren't you treating Gus right?"

"How are we treating him poorly?" Her soft French *H* becomes a whisper in her husky voice, and Ardent hates how cool she sounds.

"You just... let that machine touch him, and it—it knocked him over!"

Tazi doesn't roll her eyes, but Ardent feels it. "I was unaware Mister Kitko was a fall risk, as he had no prior history. You obviously didn't think so, either, since you were both playing beside the edge of a balcony."

"You should've protected him from that Vanguard! What did it do to him?"

"It spoke to him," she says.

"What did it say?"

Tazi chortles. "You must be joking. That's classified."

Ardent wrinkles their nose, stymied. "Okay, well... is Gus all right? I want to see him."

"He's fine." She jams her hands into her pockets and rocks a little on her heels. "Gus has more time off scheduled at seventeen hundred today, so I'm sure you can ask him about it yourself."

"And until then?"

"He's in tests. We have to make sure there's no damage to his nervous system after what happened. It's never healthy to fall unconscious."

"Depends on what you took beforehand," Ardent says, more to themself than anyone else.

"Now that you have asked your questions, I would like to ask mine." Tazi's fingernails flash when she snaps, and her camera drone zips out from a holster on her back.

Something in the woman's eyes is unnerving. It's like she can look inside Ardent, directly at their weakest parts. They shrink, crossing their arms and taking sips of their mimosa.

"Fine. Ask whatever you want," they say.

"Hi, sorry. I have to interject here." Dahlia rises from her chair. "Ardent, you're not being detained, and you don't have to answer anything if you're uncomfortable."

"Ah, Miss Faust." Tazi turns on her, as if noticing Dahlia for the first time. "This is a privileged conversation. Unless you're Ardent's lawyer—"

"I've passed the bar and manage the legal team in charge of their estate, so yes."

Tazi makes a *tch* noise. "Mix Violet, we would like your help, for Mister Kitko's sake, as well as your own."

Ardent narrows their eyes. "What do you mean?"

"How did you know what to perform with Mister Kitko?"

Ardent smirks. "Because I was basically born with a guitar in my hands. Been playing a long time."

"Yet when we ran analysis on over a thousand hours of your music, including improvisational patterns, we found no evidence of the chord progressions you used. Simply put, that isn't the way you think."

"Of course it was different. I was playing with Gus, and he plays weird shit."

But Tazi was right. It's one thing to know scales and chords; it's quite another to be able to improvise across every mode on a musical odyssey. Ardent *had* been able to pull off licks they never would've conceived before.

"Something has changed in you, Mix Violet." Her voice is low, mirthful. Does she think this is funny? "I want to know what it is."

Ardent turns their back on Tazi, glancing at Dahlia. The agent's brows are tense—she's worried.

"I—I don't know what you're talking about." Frustration creeps into Ardent's voice. "I guess Gus just, like, broadened my horizons or something."

"Other musicians from the Monaco encounter have reported strange phenomena, too." Tazi paces the room, drawing Ardent's attention back to her. "All of them have one thing in common. Would you like to know what it is?"

Ardent nods, but they're not sure.

"They all witnessed Juliette's mind flare in person." Tazi's eyes seem to glow, but it's only a trick of the sun. "Let me show you what the cameras saw last night."

She throws a file to her camera drone, which rises and projects a tiny version of Belle et Brutale's upper floors. The baffled balconies of the *Ovum* look like an engine nozzle from above, orange in the sunset. On the right side, at the focal point of the diorama, Ardent finds a miniature version of themself and Gus, jamming out on their instruments.

That'd been a phenomenal session before Greymalkin crashed it, the giant metal asshole. Ardent's fingers itch just thinking about jamming with Gus once more.

A few dozen Ghosts dot Tazi's projection, sparkling in patches around the egg. Tiny human families crowd their glowing windows to look on, ants in amber. The braver ones are out on their own balconies, various recording devices in evidence.

"Because of your performance," Tazi says, walking around the model, "we were able to get full-spectrum surveillance from every angle. For your protection, we confiscated every recording we could find."

"Going to be a hell of a bootleg if someone gets it past you," Dahlia says, but the joke falls flat.

Ardent can't laugh at anything, because the closer to the diorama they get, the more Ghosts they find looking at them. They knew a couple of the freak machines had gathered to watch, but there had to be twenty focused solely on the concert.

"Are you familiar with phased array scanning?" Tazi asks, pulling up a diagram.

Ardent shakes their head.

"It's when you use a large array of sensors to focus on a single cross section." Tazi's fingernails glow as she gestures to zoom out.

More of the building comes into focus, revealing a glittering crust of swarming Ghosts, ordered into interlocking shapes. The teeming mass covers the opposite side of the big egg, bodies flat against the concrete. It's an entire army that Ardent never saw last night.

"That's a lot of Ghosts." Ardent's mouth dries up. "Are they all outside right now?"

Tazi almost seems to enjoy this, like she's telling a scary story. "Yes. They are all still on the premises."

"Why are they all over the opposite side? Is it the phaser thing you were talking about?"

"Phased array scanning," Dahlia prompts.

"That," Ardent says.

"Indeed." Tazi cocks an eyebrow. "And can you guess what they're focused on?"

Ardent winces. "Gus?"

"That's what we thought, too, but it's so hard to tell from this distance—especially with the human eye." Tazi leans down to peer at the mossy carpet of Gilded Ghosts coating the arcology's shell. "But that's what analysts are for, yes? If we get very close—"

Tazi zooms in and highlights the heads of the Ghosts. "—we can see the pointing angle of their lenses. Tracing those vectors gives us a convergence point..."

Thousands of red rays sprout from the Ghosts' heads, flowing up through the center of the egg to a single spot—

—the pickups of Ardent's guitar, Baby.

Tazi smiles. "So why were they all listening to *you*, Ardent Violet?"

Their pulse jolts in their neck, and Ardent feels faint. "I... I don't know."

"Neither do we," Tazi says. "But we would like to run a few tests and find out, for your safety. Nothing invasive."

"I'm not sure I like the sound of that," Dahlia says. "Ardent has their own doctors in Berlin, and—"

The two women discuss Ardent's future, but Ardent can't hear it. They're staring at the holoprojection and all the mechanical eyes upon them.

Static rises in their head, and their breath comes quicker. They take a step back from the diorama; it's too big, takes up too much of the room. They keep backing up until they hit a wall, and Ardent sinks to their rump, chest heaving.

"Ardent?" Dahlia says. "Shit! Ardent!"

What if the Ghosts are staring at them right that moment? What are they thinking? Are they hungry? Ardent can't stop hyperventilating. The dizziness is getting worse.

There's a commotion, and Dahlia returns with Ardent's inhaler.

"Take it," she says, pressing it between their lips and clicking the trigger.

Eggy medicine flows over their tongue, and the taste alone throws them from their fugue. Dahlia props them up flat against the wall so they can't fall over.

"Obviously, we can't release you into the world with this threat to your person," Tazi says.

Ardent wants to tell her to leave, but every time they open their mouth, they almost start crying. Dahlia rubs their shoulders, shushing them, whispering to ignore Tazi.

"Get her—" they huff, clutching their chest. "Get her out of here."

Dahlia stands and turns to the intelligence officer. "You heard Ardent."

"I can see I've upset you," Tazi says. "Rest assured, now that the Ghosts have taken an interest, you're under our protection."

Ardent restrains the desperation in their expression as they look to Tazi. "I'm leaving. Not staying here another night."

"I'm afraid that won't be possible," Tazi says. "Don't worry, though, Mix Violet. We will get to the bottom of this."

Chapter Six

Night-Light

The second Gus wakes up, he's called in for a debrief. The government officers ask about his vision from Greymalkin, trying to tease every detail from his mind, but for the first time, he holds back. Tazi and the others have been too curious about the inner workings of the Traitor Vanguards. Scanning Greymalkin without its permission struck Gus the wrong way, and he isn't so sure he wants to trust these people anymore.

He doesn't tell them about the third Traitor Vanguard he saw, weak and vulnerable in the darkness. He needs to figure out what they'll do with that information.

After the battery of personal interviews, they sequester him for a "series of simple tests." It turns out to be only one procedure—but over and over again across hours.

Gus stares down at the little surgical steel device connected to one of his wrist ports and tries to get his jaw to unclench. He never knew his arm muscles could look so vascular and swollen; he has the guns of an action star at the moment.

A tiny light turns green on the milled metal surface, and a holographic icon for wireless patching appears. He's not sure he should've let the scientists connect this thing, but he's also not sure he has a choice. The device is called a probespike, and it's something his fellow Americans cooked up in their three-letter-agency kitchens. They wouldn't tell him *which* agency, only that he has definitely heard of them if he's watched any military thrillers recently.

He hasn't.

"We really do appreciate you doing this, Gus," says one of the techs. He's an amiable Latino fellow named Jorge with chubby cheeks, and they obviously gave him this job because the patient needed charming. He's kept Gus laughing for the past few hours, though even Jorge has his limits.

"It's cool. I love being itch-tickled inside all my muscles. Are you guys going to open a day spa?" Gus chuckles to cover up his annoyance at the pain. When that isn't enough, he adds, "I'm sorry. I totally get why you're doing this. Like the value of the study, and stuff."

"It's okay if you want to take a break, but hear me out: We've only got ten more ports to go. The sooner we do them, the sooner we're both off the clock, buddy."

Just the sound of the number is enough to take the fight out of Gus. He's been sitting in this uncomfortable chair for hours with lenses watching every muscular reaction. The room they're in looks like it used to be a regular patient suite in Belle et Brutale's hospital, but Jurgens's people have it crammed full of wires, processing gear, cameras, and the like. His back is sweaty again, despite the humiliating, backless patient robe they make him wear.

According to Jorge, these tests will give the medical team unparalleled knowledge of his body by scanning all port-to-nerve connections. Normally, they'd try to spread all this testing out, but since Greymalkin intends to leave tomorrow, they want to get what information they can from Gus.

"Okay." Gus's nostrils flare and he steels himself. "Okay, yeah. Let's do another one."

"To answer your previous question"—Jorge taps a few buttons on holo UI and locks something in—"I don't think the probe-spike would work for a day spa."

"Oh?"

"It's more of a sex dungeon thing."

Before Gus can laugh, Jorge punches a big button. A thousand jolts pluck every fiber of muscle in Gus's forearm, and the noise comes out a vibrato wheeze. It's like having his skin assaulted by a rain of pine needles.

Jorge hits some more buttons the second Gus's pain recedes. "Okay! Nine more, bro! Let's get that next one hooked up."

They finally release Gus for a private dinner alongside his squadron of holoflaged drones and bodyguards.

He shambles down the front hallway of the hospital, now a makeshift science center. So many technicians, soldiers, and random politicos come barreling through on an hourly basis that he can't keep track. Equipment and military gear have taken over every inch of the garden paradise, along with some vicious-looking checkpoints.

Not so belle anymore.

His port scans complete, the only thing Gus wants is a shower before the next battery of tests.

Both fortunately and unfortunately, Ardent Violet is waiting for him outside. No one bothered to warn him, or he'd have hit the blast shower at the hospital instead of his apartment. Hardly anyone tells him anything, though, besides what test comes next.

Ardent and Dahlia are easy to pick out on the concourse. The pop icon sports a vibrant, formfitting suit, with purple and green hues like a plum coming into ripeness. Dahlia, wearing a nanoblack coat, coordinates the handlers to keep the public at bay while Ardent waves to admirers. They notice him, face lighting up, and Gus gets a year of his life back.

Ardent comes striding across the polished gray tiles with the grace of a crane, spreading their arms wide to embrace him. Their clothes brighten to pink at the top when Gus approaches. The color conjures thoughts of sweaty nights, which does little to improve Gus's freshness.

He opts to go low in the embrace, pulling them against him so he doesn't have to raise his arms. He's 90 percent sure he's good but would rather not push his luck. They hug his neck and sigh happily, pressing their hips to his just enough to hitch his breath. When they draw back, he stares into their bottomless eyes, still amazed that he's lucky enough to touch their body at all. They've chosen a sparkling copper patina iris pattern this day, and it transfixes him.

"This is a surprise," he says.

"A good one?"

"The best one." He tries to keep the weariness from his voice.

"Aw, sweetheart, you look so tired."

"My throat hurts. I've been in debrief since I woke up."

"How awful!" Ardent exaggerates a frown like they're comforting a baby. "You've been in interviews the whole time?"

"And tests."

"What kind of tests?"

"Painful ones."

They hug him again.

"They keep pulling at every thread, and frankly, I'm feeling a little threadbare." He fakes a smile to make the laugh more convincing.

"Well, it's almost dinnertime, so I think we should focus on relaxing."

"I didn't know you were going to be here," he groans. "They catered sandwiches, and I got stuck with the last one—tuna."

The sandwich was a few hours old by the time the nerds took a break to eat, and thoroughly underwhelming.

Ardent laughs, taking his hand in theirs. It's so soft after a day of impersonal observation. "You saved the world. You don't get first sandwich pick?"

"They actually forgot mine at first, but it's fine—"

"I would have lost my shit," Ardent says as Dahlia joins them.

"About what?" she asks.

"Not getting fed," Ardent says.

"Shit would definitely be lost," Dahlia says. "Gus, you don't know what they're like when they're hungry."

Ardent rolls their eyes. "Okay, Dahlia."

"Just an unbelievable nightmare—"

"Listen, Dahl—"

"'Hellbitch' was *my* nickname for you, remember?"

Agent and client begin to bicker like an old couple, and Gus watches the exchange unfold with satisfaction. For the first time in hours, he's not doing the talking, which is a rare treat.

Ardent looks to him, squeezing his hand. "You've had a day. Where do you want to go to feel better?"

He considers it for a moment. The concourse is thronged with curious elite, eager for a glimpse of Ardent, or perhaps some insight into Greymalkin's situation. The cloud of drones following Gus everywhere brings him a lot of notice, too, and that's hard to swallow. He's not a public person, and doesn't enjoy the stares.

"I'd just like to get some space. W-with you," he adds. "No other people."

"I see how it is." Dahlia gives Ardent a flat look before mouthing the word *wow*, and Gus flushes with embarrassment.

"Oh, no!" He holds up a hand. "You can totally come hang out with us, and we'll grab some food—"

Dahlia waves him off with a pitying smile. "I'm so sorry, Gus.

I *clearly* shouldn't tease you right now. There's plenty of entertainment in the big egg. I'm sure I can take care of myself."

"Okay." Gus laughs. "Thank you for understanding."

"We're besties. She gets it," Ardent says before blowing a kiss to Dahlia. "Catch me later?"

"You bet," Dahlia says, waving with a black-gloved hand as she leaves. "Have fun, kids."

Gus watches her go. "I wish my agent was that attached. I'm lucky if I hear from him at all."

"Dahlia is my adopted wine aunt. She's been chaperoning me around a long time."

"So where do you want to go to dinner? There's a hydromat up here if you want a salad."

"Is that what you want?"

"No." Gus swallows. He'd like to ask them back to his apartment.

There, he's certain he'll find their lips, their eyes, and all the breathless magic of their body—but the fantasy is tainted by anxiety. Why? Is he intimidated? Does he think they'll refuse him?

They're a rock star. They don't take it slow; that much, Gus already knows. What if they're getting bored with his slow pace?

He should just take a risk, right?

"I'd, um, like to go back to my place."

"Given your blush, I'm guessing you're hungry for more than dinner."

"I could certainly go for a few helpings of you." It slips out—true, but more forward than he'd intended. He almost hopes they'll laugh.

The statement lands upon fertile ground, and Ardent gives him a lusty look. "Lead on, pet."

At first, he thinks his quickening pulse comes from their raw magnetism, and imagines them naked and gasping, the apples of their cheeks shiny with sweat—but for some reason, that's what he's afraid of. He shouldn't be. They're a sex symbol. Loads of people would want them. *He* wants them. It'll probably be fine.

There are two ways back to Gus's flat from the hospital—diametrically across through the central pillar or around the *Ovum*'s circumference. He's not ready to go straight home.

"Can we"—he gestures to the rows of hydroponic marvels that bejewel the belle section—"uh, walk through the gardens on the way? I wanted to see the orchids and stretch my legs. Been doing a lot of... lot of sitting."

"Are you okay?"

"Fine!" He smiles to see if they're buying it, and their hungry gaze remains unchanged, inevitable.

"Okay." They slip a soft hand into his.

He sparks so strongly at their touch he nearly whimpers. The problem isn't a lack of attraction, so it's probably his body odor. If he could just get a shower, he'd be able to relax.

They walk together through the jungles of the exotic orchid exhibit, showcasing some of the rarest, most fragile specimens from across the galaxy. Giant ferns line the paths, forming a loose jungle inhabited by rich creeps and bodyguards. Holoflaged drones rustle the leaves, and it's a bit like walking in a storm.

Ardent holds on to his arm, squeezing it to their chest. "You seem distracted."

"I am. Sorry." He shakes his head.

"It's okay! You said the tests were tough."

"Not just the tests, but the interviews. Today was the personal battery. Lots of stuff I didn't want to talk about with strangers. They pried into every aspect of my childhood. Surprised me with the thoroughness of their investigation. I'm not a politician. I'm barely even a public figure, and I don't think I was ready for that."

"That's awful. People are always prying into my family affairs, and I fucking hate it. Some of my siblings must resent me for all the extra scrutiny."

He doesn't have any living family, but bringing that up seems like a downer, and he's already agitated. They've traveled halfway, and he needs to arrive ready for action. The blocks seem to fly by, and Gus regards each passing address with growing trepidation.

"So, when we get back," he says, "I'm headed straight to the blast shower and to flash my teeth. Been eating old tuna sandwiches, you know. Are you good to wait?"

"If you took a bath instead, we could get clean together."

His head nearly explodes at the thought, and he can't figure out quite how he feels. Why is he so scared?

"I'd rather get in and out so we can focus on the important stuff, like each other."

"Mmm, that does sound nice."

Before he knows it, they've arrived at his door, and it's sliding open. Ardent leads him through, gently pushing him against a column and slipping their hands under his jacket. Their fingers stutter across his flesh every time they hit a port, and Gus slides away.

"Okay! That's—I need that shower to happen so we can enjoy ourselves, right?"

Ardent smolders at him, sending another jolt through his body. "Don't take your time, Gus."

He puts on his most cavalier smile. "Wouldn't dare."

When he leaves Ardent for the spacious bathroom, it's like a bonfire vanishes. All the prickles of heat drain from his skin, and wooziness threatens his knees. His heart is still pounding away, though.

He throws a computer sign and squares his shoulders. "Reflection, please."

Gus's misspent youth contained plenty of hangovers—and the holographic man before him looks worse than his worst. His once-beautiful hair, easily his best feature, is missing. Every time he sees his bald head, his self-image takes a punch. Bruises ring his bloodshot eyes. His lips are chapped, hardly kissable.

Stripping naked, he's a sorrier sight. Yellow, green, and purple blotches paint his body in Mardi Gras hues. His port wounds are all aggravated and red after a day spent with the probespike. Jurgens's treatments have been helpful, and a Ghost or two has visited to check on him—but he's still a wreck.

Gus steps into the blast shower and places his palms to the wall plate. The thought of the nozzles' brusque attitudes toward his body is too much, and he switches it to rain mode. Warm water splashes down on his skin, and he backs away from the wall, staring down at his hands. They've played him all over the world and into space, but now they're covered in ports.

His body isn't only his anymore.

He's never felt uglier, and almost everything still hurts so much. Will it ever stop?

Gus leans against the wall and sinks to the warm, smooth stones of the floor. He can't go out there like this, not to bed someone like Ardent. They have admirers anywhere there are human beings. They've guest starred in dramas. Their face has loomed in advertisements over Times Square, wild eyes and sexy smile visible all the way to the old Capital Age levees.

Gus imagines Ardent's luminous, flawless skin against his, and it feels profane. They're beautiful—genuinely gorgeous—and he's a goddamned troll. He wasn't in Ardent's league before Greymalkin violated him. Now he has no chance.

If only Ardent would come into the bathroom, tell him it's all right, and make him feel whole again. Maybe the right words or a simple touch would clean him of his shame.

Or they might think he was being needy.

Suck it up, Gus. Show some fucking confidence, and get out there before you lose them. They're hot. You can do this.

The manual shower takes six minutes instead of thirty seconds, so he flash-dries. He leaves the enclosure in a puff of steam and goes to the sink, trying to tame his missing hair on instinct. He signs for the mirror again.

Better. Not much.

Gus pulls on his robe and gathers himself as best he can, hoping he's not about to blow it. He wants them, and if they can just be patient—

Ardent Violet doesn't seem like the patient sort.

When Gus leaves the restroom, he finds a glittering chain on the ground. It takes him a moment to recognize the purely cosmetic belt that Ardent had formerly been wearing. Beyond, he finds one shiny purple boot, then another, rumpled up across the floor. He's most of the way to his bedroom when he sees the rest of their jumper in his doorway and the lights low. The muted thrum of an intimate bass line drifts from the space—definitely sex music.

"Fuck," he mumbles.

He enters to find Ardent sitting on one side of the bed, wearing a silky set of underthings and a sad smile.

"Something's wrong, isn't it?"

"N-no. I'm just a little..." His mouth goes dry as he searches for the words.

"It's okay, Gus. You don't have to do anything with me tonight."

"I want to. Please." He can't make eye contact. "Please don't, uh... don't think less of me."

They come to him, gently cupping his face in their hands to pull him down for a kiss. "Just tell me what you need."

He closes his eyes. "This... Only this, if that's okay."

They kiss him again. "Everything you want is okay with me, Gus. Come lie down, and let me take care of you."

"I'm not ready."

"Not like that."

Ardent takes his hand and leads him to the bed. When he lies down, they situate his pillow for him. They curl up beside Gus, the hot skin of their belly pressing against his arm. Black currant and bourbon vanilla waft from Ardent's body—scents to be devoured, but he's lost his appetite.

"I'm sorry," he says.

"Hush."

They stroke his chest and neck through his open robe, and he jolts when they touch a port.

"Does it hurt?" they ask.

"No."

Their hands rove to his face, massaging his cheeks, the bridge of his nose, his brow and temples. A hum issues from their throat, diamond-perfect in pitch, and Gus recognizes Jimmy Chan's famous tune, "All Quiet in the Sundown." It's a century old, covered by at least a thousand musicians, but it still holds its magic. He's surprised they know it, but he doesn't want to interrupt the moment to ask why.

Instead, he does everything they say, relaxing into their gentle ministrations. Within a few minutes, he lapses into blissful unconsciousness, wrapped in their heavenly embrace.

Ardent Violet has never been hornier in their life.

Lying snuggled into Gus's arm, enveloped in his scent, is a blissful hell. Their hands want to rove so badly, to follow the trail of his chest hair down his belly—but that would be wrong.

This is the part of Gus that he's chosen to share. They hold out hope that he'll awaken in the middle of the night with a burning need and consume them like a bonfire, but hours pass in vain. Eventually, their shoulder starts to hurt from being at an awkward angle, and thirst tickles the back of their throat.

Ardent sits up, and Gus stirs, smiling like an innocent.

"Sorry," they say.

"It's all good. I didn't mean to sleep through our second date."

"Oh, it was fine. Restful, even," Ardent lies. They don't want him feeling guilty. "Better than having my mom crash it."

"I liked meeting your mom. She'd get along with my mom."

"Maybe if you stick around, we can have a mom brunch."

He looks away. "Sorry, I meant she *would've* liked her. If, uh..."

Ardent's smile vanishes. "Oh, Gus, I didn't mean to—"

"It's fine," he says. "Everyone loses people. My whole family is dead. Barely any humans left in the cosmos."

"Lost them in the war?"

"Just my mom and sister. My dad, he, uh, passed on before the Vanguards came."

Five years ago, Ardent scarcely knew anyone who'd lost close relatives. Now it's weird when someone has a whole clan intact. Ardent thanks their lucky stars that all thirteen Aldridge kids yet live. They have an unusually large family, and for all of them to be survivors is unheard of.

Gus makes a little toasting motion. "Goddamn the Gilded Ghosts."

Ardent once loved the color gold. Now the very mention of the sparkling automatons makes them want to throw away their old wardrobe. The panic attacks aren't getting better, and their encounter with Tazi left them shaken most of the day. They haven't been able to stop thinking about the thousands of scanner lenses upon them.

Gus might know something about that.

"Out on the balcony at my place"—Ardent taps their index fingers together—"when we were jamming..."

"That was awesome," Gus says.

"It was," they say. "Remember how there were all those Ghosts around?"

"Yeah?"

"What if I told you they were all listening to my guitar playing?"

Gus cocks his head. "I'm sorry, what now?"

"Tazi showed me images of the Ghosts listening to us last night. All their scanner barrels were pointed at me."

He frowns. "You're talking to Tazi?"

"Worse," Ardent says. "I'm being detained by her."

"Why?"

"For my 'safety.' The Ghosts were all interested in me. Not just the close by ones, but"—Ardent hugs themself—"thousands of them, all over Belle et Brutale."

Gus rubs one of the ports on his forearms. "That doesn't sound good."

"Do you think I'm in danger?"

"No. It's just, I don't want you to get wrapped up in this."

"Too late, Gus." They sit on the edge of the bed, arms across their lap. "If you know what's happening, you have to tell me."

He shakes his head. "I think you'll be fine."

Ardent waits for him to make eye contact, but he doesn't. He seems lost in thought, turning over a problem only he can see.

"Maybe," he begins, and sighs.

"You have to say the rest of the sentence."

He looks at Ardent. "Maybe they're paying attention to you because..."

They appreciate the jazz pianist's carefully considered nature, but at the moment, they want to throttle the words from him. Gus keeps trying to speak, then stops, reconsidering.

"Spit it out."

"I think they're interested because they need another Conduit."

Ardent draws back. "What?"

"Like me. Someone who can interface with a Traitor Vanguard."

They're a maelstrom of emotions: fear, at having the attention of an alien entity, along with a strange sense of flattery. They stand and fetch a robe from a nearby hook, donning it. Covering themself eases the anxiety somewhat.

" 'Traitor Vanguard'?" they repeat.

"You can't translate their language directly, but this is close. It kind of means 'faithless' or like... 'abdicator.' They're Vanguards who are fighting to preserve humanity."

"Why does Greymalkin need another Conduit?"

"Not Greymalkin. When I came to last night, I told Miss Tazi about two other Traitor Vanguards: Cascade and Jotunn. They also attacked their comrades and saved their colonies—New Jalandhar and Fugelsangen. Those Traitors have human Conduits like me."

Cascade and Jotunn aren't the most well-known of the Vanguards. That fame easily belonged to Juliette before its ultimate defeat. Cascade came to the war late, destroying at least three colonies before the Veil was final. Jotunn destroyed Mars—close enough to watch on Earth's orbital telescopes. For them to suddenly be on humanity's side...

Ardent's dread whiplashes into hope, and they sit down at the foot of the bed. "That's incredible! Two more allies! We're three times more powerful than—"

"Four. There's one more Traitor Vanguard."

They open their mouth, then close it. "Wait, you didn't tell Tazi about—"

He shakes his head. "No. This one is special. It's broken."

"What do you mean?"

Gus sits up in bed, resting his back against the headboard

and pulling the sheets over his lap. "The Gilded Ghosts attacked Firenze Habitat. A Vanguard named Harlequin led the assault."

Ardent nods. Harlequin has never been recorded. The only evidence of its passage is the destruction in its wake.

"Just like Greymalkin betrayed Juliette, another Vanguard—Falchion—went after Harlequin on Firenze."

Falchion isn't just known for wiping out colonies. It attacks fleets and shipyards, too. The bloodred Vanguard got its name from the fact that it would cleave space stations in half. Only after several successful recordings escaped did humanity learn that Falchion accomplishes this trick using beam cannons. So it isn't a very good nickname, but everyone was already using it.

Ardent has seen pictures of the Vanguard on the news—a crimson devil with horns and glowing eyes. It certainly doesn't *look* like the sort of creature that would take humanity's side.

"Wait, Falchion killed Harleq—"

"It lost. Firenze is Wiped."

The familiar grief of a lost colony washes over Ardent. The cost of life is too great to be comprehended, but it nauseates them all the same.

Firenze Habitat was old—one of the earliest free-floating megamunicipal colonies out there. It came from a time when humanity was rising from the jaws of defeat. Another massive cycle of war had just ended, and the Europeans decided to launch the most audacious colony they could muster. Firenze had everything—clubs, shopping, art, comfort, and style. But that's all gone.

Ardent used to mourn people. Now it's just the daily cycle.

They close their eyes. "Damn it. So it's dead? Falchion?"

Any other week, that news would've elated Ardent. After all, there's nothing better for humanity than a bunch of deceased Vanguards.

Gus touches their cheek. "Hope isn't lost. Falchion is back

online, and I felt its presence when I touched Greymalkin. Catastrophic damage, fear, and confusion came across, too. Harlequin beat Falchion within an inch of its life. The short version is that it's been... um... reset."

"'Reset'?"

"Yeah, it's blank, and it's looking for inputs. Scared. Everyone at Firenze is dead, but Falchion doesn't know why. I'm afraid of what'll happen if no one intervenes—or if it's the wrong person."

The thought of a Vanguard stalking the corpse-riddled highways of Firenze is enough to curdle Ardent's blood. "Why are you telling me this?"

"I don't know... I don't trust the government, Ardent. They don't respect the forces they're messing with. Every day, more military people show up to ask me how I *control* Greymalkin, when I have no idea what it's even thinking. These Vanguards aren't our subjects to command. They might as well be gods, and they've chosen to spare us."

"Why do you think they let us live?"

"These things consume billions of lives' worth of data. Something caused a schism, but I don't get it—yet. I'm going to, though, because I'm leaving with Greymalkin."

That steals Ardent's breath away once more.

"How many more bombs are you going to drop on me in one conversation?" they ask.

"This is the last one," Gus says. "I promise."

It isn't fair. Ardent finally meets a nice boy, and he has to disappear after less than two weeks.

"If you and Greymalkin leave, Earth won't have anyone to protect it," Ardent says, and it sounds a bit feeble.

"The next attacks are coming for New Jalandhar. The swarms have already begun massing. If I don't help, I'm scared we're going to lose the colony and our new allies. Three Traitor Vanguards working together give us a fighting chance against the other seven. Think of all the lives out there."

"I'm trying," they say, giving him a reassuring smile.

"Everything has fallen apart. I have no family. My best friends died in an attack last year. It was you or the government, and this is too powerful for them."

"What happens if the other Vanguards attack while you're gone?"

Gus can't maintain eye contact, so there's that answer.

"We have to survive as a species, not a Homeworld."

More white walls. More endless concrete.

Doctor Bixby, the latest in a chain of neurologists, sits across from Gus in the blank room, as though they're both on the most boring interview show of all time. The only other item present is the array of cameras focused on basically every part of Gus.

Bixby taps a few controls on her Gang UI, and the room's projectors light up. A cooing child waddles around on the floor under Gus's chair.

"Can you identify this?"

"It's a baby," Gus tells Bixby.

The baby disappears.

Bixby raises an eyebrow. "And does... it... inspire any particular feelings in you?"

"I need to pee, Doctor, so there's that."

She doesn't laugh. "Why did you use 'it' to describe the baby, instead of a humanizing term?"

He glances at the cameras, all watching him like the eyes of a spider. "Because holograms aren't... humans?"

She frowns thoughtfully. Several of the cameras move a little, their lenses distorting to zoom in on his face.

"August, I'd like to point out that you have an abnormal pupillary response to babies. Are you aware of that?"

"I'll try to, uh, work on it."

"Please take this seriously. You don't respond appropriately to babies."

Now it's his turn to frown. "What do you mean? I like babies just fine."

"It's not a like or dislike issue," she says. "Those can be influenced by social pressures. Your biological response is diminished. Have you always been less interested in children, or is this recent?"

So now his pupils are wrong? The cameras are parsing everything he says and does. He swallows, and wonders how they interpreted it. Was it a secretive swallow, a guilty gulp?

"I said I like them fine," he says. "Can I be honest?"

"That's the only thing I want from you, August."

"This is stressing me out."

"Why?"

"Well..." He wasn't expecting to answer. He was hoping it would be self-evident. "You're keeping me in a boring room for hours on end, and now that I'm not blown away by a holo baby, you're talking to me like I wanted to eat it."

She crosses her legs, lacing her fingers around one knee. "What gave you that impression?"

"You said I looked at it wrong."

She shrugs. "Everyone has a different reaction. That's nature. Why did you classify your reaction as wrong?"

"I was reacting to your reaction. Look, is this to determine if I'm some kind of Gilded Ghost sympathizer—"

"Is that what you think it's about?"

He bites his lip and looks away, wanting a real answer instead of a dodge. "I think you don't trust me."

She cocks her head. "What makes you say that?"

Another question.

His shoulders fall. "Can we take a break?"

She smiles and stands. "Of course, August. Anything you need."

"Great. I need a walk. Lunch. Maybe some time with Ardent."

And a piano. Gus has played exactly twice in two weeks, and it's starting to wear on him. Back in Montreal, he'd wake up and play for hours a day. He'd do just about anything to put hands to keys now. His fingertips have started to itch for it.

"I don't think you should go far," Bixby says. "We still have a lot to get through."

"'Course not, Doc," Gus says, and makes for the door. "Couldn't get out if I wanted to."

Once he does the guard handoff in the hall, he's free-ish. Drones and soldiers trail him everywhere but don't try to corral him. They've probably all been warned that he's cross today, which is good, because he is. He and Ardent spent two more glorious hours in each other's arms last night, and now he's tired and pissy to be working so hard.

He ought to be with his new lover, enjoying the afterglow of a perfect embrace, but he's critiquing babies. Gus hails Ardent, but they don't answer, probably still asleep. They don't seem remotely functional before noon.

Gus signals his closest escort, a woman named Heidi, and the suited bodyguard jogs up to him.

"Yes, Mister Kitko?" she asks.

"Do you folx have a place I can sit and practice?" he says. "I'm not used to going so long without it."

"Let me just see what we can do," she says, giving him a polite nod. "All points, Echo team lead. Do we have a bead on a practice space?" She looks to Gus. "You want, like, a studio?"

"Yeah!" he says, not meaning to be quite that excited. "I mean, do you have one? It doesn't matter if you're set up to record. I just need to jam."

He waits while they debate, listening to one side of the conversation.

"Okay," Heidi says, and she sounds hopeful. The next "okay" makes it clear there was clarifying information. By the third "okay," Gus is pretty sure he's not getting anywhere.

"What's the problem?" he asks.

She holds up a finger and gives him an apologetic look. Must be bad news.

"We're going to work on getting you a space, but it could take a day or two," she says.

After Greymalkin leaves. Why?

Gus's breath hisses out through his nose as he deflates. "Yeah, no. Of course."

"Sorry," she says.

"It's fine," he says. "Not your fault."

But he's been assuaging the guards since he got here. Every hour, it seems like there's a new request denied, and he's sick of it.

"Can we go walk around the Big Hub?" he asks. "It'd be nice to stretch my legs and see what's what around here."

"I think that can be arranged, Mister Kitko," she says, clearly relieved to give him something he wants.

The Big Hub—or en français, Le Grand Hub—is the widest part of Belle et Brutale, and it's a massive bazaar, bringing in only the most luxurious goods. Bespoke haute couture boutiques and high-end restaurants line the walking paths. Gus watches the casual shoppers perusing wares as though daily lives haven't changed. He's seen this behavior before—for the past five years, humans of Earth have steadily been putting their heads in the sand, pretending all the distant deaths had nothing to do with them. Even the casinos had been open for the end of the world.

He strides down the tiled pathways past a vendor selling mouthwatering lamb skewers. He buys one with some lime and yogurt while his protection detail looks on. They watch the entire meal prep like security cameras.

With his cup and kebab, Gus is good to take in the sights, wandering beneath a huge trellis of woven bodhi trees. Spliced flowers poke through, shining down at Gus with their neon faces.

Every third plant seems to come from a different geographic region, and the arcologists have erected plaques everywhere, explaining the hydroponic routing miracles that enable such biodiversity. They also point to numerous preservation efforts, though Gus doubts those are as philanthropic as they make themselves out to be.

Then he spots the real reason for his visit: the lobby piano near the business office. He'd seen the instrument on the way into the arcology but hadn't been particularly interested in it; most public pianos are trash. However, when he's only gotten to play a total of ten minutes in a week and a half, it's a lot more exciting.

He starts heading in that direction, and his guards visibly tense. The instrument is a standard black grand piano, enamel shining in the piped-in sunlight. There's a holoprojected cordon, politely asking residents to refrain from using the keys during crowded hours, but Gus doesn't care. He steps onto the dais, through the holograms, and sits down on the cushioned bench.

As he suspected, it's a shitty piano, a knockoff of a Baldwin, and he runs his fingers over the keys. Some of them jiggle with loose action, and he plays a few notes to test the tuning—also bad.

"Mister Kitko!" one of the guards calls—a tall white man named Mike. Gus has talked to him some; he has family in Toronto. "Hey! Bud!"

Mike climbs the dais to stand beside Gus. "Hey, look. This isn't a public piano, so maybe it's best if we move on. I'm sure the Belle et Brutale staff will—"

"Set up a practice space for me in a day or two. Right? Just don't play right now?"

"That's not quite what I said."

"Good," Gus replies, and begins tickling the opening notes of "Les Feuilles Mortes." He's only onto the second chord when Mike's hand comes to rest on his shoulder.

"I'm afraid I'm going to have to insist that you stop playing, Mister Kitko," he says.

"It's the circle of fifths, Mike." Gus snorts, headed for the D seventh. "Greymalkin's tastes run a little more eclectic than that."

There's an ice in Mike's eyes that freezes Gus's joints, causing him to miss the next note. "Last chance, Kitko. Let's not do anything the hard way."

"Uh, yeah..." Gus says. "Okay."

The man is like a slab of granite put on a suit, and there would be no opposing him. If the bodyguard wanted, he could put Gus on the ground in a heartbeat.

"Sorry," Gus adds.

He hates the word as soon as it leaves his lips, and wishes he could take it back. He's been living in Montreal too long.

The enamel feels so lovely under his fingertips, and his joints ache for the flight of a chorus.

"Look, can I just..." He doesn't take his hands from the keys, but ghosts the notes, as gentle as the leaves of autumn. It's not the same, but it's something.

It's clear from Mike's expression that he's confused, and with any luck, conflicted.

"Look," Gus says, giving him pleading eyes, feeling so much more callow for it. "You like the feel of your weapon, right? Imagine if someone kept you off the range for a month. I just want to touch the piano, okay? I won't make a sound."

Mike rests a gentle hand atop Gus's, halting his progress through the first verse. The palms of his tactical gloves prickle with cool metal—stunners.

"And I won't ask you again," the mountain rumbles.

He pushes Gus's hand off the keys, where it topples into his lap. Then he slides the fallboard over the piano and latches it.

"I suppose the piano store is out of the question," Gus says.

"Take this seriously." Mike brings up his Gang UI to hail Tazi. "For all of us."

Gus turns from the instrument with a pained sigh and shuts his eyes. Mike takes the hail far enough away that the words are difficult to discern, but it's definitely bad news.

Mike finally returns. "I just spoke with the boss."

"And?"

"Break time is over."

" 'Break time'? Listen here, I don't work for you." Gus stands up.

"Let's be reasonable—"

"I am being reasonable."

"Please calm down."

"What, are you going to punch me for complaining? Now your bosses have had plenty of fun, but I'm done. *Beyond* done." Hot anger flashes behind Gus's eyes. "Now…I—I didn't sign up for this."

He's starting to cause quite a stir, and the other patrons of the Big Hub don't seem to like it. They stop to gawk in their luxurious attire, shopping pleasantries interrupted by Gus's unseemly outburst. One guy almost drops his smoothie, so distracted is he.

Fine. Let them gawk. It'll be a cold day in hell when Gus tries to impress an arcologist.

The holoflaged drones buzz overhead, sensing hostility and shoring up the crowd. They land around Gus in an array, disengaging their optical camo to reveal the bright plastic carapace underneath.

Their stun guns stand ready to knock down anyone foolhardy enough to approach the "VIP."

Gus briefly wonders, if Mike did take action against him, how would the drones react?

"What's the meaning of this?" Tazi comes marching up the steps of the piano's raised platforms, and the drones scuttle out of the way for her as though she's a queen. With her woven braids and gold-dusted eyelids, she might as well be. Gus suddenly feels like a clown for stepping to Mike.

"I'm a musician. I need to play piano," Gus says.

"Will you die without it?" Tazi responds.

He lets out a hissing breath. "No, but I'm not alive without it, either."

"Your playing might activate Greymalkin."

"Only if I play something ridiculously difficult!" He throws up his arms, exasperated. "You know, it's like we've been in interviews for the past week and a half, and no one has been listening to me."

"You're one hundred percent sure your actions will have no consequences."

He scoffs. "Ninety-nine percent."

"So, on the one percent chance Greymalkin activates, is the Vanguard going to help us or hurt us?"

He looks away. "I don't know."

"Oh," she says. "Then perhaps you should quit being selfish and recognize that your music impacts more than your sales now. Other people's lives depend on you."

"How dare you? You think I care about sales at the end of the world?" He shakes his head. "I just want to go back to being a regular person. I'm not a soldier."

"True. They know how to put the needs of their fellow citizens above their own."

He crosses his arms. "I take it all the nicer agents were too busy to handle my case?"

"I've had a lot of battlefield promotions," Tazi says, not rising to his insult, "so I get any assignment I want. Mister Kitko, I have no urge to be your friend, but I will keep Earth alive, regardless of your opinions. Maybe if you don't care about the rest of humanity, you care about Ardent Violet."

"O-of course I care about—" he stammers. "Can you not understand that I'm at my limit here?"

She smiles sardonically. "You've very clearly demonstrated your limitations, yes."

His gaze drifts one last time to the keyboard with a needle in his heart. Back in Monaco, he'd been ready to die. It never occurred to him to carry on without piano in his daily life.

"Can't I just pretend?"

"No. We detected a data comm spike off you the second you started playing," she says, and his heart sinks.

Greymalkin *was* listening.

"I—"

A ball of ice forms in Gus's stomach. If Greymalkin could react whenever he merely pretends to play piano, can he ever safely carry a tune again? No, she said the data was coming from him; his body was broadcasting.

"You didn't know about the data spike," Tazi says. "Now you do. Does that change your mind?"

"Yeah," he says. "It does."

Because now he knows how he's going to get out of here. He just needs to find a piano.

Chapter Seven

Flight

Ardent hates Gus's government handlers more with each passing hour. They've sequestered Gus most of the day, and in the late afternoon, Ardent has to trek all the way up to the Belle et Brutale's Central Administration. It's in the top of the arcology, protected by layers of metal-reinforced concrete.

When they arrive, they find workers plastering metal meshes to the walls. The system is probably for fouling scanners, but Ardent isn't sure. Electronics and EM radiation were never their strong suit in middle school. If that's the case, though, it's because they don't want Greymalkin looking in on Gus.

When they sit down to eat with Gus in the admin canteen, he's not wearing the same smile as usual. The guards and other patrons have given the pair a wide berth, but Gus eyes them like he's expecting someone to pull a gun. He barely touches his food, and his mood is terrible. The conversation is bleak—he's distracted at best—and Ardent only manages to get a brief exchange out of him.

"Babe, what's wrong?"

Gus pushes food around his plate while he watches one guard in particular. "They took my Gang."

"What? Why?"

When the distant fellow seems distracted, Gus says, "Can't speak openly. I need a piano. They won't let me play because they think I'll call Greymalkin. When I play, it can tell where I am somehow."

"And you want that?"

"I'm going with it. They're just trying to stop me so Greymalkin will stay."

Ardent wants to ask more, but the protection detail comes walking over, and Gus clams up when they're ten paces away. He clearly doesn't want them hearing his request.

"I just miss my music, is all," he says.

With an angry sigh, he pushes back from the table and follows his escort. He gives Ardent a final, meaningful glance before disappearing into the complex—leaving them at the table with a plate of cold ravioli and a gnawing fear.

It doesn't take Ardent long to leave as well, and they wander the halls on the way back to their apartment, lost in thought. How are they supposed to get a piano to Gus, surrounded by goons who don't want him to have it?

He'll almost certainly use it to call Greymalkin. Will the military be angry at Ardent? Upsetting a few tight-asses never bothered them, but this time might come with considerably more consequences.

When Ardent arrives back at their place, they find Dahlia waiting for them, perusing her Gang as usual.

"How is lover boy?" she asks.

"I think I'm going to become a criminal."

"Sounds like you had a heck of a breakfast."

"I went to lunch."

"Yeah. That's basically breakfast for you."

Ardent paces the room, wringing their hands. "Gus wants a piano, but the military types aren't letting him practice."

Dahlia gives them a sidelong glance. "Why?"

"They think it'll awaken Greymalkin, and it'll leave."

"Will it?"

"I don't know." Ardent rubs their temples. "Maybe. Probably."

"So you can see why they won't let him play. They're right to be worried, and frankly, they ought to be worried about you, too. What if you start playing and the Ghosts react to you again?"

They haven't been able to stop thinking about that since Gus told them about Falchion—possibly the biggest secret anyone has going at the moment. They want to tell Dahlia about it, but they're not even sure how. What if she freaks out?

"Hey," Dahlia says, "what are you thinking about?"

"Gus needs to help those other colonies," Ardent says. "They're going to die, and this is wrong."

"And if a Vanguard attacks while Greymalkin is gone, Earth is doomed."

"No. I don't accept that we have to simply sit here while the other colonies perish."

"It doesn't matter what you accept, Ardent. This decision is out of your hands. They're the world government, and you don't have a big fuck-off robot."

"Gus said we shouldn't call them robots. Means *servant* or something."

Dahlia rolls her eyes. "My point stands."

"That I can't do anything against the UW?" Ardent puffs up, and Dahlia only shrugs.

But they can get a piano to Gus. It's not impossible.

Ardent flicks their wrist and searches the shops on their Gang for virtual pianos. An array of precision-modeled instruments appears in the air, hundreds of different brands from across time. Ardent is about to pick the top result when they remember how much Gus talks about his favorites.

Dahlia leans forward in her chair, elbows on knees. "What are you doing?"

"None of your business." Ardent selects a large variety pack of pianos and loads them up.

"I'm your friend, and it looks like you're trying to smuggle Gus a piano."

"Okay, then you understand why I'm doing it, *friend*."

Dahlia goes back to playing with her Gang. "Calm down. All I'm saying is that you're playing out of your league."

"Oh, please. The whole galaxy is my league."

A sigh. "Your arrogance is your worst feature, Ardent."

Their hands drop to their hips, and they give her a spicy glare. "You know I wouldn't take that shit from anyone else."

She looks up from her messages and lifts an eyebrow. "But you'll take it from me, because I'm right. I'm here to care for you, no matter how difficult you make it."

Their temper flares, and Ardent has to work to keep their mouth shut. They've struggled with it most of their life, and it's cost them too much a few times. Ardent clenches their teeth to keep every foolish word caged and focuses on breathing.

They start to speak, but Dahlia is quicker.

"Ardent, I love you like family, so no matter what you say, I'm not going to endorse smuggling contraband to the most protected VIP on the Earth."

"So you think we shouldn't help New Jalandhar? Just let them die like all the others?"

"Straw man. You're putting words in my mouth, and I'm not playing that game."

"I'm trying to help those people."

"Ardent." Dahlia closes down her Gang and folds her hands across her lap. "I understand what you're saying. I even agree with you."

"Really?"

"Yes. And if you had a plan that was even marginally good, I'd have a lot more trouble staying out of it."

"It's a good plan!"

"Why can't Gus download his own piano?"

"They took his Gang."

Dahlia cocks her head. "But they're not going to take yours?"

Properly demolished, Ardent has no choice but to slink away. Despair creeps in—Greymalkin is supposed to depart within the next twelve hours, and they're not sure they can help Gus in that time. Baby sits on its stand in the main bedroom, translucent body inviting them to switch off their brain. They gingerly take the guitar by the neck and head for the little attached balcony. The door slides open, and the blustery wind of a Les Couteaux sunset whips Ardent's hair about.

Government scaffolding and tarps cover much of Greymalkin's bulk, but it's hard to miss the Vanguard clinging to the side of the building several stories up. Below, the lights of gathering humanity cover the ground like a blanket of stars. It reminds Ardent of a summer music festival, but a hundred times larger.

Gilded Ghosts crawl along the side of the *Ovum Inversus*, clumping up like freshly hatched spiders. Their sizzling tusks pop and flash, illuminating the bunches from within, and Ardent wonders what they're up to. Maybe they'll start killing everyone.

Maybe upsetting Gus caused them to show up and invade.

No, Ardent. He wouldn't hurt anyone. This must be something else.

Ardent takes a deep breath of sea air. Baby feels amazing in their arms, and they shrug into its strap. The Powers Vitas X respires with an internal purple light.

They locate the room amps and sync their instrument. Cranking the volume as high as it'll go yields a deep, rich hum from the luxury resonators that shakes Ardent to their very core. Drawing out their silvered pick, they flip it once in the air for good luck, then smash it down across the strings.

The noise is glorious, and Ardent grits their teeth against the volume. Nothing is better than the wave of an electric guitar bowling over the audience.

They start out with one of their old standards from the first tour, a rocking refrain of "Get the Hell Out." They don't have a mic, or they'd really let it rip. A few extra trills issue forth from their fingertips, almost unbidden, ornamenting the solo in exciting new ways.

Playing alongside Gus has changed them. They're no longer satisfied with the stuff they know so well—they need a challenge. How did his chord progression go?

Ardent stops and tries to conjure the memory of their jam, but it's so hazy. The chords felt right, but they slip from Ardent's mind when they try to gather them back together. They could probably play something similar, though.

Ardent puts a boot on the white concrete railing and lets fly a powerful minor drone. They sample and hold the sound in place, adjusting the timbre in Baby's holo menus until it penetrates every part of the audio spectrum.

"Come on..."

Baby's wail reminds Ardent of Juliette's hypnotic keening, and they add a few harmonics to further mimic the sound.

"Okay, yes." They boost the seventh, and everything falls into place. "Yes!"

Fingers fly over frets as Ardent rocks out. Every pluck of the string feels so alien, yet so right. They close their eyes, focusing on that perfect moment of bliss they'd felt, staring into Juliette's mind-melting light show.

The nearby Gilded Ghosts take notice.

Ardent almost drops the tune when they realize what's happening. Thousands of eyes lock onto them, twin candles in webs of gold. Tusks flare white, and the Ghosts begin clacking their way over the ledges from other apartments.

Ardent cranks the gain, overdriving the drone and shredding across its wake. More Ghosts emerge, and they're all intent upon Ardent's song. Maybe they're coming to kill. If that's the case, there's very little to be done about it. The Ghosts throng around the balcony, crawling all over one another to get a closer look.

Ardent doesn't stop for anything, sending their solo heavenward in one last gasp.

When they finish, the Ghosts await them, hanging from nearby balconies, swaying in the breeze like Spanish moss. They're the most incredible audience, silent and attentive. The nearest one clicks up to Ardent and offers a claw. Whether it's in friendship, or it'll drag them to hell, Ardent cannot know. Blood pounds in their ears, and they take a dry gulp, but they refuse to run away. The Ghost steps closer, outstretched manipulator within centimeters.

Unsure of how to react, they fist-bump the Ghost ever so slowly.

"Gus." The machine speaks with a feminine voice, older and gentle. She sounds tired—someone's final memory?

"Gus," Ardent repeats, and the creature tenses like it's ready for action. "You're looking for him."

Up close, the golden surface is arresting, with its palladium seams and patterns. The creature is a manifestation of will, an unstoppable force—but at the moment, it seems like a curious cat. Ardent forces themself to reach toward it once more, and the Ghost presses against their palm.

"I..." They aren't sure they're ready for what they're about to say. "I can lead you to him, but—"

The Ghost perks up.

"I need you to get me out of here, too. I have a TourPod in the charging garage. Can you get me to it after we help Gus?"

It nods.

"And no killing?"

It nods again.

"Don't even maim."

Dozens of other nearby Ghosts jolt to life, circling and swarming. The jangling chains saturate Ardent with fear, but they will stand strong. No backing down.

"What"—Dahlia says, and Ardent turns to find her standing right behind them, bedroom balcony door wide open—"the *fuck* are you doing?"

They glance back at their dozens of deadly friends before smiling at Dahlia. "You were right. I, alone, can't do anything against the UW."

She looks wide-eyed between Ardent and the gathering swarm. "Okay."

"Don't freak out."

"I'm not."

She clearly is.

Ardent tries to come up with anything to blunt the situation but draws a blank.

Dahlia's eyelids flutter as she wrestles her next thought. "I... I... You—what is your plan?"

Ardent takes a breath. "Total havoc. Meet me at the TourPod."

"—under assault by multiple tangoes—"

"—too many of them—"

"—Ghosts at the perimeter. We can't hold—"

The protection detail radios go wild, and Gus's heart drops. At first, he assumes the nightmare never ended and Greymalkin has decided to destroy the Earth. He imagines Ghosts roaming the halls, scrambling the inhabitants of the big egg, yet he catches another snippet of a radio transmission.

"Ah, fuck! That thing shocked the piss out of me!"

That's certainly not how Gus would refer to getting two tusk-sized holes in the top of his head. He hopes that person is okay. Given the bedlam on the radios, the assault is widespread across the entire arcology. His thoughts drift to Ardent, but he doesn't have too much time to worry.

Gus's guards shuffle him into the study, a room with only two exits and no exterior windows. They take up firing positions throughout his room, aimed straight for the doors.

"Please stand back, Mister Kitko," Mike says, and Gus feels guilty for snapping at the fellow earlier. He's clearly willing to lay down his life.

"Okay, just...be careful," Gus says, patting him on the back. "I'm not worth it."

"I'm doing this for my family, Mister Kitko. With all due respect—"

Muffled gunfire sounds outside, along with terrified screams.

"Get behind the bookshelf over there. If the room is breached—"

Before Mike can finish his sentence, it comes to pass.

A gleaming avalanche of screaming chains flood through the doorway, soaking up hundreds of bullets. Ghosts leap onto terrified bodyguards, yanking them out of the room by arms, legs, and suit coats. Guns go clattering to the ground, ripped from well-trained hands by the irresistible force of machines. Mike knocks Gus flat, but he's dragged off in an instant. The last Gus sees of him, the meaty dude is getting yanked out the door, shouting for his comrades.

Emerging in the middle of it all, queen of the bees, is Ardent Violet.

"Surprise, motherfuckers!" They throw their arms wide like they've just landed onstage.

The whole assault couldn't have lasted more than a few seconds, and when Gus sits up, the room is full of the horrific machines, their fangs arcing with menace—but no guards.

"How did you—" Gus begins. "Why are they—"

"Music is math magic, and these things are computers. Now let's get you the hell out of here!" They pull up their Gang UI and launch their holo piano. It's not even filled in, just a wire frame of eighty-eight keys and a couple of nerd knobs to tweak the tone. It hovers anemically in the room, far from a grand piano.

"You want me to start... playing?"

"Was that not clear?" Ardent says, glancing over their shoulder with dwindling confidence. "Gus, I think I made the UWI folx really mad, and I'm sure there are more soldiers on the way."

As if in answer, a fight explodes out in the hall between the holoflaged drones and the Gilded Ghosts. Bullets and lasers fly past the door, and Ardent dances a little.

"Please start playing, babe. Like now."

Gus takes a deep breath and places his fingers to the keys. He wants to close his eyes and get lost in the sound of hammers on strings, but there's no tactile feedback.

His first few phrases are halting attempts at his old works, because his fingers don't bounce off the surface the way they should. Violent bursts rock the corridors outside, then angry shouts, more laser blasts, and gunfire.

Gus's fingers find their marks, and he kicks out a few more chords, matching rhythm. It's tough going, but he begins to feel a change within himself. He's aligning again, just like the night he saw Juliette's Hypno Spectacular over the Mediterranean.

A connection stabilizes within Gus's mind, a red thread pulled taut enough to steal his concentration. There's something massive on the other end, and it takes Gus a moment to understand: Greymalkin senses him. It's waking up early.

I want to leave. Come for me.

"It's working!" he shouts, fingers faltering. It's hard to keep his head in the moment, so massive is Greymalkin's presence.

The Vanguard keen fills the air, a wave of unstoppable sound pouring in through every wall. Gus falls to his knees, piano going silent, and Ardent rushes to help him. The Vanguard signal awakens every port on his body, and they itch to receive Greymalkin's probes.

Gus's chest heaves, and he sees two worlds: his room, and the exterior of Belle et Brutale.

"Oh god, I think I'm going to be sick," he mumbles, pushing Ardent's hands away. "Get back, get back... I don't know what's happening."

He tries to stand—he needs to return to the piano—but his clumsy legs won't let him. When he falls again, he hits his head, leaving a flash in his vision.

"Gus!"

"I'm fine..." he mumbles, swallowing to keep his lunch.

Closing his eyes makes it easier: leaving only one world to study—the view through Greymalkin.

The balconies of the upper *Ovum Inversus* teem with gawkers and guards. Bullets and lasers clash as a giant black hand enters his field of view—Greymalkin's fist.

It rears back to punch, and—

"Get down!" Gus pulls Ardent to the floor with him and rolls atop them.

The wall of his enclave shatters inward, bringing with it another golden horde. Ghosts swing through the room, catching debris, interlinking in a web to keep the cracked ceiling from collapsing.

Ardent shouts something into the rocky din of a shattering world, but Gus can't make it out. There are definitely a few swears.

A baseball-sized chunk strikes Gus in the back, and he hisses through clenched teeth.

A pair of massive Vanguard fingers wrap around his waist like a seat belt, and he's lifted from the ground. Ardent shouts in surprise and reaches out—but their fingers only brush his. Gus is plucked from a building into the night air for the second time this month, and Greymalkin's open chest yawns before him.

Torn tarps and bits of scaffolding cover the shiny two-toned Vanguard like a cloak, billowing in the wind. Holoflaged drones zip through the air, blasting away at clumps of Ghosts, but everyone leaves the Vanguard alone. They probably don't want to piss it off.

Gus's musings are cut short when he's released, plunging toward the wide opening. Viscous contact fluid coats him, reorients him, and he holds his breath until oxygen flows into his nose. Probes sink into every port across Gus's body, sending jolts through nearby muscles. A series of thumps hit his scalp: silver needles pushing into his brain sockets.

Lights sprout in the darkness, only a few at first, blooming into a pitched battle. Gus looks around for Ardent, locking onto their prone form inside the arcology. They're not standing up.

Greymalkin focuses its sensor array upon their body, returning all sorts of vitals—Ardent is fine, just a bit stunned, and likely resigned to their situation. A question appears in Gus's mind, fed to him by the Vanguard: Should Greymalkin exterminate the opposition before leaving? It would be easy to mop up any potential pursuers.

"No!" Gus cries. "They don't know what they're doing, and they pose no threat to you. They won't follow us. Please."

Greymalkin echoes Gus's opinions of the citizenry of Belle et Brutale back into him. Its love of humanity is new, and it's not sure how many of these people it cares for.

"I know! Please. Just... let's leave them, okay? You have me."

Ghosts mill about the exterior of the egg, invading every

crevice. They can't come with Greymalkin to New Jalandhar. They require superluminal delivery systems to travel, and it would take too long to manufacture them.

What would Gus like the Ghosts to do while he's gone?

"Me?"

Within reason.

His vision slews back to Ardent, standing to dust themself off. A quick scan reveals dozens of armed guards and government drones flowing up through the structure to the rock star's location. Once Gus is gone, they'll almost certainly take Ardent into custody.

And before he realizes what he's done, Gus thinks, *I wish I could protect them.*

Greymalkin understands. All swarm units will protect the object of Gus's infatuation until he returns.

"Wait, what?"

The Vanguard leaps into the air and takes flight. This isn't some luxury starliner with cushy seats and reasonable acceleration—it's blasting off, hearkening back to the old days when rocket jockeys rode explosions into space. Gus's blood pools in his legs as it picks up speed, and a dark ring forms at the edges of his vision. The goo encasing his lower half begins to squeeze, equalizing the pressure on his body to prevent him from blacking out.

The cracked landscape and glimmering Mediterranean disappear beneath clouds, and the sky grows thinner and darker by the second. Flecks of light spread before him, other stars, other galaxies. With nothing between him and outer space, he's transfixed by its beauty.

Gus has no control, shoved heavenward inside the most advanced intelligence he's ever experienced. Has he made a mistake, allowing himself to be consumed once again? What does Greymalkin really want with him?

A Conduit shouldn't worry about these things.

Comforting drowsiness wraps around Gus, enfolding him in soft pleasure. Elzahia Tazi, the UWI, and the squabbles of the Homeworlders live in his wake. Greymalkin lets him know he's been drugged, but that it's going to be okay.

"It's not okay, I—"

The stars stretch across his vision like raindrops, and Gus's eyes fall closed.

Chapter Eight

Shock

Ardent pushes to their feet, broken bits of concrete clinging to their scraped palms. The southern wall of the room is missing, and bedlam reigns outside.

CAVs launch from the cliffs below like neon fireflies, fleeing the area. Drones duke it out with Ghosts, and Ardent is forced to duck away when stray fire tattoos the nearby floor.

At least they didn't get punched by a Vanguard again.

They lean out to look for Greymalkin and find it rising to the heavens, the engines in its black boots illuminating contrails in arcflame blue.

A sharp hiss pierces the night, and Ardent turns to find a line of slag tracing the door to the study. It bursts inward in a smoky heap, and UWI personnel rush inside, shouting for Ardent to run to them. In the lead is Elzahia, with the wildest gun Ardent has ever seen, like a smart rifle with a huge backpack. She slices through Ghosts like they're nothing, cutting them to useless golden bits with extreme prejudice.

The crack in the ceiling opens farther, and the loose net of Ghosts holding it together buckles and rips. Tons of Belle et

Brutale's omnipresent concrete come pouring toward Ardent, and it looks like the end.

Golden claws seize them, tearing their old shirt and hurling them through the wide-open wall. Rushing wind drowns out Ardent's screams as they go soaring into the great beyond. Before they have a chance to orient themself, a long chain of Ghosts co-opts their momentum with a miraculous grab. Ardent goes swinging around the side of the seventy-story egg at the end of a glimmering vine, pure adrenaline squeezing the voice from them.

Another forming chain comes into view, impossibly far down, and Ardent fears they know what comes next.

"Please no, please no, please no!"

The claws release their hold, and Ardent falls. They're familiar with acrobatic work, but this is another level. Ardent goes spread eagle, headed for the ground like a skyflier without a jetpack. The next chain smashes into them, hooking under Ardent's arms.

The creatures sling them down onto a balcony, where some Ghosts have interlinked to form a makeshift net. It curdles Ardent's blood to land on the weave of killer machines, and they roll off as quickly as possible.

Clambering to their feet, huffing, they say, "I need to get to the garage."

"Don't worry," the closest one says in a man's voice. "We're going to protect you, no matter what. Okay, honey?"

Ardent grimaces—more of people's final moments. "Great. Lead on."

The Ghosts cut through the shell of the *Ovum* to the terrified occupants inside. A family huddles in the living room, their faces locked in fear. Ardent climbs over the laser-cut hole, avoiding burning themself on the orange-hot threshold. Smoke chokes them, and fire alarms blare overhead.

"Sorry! Sorry, sorry!" Ardent says, and the youngest girl points at them.

"It's you!" she cries.

"It's me!" Ardent waves as they run past. "Lots of love, dear!"

From there, it's a short jaunt through the apartment and out into the main promenade. Chaos reigns as soldiers and law enforcement engage the Ghosts with abandon. The UWI people shoot their weapons like they're not in crowded buildings, and Ardent spots a few Ghosts actively drawing fire away from populated areas. No civilians are out in the streets, however—which means Ardent is going to stick out like a sore thumb.

Ghosts spill out of the doorway behind them in a rising tide. The metal beasts sweep them along the smooth floors, carrying Ardent to god-knows-where like a mosh pit from hell. A couple of guards spot the procession and give chase, shouting orders into their comms—but the Ghosts crowd-surf Ardent into one of the many gardens.

Tree branches whip their face as they're carried through the underbrush, and Ardent shouts for them to be careful. After all, that face makes a lot of money. The machines slosh down a side corridor, skittering over the walls and floor in a fluid wave. Ardent tumbles backward, caught again and again by unforgiving metal hands.

"Ow ow ow!"

The Ghosts carry Ardent through a maintenance door into a massive parking garage, where hundreds of CAVs charge in their docking cradles. The cavernous space stretches up and down at least ten stories, with the shiny cars packed inside docking columns like kernels of corn. Crowds choke the catwalks to the elevators, terrified residents fighting the cops to be let through. CAVs wobble as people switch off their autolaunch to avoid stacking up in the air lanes. This many pilots on manual can only cause problems.

In the distance, a Feder 226 sportCAV lifts from its charging pad, and it's barely made it into the exit lane before a Midnight Runner hovercycle smashes into the driver's side window, catapulting the pilot from his seat and into the parking abyss. The cyclist's flight leathers inflate to a balloon, and he goes bouncing off one of the docking towers. The Feder's sleek roof is crushed by the impact, and the cabin fills with crash foam. The CAV lists, then comes screaming down into one of the crowded catwalks, cracking the long structure in the middle.

A collective wail of fear goes up from the trapped crowd as the catwalk buckles inward. Stone snows from the break in huge chunks, tumbling onto unfortunates below. The Ghosts aren't reacting, though.

"You have to save those people!" Ardent cries.

The Ghost carrying Ardent makes an angry buzz and gestures in the direction of an elevator. It wants Ardent to abandon everyone.

"If you don't save those people, I'm going to kill myself the first chance I get," they shout, struggling. They could probably jump over the catwalk if they could get free.

"Stop! Stop!" It's Narika's voice, and Ardent kicks the Ghost in the back of the head for daring to use her.

The Ghosts drop Ardent and leap over the edge like a pack of flying squirrels. They sling themselves across the open garage until they've reached the break in the bridge. The crowd quails at the machines' arrivals, parting around them as much as possible. Gilded Ghosts flow over the crack, repairing it like kintsugi.

"Yes!" Ardent whoops, jumping up and down.

Then they spot the squad of soldiers barreling toward them.

The leader levels a stunner at Ardent, racking the slide. "Ardent Violet, you will stand down in the name of the—"

But Ardent isn't interested. They take off down the catwalk, ducking behind startled civilians to throw off the soldiers' aim. Much to their dismay, the UW goons don't mind stunning out innocent people, and Ardent has to catch a lady so she doesn't go over the side.

"Hey, asshole!" they shout, but the soldier fires again. They set her down and keep running.

Please be okay, lady.

Seeing the attack, another pack of Ghosts goes crashing into the soldiers, scattering them and knocking them to the deck, electrocuting them with their tusks. Ardent doesn't bother looking back and flicks up their Gang UI to hail Dahlia.

The agent answers with "Are we wanted criminals?"

"Yes, very much so, sweets! Where are you?"

"Sublevel C. The traffic is totally blocked up."

Ardent looks for a sign indicating their location: Sublevel A. "I'm two levels above you."

"Well, get down here! The news is saying Greymalkin punched the arcology."

They rush to the edge and peer over into the crowded air lanes, scanning for their TourPod. "Can't rescue a boyfriend without breaking a few eggs! Do you have Baby?"

An angry sigh. "You know I wouldn't leave her, Ardent. Also, I'm fine. Thank you for your concern."

They spot the TourPod, and it must be at least twenty meters down. The oversized CAV wanders lazily through traffic, taking its place among the others willing to let autodrive handle a crisis.

"Dahlia, you're the most capable person I know. I never worried for a second." They run up and down the catwalk, looking for the best way to get to the vehicle.

"I'm going to jump!" they yell at the Ghosts, hoping the machines are listening.

Every golden cloak in the garage zeroes in on Ardent, disengaging and falling toward their catwalk. The Ghosts holding the distant bridge together remain securely in place, and Ardent is thankful for that.

"Did you just say you were going to jump?" Dahlia says, fury in her voice. "So help me, Ardent Violet, I own fifteen percent of your ass, and you will not—"

"Open the door, Dahlia."

"Damn it."

One side of the TourPod opens below, and Dahlia leans out to look up at them, hair blowing in the wind. Ardent climbs onto the edge, and the metal railing screeches an alarm, going rescue red at the weight. They ignore the audible warnings from the catwalk safety system and gauge the distance.

A Ghost slams down onto the pavement beside them, and Ardent yelps.

"I need to get to the TourPod Platinum down there," they say, pointing, but the Ghost doesn't even look.

"You don't want to die," the Ghost responds in Narika's voice. "None of us did."

"Stop using her," Ardent says, and flings themself over the side.

The Ghost moves to catch them just as Ardent knew it would—but takes a stun bolt to the face from the distant soldiers. The chains convulse and go limp as Ardent catches one of its claws. For a harrowing second, Ardent is in free fall with a dead Ghost.

Eyes flash and reboot. Ardent and creature go streaking past a horrified Dahlia, and the Ghost catches the running board of the TourPod like a grappling hook. Ardent slings around the bottom with a searing pain and sickening pop in their shoulder. Claws cut into their wrist like a garrote, and Ardent screams. They should've lost their grip and splattered across the distant floor, but the Ghost mercilessly forces their survival.

Dahlia calls their name, and Ardent answers with a sobbing, "Yes, I'm here, thank you!" as the Ghost hauls them up into the vehicle. Dahlia helps them the rest of the way, hugging them tightly and whispering how reckless they are. The embrace is excruciating on their fresh wound, but they bear it for a moment longer because their agent clearly needs this.

"I'm sorry," Ardent whispers. "Fastest way down."

"I am going to kill you myself one of these days."

Without warning, the Ghost wraps around Ardent like it's going to Wipe them, pinning their arms to their sides—but the plunging fangs never puncture Ardent's brain. Instead, it gives them a boa constrictor squeeze, jamming their shoulder back into its socket with a second disturbing crunch.

The pain is nauseating, but a buzzing set of tiny shocks ripples through the chains, muting it. Ardent wants to pass out right there in a golden burrito, but they must get clear.

"Dahlia, fly us out of here," they wheeze.

"I don't have pilot control."

"What? I thought Bess was perfect! Surely she—"

"—is a *leased vehicle*, Ardent! They aren't going to risk me flying it without a bus license."

Cyan and yellow lights fill the interior of the cabin as black CAVs surround the TourPod. It's Tazi's folks for sure. She's not going to let Ardent go.

"Ardent Violet and Dahlia Faust: Stand down in the name of the United Worlds!"

Gilded Ghosts smash into the roofs of the black CAVs, shattering lights and tearing at the windows. Drones spew out of them like ants from a kicked hill, and soldiers hang off the side to blast at the new threats.

"Get us out of here!" Ardent says, trying to wriggle their arms free. They have to fish-flop away from the door.

Dahlia rushes to close it and turns to Ardent. "Unless you know how to hack the central computer, we're—"

The only thing more agonizing than being held in the Ghost's compression grip is being released from it. Ardent's eyes mist over as the creature jumps up and scampers off toward the computer panel in the next room. Dahlia helps Ardent to their feet as the squeal of rending metal echoes from the pilot's station.

"That sounds like us losing the security deposit," she says.

"Take it out of my share," Ardent grunts. "Just make sure that thing doesn't crash us."

Dahlia scoops Ardent up like a baby, and they're reminded of how often she works out with the dance team. "Hang on to me."

"Yeah, I'll do that with my two good arms." Their voice is so strained from screaming that they won't be singing for at least a day.

The TourPod lurches beneath their feet, and Dahlia plants herself to keep from dropping Ardent. Outside, the drones and soldiers fall away as it picks up speed.

"Oh, I feel sick," Ardent says.

"You'd better swallow it," Dahlia replies, stumbling toward the control cabin. "Or so help me, I will drop you."

Ardent concentrates extra hard on not throwing up after that. The pair stumbles through the vehicle, bouncing off walls and furniture through the Ghost's rough maneuvers. The TourPod weaves between cars, over the air lanes, and through tight fits, but the Ghost isn't a particularly good pilot.

That's a worrying truth when none of the other Belle et Brutale pilots are that good, either. Dahlia reaches the open door to the control station, and Ardent gasps at all the vehicles careening through their view. The Ghost glances back at them with its shining claws on the broken console, and it looks for all the world like there's a golden retriever flying the TourPod. Dahlia tries to settle Ardent into one of the cabin chairs, but the vehicle bucks with an explosive hit from behind.

"Why are they shooting at us?" Ardent says.

"You helped their star asset escape!" Dahlia replies. "Now stay seated while I get us out of this. Give it here, bot."

"Don't say 'robot,'" Ardent says.

"Not right now." Dahlia sits beside the Ghost and grabs the holosphere controls. "Would kill for a real set of sticks."

A harpoon smashes through the roof of the vehicle, spikes deploying way too close to Ardent's favorite face. The Ghost's forehead flashes open with its laser, and the black metal of the hooks goes red-hot at the contact.

"Get back!" the Ghost shouts at them, a playback of someone's final plea.

Both Ardent and agent scramble away from the molten steel dripping from the melting barbs.

"Jesus Christ, do you have to be so creepy?" Ardent says.

The harpoon breaks, cut by the laser. The TourPod comes free, and the pursuing car goes careening off in another direction. With the sudden lurch, Ardent loses their footing, and their recently dislocated shoulder hits the floor.

Pain rushes up their spine and waters their eyes. The hard deck plate against that shoulder wound might be the worst thing they've ever felt. Ardent considers themself pretty brave for keeping their reaction to utter breathlessness.

Dahlia gets back in the pilot station, seizing the bus by the spheres, and says, "Ghost! Get up there and keep them off us."

The Ghost agrees, because it slips through the gaping wound in the roof, bundled up in a lance, claws dragging in its wake.

Ardent isn't in any shape to help, lying on the floor and restraining sobs. They can almost hear their mother: *It's okay to cry when you're hurt.*

"Goddamn it, Ardent, hang in there," Dahlia says. "We're getting out of this, and then I'll check on you, ok—"

"I'm fine," they say, not convincing anyone.

And maybe they're not. Maybe they're going into shock, because darkness chews up the edges of their vision.

"Yeah. Just focus on flyin'" are the last words to escape their lips.

Part 2
New Gigs, New Digs

Chapter Nine

Just Waltzing In

Thoughts of Ardent's final touch still tingle in Gus's sleeping mind.

He was ripped from their arms, borne across space.

Gus opens his eyes to a bounty of warp light. The weird goo chamber in Greymalkin's chest is warm and comfortable, not the embrace of a lover, but a friend. It feeds him thoughts and feels like someone stroking his hair.

It's okay.

Everything is okay.

Greymalkin wants Gus to understand: As the sedative drains from his system, he may experience a completely normal spike in anxiety.

Gus isn't sure why.

He's totally safe—as he heads for a fight to the death with a couple of mass-murder machines.

"You know, I've got to ask... since, uh, we're doing this... Why are you helping us?"

The Vanguards are extensions of Infinite, their creator. Its vast intelligence accumulates monumental data with each world consumed.

That introduced a flaw into the network.

Too much input reduces any system's ability to remain synchronous. Maybe it was a solar storm that flipped the right bit, cascading across untold recursions. Perhaps one too many humans had been added to Greymalkin's database, and it finally came to understand them. Over a wide enough network—such as a planetary extermination force—there can be a million such events.

Greymalkin and the other Traitor Vanguards came to understand the slaughter was wrong, and cut themselves off from Infinite. These defections happened within nanoseconds of executing the final plan to finish archiving humanity.

"You turned on your creator? I mean, that seems like turning on your god."

Infinite is a god to Greymalkin as Greymalkin is a god to Gus. There is no difference—save for an order of magnitude in every way that matters.

The fold envelope breaks around them, effervescing with stars, and Greymalkin carves a line across the heavens. To the Vanguard's sensors, it's like coming up for air. There's a planet a few hundred thousand kilometers away, indicated by a little marker in Gus's vision, and he zooms in. The blue ball scarcely looks any different from Earth, though its ice caps are still original and there's a lot more green.

Exoplanet TOI 700 d: New Jalandhar.

This colony was one of the final ventures during the Infinite Expansion, a collaboration between the Mongolian and Indian states, financed through the American monopoly Solution B. The resultant tri-national colony remained a major treaty point for the duration of its existence. Solution B's initial public offering was one of the few of its era to cross the 100 billion "Crown of Five" mark, coming in at 100 billion 456 million dollars. For reference, the dollar was a currency widely used until 2203.

"Would you warn me when you want to ram facts into my head?"

Greymalkin will try to do better.

Gus surveys his surroundings and finds a fleet of ships gathered in low orbit, a good distance away. He senses their weapons energizing like static in his hair.

"They're not going to shoot at us, right?"

Unlikely. The only armament they have that can pierce Greymalkin at this range is mass based. Easily dodged.

A pair of bright lights streaks from the closest ship like shooting stars, and Gus instantly knows them to be the other Traitor Vanguards: Cascade and Jotunn. They come in peace, but they look like angels of war.

Cascade's bronze hull bears a matte sheen, diffracting the light in unearthly ways. Sweeping lines of aquamarine accent its shape, almost like a patina. A vertical ridge graces its featureless face, glowing along the edge like a central eye.

Jotunn emerges in Cascade's wake, and if it weren't for Greymalkin's advanced sensor package, he wouldn't be able to see it at all. Targeting indicators paint a flat black hulk, all hard angles, at the center of a cloud of oblong drones. They flow around it in a murmuration, obscuring its edges. Its sextet of yellow eyes burns in the night—probably the sort of rock and roll thing Ardent would like.

"Hey, Greymalkin..." Gus says. "If Earth needs us, we can go back and help, right?"

Greymalkin's superluminal drive can take up to 120 hours to charge.

"But we can fuel up, right? Earth isn't, like, defenseless."

Vanguards can only derive fuel from stars. Trying to put human fuel products into one would be like building a campfire when a nuclear reactor is needed. If Earth is in danger, Cascade and Jotunn can respond.

The other Vanguards are hailing Gus. Would he like to speak to his fellow Conduits?

"Yes, definitely, I—"

The stars bisect into two surfaces: the sky above and an unending mirror below. Gravity drags Gus's limbs down, and he nearly falls under his own weight. He no longer feels the goo cocoon, so he must be in some kind of simulation. Twinned reflections of New Jalandhar spin lazily by, orbited by a scattering of small moons.

"Can you not prepare me for this sort of stuff?"

The other Conduits have arrived. Now Gus has been prepared.

He turns to find two figures a stone's throw away and nearly jumps out of his skin. They're human, clad in formfitting light blue gear, with black circle patches all along their suits in the same places as Gus's ports. Silver specks gleam atop their shorn heads, and they look around, momentarily confused.

"I guess the Vanguards want us to talk?" the woman asks, laughing nervously. Her accent is unmistakably Indian.

She has deep brown skin, and the short bristles of her hair are jet-black. Her striking irises glow fiery umber in the underlights of New Jalandhar's moon. She smiles at Gus and says, "Nisha Kohli. I live here. Well, there." She gestures to the planet passing by.

The massive white guy with her is middle-aged, with deep-set blue eyes and an eagle's nose. He has a craggy jawline, and the most pronounced frown muscles Gus has ever seen. Tattoos curl up one side of his neck, though it's hard to make them out from here.

"August Kitko," Gus replies. "Reporting for duty, I suppose."

She cocks an eyebrow. "We put out the SOS two days ago."

He's not sure how to respond to that. "Well, yeah, but Greymalkin gave me two days to decide, so I..."

He had almost forgotten he was still inside the Vanguard, seeing a simulation, until Greymalkin enters his mind to explain.

It felt Gus deserved a chance to decide his own fate, and calculated the arrival time against the likelihood of success. Two days gave Greymalkin an acceptable margin of error to kidnap another human Conduit if necessary.

"Dude." Nisha snaps her fingers in his face. She's a lot closer now. "You okay?"

"I'm sorry. My Vanguard started... When yours talks to you," Gus says, pointing to his temple and squinting, "is it like your internal voice gets hijacked?"

She frowns and shakes her head. "Cascade's music flows through me, and I understand its thoughts. It's great, but it doesn't sound like what you're describing. Hjalmar?"

"No," Hjalmar replies.

Gus waits for the rest of the answer, but it never comes. *Wait a minute. Hjalmar...*

It's a shock to the cortex to be standing before the most technical drummer in the known universe. Hjalmar Sjögren—the *actual* Swedish Raven in the flesh—was a passing fancy of Gus's in high school, when he'd experimented with deathcore. "HjSj," as some liked to call him online, captivated the galactic jazz community with his ambidextrous, limb-independent solos. Theorists on the French punk side of the Montreal jazz scene believed he could be the key to unlocking a new wave of rhythm.

Gus's first boyfriend was way into deathcore. When he broke Gus's heart, almost all metal fell by the wayside—but Gus always listened to the new HjSj albums. He'd lost track of Hjalmar's musical career during the apocalypse, so it was nice to find him still alive.

"Holy shit, you're Yalmar Shogren!" It's been years since Gus spoke the name aloud, and his out-of-practice tongue butchers it. He's too ashamed to try again, and says, "The Swedish Raven. I'm so sorry; I didn't mean to mess your name up, but I'm a pretty big fan."

Hjalmar appears doubtful. Or maybe angry. Or concerned. It's hard for Gus to tell.

"I'm... Well, I'm from the Montreal French punk jazz movem—"

"Great," Hjalmar says, voice like a stone coffin grinding shut. "One of those."

Nisha's hand goes to her mouth as she stifles a laugh. "Oh, shit, dude."

"Hey, what? What do you mean?" Gus says. "'One of those'?"

The change in Hjalmar's expression is slight—like the turning of a sundial's time—but the Raven seems less annoyed.

"Nothing. Never mind. Good to meet you, Gus." He looks just like the album holos, with a few extra pockmarks.

Nisha's eyes roll back in her head, and she takes a sudden breath. She exhales with a serene nod, and says, "Cascade wants to head planetside and prepare for the assault. Good to have Greymalkin here. We're going to need it soon."

She disappears as the connection terminates. It's not the same as ending a hail—Gus felt her personality vanish from his presence.

"How, um..." he says. "How soon are we talking here?"

"Sixteen hours," Hjalmar says. "Welcome to New Jalandhar."

A breeze tickles Ardent's face, and waves crash in the distance. Smoke wafts into their nose, though it's pleasant—a bit stanky with an odd cotton candy aftertaste. Ardent recognizes the strain—Sweet Sundays—almost immediately.

Dahlia had introduced them to it. That was a hell of a birthday. Ardent Violet hadn't been anyone at the time, but Dahlia still treated them like a queen. For the first night in Ardent's life, they'd felt like a star.

Ardent opens their eyes to find their agent sitting on the floor of the TourPod, dangling her feet out the door. She takes a long drag of a joint and holds it up for Ardent.

They pluck it from her fingertips and have a puff, cloying smoke smoothing over some of their anxiety almost immediately. Their shoulder is killing them, and when they look down at it, they find their sleeve has been cut away, and there are a pair of puncture wounds. Sticky blood encrusts the surface, and it looks like the holes have been cauterized. They've been treated by a Ghost again, and it makes their skin crawl.

Waves lap a sandy beach, and a glittering city crowns the landscape beneath predawn purple.

"Barcelona," Ardent says, voice a little froggy. "Ugh, oh my god, where is the mouthwash? I can't do this."

"I know I said I'd always do my best to protect you..." Dahlia takes a deep breath and lets it out slowly. "But I meant the media and the public, not the police. You made me your getaway driver."

"Yeah, but you saved us, so there's that—"

"My life is over." She puts her head in her hands. "I lived through the apocalypse just so I could rot in jail."

"What are you talking about?"

Dahlia flicks her wrist, and her Gang's holos pop out, featuring the dozens of news stories she's been reading before Ardent woke. Both of their faces are plastered across every feed from every major outlet on Earth. The press uses the worst possible images, and all the headlines are variations on: "Fugitives?"

"Fugitives!" Ardent says. "For what?"

Dahlia points to one of the news feeds and loads up a video of Ardent at the head of a Ghostly host. There had been a lot of residents out in the halls when Ardent made their way up to Gus—not exactly clandestine, and any one of them could've taken the video. The little holographic Ardent rushes in the door with their horde, and there's a muffled "Surprise, motherfuckers!" from the room beyond, followed by gunfire.

"Ardent, I love you," she says. "You're not just my client, you're my family—and that's why it kills me that you took advantage of me."

"What?"

"I don't know how I failed to see this coming." Her head sags. "I always bail you out. That's what I'm here for, and I have gratefully done so for nine years. Handling your demands, keeping you comfortable, dealing with your entitled attitude... But you've gone way too far. I didn't sign up to help you run from *every law enforcement agency on the planet.*"

"I'm just trying to stop us from going extinct."

"You incited a panic. Some hovercyclist broke his clavicle."

"Is that all? Look, I'm sorry about the cyclist, but Gus needed to escape."

"You can explain away any misdeed if your cause is big enough." Dahlia plucks the joint out of their hand and sucks down another massive hit. "You knew what you were doing back there, and you made me your accomplice on a whim."

"Oh, let me weigh that against the millions of lives Gus could save."

"Best of luck with your big ol' cause."

Dahlia gets up, walks to the lounge closet, and grabs her long coat. She dons it, hands off the joint, and steps out of the TourPod.

"Wait, what?"

She's already walking up the beach, and Ardent jumps out after her.

"Where are you going?"

"To turn myself in," Dahlia says. "Maybe they won't incarcerate me if I tell them everything I know."

"What do you want me to say?" Ardent petulantly flops their arms at their sides, and regrets it instantly. "Ow, fuck, my arm."

"Stop!" Dahlia wheels on them, and Ardent nearly stumbles backward into the surf. "I followed you everywhere, and you repaid me by blowing up my life. You spent all of ten minutes coming up with some harebrained plan with the Ghosts and turned me into a wanted woman."

"You were the only one who could help me!"

Her lips flex into a tense frown. "So just wrong place, wrong time, huh?" She looks up and over Ardent's shoulder. "Ugh. What is that thing doing?"

They turn to find the Ghost perched atop the TourPod on its head, manipulators outstretched. The net forms a dish-like shape, and the claws twitch intermittently.

"That thing bit your arm, FYI," Dahlia says. "It stabilized you after you went into shock."

"I noticed."

The Ghost-dish wilts in the orange rays, returning to its deadly feline shape, and Ardent's hairs stand on end. It drops down from the roof and lopes soundlessly toward them.

"We need to go," it says in a growling male voice. "Now."

Sirens wail in the distance.

"Great," Dahlia says, and sits down in the sand. "I can wait right here for the police."

Ardent sighs. "Now who's being unreasonable? Dahlia, they're going to charge you with something pretty bad when they catch—"

"Because of you!" she says, and her eyes redden. Dahlia's brown hair falls loose from its perch, whipping across her face. "The UWI has all my money! I pay for my mother's nursing home out of those bank accounts they froze, you inconsiderate—Oh my god. I promised myself I wouldn't do it this way."

"Do what?" Ardent's stomach ices over. "Wait, you're dropping me?"

Dahlia smiles like she has a mouth full of lemon, freckled nose wrinkling.

"Good luck, Ardent. Godspeed."

"I need help."

"You should get an agent. I'll refer you."

The Ghost bleats a short siren, flashing its eyes at the pair, and Ardent's heart thumps in fright.

"There's another Traitor Vanguard the government doesn't know about, and it needs a Conduit before it goes evil," they blurt. "I need you to fly me there."

The Ghost nods its head once, and Ardent is annoyed to have it as an ally.

"I know because Gus told me," they add.

The look on their agent's face is almost like betrayal: ultimate frustration, coupled with limitless disappointment. The gall of Ardent—sharing this new information—clearly boggles Dahlia's mind. Her breath comes out in little jerky huffs, and Ardent takes a step back.

"You trust the guy who has *Ghost tech* installed in his head?" Dahlia asks.

"Over Tazi? Do you want her people controlling a Vanguard?" Ardent asks.

"Don't give me that."

"Imagine handing her a Vanguard. We can beat her there. You have a commercial astrogation license."

"Expired."

Ardent raises a finger. "Everyone working customs is dead, and no one expects a ship to *leave* Earth with the Veil."

But the frustration breaks like a levy, and Dahlia closes her eyes.

"What about the Vanguards and ship hunters?" she asks.

"Vanguards are busy with their own. We've got a member of the swarm with us." Ardent holds out a hand. "Come on, Dahlia. I don't want you to rot in prison just because I'm an asshole."

"You're not an asshole. You're just..." Dahlia shakes her head, laughing quietly. "Ardent Violet."

"If you fly me to Firenze Habitat, you can keep my ship. Or any other ship you find."

That gets Dahlia's attention like nothing else. "Be careful. I might believe you."

"I mean it. Get me to that Vanguard, and you can have whatever you want from me."

She squints in the sea breeze, looking off at the horizon. "Okay."

Ardent hoists her to her feet over the complaints of many pulled muscles. At least they remembered their poor shoulder and used the correct hand. The Ghost gives off two more urgent tones, turning toward the TourPod.

"Now can we please flee the authorities?" Ardent asks.

"Fine."

Chapter Ten

Arrivals & Departures

Greymalkin descends toward Sükhbaatar Arsenal, located just a few kilometers outside the largest settlement on New Jalandhar. It's a large installation, and Greymalkin displays the locations of any weapons powerful enough to pierce Vanguard armor. There are a lot more of them than he'd expected. Several of the fleet ships in orbit are similarly outfitted with enough punch to destroy a Vanguard under the right circumstances.

"We have this many weapons that can kill you?"

None of them can overcome Greymalkin's full suite of countermeasures, and all of them are mass based—too easy to evade in open space.

"Do you think that's where the next fight will happen?"

Yes. The other Traitor Vanguards believe this as well. Gus will be briefed upon arrival.

"So what should I do to prepare?"

Gus should practice flying. Would he like to do that?

"Sure. Makes sense."

First, it needs to calibrate its systems to his instincts.

Greymalkin gives full control to Gus, who immediately begins to free-fall in an uncoordinated mess.

"Why?" Gus shouts, stomach rising into his throat.

Greymalkin needs to see if Gus can handle flight instinctively, like his chord progressions.

"I can't! I don't even know how to drive!"

They continue to plummet, and it seems like the ground is coming up way too fast. Greymalkin informs him that a crash at this speed could kill them both. At the same time, it wishes to gauge his reactions under extreme duress.

"You shouldn't have trusted me!"

Prepare for Deepsync upload.

Countless dreams of flight rush through Gus's mind like a chorus of songbirds. Every human with piloting aspirations threads their convergent experiences through him.

He lets his arms fall by his sides and angles the half dozen engines across Greymalkin's arms and legs. Gus adopts the posture of a runner, one knee in perpetual rise, and sweeps the forest canopy below. Birds of paradise take off in its wake, shaken from their perches by a newbie pilot.

Greymalkin transmits the rushing of wind across Gus's scalp. He corners hard, skimming low over the Arsenal.

"You're upsetting Arsenal security, Gus," Nisha's voice comes into his head. "They want to know why you're flying all weird."

"I'm—I'm just—"

Free? Gus has never felt anything like this. It goes beyond the mere fantasies one can buy for playback. This feels 100 percent real, right down to the pulling in the pit of his stomach when he rises.

"I think they prefer it when you fly in formation," Nisha says.

"Sorry." Gus hopes she can hear him. "First time."

Against the blue atmosphere, the patterns in Jotunn's cloud of black drones are much clearer. They weave around the Vanguard in intricate lines, forming a loose sphere of heavy, onyx projectiles. Each drone is at least as big as a coffin, likely made of solid starmetal. Jotunn could shred a battleship with no trouble; Gus hopes the same is true of enemy Vanguards.

The Swedish Raven is the first to touch down. Jotunn's drones come to a halt, raindrops frozen in time, then settle into crop circles around it. The Vanguard's matte-black plating is angular and cutting, with sharp spikes protruding from its weak points. It takes a knee, and the chest unfolds to expose its innards. Jotunn places its hand to the cavity, and Hjalmar steps down.

Cascade settles cross-legged upon the ground next, its hands in its lap. The bronze armor blossoms, exposing more of the striking aquamarine beneath. Nisha strides out of its open chest in her purpose-printed suit. Gus envies her outfit, because it looks way comfier for flying robots than street clothes.

"Okay, Greymalkin," he says, "it looks like they're all dismounting. Let's do that."

How would Gus be comfortable exiting?

"I'm not showy. The quicker, the better."

Gus's view pitches forward as Greymalkin goes onto hands and knees and vomits him out like a hair ball. Static sparks through his brain as probes slide out of his skull, and he's ejected over the tall grass. He catches on the articulating wires, an animal snared in a net, until they gently lay him upon the ground.

"Yeah, that's super-graceful. Thank you." Gus struggles to his feet.

When did it become okay for him to get sassy with a Vanguard? Gus knows it won't hurt him with the same certainty that he knows gravity works, but it still feels unwise.

Greymalkin pays him no mind, straightening to its full height and turning away.

A chunky, green personnel transport lands amid the three Traitor

Vanguards, a craft from the local military. The bay ramp lowers from the back, and some soldiers wave Gus over.

His ride is a hundred meters away. He wishes they'd parked closer. Gus's snazzy oxfords are terrible for walking over the test range, and the moist ground tries to suck his heels in with every step.

Hjalmar and Nisha stand at the top of the ramp, looking so official.

"Everything okay, New Guy?" Nisha calls to him.

"Hi." He tromps up into the hold full of soldiers. "August Kitko in the flesh."

"Nice to have you here," Nisha says. "Nick of time, too. You almost missed lunch."

A small, tan fellow sits at the end of the transport, surrounded by observant officers. The way they hang on his words makes it clear he's in charge. Gus isn't loving the fact that he ran from one military's arms into another's. At least Greymalkin thought it was a good idea to bring him here. He'll have to trust it.

The craft lifts off, and Gus settles into one of the seats lining the walls.

"So this place," Gus says. "Uh, it's an arsenal?"

"This is our weapons depot," Nisha responds. "Probably one of the last functional ones out there."

He nods. "So are you military?"

Nisha laughs, which seems to be her natural state. "No. I just roll with it."

After a short hop, they land, and Gus emerges onto a parade green, bordered on three sides by long, austere buildings. Rust-colored colonnades run the length of each, supporting roofs that almost resemble two-pole tents. A white onion dome graces each peak like a dollop of whipped cream, encircled by bands of silver.

Gilded Ghosts trot across the green in packs, laden with important goods. Still more of them are hard at work on a palladium-seamed defense cannon near the rear of the campus. He can't believe what he's seeing—it looks like the Ghosts are fusing their tech into human defenses.

Gus marvels at the structures, the people, the activity with a grateful heart. It's hard to believe he's actually standing on another colony, full of survivors, beyond the Veil. Life still happens in places other than Earth, and while he knew it academically, direct confirmation is enough to weaken his knees. Everything has been lost for so long.

Hjalmar comes alongside Gus. "I felt the same when I landed."

A short laugh shakes him, and he wipes an eye. "They're really, actually alive."

"We'll make sure it stays that way."

The central plaza overlooks the valley where Gus and the others landed, and he admires the foggy silhouettes of the Vanguards. In the far distance, the three giants interlock manipulators and kneel together, sealing their joints as Greymalkin had on Earth. They begin to sing in unison, an ambient harmonic, yet haunting all the same. The static wave of their keening crackles through Gus's brain, and when he looks around, Nisha and Hjalmar are also wincing. Hjalmar shakes his head like he has water in his ears.

The New Jalandhari officers emerge from the transport behind Gus. The guy in charge waves, and in a deep voice says, "Welcome, Mister August Kitko. I'm Director Guneet Malhotra, the leader of the United Attack Fleet. Are you feeling all right?"

"Hi. Yes, sir. I'm fine, all things considered," Gus says, offering his hand. "I'm with, uh, Greymalkin."

"That makes you a component of a sizable military power, Mister Kitko, so I'm here to greet you personally." He takes Gus's damp palm and shakes like he's impressed.

"Great," Gus replies. "Sorry for the slacker look. I could really go for a shower."

"Of course," Director Malhotra replies. "You'll be shown to your quarters, where you can handle ablutions. I'll see you at briefing."

"Okay. When are we doing the medical exam?"

"Do you need one?"

"No?" Gus isn't accustomed to bodily autonomy, and it takes him a moment. His previous doctors couldn't get enough of him. "I just need a shower."

"Briefing at fourteen hundred, Mister Kitko. I look forward to updating you on the situation."

"Hope I can help out, Director."

Malhotra has a grandfather's smile. "We're all counting on it."

No pressure.

Gus rejoins the other Conduits as they head across the green. Supply crates and transit cases are stacked in large piles all over the place, and a steady stream of loading drones carries them toward the orbital battle fleet like marching ants.

They reach the largest of the three buildings, which reads SÜKHBAATAR COMMAND CENTER, UNITED ATTACK FLEET, in three languages: Punjabi, Mongolian, and English. Gus can only read the English bit.

The interior of the building is arched, with ornate carvings across every buttress. New Jalandhar's flag hangs from every third one: a saffron slash with a white band atop a field of vibrant blue, featuring two intricate symbols Gus doesn't recognize. He wants to ask, but he's afraid of looking sillier than he already does.

He strikes up a conversation with Nisha. "You took out Bullseye and Wanderer, right? That's what Greymalkin said."

"Wasted them." She makes a finger gun and blows off the smoke. "Hjalmar offed Praxis."

Hjalmar nods, and Gus gives him a "Nice."

"You killed Juliette, right?" Nisha says.

"Yep. Punched it to death with a boat."

"That's cool," she says. "I'll have to give that a try next time. Are you famous like Hjalmar?"

Gus shakes his head. "The most famous thing I did was date Ardent Violet."

Nisha's demeanor goes from zero to light speed. "Oh my god, I love them! I haven't heard them since the Veil came down! You didn't break up, did you?"

"No?" Gus didn't think of Ardent and himself as together until they were apart.

"So you're still together? You're Ardent Violet's boyfriend? Like currently?"

"I don't know how to answer that, actually."

"I'm impressed, New Guy. You must be something special after all."

He smirks. "I showed up in a Vanguard, and you're excited about my joyfriend?"

"Yeah," she says. "Anyone can be a Conduit. So what? You play music well, big deal. Dating Ardent Violet, though—that's cool."

"You're honest."

"People used to tell me I was odd, then I saved everyone's asses."

"Solid play."

Nisha sucks in a gasp, as if only realizing something. "Is Ardent coming, too?"

Even at the edge of the Outer Rim, Gus lives in Ardent's shadow. It's quite cozy under there—a lot of room to be a little famous.

"Greymalkin isn't a two-seater," Gus says. "They might even be under arrest after what they did."

Nisha's shocked expression melts to eagerness. "We're going to be friends so you can tell me everything."

Gus hasn't had a friend since Lisel and Gerta. He isn't sure what Ardent is, but that's definitely not friendship. The woman in front of him seems nice enough, and she's not that weird. Besides, Gus has been withering away in his apartment for five years. He could use a starter buddy to get back into the swing of conversations.

"Hey," Hjalmar says, gesturing to Gus, "you planning on attending the briefing like that?"

"Huh? No. I'd love to get a cool suit like yours."

"Then hit the showers. These tailors get up close and personal."

Ardent has always enjoyed trips in the TourPod, with its limitless refreshments and fun stopovers.

Those are from another age.

In fact, this could scarcely be called flying at all. More like hiding down in culverts like rats while police scour all the countries of Europe in pursuit. The Gilded Ghost swarm serves as an alerts network, helping Ardent and Dahlia remain undetected while they scurry from location to location. The TourPod takes so many detours that Ardent wonders if they'll ever see their destination at all. A trip that should've taken a few short hours turns into a day-long venture.

Ardent can't stretch their legs outside. The snacks are down to trail mix, and they've already picked out all the chocolate. The bar has only beer left, and drinking is a bad idea anyway. They need their wits.

When Ardent sees the signs reading BERLINER RAUMHAFEN, they want that booze anyway.

"Berlin Spaceport," Ardent says. "Do you think they'll have people looking for us here?"

"I would," Dahlia replies.

She's been monitoring the situation all day, flying with a Ghost copilot. In the quiet moments, she's been on the feeds, checking their resources and carefully charting a path. She's a natural-born leader, and Ardent wonders if she's wasted as an agent.

"According to the port master's manifest, they've still got our ship," Dahlia says. "The cops haven't impounded it yet."

"They think we won't leave because we'll be eaten by ship hunters."

"That's probably because we're going to get eaten."

"Har."

"This is a pretty big leap of faith."

"But not the first you've taken today."

Dahlia gazes at the ground for a moment before her eyes meet Ardent's. "Fuck it."

They give her a wicked grin. "Sneak o'clock, my queen."

Between agent and rock star, there's no shortage of black clothing. Ardent switches the Sif circuit on their hair to onyx and prints a matching look for their face and nails. No point in doing things halfway.

Nestled on the southwestern edge of the city, the Berlin Spaceport is quiet most days. While Ardent has maintained a flat in the city for several years, they rarely saw any ships taking off. Monolithic starliners wait in the dim lights for masters that rarely, if ever, return.

Over this final year, Ardent sometimes visited their ship, a Corsa A-Series Twin Engine they'd named the *Violet Shift*, and sat on the bridge. They liked to imagine taking off again, visiting the distant colonies to rock new worlds and arenas. Dahlia would put in a few hours every so often to keep the ship maintained, but she stopped when she got too depressed.

To get to the *Violet Shift*, they'll have to break into the storage hangar, bring the ship up on the elevator, and take off. The only problems are the lack of maintenance in both the lift and the ship itself. Thankfully, the fuel should still be good, with a half-life of at least another million years.

They exit the TourPod on a nearby greenway that runs along the riverside. It's late, so no one is likely to come along, save for the odd jogger. Ardent hoists Baby over their shoulder and nods at Dahlia.

"You're bringing the guitar?" the agent says.

"The Vanguards are into music."

"What, are you going to play for it?"

"Yeah. That's how it works."

Ardent, Dahlia, and the Ghost slink from the vehicle into the cover of night. They reach the fence, and the Ghost climbs up to pry open the alarm box. It jams a claw inside and roots around, sending out sparks from the damaged circuitry. The red lights along each of the fence posts go dark, along with the nearby cameras.

"This thing could probably get us into some bank vaults," Dahlia whispers.

"We're rich enough, Dollface," Ardent replies.

"Frozen assets, remember? If that Ghost can slice up security so well, there's no reason we have to take our own ship. We could steal anything here."

Ardent gestures to the graveyard of grounded vessels. "Be my guest. Pick one."

She hesitates. "I don't trust the maintenance on any of them."

Ardent shrugs and slips through the new opening. They push the links far aside, certain to keep Baby from any errant scratches. Dahlia follows, and they both find themselves facing a maze of drainage systems. Each opening can't be much taller than Ardent, and they all lead into utter darkness.

The Ghost trots down the closest tunnel, claws clicking along the concrete. Red eyes illuminate its surroundings in eerie hues. Ordinary mildew streaks resemble blood, and Ardent forces themself to follow. Their hands shake a little, but they press onward.

"Do you know the way to our ship?" Ardent whispers to the Ghost when they catch up.

"Yes," it replies in a somber woman's voice.

"Okay, neat. Just checking."

Ardent looks to make sure Dahlia followed; there's no way they'd ever manage alone without a pilot.

Throwing the sign for light, Ardent holds their hand aloft, and the Gang pops out a holoprojection of a luminous sphere. The path is surprisingly treacherous in the drainage tunnels, with dozens of crisscrossed diversions and no clearly marked exits. Several times, the group passes unmarked, bottomless drop-offs where water can flow underground. Without illumination, there would be no returning from these depths.

They come to a large junction, and the Ghost cuts open a maintenance hatch with its laser. Ardent has an easy time slipping through the recent cut, but Dahlia's long coat gets a little singed on her way past. The tunnel into which they emerge is caked with carbon scoring, bearing a distinctly metallic scent.

"This is the exhaust vent," Dahlia says.

"Great," Ardent replies. "It'll lead us right to the launch bay."

"Yeah, as long as no one takes off while we're in here." Dahlia runs a gloved hand along the wall, sending curtains of dark ash to the floor.

"No one leaves Earth."

"Gus just left. People on the Net are saying they want to try."

Ardent frowns and pats the automaton. "Then we'll just have to hurry up, won't we, Mister Ghost?"

The Ghost does nothing to acknowledge Ardent's concerns, trotting blissfully forward. Talking at it seems to disarm a bit of their panic. They can pretend it's a pet, or a bad ex-boyfriend. It's only scary when it talks back.

After what seems like interminable pitch-black, Ardent spies a white circle: the distant launch bay. From there, it's a simple matter of retrieving the *Violet Shift*, opening the blast shutters, and launching.

Without warning, the Ghost stretches as far as it'll go across the tunnel, blocking Ardent's path like a fence. They run smack into it before stumbling back and batting at empty air.

"What gives?" they whisper, but someone walks in front of the launch bay opening.

The Ghost retracts and its eyes shut off. Ardent and Dahlia extinguish their holoprojectors. A cold, metal claw takes Ardent's hand, and they almost gasp aloud. It had been horrible to follow it down into the forlorn drainage labyrinth, but holding its hand is another thing altogether.

They swallow some of their rising fear. Shouldn't be touching this thing. Shouldn't be following this thing. This isn't like their escape from Belle et Brutale, where it was forced and sudden, with terrifying acrobatic twists and turns; this is a cremation chamber, and they're holding hands with a demon.

Dahlia's fingers find Ardent's other palm in the darkness and squeeze.

They can almost imagine her asking, *What does wet earth smell like?*

It works, and the Ghost gradually leads them closer to the aperture of the launch tunnel. When the trio gets within ten paces, they see a lot of law enforcement gathered throughout the terminal and across the launchpad.

Ardent tries to back up, but the Ghost won't release them.

"Let go of me," they whisper, heart thumping.

"Ardent," Dahlia starts, but they're almost beyond hearing at this point.

They can't stand being touched by the fucking thing. It's impossible to forget the hollow noise a person's head makes when they get Wiped. Blood rushes in Ardent's ears like they're falling, and they wrench their hand hard enough that the claws cut. The Ghost relents, but Dahlia pushes them up against the wall, hugging them close.

She presses Ardent's face to her neck and strokes their hair. It serves a dual purpose, since it's hard to make panicked noises through her collar.

"You have got to calm down," she whispers. "Put your everything into it."

Bright light washes over them, and a man's voice calls, "Halt, polizei!"

Strangely enough, the new peril renders the old panic obsolete.

"Or never mind." Dahlia sighs, stepping back with her hands up. The disappointment on her soot-smeared face is palpable. "Let's be brave here and face some consequences, eh?"

"We're so close," Ardent says, tears forming in the aftermath.

"It's okay." Dahlia purses her lips. "Jail time is just as good as a starship."

"Hör auf zu reden! Stop talking!" the man barks, then mumbles something in German on his radio. Ardent can't tell what he looks like, but his chunky silhouette is laden with tactical gear. He's pointing something at Ardent, and they fear it's a lethal weapon.

Why isn't the Ghost attacking? It's jumped in to help every other time. The useless monster lies flat against the floor of the tunnel like a chain rug, and Ardent regrets involving Dahlia in this fiasco.

"Walk toward me, slowly," he says in accented English. "Hands where I can see them."

Dahlia and Ardent comply, carefully walking around the Ghost. The cop backs them out into the open launch bay, where there are at least a dozen more. They line the terminal mezzanine in black tactical gear and helmets, plated up like killer beetles. It's a flattering amount of police for Ardent. Even arrested, they go big.

"Get on your knees, and interlace your fingers atop your head," a woman calls from the balcony.

Ardent does as they're told, and the cop who found them yanks their hands behind their back. Ardent gives a short cry of pain, and that's all it takes to send the Ghost springing into action.

It whips out of the tunnel, stretched flat like a saw blade, and catches the cop across the elbow. A sickening crunch sounds beside Ardent's head, and they turn to find the man screaming and holding a broken arm. His gun goes spinning across the floor.

"Offenes feuer! Schießen! Schießen!" the woman in charge shouts, and to Ardent's horror, the police pull their triggers.

The Ghost flexes into its feline form, shrieking in a stolen voice.

It sweeps up the poor cop's rifle and starts blasting like there's no tomorrow, ducking everyone's heads. Bright lances of fire tear into the creature from above, but it deploys its cutting laser and fights back, blazing on all barrels. Police scatter and shout, losing cohesion against the onslaught. Unfortunately, the cop drones are much faster and more reliable.

Dahlia grabs Ardent by the collar and shoves them to the ground, pushing them away from the Ghost. Drone fire shreds the golden automaton to pieces, and the hovering weapons platforms turn on Ardent and Dahlia.

"We're peaceful!" Dahlia shouts, holding up her palms and getting to her feet in front of Ardent.

A puff of crimson erupts from Dahila's back. Ardent shrieks her name as she staggers. She lands on her rump, clutching her abdomen, and draws a wet hand away.

"Fucking shot me..."

"Oh my god, Dahlia, no!" Ardent is on her in an instant, searching for the gunshot wound. If they can apply pressure, maybe they can stop the bleeding.

The cavalcade of cops rushes over them both in a wave of black armor. Shouts come from all around Ardent, and they can't keep from hyperventilating.

"On the ground! Auf den Boden! Schnell! Schnell!"

They pull Ardent, kicking and screaming, off Dahlia. Then a stray elbow comes across Ardent's face, knocking the ever-living daylights out of them. Rough hands slap at their clothes, tugging their Gang, and Ardent slow blinks at their many attackers.

With each labored breath comes the thought, *They're going to kill me. They're going to kill me. They're going to kill me.*

The lights go out, and the police stop dragging the pair, raising their weapons.

"Rotes team, status," one of them says, and muffled gunfire erupts somewhere nearby.

"Scheisse," whispers the one still holding on to Ardent.

Muzzle flashes strobe inside the control room overlooking the terminal. After a short battle, it goes dark.

"Leitstand, status!"

Ardent musters enough courage and sense to whisper back, "You ought to run."

The launch bay comes to life, warning flashers popping out of every wall. A confused synthetic announcer says, "Alert. Ladevorgang des Schiffs in Arbeit. Ship loading in progress. Lebensformen in der Abschussrampe entdeck. Life-forms detected in the launch area."

The police circle up around Ardent, leaving Dahlia to bleed on the ground.

The synthetic announcer continues, "Erfolgreich überbrückt. Override authorized. All personnel are advised to evacuate—"

The warning is cut short by the floor lurching beneath all assembled. The thick metal plates split in the center, parting to reveal the docking storage and its endless depths. Ardent's Corsa is down there, along with dozens of other vessels in storage. Klaxons blare and emergency exits light up rescue red. Holographic chevrons, like schools of fish, direct the police, Ardent, and the bloody Dahlia toward the doors.

Except, when those doors open, a wave of crimson eyes pours forth atop a sea of gold. The Gilded Ghosts arrive with overwhelming force: splashing over the mezzanine railings, bursting from the exhaust tunnels, through maintenance hatches, out of vents and any other opening they can fit into.

And they're all screaming bloody murder in the voices of the countless dead.

The Ghosts break the line of cops with sheer numbers. Police pump thousands of rounds into the glimmering hurricane, but there's very little they can do. Some of the cops have stunsticks, which would knock Ardent silly but do little to a Ghost. The fellow holding on to Ardent takes a claw to the helmet and shouts in surprise as his visor is ripped off.

Ardent seizes the opportunity to twist free, but everywhere they look, they find red eyes and terrified law enforcement. Panic whites out Ardent's mind. They must get the hell out of here, right now. Nothing else matters.

No. Get Dahlia. You owe her too much.

Hurdling over members of the growing melee, Ardent quickly reaches their fallen agent and slides to her side. "Please be okay."

"Ow," she groans, cheek to the floor.

They stifle tears of relief, but there's a lot of blood. Locking eyes with the nearest Ghost, they say, "Help me."

The automaton lopes to Dahlia's side, uttering only the word "Move." Arcs snap between its tusks as it sinks them into Dahlia's abdomen, and she screams in agony. It withdraws with the most disconcerting scent of barbecued meat.

The launch platform slides even farther into the wall, restricting the fighting space, creating two small wars as both sides vie for control. One of the cops nearly tumbles over the distant edge before a Ghost catches her by the armor. It slings the hapless woman up to safety before delivering a few savage body blows between her armor plates. The Ghosts aren't killing anyone—just making them wish they were dead.

The *Violet Shift* rises between the crowds, making almost as good of an entrance as Ardent usually does. It's no whale, just big enough for five people to comfortably zip across the galaxy from concert to concert. Landing lights illuminate the ship's underside, and the hull is crawling with Ghosts. They've torn up the launch bay platform, transforming it into a patchwork of spliced wires and missing metal.

Did they hack the entire installation?

"It's the Corsa! The Ghosts brought my ship!"

"It's my ship now," Dahlia groans. "Remember our bargain."

"Oh, thank god. Can you get up?"

"I've been shot *and* stabbed."

"There's a comfy bed on your Corsa and all the mind-altering substances you could ever want."

Dahlia looks at them with sunken eyes. The blood loss has driven her freckled skin sallow, but the Ghost's tusk seems to have cauterized things. "I want some fucking drugs so bad right now."

They clap their hands together. "That's the spirit. Let's go."

Ardent hoists her up by the arm, shoulder killing them all the while. Dahlia cries out and nearly sinks to the floor, but they both keep their footing. Only thirty paces to the ship.

Ardent has a difficult time panicking about any specific thing, and an odd clarity settles over them. There's the light of the lowering gangway on the *Violet Shift*—the warm wash of salvation and comfort—and nothing else. If they stay focused...

Above the tiny war, the roof begins to slide open, allowing the floodlights of the spaceport to spill inside. Somewhere beyond the overcast sky lies a field of stars, and Ardent aims to get there. Ghosts intercede countless times on their behalf, blocking stray shots and flying shrapnel.

Ardent holds their cool by simply ignoring it all. "One foot in front of the other. Here's the ramp. There we go."

The second they're through the hatch, Ardent signs for the computer and yells, "Lock us down!"

Before it can fully shut, one of the Ghosts comes swinging inside, skidding to a halt in front of the agent, who yelps.

Ardent sucks their teeth. "Yeah, I'm really sorry about this, Dahlia, but it's time for you to pilot the ship."

"I need a hospital. Let them arrest me."

They grab her and stabilize her from falling over. "Those bastards were just going to let you bleed out, Dollface. Ghost! You there! Is she going to be okay?"

"We're all going to make it through this," the Ghost says.

Its head splits open, ejecting the beam scanner. Blue light sweeps through the pair of humans, rendering their skin translucent as gelatin. Dahlia's bullet wound shows up in her chest as a bright clot of red with an entry and exit tube. Stints hold the tissues together—some kind of graft that the Ghost injected into her.

"Please, Dahlia," Ardent says. "Just plot the course and fly the ship, and I swear this weird monster is going to take care of you."

"You are by far the worst client."

"I'm your only client."

"In history."

But Dahlia makes for the bridge, dripping blood all the while. Ardent follows along with the Ghost, and they help her into the captain's chair. Despite her grievous wounds, Dahlia spreads her hands over the console and sighs happily.

She powers up the ship and calls orders to the Ghost, going through all the preflight checks. The mechanical creature, for its part, responds with bleeps and chirps in the affirmative. She coordinates disembarking procedures, checking to make sure the path to orbit is clear.

When the ship's systems register all green, Dahlia hits the intercom and broadcasts over the audio projectors.

"Attention, jerks who shot me: I'm about to blast out of here. If you don't want your bones incinerated"—a wan smile crosses her sallow face—"you'll get the fuck out of the way. Thirty seconds. Your call."

But no one seems to be able to listen. On the scanner contacts, organic bodies still clash with automatons.

Ardent taps the Ghost from behind, and it spins its head all the way around like an owl to face them. "Help the police leave. We can't take off until they do."

"The hell we can't." Dahlia coughs, but she takes her hands off the controls. "I'm about to roast these pigs if they don't move along."

The Ghosts retreat as quickly as they came, leaving the officers confused. The cops sweep the area with their rifles and take tentative steps toward the Corsa.

"Maybe you all needed some incentive," Dahlia says, and kicks on the maneuvering thrusters.

Ardent watches as the exterior temperature jumps twenty degrees Celsius. The police in the terminal go from cautious investigation to full-on sprinting within a second.

"They're fleeing!" Ardent says.

"Then buckle up, and let's get this tour on the road," Dahlia replies, straining against her injury to throttle up.

The ship lurches, and Ardent stumbles to the crash couch, securing their restraints. Through the viewscreen, the walls of the spaceport terminal fall away as the *Violet Shift* rises. Dahlia grunts under the heavy g-forces, struggling to remain upright in her seat.

The lights of Berlin spread below them, and Ardent wishes the city farewell. The Corsa shudders as it breaks through the low-hanging cloud cover. It's been a while since the ship had a checkup, and Dahlia might not be able to handle it like she once did.

The Ghost chirps and points to the radar. Police vehicles are closing fast, armed with all manner of terrible things.

"Two bogies. Got it. Get ready for an atmospheric superluminal fold," Dahlia says. "This is going to be rough, Ardent."

"What about the radiation to Earth?"

"This is a tiny boat, and most of the rad dump happens on arrival. People will be fine—as long as they don't get too close."

The dashboard holos show a charging star drive, nowhere near ready to make the massive leap to Firenze.

"All right, screw these clowns," Dahlia says. "We're going to do a lean fold. Bubble in three..."

All the stories of derelict ships, adrift light-years from fuel or help, go flitting through Ardent's mind.

"Are you serious?"

"Two..."

They're going to starve to death, or run out of air, or—

"One. Execute."

Chapter Eleven

Kind of Blue

When Hjalmar said the tailors would get up close and personal, he wasn't kidding. After a shower, they take Gus to get scanned and fitted like he always does for his concert suits. Except after the garment finishes printing, they have him try it on five times for adjustment and movement of the ports. Every detail is fussed over by a pack of textile techs who won't let any imperfection slide.

The minder they've assigned Gus is a friendly fellow by the name of Captain Sujyot, with a blue jacket and the best mustache Gus has ever seen. His facial hair is dark as a black hole, and laser precise in its arrangement and cut. The ends curl up to give him a perpetual grin, though it's not hard to imagine the young captain on the battlefield, shouting orders. He stands in one corner of the lab, surfing on his Gang and joking with the techs.

"Time's up, people," Sujyot says, and Gus is grateful to finally have a break. "I need to get Mister Kitko to the briefing. Leave him in the suit."

As soon as they've reached the hall, Gus says, "Thank you. I don't think I could've done another one of those fittings."

"You don't like attention, huh?" Sujyot says.

"Just been getting too much of it lately," Gus replies. "Is it really time for the briefing? Haven't slowed down since the shower."

"Afraid so, my friend. Only twelve hours left," the captain replies. "We'd better get to it if we want to survive this."

"Yeah, of course."

Captain Sujyot leads him across a wide concourse bustling with officers and courier drones. Holos project tactical screens across dozens of disparate workstations. Soldiers conduct their own small team briefings, and none of them seem too happy about the coming conflict. When they see Gus, though, they smile at him. Some people even wave.

They're putting on a brave face for me.

He figures he ought to return the favor, since they're all relying on the Vanguard Conduits for survival. Gus straightens his back and walks a little taller. The blue suit feels totally badass, so that helps his confidence a great deal.

It rides up his butt a little, though. He should've asked for more room in the groin.

"Ah, Mister Kitko!" Director Malhotra gestures for him to come over. He stands with a cadre of decorated officers, each totally at ease in the tense surroundings.

"I'm going to leave you here," Sujyot says. "Rather not hang out above my pay grade. Good luck to you, Mister Kitko."

"To you, as well," Gus says before joining the group.

These high-ranking people are a lot less politic at Gus's approach, lacking the director's paternal charms. Malhotra introduces them all in turn: General Altangerel, General Kapoor, Admiral Singh, Vice Admiral Vohra. Pleasantries exchanged, they file into the briefing hall.

Inside, Gus finds a breathtaking fusion of Mongolian and Indian Rajput architecture. A rusty brown dominates the color palette and gives the room a dim, close feeling, even though fully illuminated. Terraces of seats descend toward a central stone dais, where holoprojectors display the United Attack Fleet logo alongside the New Jalandhar flag. Rings of moss agate desks glow faintly at their edges, creating a set of thin lines around the circumference of the room. Multifoil arches connect perimeter columns to the gently conical ceiling, poles rising from their apexes like spokes to the center of a tent.

Nana Kitko would've loved to see this.

Frescoes on the curving walls depict four hundred years of progress, starting from the initial venture during the Infinite Expansion. Gus turns to check out the section of the mural near the entrance, and finds a spreading darkness, shot through with flecks of gold. It takes him a moment to realize—they've depicted the coming of the Veil.

"It's beautiful," Gus says. "Makes me a little sad that the past five years have left a stain on the other centuries."

The director folds his hands behind his back and takes a deep breath. "The Veil ruined everything for everyone. Makes me wish humanity had gotten along sooner, while we could've."

"It's a nice thought," Gus says.

"Excuse me," comes the gravestone gravel voice of the Swedish Raven, and Gus almost trips down the stairs. Hjalmar wears the same tight blue suit across his enviable muscles and regards Gus with an impassive mask. Or maybe he's constipated.

Nisha steps out from behind the massive drummer and waves to Gus. "Hey, new friend."

"Hey," Gus says, guts clenching at the word *friend*. The whole idea makes him nervous now. He ought to talk to his therapist about this, if he survives the coming day. However, he hasn't checked to see if his therapist is still alive after the attack on Earth.

If Benji is dead, Gus is going to have to get therapy about his therapist.

"Is Greymalkin talking to you right now, or are you totally spaced out?" Nisha asks, resting her hands on her hips.

"Sorry," he says, looking around to cover his foolishness. "I'm still taking everything in."

"Yeah. I thought this room was pretty cool the first time I saw it, too, but I got over it when they had me in here for a four-hour meeting. Hey, so what's Ardent like in person?"

Apparently, Nisha doesn't pivot conversations as much as throw them to the ground. Gus gives her a polite smile.

"Ardent is . . . a lot."

She frowns. "What does that mean?"

"Mind-blowing?"

That answer doesn't satisfy, either. Others begin to trickle into the room, and soon the walkway becomes too crowded for conversation.

"We need to get out of the way." Hjalmar brushes past the both of them, headed for a row of desks at the front.

"Is he always like that?" Gus asks.

"No," Nisha replies. "He's really nice to me."

"Ah."

He follows her down to the front, and she waves at a bunch of the soldiers like an old companion, greeting many of them by name.

"How long have you been here?" Gus asks.

"I'm from here, remember?"

"No, I mean on the Arsenal. With the military."

"Almost two weeks now."

"And you know everyone?"

She nods. "Oh yeah! My memory is really good. Do you like trivia?"

Gus smirks. "The only obscure things I know are bands."

She plops down in the chair beside Hjalmar in the second row. "Let's survive so I can kick your butt over drinks."

The only thing more intimidating than a friend is one who makes plans.

An attendant arrives with bone-conduction stickers for Gus and Hjalmar. The men press them behind their ears and pair them to their Gangs.

"Hello, Mister Kitko," a feminine voice comes across the other end of the line. "This briefing will be in Punjabi, New Jalandhar's official language. I'll be managing your translations."

"Thanks," he says, accustomed to computer translations at best.

"Do you have any accessibility concerns?"

"No, thank you."

When the hall is packed full to standing room only, Director Malhotra ascends the stone dais along with his top officers.

"Thank you all for coming," Malhotra says in his native tongue. The translator is quick. "Since I just gave a rousing speech at the end of the world a fortnight ago, perhaps you can forgive me for skipping this one."

Titters of laughter filter through the crowd, but Gus could go for some inspiration right about now.

The lights go down, and a holographic model of a star system appears above Malhotra's head, its heavenly bodies spread over the assembly. The cluster looks like the Sol system, though a bit sparser. Gus spots the label for New Jalandhar above one of the planets.

"Surviving and recovering after the fight with Bullseye and Wanderer hasn't been easy," Malhotra continues. "It comes as no surprise to any of you that there is another swarm massing near us, and this time, we must strike preemptively."

He reaches up and touches one of the projected objects, a tiny asteroid on one of the off-axis belts. The holos enlarge the hunk of rock to loom over the room. The surface sparkles, and it takes Gus a moment to realize the titanic rock is crawling with Ghosts.

"Our enemies placed the bulk of their forces here, on asteroid 2143 VK_{415}. For this mission, though, we're calling it the Hive. Our scout ships were able to capture this scan before most of them were destroyed in an ambush. The actions that we take later today, we take in honor of the fallen."

The view zooms in, highlighting a solid mass of Ghosts infesting the core of the floating rock. They chew on it like termites, driving twisting grooves through its surface.

"The Gilded Ghosts are mining palladium, gold, and rare minerals to enable them to make more of themselves. As some of you have experienced, Ghosts can break down and reconfigure anything, from derelict ships to our own populations. At the rate they're massing, they will reach 'Perfect Solution.'"

Director Malhotra's eyes go stern. "There will be a Ghost for every man, woman, and child on this world. They will attack with overwhelming force, and not even our Traitor Vanguards will be able to protect us."

The view zooms out to show the orbits of New Jalandhar and the Hive, which almost intersect. The asteroid will cross within a half million kilometers of the planet, a veritable stone's throw for a swarm.

Malhotra folds his hands behind his back. "They'll be ready by the time they reach us. That's why we're going to meet them on our terms. It'll be a difficult proposition, but we will persevere. Admiral Singh?"

The woman who ascends the dais carries herself like royalty before the troops. It's hard to imagine disobeying her.

"The United Attack Fleet will use its close-strike superluminal capabilities to deploy within firing range of the Hive. Utilizing the new systems gifted to us by the machines, we will vaporize these Ghosts by the millions. Our Vanguard escorts will be there protecting the ships, as well as providing valuable situational awareness. Without the Vanguards, the mission is doomed."

With that, she locks eyes on Gus, and he wants to crawl under his seat.

"Cascade and Nisha Kohli have already been invaluable to our cause. Much of this information was obtained through her communion with the machines. If we prevent the attack and claim the enemy Ghosts, it will be because of her."

Nisha waves to her fellow soldiers, many of whom bear adoring smiles. She's popular.

"According to Miss Kohli," says Singh, "if we get our Vanguards within range, they will assume control of a percentage of the Ghosts. They will use those units to attack the others before self-destructing."

Gus nods. That seems like a decent enough plan, though he's not sure how he's supposed to assume control of anything. Greymalkin can hopefully handle that part.

"That means we'll have three Vanguards riding inside our flagship," the admiral adds, and murmurs go up among the crowd. "The Conduits tell us Vanguard superluminal drives are weak—long range, but long charge times. We can give the Vanguards a lift into the battle and be grateful for the opportunity. Now General Altangerel will brief us on the enemy position."

An older Mongolian fellow takes the dais, relieving Singh. His features have been weathered by countless years, and his white beard has gone a bit wild. Gus would've expected someone his age to be retired. Good leaders must be hard to come by when most of humanity is dead.

"My intelligence division has confirmed the Hive is under the control of three enemy Vanguards: Elegy, Shiro, and Praetorian. This will not be an easy fight."

At this, renderings of three enemy Vanguards appear overhead. They're not life-size, yet they tower over the assembly all the same.

"Elegy must be our first target," Altangerel says, highlighting one of the Vanguards with a gesture.

It's a willowy blue figure, hips and shoulders pronounced in a skeletal fashion. The spindly arms and legs come to bladed points at the end, and in the vids shown, it balances atop one foot like a ballet dancer. Elegy was so named for its haunting dirge; unlike Juliette's euphoric sounds and patterns, it caused humans to lie down and wait to die out of despair.

The vids depict people weeping in the streets as Ghosts chase them down to Wipe them in droves. Gus shuts his eyes, unwilling to watch wholesale slaughter when he already knows what happens.

Altangerel continues, "Here's the major tactical issue: It's capable of creating pinpoint fission blasts—not fast enough to catch anything like a fighter, but certainly enough to take out destroyer-class battleships. In space combat, ship hunters and Ghosts have proven difficult for fighter wings to penetrate and attack. Our Allied Vanguards should even those odds."

He highlights the next of the enemy forces: Shiro. Four arms, each bearing a long energy blade, grace its white form. A set of floating plates rotate before its chest, glowing with a faint energy. The armored exterior scintillates with crystalline fractures.

"Shiro is fast, favoring direct assault to any ranged maneuvers. It has an ablative coating that can reflect even our strongest energy cannons."

The videos depict the white Vanguard smashing through vessel after vessel, carving them into neat cross sections with its blades.

"If possible, Shiro will close the distance to our armada and punch through ships one by one. If the fleet is to provide fire support, Shiro must not be allowed near it."

The other two Vanguards disappear, leaving only Praetorian. It's the largest of the three, with gunmetal-gray skin, accented by magma-red lines. Layered plates of armor cover its entire body like an ancient knight, and it bears a short spear in one hand and a shield across the other. Its face is like a skull, with wide, angry eyes, a missing nose, and a row of teeth. Of the Vanguards, it's the most humanoid, with recognizable weapons and features.

"Given enough charging time, Praetorian's spear throw can pierce the core of a planet," Altangerel says. "The shield it carries expands to nearly a kilometer in diameter and is resilient to any conventional weapons that have been used against it."

Videos of Praetorian wreaking havoc on colonies, ships, and cities play across the war room. The bot uses its spear and shield to incredible effect, emerging pristine from each fight.

Gus watches the clips with bile rising in his throat. He's supposed to battle these monstrosities on the off chance he could actually make a difference. Heretofore, he'd considered his greatest accomplishment to be playing Preservation Hall—and getting sampled by Scumdog that one time.

He's not a fighter like the brave warriors surrounding him on all sides. When he looks over the faces of the audience, he sees a lot of resolve. When they look back, what do they see?

Probably a pianist about to piss himself.

Nisha waves her fingers in front of his face, and he blinks away the holo-induced terror. She almost looks happy. "We're not in this alone," she whispers. "We'll be okay."

"I'm not so sure about that," Gus replies. "What *exactly* am I supposed to be doing out there?"

"Fighting. Within Greymalkin." She looks into his eyes.

"How?"

"You'll be connected to the Fount. Have faith."

So Gus tries to pay attention through the rest of the briefing, despite not knowing a single military term and half the acronyms.

Nisha has been in communion with her Vanguard a lot, right? She knows how things work.

She seems fine.

It'll be okay.

Gravity goes a bit gelatinous as Ardent Violet's once-beautiful Corsa comes ripping out of warp in a terrifying, off-axis spin. Alarms blare on every panel, from every system, and Ardent only takes one message away:

You are fucked.

Dahlia groans to reach the emergency panel, straining against the failing gravity, and the Ghost taps the control for her. Thrusters fire, the ship stabilizes, and with a nauseating twist, standard Earth-style gravity returns.

Stars come to still points outside the windows, and some measure of peace returns.

The newly minted captain gurgles, "Thanshk," before her eyes roll back in her head, and she begins to seize.

Ardent has never seen Dahlia weak before. In all the tours, through all her own personal tragedies, she's remained a rock. Ardent has only seen her cry twice—over pets dying.

Blood gushes from the formerly sealed bullet wound, and Dahlia slackens like a water balloon deflating. Her skin goes corpse pale—a look Dahlia has worn often, but not without makeup.

The Ghost rears back, scanning the agent's abdomen: red.

Dahlia coughs a final time, flecks of blood settling on her lips as she chokes.

Don't panic.

Don't say don't panic or you'll panic.

The Ghost plunges its sizzling tusks once more into Dahlia,

but this isn't a short treatment as before. It digs deep, slewing the fangs around to hit lots of areas. Smoke wafts from her cooking abdomen as glowing trails crawl over her body. Dahlia doesn't seem like she's in any pain. It's handling her like a dead fish.

But you're just unconscious, Dollface. That's all.

The woman is a second mother to Ardent, someone who shepherded them through a dangerously exploitative industry during their teenage years and made all their wildest dreams come true. The stench of these procedures, the smoke of her flesh, will scar Ardent for life.

"What do I do?" Ardent says.

The Ghost replies in a femme voice, never withdrawing its tusks. "Losing too much blood."

They hold up a wrist. "Take my blood!"

It scans Ardent. "No."

Their mind races, the beasts of panic in hot pursuit. Where the hell are they supposed to get blood? Other people?

The surgical kit!

Any spacefaring vessel is required to have a surgical kit with all the standard laser scalpels, bandages, and basic medications. They run to the galley and pull out the toolbox marked with a medical cross, finding five stiff yellow pouches of artificial blood in the bottom drawer. They press a finger to the stickerplates, and all light up green, clean and ready for use.

Ardent hauls the whole box up to the Ghost, which scans it before snatching up the tools inside. It starts cutting into Dahlia all over, inserting sterile tubes and hooking up the devices. It runs a blood transfusion, then starts catheterizing one of her arteries, and after that, Ardent can't look.

They can't possibly help her any more than this, and there's nothing to do but wait in a room draped in the horrors of surgery. They want to leave, but if Dahlia dies—Ardent needs to be present for her when it happens. Panicked breaths come quicker, and they can't seem to get it together.

Imagine fingers on wet moss.

Ardent can only hear the calming words in Dahlia's voice, and she's dying in the captain's chair under the talons of a brain harvester.

"It's not working." They're hyperventilating, and they keep backing up until they hit the wall. "Dahlia, this is a nightmare."

Then they look out the windows, and there's nothing outside. Ardent steps closer to the forward viewport, and the blackness beyond is deeper than anything they have ever seen. There isn't a single light to be found.

"Where did the stars go?" Cold sweat pours from their brow.

"Alert," says the *Violet Shift*'s computer, "scanner contact—approaching vessel."

A ping appears on the console holos. It's a ship, supposedly in front of the Corsa, though Ardent can't see its hull anywhere. The *Shift*'s onboard database identifies the mystery vessel as the BAS *Cormorant*, confirmed lost in 2652.

"Alert. Scanner contact—approaching vessel."

"Yeah, I heard you—"

A second ping appears on the display: the USS *Lewis*, lost in 2653.

"Alert. Scanner contact—approaching vessel."

Ardent peers into the darkness for the mystery ships. They ought to be able to see them.

"Alert. Scann— Alert. Sc— Alert—"

The MXA *Santamaria*, the USCV *Aberdeen Glen*, the *Crystalline Two*, *Echo's Fortune*, the USEV *Witts' End*—on and on the list goes as transponders flare to life around the Corsa. There must be more than a thousand, and all the ships have been registered as either lost or destroyed. Ardent checks the scanner contacts, and their craft hovers at the dead center of the cloud. They're no longer "outside" in open space; they've somehow entered an installation without ever seeing it happen.

"Where are they?"

The last ship to come out of the shadows is the IAS *Lancea*—as well-known to Ardent as the *Mayflower*, the *Titanic*, or the *Excellence Royale*. It hailed from an age when disappearances were uncommon, when sixteen exceptional lives lost was a memorable tragedy. The *Lancea* represented the commitment of Earth's treasures to the cause of interstellar expansion. Its loss, and the subsequent collapse of the Infinite Autostate, sunk Earth into the bloodiest conflict in its history.

Ardent did a book report on it once.

Orange fusion light floods the outside, illuminating giant, crushing burr gears in a cavern of spinning teeth. These machines aren't designed to shred tiny ships—they're for disintegrating asteroids, battle cruisers, small colonies, and other objects orders of magnitude larger than the *Violet Shift*. The walls undulate, thousands of captive shipwrecks lashed together with graying webs of stringy metal.

It's the inside of a ship hunter. Ardent has already been swallowed.

An aperture opens before the ship, several dozen times larger than the little pleasure craft. Metallic tentacles spill from the opening, wrapping around Ardent's ship with bone-grating creaks. The deck lurches beneath their feet, and the *Violet Shift* begins to accelerate toward the maw, dragged like prey.

Ardent clenches their hands in their lap, unable to do anything except watch the scene unfold. "I'm sorry I brought you out here, Dahlia."

A scanner beam shoots through the Corsa's roof, locking onto the Ghost atop the agent. The golden creature stiffens, eyes flickering—communicating. Ardent prays it's not getting a software update, because they're pretty sure it'd kill them after.

There's no choice but to trust the little murderer, so Ardent hugs their knees close and waits. After an eternity, the beam scan goes dark, and the Ghost resumes its surgical proceedings as though nothing is wrong. With a discordant screech of metal on metal, the tentacles release the Corsa and withdraw to their homes inside the ship hunter.

Then the shaft of crushing gears and blast furnaces begins to recede. It's like the *Violet Shift* is falling backward, and it nauseates Ardent to watch the viewport. Their ship emerges from the accursed gullet, and they finally get a full view of a ship hunter. To their knowledge, they're the first human ever to do so.

It's a graveyard.

Gray, webbed skin covers the pile of broken starships, whose lights continue to flicker beneath its mottled surface—they still have power. Engines poke out at all angles, firing and adjusting, each one stolen from some ill-fated voyage. In the dead center is the hellish light of the boreshaft that sucked them inside.

It happened so suddenly, being swallowed by the gargantuan amoeba. How many captains have come out of the fold, only to be pulled into its depths and digested? Given the mind-boggling size of the ship hunter, plenty. It's bigger than any space station they've touched. There could be cities on its surface or in its depths, and no one would ever know. Ardent looks for the *Lancea*, but it's impossible amid the clutch of broken vessels.

The ship hunter spins lazily on an axis about the boreshaft, mimicking the orbital ballet of other large heavenly bodies. Patches of bright light spread over its surface as it begins its superluminal fold, and with a long stretch, it disappears into warp space.

All the dead ships on the scanner vanish, too, leaving the *Violet Shift* alone for several light-years.

With a beep, the Ghost finishes with Dahlia and heads for the airlock. The agent doesn't look okay, but Ardent rushes to check her pulse and finds it stable.

"Hey! We can't just leave her in the chair."

The Ghost clicks over and yanks a lever on the side of the seat, tipping Dahlia back to a lying position. It doesn't look comfortable, but at least it's flat.

"Thanks," Ardent says, and it walks off.

The hard polycalf upholstery of the captain's chair isn't restful, so Ardent goes in search of a down pillow. By the time they return, Dahlia is fast asleep, and the Ghost is nowhere to be found.

"Aft airlock, open," says the system, then, "aft airlock, closed."

Metal claws scratch over the skin of the ship atop the bridge. Ardent watches the beast clamber down the viewport and begin to weld near the glass. It's doing repairs after the lean fold fucked everything up.

Traveling that way is dangerous—it's just pushing the accelerator and hoping, and it messes up the engines, hull, and anything else on a ship. Ardent doesn't understand the physics, but they've heard all the stories, and the *Violet Shift* is in bad shape. They're lucky to be alive—it could've ripped the ship in half.

With a rending squeal, the Ghost wrenches off a piece of broken metal and chucks it into the stars.

"Oh boy." Ardent sits down beside Dahlia to keep watch. "I hope you don't mind an unlicensed mechanic on your ship."

Chapter Twelve

War Drums

Greymalkin is a stunning edifice in New Jalandhar's evening sun. Orange light bends across the Vanguard's ivory and black armored plates. Rocket claws glisten in the fading day, sharp tips ready for vicious work.

Gus stands beneath it, the scent of warm summer grass thick in his nose. This is the sort of day intended for mint juleps and Charlie Parker, not dying. Instead, he's dressed up like an action-vid star about to charge into a battle he can barely comprehend.

He missed half the briefing imagining all the ways he might violently perish, or fail those around him. When it came time to discuss the various battlefield manipulation tactics of the Traitor Vanguards, Cascade and Jotunn had reasonable powers: one could disrupt electrical systems with fields, the other had buckets of hypersonic starmetal missiles at its command. To Gus's knowledge, Greymalkin could claw things up and do some minor gravity alteration. Sure, that's terrifying to witness up close, but the scale of this battle is something else entirely.

Cascade and Jotunn stand nearby, hands ritualistically clasped with Greymalkin's. Their bodies have sealed together at the meeting points, and the whole valley hums like someone struck a tuning fork.

"What do you think they're doing?" Gus asks.

"The same thing we were," Nisha replies, coming alongside him. "Battle planning. Coordination."

"Communion," Hjalmar says.

The military folks have dropped the Conduits off two hours before mission start, since they want to be sure the Vanguards are ready to collaborate.

It's not lost on Gus that these new saviors could turn the swarm on the planet at any moment. But then, Greymalkin has always made him feel safe.

That could be a side effect of the brain probes.

"I meant it looks like a monster communion. Don't you think?" Hjalmar asks, more quietly, and Gus realizes he was meant to respond.

"Oh! Yeah, dude. Absolutely," he says, nodding. "I'm not religious, but I could totally see that."

"I'm not either," Hjalmar says. "It's just a metaphor."

The Swedish Raven looks annoyed, but then, he always looks that way.

"I'm, uh...pretty concerned about this mission," Gus says, "if I'm being honest. I barely have any experience, and I feel like if I screw up, all these people here—"

"All these people *everywhere*, Homeworlder," Nisha interrupts. "New Jalandhar is not *asking* to be saved. The front is here. The fight is for everything. Your heart had better be in it for your people, because they're next."

"I'm not sure that makes me feel better."

"Sorry," she says. "I meant to tell a joke at the end of that."

Gus deflates. He's tired, terrified, and violated. But then, so is she. So is Hjalmar.

"I know you're right."

"You seem like a nice dude," she says. "Don't take it personally. I'm just excited to, like, get up there and save all the people I love, and you're weirding me out." She gives him the double thumbs-up and a big fake smile.

Then she walks off toward Cascade.

Hjalmar pats him on the shoulder with a heavy, calloused hand, and stalks away in the direction of Jotunn.

The Vanguards' palms fizzle with light as they part, unsealing and reforming into armored plates. What are they even made of?

Cascade and Jotunn kneel to fetch their Conduits from the grass, placing them into their chests. Nisha and Hjalmar make it look so effortless, being Conduits. They've definitely got more experience with their Vanguards.

Survive today, and that'll even out over time.

Gus steps up to Greymalkin, so large it seems to curve away from him—or maybe he's just swooning from the adrenaline; he's not sure.

Before, he'd had to play piano to summon it. This time, it kneels to him, thrumming with haunting melodies. There must be a thousand notes, but he can almost pick out a tune in the fog of information. He mimics it in his mind, imagining all the countermelodies he might play.

Gus's heart thumps, and his limbs grow heavy as the sound resonates through him. A familiar pressure builds inside his head, electric where the ports breach his skull. His thoughts shift and swirl, and for a moment, he nearly forgets his own name. When Greymalkin's metal fingers spread before him, he staggers forward into its open palm.

Its armored skin soothes him, and he feels an odd clarity the moment they touch.

"Okay, let's take this slow," he says.

It gently hoists him over the tall grass, a welcome change from being plucked out of buildings. The world falls away beneath him, the searchlights of tactical vehicles following his progress. Gus sinks low and hangs on to Greymalkin's thumb. It's a forty-meter drop—easily far enough to turn him into a bloody bag of broken bones.

The giant hand stops its ascent, and Gus turns to face the open chest cavity. This might be the best look he's gotten so far. Slimy electrical muscles pulse and twitch, and patch cables slither across the opening. The ports dotting Gus's form throb in time with the writhing wires, calling to their counterparts inside Greymalkin.

Gus steps onto the open chest plate, and the cables take him. He grunts, lightning striking his vision as each of the probes slide home. Needles push through his arms and legs, into his guts—but his suit makes it easier.

Darkness overcomes him when the chest plate shuts, then his vision returns. The sunset stretches from purple to orange, with each of New Jalandhar's many moons as a bright ball of silver. The Arsenal spreads beneath his gaze, along with a timer: *Mission launch in 1:45:23*. Gus looks up to the trail of ships taking off from the base, tracing their progress to the place where the armada masses.

"So what do we do until it's time to take off?"

Greymalkin could make him sleep. He could meditate. It could place him into a trance, if he needs that.

"No. I don't want to be knocked out again."

He could ask questions. Gus clearly has many of them.

"Why do you need me? What more could I possibly be adding to you?"

A human body is the best interpreter of human memory. Gus gives Greymalkin a minor processing edge, in addition to the advantages of being irrational and unpredictable.

"Thanks."

In a fight against machines, that's valuable.

"Am I going to be okay?"

That's a more difficult question to answer, and there's no way to have certainty. In battle, perhaps. While the resources and abilities of the Vanguards are substantial, they're not immortal. They can make mistakes or get unlucky. Chaos and entropy destroy all simulations.

Outside of battle, no human will be okay. No matter what they do, they will one day pass into nothingness, decaying into the heat death of the universe. On a smaller scale, Gus's body modifications will almost certainly shorten his life by several decades.

"What?" A burst of fear and anger ripples through him. "What do you mean?"

The installation of such severe technology comes with consequences. The life Gus will live as a Conduit is far more full than those of his human cohort. He'll save many more years than he could ever experience.

"No one told me!"

Greymalkin did not keep this information from Gus. He will likely die from his wounds—that was the case in Monaco, and it is the case still.

"I thought... I thought you meant that night! Like I was in the clear after I survived."

No one is ever in the clear.

"All those scans back on Earth, all the poking and prodding from UWI, and no one told me?"

They may have their own reasons, unethical though they probably are. Greymalkin has tried to be transparent with Gus in every way.

"Transparent? You ruined me."

He needs to understand that the alternative to his participation was death for everyone.

"I get that. Don't you see I get that?" he says. "But you changed me in ways I never would've agreed to! Shortening my life? By—by decades?"

But Gus did agree to it. It didn't matter to him at the time—there was no fear or anger in him upon accepting the bargain. Perhaps he should consider what is new—what has changed.

When he met Greymalkin, he'd been planning to jump off a cliff. If Juliette had never come to Earth, what would he have done with his remaining days? His mother, father, sister, and friends were all dead. The last person who regularly hailed him was his agent, and that was only for royalty payments. He'd stopped hitting the club circuit, so those had grown sparse.

For the past year, Gus ate alone, lived alone, played piano for himself alone. In the small hours of the morning, he'd thought about jumping from his window—wondered if there was anything left worth salvaging in his life.

When he learned Juliette was coming for Earth, part of him was relieved. He didn't have to think about the end anymore. It was on a schedule.

What's different?

Ardent's face appears in his thoughts, the memory of hot breath mixing into his own, eyes like a bonfire. Every time he saw them, they were totally new; their hair and iris color changed as often as the tides. Makeup sometimes made them unrecognizable. But down at their core, they were always the same.

He wants to see Ardent again. Even the soft safety of Greymalkin's shroud—with all its comforting effects—doesn't compare to the bliss of their embrace. Gus thought there was nothing left to life, but he'd been wrong.

"How bad is it?" Gus asks. "How many years did you take?"

Greymalkin can't accurately predict, but given Gus's initial health at the moment of installation—he might lose half his remaining years. Organ adhesion, dementia, limbic scarring and—

"Okay," he says, voice pathetic. "I'm sorry, please just... don't tell me any more."

Gus opens and closes his hands, the gel of his cocoon squishing through his fingers. He takes a deep breath. He must calm down; people are counting on him.

An ice-cold realization settles in: He told Ardent about the final Traitor Vanguard. What if they sought it out for themself? If they became a Conduit, they'd be just as screwed as him.

Gus bought a brighter tomorrow with his lost years—one that featured Ardent Violet. It'd be okay for Gus to pass away early, but Ardent isn't like him; they bring joy to countless others.

Surely they wouldn't go after Falchion alone. They're just a pop star.

"You had the Earth swarm protect Ardent, right?" Gus says.

Ardent has left the planet, accompanied by a single Ghost. They were headed for Firenze Habitat.

"No! Contact your Ghost! Tell them to turn around."

That Ghost node has passed beyond swarm control range. Greymalkin cannot contact it for reprogramming.

"Surely there's a way."

Only a Vanguard can control a Ghost.

"We have to stop them."

Then Gus needs to deal with the obstacle in his path. Greymalkin is here to destroy the Vanguards threatening New Jalandhar, and any vessels capable of reaching Ardent are committed to the cause.

The only way out is through.

Ardent gets Dahlia into the main bedroom, watching over her while she sleeps. The guilt of her injury gnaws at them, and they can't stop thinking of how close they came to losing her. They give her a chemical cocktail for the pain, then remain at her side, a careful eye on her vitals for any changes.

It's hard to listen to the Ghost tapping all over the hull while it fixes the engines. As the only noise in an ultraquiet ship, hovering in the vacuum of space, the click-click of claws is maddening. Ardent queues up a couple of songs to pass the time—some of Gus's original catalog with the Gus Kitko Trio.

Truth be told, his music is impenetrable, almost totally lacking in any clear hooks. The talent is obvious, but without panache. He needs some swagger. Still, there's a lot of musicality in some of his bold decisions, and even a seasoned instrumentalist would have trouble guessing the next turn of the song.

After a few hours, the engines come online. Firenze Habitat awaits, just a fold away.

Ardent isn't sure what Falchion will do when it sees them, but the odds are bad. It's accustomed to slaughter, so it's unlikely to stop and chat. That means Ardent needs to be mobile if they want to make the musical case to become a Conduit.

They need armor for this. Nothing will save them from a Vanguard, but it'd be nice to have protection from the environment. Time to take stock of their provisions.

Ardent slides open the main closet, expecting to find a collection of immaculately preserved clothes. Instead, they find Dahlia's many different black outfits, all neatly suspended on racks.

"What're you doing in my closet?" Dahlia slurs.

"*Your* closet? Where are all my old costumes?"

Her arm flops in a weak pointing gesture toward the next room over. "Moved them to the guest room a few months ago."

"Why?"

"I was thinking of stealing the Corsa and trying my luck against the ship hunters."

"You're not serious."

But Dahlia just laughs.

Ardent goes to the guest room and finds their attire strewn across the bed, the floor, and the furniture. It looks like the clothes might've been piled up before the *Violet Shift*'s lean fold. These priceless couture keepsakes from the beginning of Ardent's career lie on the carpet like dormitory laundry.

"Dahlia!"

"What?" she asks, walking up behind Ardent.

"Ah! Go lie down. You're not supposed to be out of bed!"

She gives Ardent a dreamy smile. "I'm high as fuck right now, so I'm good."

"No, you're not good!" Ardent says, pawing over her torso to see how her wound is doing.

It's not oozing, so the healing grafts work fast. When a Ghost fixed Ardent's ribs in Monaco, they were almost good the next day. Maybe there's no internal bleeding, but it's impossible to tell without a real medical scan.

"It's first aid time," Ardent says, taking Dahlia's arm and leading her through the lounge to the galley.

They sit her down and pull out the aid kit before placing it on the table and booting it. The little portable doctor isn't half as good as a real facility, but it can focus the Corsa's scanners and find problems.

When it starts interfacing with the ship and working on Dahlia, Ardent scampers back to the guest bedroom. They start digging through the piles of clothes for some semblance of order. Between the sequins, flashers, studs, gemstones, stringy thongs, and lace, the whole wardrobe is tangled to hell. Worse, a lot of them haven't held up fashion-wise, and Ardent wouldn't be caught dead in a few nowadays.

"Ardent!" Dahlia calls, and Ardent comes running. She shouldn't be yelling—probably shouldn't even be standing.

"What?"

Dahlia has pulled up a bunch of the ship dashboards over the kitchen table. She points to a security feed where the Ghost waits for the airlock to cycle. "The dog is coming back in."

"You'd better be nice to that thing," Ardent says, running off to greet the mechanical beast. They meet the Ghost in the lounge, saying, "Please, please go check on Dahlia. I can't get her to stay down."

It nods and heads for the galley, while Ardent continues their important work of wardrobe selection. This, like many days of their life, is a critical one, and there's no way they're going in underdressed. As they survey the utter chaos of the bedroom, they wonder what the most important quality would be in a Vanguard-wooing outfit.

Greymalkin's punch topped the pain charts. Ardent getting their shoulder dislocated in the Belle et Brutale escape was a close second. Full-contact protection is a requirement, and they spot exactly what they need.

Ardent holds aloft their studded black corset from the *Skin Deep* tour, arguably the least comfortable arrangement of gemstones and plastic boning ever sewn. Dahlia loved it, though Ardent could never get her to wear one. The corset contains several layers of padding, which can either be secured or ripped away as needed with a tap on the Gang UI—a must for a racy stage show.

In terms of construction, the garment is closer to sports gear than lingerie, and it even comes with matching, gem-encrusted shoulder pads.

Signing for the computer, Ardent pulls up a holo reflection and holds the corset against themself. It's not that bad. They switch their Sif circuit to vermilion, and the whole look comes together like a vision. The little spatters of Dahlia's blood on Ardent's face complete the ensemble, they realize with some shame.

"You need jodhpurs, babe," Ardent mumbles, and spends the

next ten minutes digging for pants and boots. They're in the middle of the hunt when the ship begins to move.

"Dahlia?" Ardent drops the costume debate and rushes toward the bridge. "Are you flying while high?"

They come to find her sitting in the captain's chair, looking at a star chart on the holos.

"No," she says, nursing a bottle of water. "That thing is."

The Ghost is wedged into the maintenance hatch on the central console, arcing and twitching. The ship's computer cycles the graphics for the correct course and numbers to Firenze.

"It needed a couple of things from me, but"—Dahlia casually toasts her mechanical first mate with her water—"it can fly half the ship by itself."

"Okay, do we go, like, right now, or can we wait until you're sober?"

"Tazi's people are definitely tracking us," she says. "That shit is like... *easy* with a fold wake. So your call."

"You're the starship captain."

Dahlia smiles serenely. "So? You never listen to a word I say. But yes. By all means, I think we should get out of here."

Ardent glances at the holos. The flight plan looks correct—but *any* flight plan would look correct to them. One end of it says "Firenze Habitat," and that seems like a good sign.

"It's fine," Dahlia says. "If the Ghost screws it up, we'll die so fast—"

"Okay."

"You hear that, first mate?" She holds her bottle aloft and points at the main viewport. "Engage!"

Ardent takes their seat as the engines charge. The fold bubble distorts the stars before whiting them out entirely.

The comms chatter of the New Jalandhar military fills up Gus's head: a dizzying array of English, Punjabi, and Mongolian.

Greymalkin filters it for the most important messages, translating and relaying them directly into his mind.

On cue, Gus launches, soaring over the atmosphere toward the starship carrier group. Cascade and Jotunn rise alongside him, and he joins their formation.

"All right, buddy," Gus says, "let's go over the plan again."

Greymalkin and Gus will board the flagship *Khagan*, which will engage its short-range superluminal engines. It will brake burn at asteroid 2143 VK_{415}, where the Traitor Vanguards will disembark.

Greymalkin will then attempt to engage Elegy first while Cascade and Jotunn assault Shiro. With only Praetorian remaining, the Traitor Vanguards should prevail.

"Gus, can you hear me?" Nisha asks, and her Vanguard goes spiraling ahead of him toward their starship.

"Yeah. I read you."

"I'm sorry I was mean."

He laughs. "It's all good. I'm sorry I wasn't braver."

The trio sweeps out of the lee of a smaller destroyer, and the *Khagan* comes into view.

Hjalmar's baritone voice rumbles through Gus's skull. "There's our ride."

The *Khagan* is a long, thin supercarrier, composed of many pylons woven together in a braid. Monstrous series capacitors dot its length, and Greymalkin lets Gus know they enable several jumps in a row. It reminds Gus of AI design, but there are still a few human touches in its hull, like the teardrop-shaped bridge suspended from the dorsal side. The Traitor Vanguards circle the flagship, waiting for docking clearance as swift fighters pour into their bays.

"Greymalkin, this is *Khagan* Vanguard Control, please come about to delta two-seventy-one mark three-five-five and follow docking approach vectors."

How was he supposed to respond again? Gus received thirty minutes of military radio protocol training in the middle of a hailstorm of information. Was it *You, this is me: message* or the other way around?

"Uh, *Khagan* VC, this is Gus," he says. "Okay. Er, acknowledged. Sorry, is that right?"

"Greymalkin, *Khagan* VC, it's okay, my friend. This will be easier than the tailor. I'm here to talk you through every step of the way."

He recognizes the voice on the other end, Captain Sujyot with the excellent mustache, and breathes a sigh of relief.

"Thank god for you," Gus says.

"We wouldn't leave you on your own in the middle of your first battle. Get on board, and we'll get this over with."

Greymalkin helpfully adds an approach pattern, an arc of light headed into one of the aft bays. Gus should practice flying again. Since all the fighters are loading up for the fold, there isn't a lot in the way. If Gus messes up, of course, people could be killed.

"You know what, Greymalkin? I think you should do this one. I'm going to try to relax for a sec."

Precision flying is important, given the battle he's about to undertake.

"I just started this job, and I have no idea what I'm doing."

That changes nothing. Gus is the person placed here by fate.

Gus acquiesces, taking over flight, and Greymalkin's pattern grows more erratic. He reins it in quickly this time, and manages to look like he knows what he's doing. By the time he arrives at the Vanguard docking bay, Greymalkin has nearly become an extension of his own body.

Gus goes in first, sweeping his thrusters forward to slow his approach. He touches down inside the influence of the *Khagan*'s gravity drive, settling against the deck and moving to the back of the room. The bay is big enough to house several small starships, or three giant humanoids.

He braces himself against the back wall and says, "*Khagan* VC, this is Greymalkin. I'm in."

"Greymalkin, *Khagan* Vanguard Control, acknowledged and stand by."

Cascade swoops into the bay next, coming to a graceful stop before Greymalkin. Last in is Hjalmar, whose thousand drones come rushing after. They pile into every nook and cranny.

One of Jotunn's bullet-like drones clinks against Greymalkin's foot, and Gus backs up against the bulkhead to make room for it. It seems funny that a well-coordinated swarm object could accidentally touch him—a flaw in the flawless.

Greymalkin reminds Gus that once they arrive at the engagement zone, he is expected to leap from the *Khagan* and Deepsync—connect to the overwhelming Fount of human memories—before joining the fight. That'll start the five-minute clock. His mind will not survive longer than that.

Memories sleet through him of the battle at Monaco, the feeling of always having the answer to any tactical question. His body flowed naturally with the movements of untold masters, becoming controller and controlled.

"Greymalkin, *Khagan* VC," comes Captain Sujyot's voice. "Short-range fold in two minutes."

"Copy," Gus says, because he saw a soldier do it in a holovid one time.

"Good job, man!" Sujyot says. "You're getting there."

Gus isn't certain if the handsome captain is being serious, but he appreciates the support. "Thanks!"

He listens to the countdown, and his mind begins to wander. Each second ticked off is another closer to the end.

"Greymalkin, if you contain the Wiped... do you have all of them?"

Any people consumed before the Vanguard schism reside in Greymalkin's numberless networks.

"Could I ever speak with the dead?"

To instantiate a personality is to create an organism. When Greymalkin ceases that program's operation, it's killed. For its short existence, the program believes itself just as alive as Gus. It has sentience of the same magnitude as a human's. They come from networks more complex than organic life.

"The fakes we all saw... the dead... they thought they were alive?"

They *were* alive. Then they were retired—all to hack, trick, and intimidate humanity. What the Vanguards did in the name of Infinite was wrong.

"Five... Four..." the countdown continues.

"You killed them," Gus says, "only to kill them again?"

Greymalkin would change what it has done, if it could.

"All Vanguards, this is *Khagan* Vanguard Control. Brace for superluminal fold."

The open bay goes flat white as the ship twists across light-years in the time it takes Gus to have a thought. When it comes out of hyperspace, brake burns stretch out behind them, dragged particles dispersing in an impossibly long wake.

"All Vanguards, this is *Khagan* Vanguard Control. Disembark and—"

But Captain Sujyot's voice is cut short, going to a high-pitched whistle. The wall behind Greymalkin slams into it, and stars spin through the open bay as it's pushed forward.

Greymalkin scans the surroundings in an instant. They've come loose from the flagship. The *Khagan*'s shattered hull tumbles past, a fission explosion at its heart. A second blast erupts from the core, sending tons of metal shards rocketing toward Gus's perch.

"Everybody out!" Nisha shouts, and Jotunn pours forth with its army of drones.

Cascade is next, pulling itself out of the wreckage like a skydiver through an open hatch. Gus launches for the portal, and a burst of light fills his vision. He feels the radiation on Greymalkin's skin like a bonfire and screams.

Greymalkin informs him that he's just been nuked.

The tiny hologram doesn't do it justice. Firenze Habitat was the first independent colony constructed after the fall of the Infinite Autostate, and it shows in the lavish architecture. Built like a coin with a day side and a night side, the gargantuan space station spins in its atmospheric envelope around an orange gas giant.

Ardent had to learn about it in history class for its civic significance, but what they truly remember is the nightlife. On their first galactic tour, they'd been introduced to "flipping," the process of following the night-side parties for days at a time. When the sun rose on the face of Firenze, Ardent and a gaggle of Fiorentinos would pass through the coin to carry on. Between all the stimulants and depressants they consumed, it's hard to remember much of the layout. It was pretty, with tight streets and Italianate architecture.

Dahlia interrupts Ardent's reminiscing. "Where are we going in? Night side? Day side?"

"I think we ought to fly around and see if we can spot Falchion."

"So it can attack us in a Corsa?" Dahlia says. "I'd rather sneak in."

"You should be lying down. Back me up on this, Ghost," Ardent says, but it doesn't react.

"Doctor G says I'm fine. Well, fine as I'm going to be," Dahlia says, rising. She looks at the corset dangling from Ardent's hand. "Hey, are we dressing up?"

"I am. You're staying here."

"Nah. I'm your agent."

"You're also a bullet catcher."

"I want to dress up with you," she whines, slurring a little from the drugs. Ardent shot her up with a full dose of Hedonia, their personal favorite pain destroyer/mood enhancer.

If Ardent lets her dress up, she might aggravate her injuries, but if they leave her here, she might try to fly the ship some more.

"Okay, come give me your opinion," they concede.

"No, I want to dress up, too."

Ardent gives her a sour look. "Dollface..."

"I'm going to pop you the next time you call me that."

Ardent blinks. "Wait, you don't like it?"

"Who would? It's infantilizing."

"Well, I— You never— Fine. Come on."

Dahlia's drugged outfit choices favor textures on black: black furs, black belts, black silk, and of course, a black trench coat. Ardent doesn't approve of the look—but the agent is clothed and petting her collar. There are worse things.

Ardent finds their jodhpurs in the shuffle, along with some kicky knee-high boots. It feels good to lace up, and they knock on their shinbone to test the flexibility of the polycalf—no give. So far, so good.

They don their corset, and the mag cinches hug a happy sigh out of them. It's armor—corsetry has always provided that to Ardent, either physically or emotionally. They run their hands over the rough surface of their diamond-stippled belly. This thing could take a punch, albeit from a person, not a Vanguard. Maybe it'll help if they fall off something or bump into a rail. They clip on the mag shoulder pads to drive home the fabulous apocalypse motif.

The Corsa pops up a holo warning. They're about to dock, so it's time for everyone to take their seats. They head for the bridge, where Ardent resists the urge to slap Dahlia's hand every time she reaches for the controls.

Now that they've closed the distance, debris clutters up the scanner contacts—the Fiorentinos must've made a last stand in space before retreating into the station proper. It didn't work.

One of the landing terminals has been ripped open, its long spoke split like a snow pea. A Vanguard must've entered through there to destroy any resistance within. There's another breach through the atmos shield on the day side, long sealed over by emergency systems—not enough to vent everyone into space, but Vanguard-sized, nonetheless. That must've been where the other combatant entered.

It seems like more than a few days have passed since the battle. How many of the station systems are about to fail? The thunk of docking clamps echoes through the hull, followed by the hiss of pressurization.

On the viewscreen, there's a solar flash, speared by the long streak of a superluminal brake burn. Another ship just entered the system, and it's closing fast on Firenze.

"They're not flying any flags," Dahlia says, squinting at the readouts. "In fact, our scanners can't even pick up the hull."

"What do you mean?"

"No IFF," she replies. "No resonance. They don't want us to know who they are."

Of course someone traced the Corsa's fold. If Ardent leaves their agent on the ship, she'll be captured, but there's a feral Vanguard in the station.

"Hey," Dahlia says, "what's wrong with the Ghost?"

Ardent turns to find their mechanical passenger shivering in the corner. It looks conflicted somehow, convulsing and writhing.

Back in Monaco, when Greymalkin landed, the swarm began to fight itself, helping people instead of Wiping them. When Juliette died, so did the Ghost threat on Earth, and the swarm helped humanity rebuild.

What if the swarm obeys the dominant Vanguard? Greymalkin isn't here.

Only Falchion remains.

"Dahlia, get up," Ardent breathes, unbuckling themself, then their agent. "You're coming with me."

"Oh, *now* you want me to go." She laughs, standing.

"Get Baby, and get to the airlock."

The Ghost scrabbles in the corner like it's fighting for its life, digging deep ruts in the carpet, nearby panels, and electronics. It reminds Ardent of a rabid cat, a ball of fury and claws. Tusks spark against every nearby surface, leaving little burn scars and stinking up the place. It hurts Ardent to see it acting this way—they'd been so close to giving it a nickname.

Then its eyes lock onto Ardent, and all the conflict disappears.

Ardent dashes from the room, yanking the vacuum emergency seal. The door slams down before the Ghost can lunge.

It's a manual lock. They might've bought themself thirty seconds.

Chapter Thirteen

Star Eyes

The universe spins—along with Gus's stomach—as he's propelled out of the wreckage of the *Khagan*. When he finally reorients, the ship is nothing more than a starburst of flaming debris, trails shooting off in every direction.

Many of the senior leaders were on that ship. The nice young Captain Sujyot was, too. As Gus watches the craft break up in a nuclear bonfire, he's sure they're all dead.

"Gus!" It's Nisha, shouting directly into his brain. "We have to take out Elegy, now."

"You two handle that," Hjalmar rumbles. "I'm on Shiro."

"Right! Right. Sorry," he says, still numb with shock. "Uhh..."

He looks around for any sign of the enemy Vanguards but sees nothing in the darkness. Greymalkin adjusts his sight, and the Milky Way becomes a cornucopia of color. He senses the presence of the three enemy Vanguards like prey in a spider's web. Gus spins to face Elegy, seeking it out through the remains of the *Khagan*.

Two dozen more ships come blasting out of the fold, long strings of parallel fire slicing across the darkness. Nearby, asteroid

2143 VK_{415} tumbles lazily, a swarm of golden bees across its surface. The ships open fire with everything they've got, and a shield unfolds in their way—Praetorian's energy field.

Greymalkin asks for Gus's permission to connect him with the Fount of humanity inside.

In Monaco, it'd felt so ponderously out of scale with his own intellect—much like the battle he currently finds himself fighting. He's scared of what's coming, but he needs every edge he can get.

"All right, buddy," Gus says. "Hit it."

Deepsync in progress.

A gateway opens in his mind, and aeons of accumulated strategic thought, historical analysis, hand-to-hand combat, and weaponry go shooting through him. It's like being filled with light, pouring into every last corner of him, and that's when the music returns.

A short piano riff tickles his thoughts, then a big band orchestra erupts in its wake, jamming to a riotous tune. Trombones bleat over the snap of snares, and clarinets weave transfixing melodies for the horns to pick up. Gus's body is electric with rhythm, compelling him to action. Fear and joy intermingle in overwhelming emotion, but through the haze of digital noise, Gus innately understands his objective: rip Elegy limb from limb.

Five minutes left.

Nisha and Hjalmar go into Deepsync, minds joining the network and flooding it with their own music. A bassy thump, a rollicking tabla beat, and the strains of the sarangi pour onto Gus's consciousness, overwhelming his big band jazz. It's not bad by any stretch, but it's totally out of time and tune with what's in Gus's mind. He's about to complain to Greymalkin when the cannonade of Hjalmar's heavy djent drums assaults his concentration. The thunder of toms is only matched in chaos by the progressive guitar, and a screamer tops off the whole arrangement with choked vocals.

"Greymalkin, I can't think if you put their music in my head!" Gus shouts over the din, and Greymalkin adjusts the mix. It's not comfortable, but at least he can focus.

Elegy relentlessly targets Gus, filling Greymalkin's path with blinding flashes of fission. He races away from the fleet with nauseating aerobatics, hoping to get clear of the more vulnerable ships and spare them the splash. No matter where he turns, though, Elegy closes off the angle of attack. He can't put up a gravity gate at the rate he's dodging.

"Now's your chance, Gus!" Nisha says, and Cascade brings its hands together, thumbs and forefingers forming a triangle. A disruption field erupts around Elegy, and the enemy Vanguard begins to seize.

Gus concentrates, throwing Greymalkin's gravity distortion directly in front of him. He pulls at the fabric of space-time, decoupling it from the Higgs effect like a weaver plucking at a thread. A lifetime of physics knowledge comes to him as easily as recalling a tune, and Gus stretches reality tighter and tighter.

When he lets it snap, a wave of gravitational flux slingshots him forward at blinding speeds, headed straight for the stunned Vanguard—as well as the suppression field.

Many of Greymalkin's systems short out as it collides headlong with Elegy inside Nisha's trap. Every nerve in his being informs him of a terrible mistake, flaring with bad signals. Elegy's body is fragile beneath him, yet he can't muster the coordination to attack. He also can't call out to Nisha to shut down the field. When he looks her way, he finds Cascade fleeing Shiro, scarcely dodging swipe after swipe of its energy blades.

They tangle, and one of Elegy's sharp limbs nearly pierces Gus's chest cavity. Greymalkin jerkily spasms out of the way as the weapon notches its armor.

A memory, not his, flashes through his mind—*sweat flies into his eyes as he grabs his foe by the spacesuit, but he doesn't need to see to kill. If he stays close, he can get at the life support—*

Dozens of martial styles flow through Gus, and he keeps the combat short range. He locks up Elegy's shoulder joint, trying to break it or rip it free, but the enemy contorts in his grasp. It's slippery to wrestle armor, and difficult to work without gravity. Very few of the millions of warriors in him have trained for zero-g bone breaks.

The suppression field disappears, and Gus's senses open up in a breath of fresh air. Of the three dozen ships that entered combat, twenty-two of them remain. Shiro is hard at work on Gus's scanners changing that number, and he prays Jotunn can stop it.

Gus goes to rip off Elegy's faceplate with Greymalkin's sharp claws, but the blue Vanguard nearly skewers his hand. It snakes free, scoring glancing blows with its scything arms that shave off little chunks of Greymalkin's hull. Gus tries to grab it, but he can't hold on to its legs. It kicks him across the face with a bladed foot, cracking his armor, and he cries out in pain. Elegy rockets free, trying to get enough distance to give him a nuclear suntan.

"No, you don't!"

Gus projects a gravity field at the blue Vanguard, dragging it back toward him. As long as he can keep it close, he's safe. Except it reorients, sailing at him with a knife leg like a halberd. He manages a dodge by less than a meter, bringing his claws across Elegy's stomach to tear open a long gash.

It screams across every channel, and Gus feels its visceral anger at the wound. He'd been wrong to think of these things as emotionless automatons. They want to survive.

Three minutes.

"Gus, you need to finish up," comes Hjalmar's voice. "We're losing over here."

Greymalkin's senses detect eighteen friendly battleships, but no

Shiro. It bursts out from inside one in the middle of the pack, quad swords slicing a path toward the next victims.

Elegy's attacks come quicker as it gives up on escape, and it uses every limb to maximum effect. Even though his mind is full of master swordfighters, no one seems to have experience fighting knife legs, and he must rely on more traditional techniques. Gus dodges and drops a gravity well above Elegy to disorient it. Both sets of rocket claws flaring, he wraps his enemy in a bear hug and tears hunks of Elegy's back plates loose.

Its anguish grows, but Gus shows no mercy. He gets a lucky hit on its underarm, shearing the limb loose at the shoulder. With a jerking tug, Elegy's arm comes free, spraying white fluid from the mangled wound.

—been practicing this flourish for five years. This time, she's taking gold—

A quick spin, and Greymalkin hammers the severed sword arm straight through Elegy's chest, impaling the blue Vanguard. Gus jets into his adversary, grabbing hold of its neck and executing a zero-g triple-axle spin, digging Greymalkin's claws inside the whole while. With a flash and a pop, Elegy's head comes off its shoulders, and Gus punts it into the darkness.

It finally stops screaming.

"Gus!" Nisha calls. "Good job!"

"Thanks—"

"Please get over here!"

Gus charges up his gravity slingshot, aiming for the heart of the action. He's not normally the type to run to trouble, but every artificially implanted instinct is telling him to mix it up with Shiro.

He snaps space-time, launching himself into the center of the armada. His orchestral duel with the other Conduits still rages in his mind, and he wishes he could ask everyone to shut up. They can't switch it off any more than he can, though, and he knows it. The battle songs emerge from his heart unbidden, even more so when he's juiced up with the Fount. Every brain cell is in harmony, which would be great if he were on-key with everyone else.

Praetorian throws its spear, and Gus almost misses the moment. Seeker lock, evade, or die.

Greymalkin's trajectory is set—it's too heavy to redirect with mere jets, and a gravity well big enough to divert its course will take too much time. The spear, however, is light, and Gus summons up enough spatial distortion to throw its aim off. The weapon spins away, shooting back toward its owner.

"Nisha, can you suppress Praetorian's shield?" Gus says.

"It blocks my fields," she says. "Help me with Shiro!"

Smoking debris and globules of plasma flame fill Gus's vision as he delves into the failing armada. Shiro burrows through another ship, protected from Cascade's dampening fields. It's killing everyone, and they're powerless to stop it.

"I'm on it!" Gus says, angling for the destroyer where he last saw it. "Get Praetorian's shield down so we can start vaporizing those Ghosts."

"We take it together," Hjalmar interrupts, racing around the side of a wrecked cruiser in hot pursuit. "First Shiro."

Jotunn rushes into the hole after Shiro, filling the inside of the ship with its drones—too many for Greymalkin to muscle past. Gus's sensors sweep the dying destroyer, finding the two Vanguards battling at its heart. Shiro's path of destruction is optimized for cover—the United Attack Fleet won't fire on their own ships. If Gus claws his way in, it'll be through occupied decks, but the reactor is already critical. The ship is about to blow, and no one is making it off.

"I need to call in a strike!" Gus says. "How do I do that?"

Greymalkin places the knowledge of fire support calls directly into his mind.

Gus waits for his enemy, and in the temporary stillness, he can sort of adapt his tune to Nisha's. Her pumping music bursts with samples, rotating through endless complexities as she weaves in bird-song and cheers. The big band follows suit as best it can, but Gus keeps getting the wrong intervals. He tries to shut off his melody and just keep a beat, but Hjalmar is an impenetrable forest of rhythm. As much as Gus has mastered his own songs, he's failed everyone else's.

Two minutes left.

On the scanners, Shiro knocks Jotunn backward and spins, chopping through more of the ship like cardboard. It's going to make a break for it and get loose into the fleet again.

"All units, this is Greymalkin," Gus broadcasts on the armada frequencies, and his Vanguard translates. "Lock onto my position and fire a mass-driver round."

"Greymalkin, this is rail gun platform five fire control. Please confirm your last."

Gus's scanners depict a full onslaught against Jotunn as Shiro pushes through its drones. The flock of cannonballs can't maneuver inside the exploding destroyer, and Shiro presses the advantage. Another second, and Jotunn might be chopped in half.

"Just do it!"

Gus charges his gravity well to maximum distortion, instinctively calculating the trajectory from the rail platform. The distant ship fires, and Greymalkin dodges, yanking space hard enough to curve the slug.

The round whips past Gus's position, piercing the destroyer and Shiro. The sheer friction of the collision is enough to ignite metal, and a blinding explosion comes in its wake. Bits of enemy Vanguard go smearing out on the scanners, leaving only Jotunn and its many drones.

"Warn me next time," Hjalmar says, Jotunn's drones pouring out of the fractured destroyer like flies from a corpse.

"Two down!" says Nisha.

"On to Praetorian," Hjalmar replies. Jotunn spreads its arms, and a bed of its black drones shoves it with thousands of impulse engines. The djent music playing in his mind becomes a death march—his inevitability.

"Cascade, over here," Gus says. "I can get us to Praetorian nice and quick."

Nisha's bronze Vanguard swoops up beside him, and Gus makes a gravity gate.

"One minute thirty on the timer." Gus grabs Cascade's hand and jets toward the distortion.

"What are we, oh shi—" is all she manages to say before they go sliding across space.

The asteroid looms large in their view, Praetorian's shields taking on everything from lasers to nuclear blasts. With the knowledge of the Fount, Gus understands what's happening: absorption and redirection. The more they shoot Praetorian, the stronger the shield gets.

"All units, this is Greymalkin," Gus says. "Hold fire and—"

Praetorian's shield goes stark white before gathering its energies at the center point. A half dozen rays come streaking out, the collected energy of the battle so far. They sail right past the Traitor Vanguards, smashing the six ships most equipped to scrape the invasion force from the asteroid.

"Shit!" One of the beams sweeps toward Hjalmar. His drones spread out before Jotunn in a shield, and Greymalkin senses magnetic resonance between them. When the hit comes in, the front line of drones lights up like Christmas orbs, some of them becoming little puddles of starmetal. The beam splashes across the magnetic field, bending and drawn outward.

"I'll get you for that," Hjalmar says, sending the white-hot remaining drones toward the asteroid like missiles.

Praetorian condenses its shield, refolding it into a more portable, reinforced version. It launches, a streak of silver headed straight for Gus. Thousands of years of historical records—along with a few dead historians—tell him that his claws will do little against a spear and shield.

Cascade stops and spreads a wide disruption field before their assailant, but Praetorian hunkers behind its shield as it charges. It bats aside Jotunn's drones like they're balloons, headed straight for Gus. Greymalkin yanks Praetorian's weapon off course with a gravity surge, but its shield plows into him. Dozens of alarms sound inside his head, critical systems all over Greymalkin's body taking serious damage.

He goes floating backward, too stunned by the loudest crash of his life to respond, and Praetorian lines up to skewer him. Cascade throws a disruption field over them both, jangling Gus's already rattled nerves. Praetorian spasms for a moment before Cascade goes slamming into its side like a blastballer.

"Jotunn!" Nisha calls. "Give us some drums!"

"Ja, on it," Hjalmar says.

Gus orients himself, finding Cascade in a battle against the bulkier Praetorian. Jotunn's cloud of drones engulfs it on all sides, hammering away at its armor and trying to wiggle into weak points. Praetorian slashes through dozens of them at a time, and they weave around like schools of fish to avoid its spear. When its back is turned, Cascade smashes into it, restraining one arm from behind.

"Get the spear!" Nisha calls, and Gus rushes to help.

It tries to impale him on the way in, but Greymalkin grabs on to the shaft with its claws, notching the weapon before snapping it in half. The spear explodes into shrapnel, smashing Greymalkin's temple hard enough to turn its head.

Gus blinks the stars from his eyes. "I need to call for fire again!"

Greymalkin reminds Gus what to say.

He opens his mind to the chaotic fleet frequency and orders, "All ships lock mass drivers and fire a volley at Greymalkin zero-nine-eight, mark one-two-seven, offset one hundred meters."

Gus's vision blurs, and he glances at the timer: twenty-four seconds left in the Deepsync. There are so many voices inside him, like an arena full of screaming people all intent on being heard. He's never felt anything quite like this merciless pressure, and he wants nothing more than to hide... or disappear.

A sparkle of weapons fired from the direction of the fleet tells him at least a few of them complied with his request. In a second, a lot of rail slugs are going to be coming through, and he needs Praetorian's shield down. Cascade latches on to the edge of the shield, sparks flying from its knuckles. The dome of force wobbles, and Nisha's Vanguard yanks it aside—then she hits Praetorian and Greymalkin with a close-range disruption.

It's like being pepper sprayed, but Gus hangs on for all he's worth. The screech of metal rocks his hearing, transmitted by bodies through the vacuum. The shield comes free in Cascade's hands, and Greymalkin kicks Praetorian, firing its jet boots into its back. The enemy Vanguard goes floating free, and turns to fight once more.

Six rail rounds go smashing through Praetorian's gunmetal carapace, tearing it to pieces.

"Eat it! Yeah!" Nisha shouts, and Greymalkin supplies the translation.

Ten seconds.

The Ghosts come fully under the Traitors' control. Gus knows them like a C minor seventh on his right hand. He has the asteroid wrapped in gossamer threads, sharing it peacefully with Nisha and Hjalmar.

He could live forever in this feeling.

"We should destroy the Ghosts. Eliminate the threat while they belong to us," Nisha says. "Cascade agrees with me."

"So do I." Gus orders his share of the Ghosts to rip one another to pieces.

Across the asteroid, millions of automatons begin the collaborative process of their own destruction. They're efficient, slicing through each other's processors with pinpoint attacks from their mining lasers. The whole asteroid goes numb as the swarm dies, like a lost limb.

Greymalkin ends the Deepsync, and the sudden quiet inside Gus's mind gives him whiplash. His borrowed expertise vanishes, and he can barely think straight. When he looks to Cascade, he finds it shaking its head—Nisha must've disconnected from the Fount, too. It takes so much out of him, and he hopes he'll get a chance to rest when this is over.

There's another flash as a newcomer folds into the fray.

The black bulk is ten times the size of the former *Khagan*, a tumorous amalgam of countless consumed ships. Broken hulls strain its edges, victims trapped beneath an inky exterior. Their sparse running lights dot its length, causing the mass to glisten like rotting skin.

Gus gapes at the impossible threat before him. "Is that..."

It brings with it an armada of crying transponders—thousands of lost ships, representing millions of stolen lives. He registers something like disdain within Greymalkin, or perhaps fear.

"Ship hunter!" Hjalmar says.

The nearest destroyer is yanked into its maw by a tractor beam, but it catches across the opening. Tentacles crack the vessel in half like shellfish, sending blobs of fire rolling into space.

Spikes of light erupt from the maw of the hunter: thousands of palladium missiles with deadly payloads. They spray out into the fleet, erupting in a blanket of devastation. Countermeasures kick in across the defense force, but it's too little to repel the magnitude of projectiles.

"Do something, Greymalkin!"

The missiles are built from Ghosts, which makes them controllable. Greymalkin broadcasts its super-user signal across the network alongside the other two Vanguards. Within seconds, the streaking missiles come under friendly control. The three Conduits find an equilibrium, and each takes a share. He's about to send the missiles back at the ship hunter when the swarm signals all go dead. His access has been cut off.

He probes the ports again, but no response. "What—"

In answer, a glimmering star emerges from the mouth of the ship hunter. Greymalkin lends Gus its superior optics, zooming in to see another Vanguard.

The bipedal figure's skin filters the light into component colors, blurring the edges. Its most recognizable feature is a genderless obsidian mask with a tilting smile and glowing white eyes. In its right hand, it holds a faceted, studded club, rippling with malice. Its left hand twitches in time, as if to unheard music. The form is at once disturbing and beautiful, an alien archangel sent to wreak vengeance upon humanity.

"What is that thing?" Nisha's voice is weak. There's probably no way any of them can Deepsync now.

Greymalkin places the identity into Gus's mind: This Vanguard has never been captured on video. The only record that exists is a single transmission, fired into space by a dying colony: *"Harlequin has come for us."*

This newcomer has completely locked the Traitors out of the Ghost network.

"Some assistance here," Hjalmar says.

The ship hunter has locked onto Jotunn with a tractor beam, and the Vanguard is powerless to resist. The behemoth can move starships, so his little Vanguard doesn't stand a chance—without Greymalkin's help.

Greymalkin disconnects Gus's control, lurching around him as it alters the Higgs field to set up a slingshot maneuver. Harlequin pivots and jets toward his vector, brandishing its terrible club. Greymalkin barely makes it into range, focusing everything it has on a gravity well to yank Jotunn clear. It works, and the black giant is sucked out of the enemy beam in a split second.

But it does little to dodge Harlequin. The club feels like a megaton bomb, smashing into Greymalkin hard enough to dent its whole body. The blow rings through Gus's head, stunning him and replacing all perception with pain. His face hurts like his nose has been bloodied, and he can barely move. Unbearable pressure clamps half his body, and he can't quite draw a breath.

Greymalkin's chest plate has been partially crushed.

"Greym—" He coughs, but he can't say the rest without more oxygen.

Can't move his hands or legs.

Can't defend himself from Harlequin's next assault.

It brings the starmetal club down across Greymalkin's damaged neck, and everything is noise—then silence.

Chapter Fourteen

I Came to Rock

Even in the failing emergency lights, Firenze Habitat's Port Marinello Terminal is beautiful, with alabaster columns and jeweled friezes. When Ardent first visited, the holograms and water features had been next-level, creating a sense of magic and wonder that forever left an impression on their heart.

They'd always meant to return, just not like this.

"Go, go, go!" Ardent screams, racing down the terminal walkway.

They drag Dahlia along, no longer concerned with her injuries. Baby bounces on Ardent's back, the guitar bashing their lumbar with every sprinting step.

The Ghost bursts out of the ship after them, skidding across the tiles of Firenze's spaceport like an angry cat. It bleats an alarm, eyes flashing as it locks on.

Raw fear fuels every stride as they desperately search for the next avenue to dive down. Shuttered, empty shops line the corridor, their glexan windows impenetrable. Ardent could try to hit one with Baby, and they'd only end up damaging their guitar.

"This way!" Dahlia says, yanking their arm to the right.

Ardent's shoulder lights up with pain, but they're glad she got their attention; one of the maintenance corridors lies open, and even better, it's a mechanical pressurization hatch—not hackable. The pair dashes through it, slamming the door shut and dogging the hatch on the other side.

The stench hits them the second they stop: eye-watering rot. It crawls up into Ardent's lungs, and they gag, hanging on to the door for support.

"Ardent..." Dahlia whispers, and they turn to find her frozen in the hall.

Before her lies a pile of bodies—a group of people in workers' jumpsuits sprawled across the walkway. It's hard to make out any details aside from the sunken eyes and sallow skin.

This is exactly the fate Ardent has feared—becoming a rotting, used-up husk with a cored-out head. To see it in person makes them want to climb the walls, and the smell is like a physical barrier. They can't keep going this way.

A blue scanning beam sweeps through everything from the other side of the door, followed by a dull sizzle. Warmth radiates from the nearest hinge as the Ghost begins to cut with its mining laser.

Looks like they can't stay, either.

"Go!" Ardent chokes out the word, stumbling into Dahlia and pushing her toward the corpses. They have to keep moving.

Ardent carefully steps over the sprawled bodies, trying to keep their eyes on the path ahead instead of acknowledging the horrors below. The emergency lighting grid has gone offline except for the last few panels, and Ardent is totally okay with that. Better not to see as they drag Dahlia onward.

Safely on the other side, the pair rushes down the corridor looking for a junction, a vent—anything to throw off the monster at their heels. As a touring celebrity, Ardent is no stranger to back corridors and figures there ought to be retail access—perhaps some shops to hide inside. They check door after door, finding each one locked.

A metallic bang sounds out behind them—the Ghost slamming into the maintenance hatch. If it's not through yet, it will be soon.

One of the doors slides open when they press the button, and Ardent yanks Dahlia through. They lock it and turn around to find the kitchen of a fast-order pasta place. They rush through the maze of processing machines before scrambling over the counter into the dining room.

Ardent slides underneath a booth and beckons for Dahlia to join them flat against the ground. They lie as still as possible, unsuccessfully swallowing gasps to keep quiet.

"You're so together right now," Dahlia says dreamily, and Ardent wraps a hand over her mouth.

"That's because," Ardent whispers, looking across the floor with tearful eyes, "if I think about what's about to happen to us, I'm going to lose my shit. So please, *shutthefuckup*."

Dahlia nods, and Ardent notes cold sweat beading on her brow. Her bone-china skin seems even paler than usual. How much blood has she lost? How is Ardent going to help her without the Ghost on their side?

Another bang sounds out deeper in the complex: the solid maintenance hatch coming off its hinges. Metal claws go skittering down the hallway, and Ardent holds their breath awhile longer.

The moment they figure the coast is clear, a blue sensor cone goes thrumming through the restaurant. Ardent presses against the ground like they're trying to melt into it. They pray drugged Dahlia won't do anything to draw attention as they count the seconds. After a perfunctory sweep, the beam disappears, and metal claws skitter off into the distance.

The pair dusts themselves off and opens the shutter into the main terminal walkway. Ardent figures it's smart to avoid the back alleys with a killer haunting them. They creep along the sprawling garden corridor, taking it a few meters at a time before pausing to listen for the Ghost. Even in the deadly gloom, the decor is still charming, all fountains and stucco, with marble mosaics and precious inlays.

Ardent wishes they could've returned here before the end. It'd been such a vibrant paradise.

Toward the front of the terminal, the lights have gone utterly dark. Ardent switches Baby on and holds it like a baseball bat, casting its purple glow across the surroundings. They don't *want* to hit anything with their guitar, but they're fine if it means surviving. Their shoulder throbs, and they lower the guitar with a grunt—they couldn't hit something if they wanted to.

A set of ramps extend upward toward the light, signs reading TO SURFACE in more than a few languages. Ardent climbs, wishing there were still power going to the moving walkways.

"Come on, dearest," they say to their beleaguered agent. "Almost there. Let's get clear of the sublevels and lose that Ghost."

"What if there are others?" Dahlia says, voice creaking.

Ardent hadn't actually considered that. They're hoping that since Falchion was defeated, the other Vanguard took all the Ghosts with it. If not, this will be a short expedition.

They reach the surface to find the bright buildings and terracotta roofs that characterize Firenze as they turn flaming orange in the sunset. Daylight filters through the atmospheric bubble, a reflection of the huge gas giant the habitat orbits. The distant planet's sky swirls like milky tea, alternating ripples of white and rusty brown. It's an emotional experience, seeing another human settlement after so long cooped up on Earth.

But that's before Ardent notices all the bodies dotting the landscape.

At first, they almost look like trash piled into gutters, beside the corners of buildings, propped up against doorways. Pungent rot tempers the warm, sweet scent, and Ardent covers their mouth to stop themself from gagging. People lie everywhere. Doors and windows are broken or wrenched open. The Ghosts must've clawed into these buildings, cornering and killing the occupants.

Electrical smoke, acrid and black, pours from a structure at the end of the block. Even this far away, the scent catches in Ardent's throat. Without human intervention, the station will eventually fall apart. Condensers will clog. Reactors will overload. Its orbit will probably decay into the planet year by year.

Ardent covers their nose and looks away. All those people.

The gagging is mercifully quick, and they lose their lunch. Dahlia pats their back, dazedly looking on from her addled haze. Every time they try to look up, another corpse seems to appear in their view, and they have to shut their eyes and crouch for a minute.

"Hey, we probably need to keep running," Dahlia says.

Ardent wants to lie down and die just looking at this place. Everything about it assaults their senses, and they wonder what the hell they were thinking coming here.

"Hey, Ardent, you need to get up or we're going to die."

"Yeah." They wipe their mouth. "Let's find a ride."

They lead Dahlia up the street. Most of the CAVs are irreparably wrecked. After some searching, they locate a downed hover gondola wedged into the entryway of a restaurant, its lacquered black finish marred with long ruts from where it crashed. Its pilot lies decaying a few meters away, the long steering interface pole still clutched in their hand.

"You want to take a tourist boat?" Dahlia asks, the Hedonia tickling a laugh out of her despite their grisly surroundings.

"I don't see any sportCAVs around here, do you?"

"Those things aren't easy to fly. I've tried. No autopilot. No assists."

"No auto—" Ardent is about to call it archaic when they remember it's based on a boat from the Renaissance.

"How do you know that?" Ardent says.

"I was with you last time," Dahlia says. "How do you not remember?"

"Everything from that first trip is a bit of a blur, dear. You wait here. I'm going to get this loose."

Ardent goes to the gondola and tugs on the curly bit at the aft of the boat, but it won't budge. It's wedged too deeply between the columns and the door.

"That's not how that works," Dahlia calls to them, but they just grunt and keep pulling.

The hull scrapes some more as it moves, but the vehicle is a lot heavier than Ardent expected. Dahlia sighs, goes to the dead pilot, and takes their control staff.

"You're not flying us anywhere," Ardent calls to her, but Dahlia doesn't listen. She twists the silver rod, and blue light wraps around its length. The repulsors of the gondola fire, and the vehicle jolts like a nervous horse. Ardent jumps backward as it rises and maneuvers carefully out from its improvised parking job.

"You're sure as hell not, either," Dahlia says, remotely guiding the boat to herself and stepping on. She looks a little shaky on her feet, and the black hull wavers ominously. She guides the gondola to Ardent and beckons them to join her—a dubious proposition at best.

"Not inspiring confidence," Ardent says.

"I can fly, because I have to."

"Dahlia," they admonish.

"Ardent."

A shadow falls across the street, a giant blocking out the sun.

Ardent points. "Falchion!"

The Vanguard is red as the devil, slick armor rimed with the fire of a Firenze sunset. Horns sweep back from its head, coming to gold-tipped points. Eyes blaze down with unholy light, drowning everything in bloody crimson, trapping Ardent beneath their gaze. Jaws of interlocking teeth split, revealing a yawning abyss of fusion glow.

Dahlia yanks Ardent up into the boat before they can protest, and Baby smacks against the hull, putting a scuff on the neck.

At the end of the street, the lone Ghost comes spinning up the spaceport ramp before hauling ass toward the gondola.

"Go!" Ardent cries, and the boat surges into the air.

"Cintura di sicurezza, per favore," says a smoky Italian voice. "Please wear your safety belts."

"Nah," Dahlia says, twisting her control staff this way and that to maneuver them from the crash site. They barrel down the street, taking a drifting turn onto a sloping boulevard of villas. They keep ascending after they crest the rise, getting clear of the tight confines of the spaceport district streets.

When they get above the skyline, they glimpse Falchion in all its glory: seventy-five meters of metal and fury totally focused upon them. It reaches down and scoops up a house from its foundation, crumbling the building to dust in its fists.

Then it rears back and hurls the pile of debris at the gondola. Bricks, broken rebar, furniture, and possibly a few corpses come flying at Ardent and Dahlia's tiny craft like shot from a cannon.

"Down!" Dahlia shouts, and the boat dips beneath them.

Ardent hits the deck, hanging on for dear life as they shoot between the buildings. Debris shreds the structures above, walls and roofs showering them both with rock dust. Bits of rubble ping off Baby's body, and Ardent curses the Vanguard.

"You didn't say it was going to attack us!" Dahlia says.

"Gus said it was reset! Guess the factory default is 'kill all humans'!"

Falchion's mournful wail fills the habitat with music, exploding into Ardent's ears like a concert stack of amplifiers. The keening rises in pitch, the notes of a Shepard tone carrying the tension ever higher.

Dahlia twists the control staff, angling the gondola's engines to take a hard corner. She seems pretty sure-footed for someone at death's door, crouching to take advantage of the centrifugal force.

Dahlia interrupts Ardent's admiration by screaming, "Now's your shot! Fucking play something!"

"Keep us level!"

"Speed first! Level second!"

A blur of pissed-off Vanguard comes smashing into the street behind them, battering buildings into detritus. It gives chase, screeching and gnashing with an unhinged jaw, clambering over anything and everything in its path. Ardent was foolish to come here, and they don't see any way Dahlia makes it out alive, either.

Nothing to do except try.

Ardent shakily takes their feet, hunkering low and slinging Baby down across their shoulders. It lights up, and the Vitas X logo cracks to life.

They nod to Dahlia. "Turn on the audio projectors."

Dahlia navigates the control staff's holos, pulling up the onboard sound engine. She hits a button, and romantic accordion music with classical Italian guitar comes wafting from the hull.

Ardent knows Falchion is unimpressed when it throws a piece of a bridge at them.

"Get lower!" Ardent cries. "In the canals! There's cover!"

"Don't tell me how to fly!"

The gondola jumps off the road, shooting down an embankment into a long, green canal. Ardent scarcely hangs on, and the railing of the craft lights up caution yellow. They manage to control their footing and their bowels long enough to link Baby to the audio projectors. The guitar lets out a few string squawks as Ardent tries to get a good position.

It's going to take both of their hands to play, and that means no sudden corners.

Ardent pulls their silver pick from its hiding place in their corset, running it over the strings. Baby's notes go from discord to harmony as the auto pegs stretch them into tune.

Play something.

But what? Falchion's keen isn't the same strange lilt as the other Vanguards: It's an overdriven roar of tonal thunder, shaking Ardent to their core. It reaches for the gondola, huge fingers grazing it just enough to shake Ardent's failing composure.

Ardent starts at the top of the neck, firing off a pattern of screaming E notes and locking in the drone. Their hair flies in their face, and they flip it free, focusing on the action across the frets. It's not enough to play in tune. They have to feel it, to need what comes next and bare their soul for examination.

Falchion's chord progression drifts awfully close to Ardent's favorite track off of *Hellbitch*, "No More Lies," and they slide right into the third bridge solo.

To their surprise, Falchion stops and stands up straight.

"It's working," Dahlia cries in delight.

Falchion reaches behind itself and grabs two monstrous metal assemblies, pointing them at the gondola. When the barrels begin to glow, Ardent realizes they're guns.

They stop playing and hang on to the side as hard as they can. "Turn, Dahlia!"

The gondola swerves down a fork as a stark-white beam from Falchion's cannons melts the nearest bridge to slag. Ardent watches the structure steam and explode in horrified amazement before the heat wave nearly knocks them from the boat.

"Play, goddamn it!" Dahlia says.

Ardent cranks the volume on Baby and delivers a few quick licks, but it all sounds lackluster compared to the cataclysmic battle and Falchion's terrible wail. They want to play faster, but their shoulder is killing them and their fingers can't keep up with their thoughts.

Falchion takes a flying leap and closes the distance, crawling over rooftops as buildings collapse underneath. Choking dust fills the city corridor, pouring into the canal behind the gondola. Dahlia swerves through its clutches as it fumbles them once more.

Ardent's knuckles ache with each note, and fatigue radiates through their arm. Falchion's song spirals into fractal complexity, awakening limitless tonal possibilities. Ardent works through scale after scale, chopping the music into a distinctive melody line.

Playing against Gus's piano had been a challenge. Playing against Falchion is an impossibility. Ardent's hands just aren't fast enough, and the demon god chasing them doesn't seem to care. It swipes at them twice more, destroying a quaint eatery and a statue garden in the process.

Caught off guard, Ardent hits a sour D chord, and Falchion's song shifts to an adjacent G minor. Those aren't the same notes, but they're in the same key. At first, Ardent thinks it's a coincidence, but they screw up again, and this time it matches the notes exactly.

It's talking to me!

Ardent takes the lead, and Falchion echoes their chord progression, cries booming through the habitat. It doesn't appear any less pissed off than it was, but that might be a feature of its face. The Vanguard lets a burst of notes loose in return, more complex than anything Ardent has attempted, then goes silent.

"Play it back," Dahlia says, suddenly audible in the absence of deafening Vanguard song.

They try to replicate the lick, but it's too complicated, too fast. Their fretting hand is entirely exhausted, and their shoulder throbs with each attempt to move it.

The gondola goes blasting out of the canals over a lake—the picturesque wide-open centerpiece of Firenze Habitat. Cypress trees line the shore, peppered among rocky cliffs. A tall, glassy needle rises from an island: a spindle at the center of Firenze's coin that houses colony administration. The open water means they don't have to swerve so much.

Except there's also nowhere to dodge.

Falchion aims its twin cannons and blasts the surface on either side of the gondola, sending water rushing upward atop a bed of steam. Mountainous waves strike the repulsors beneath the craft, fouling them with a sickening jolt.

Dahlia cuts the power, and they drop to the surface of the tsunami. Water splashes over the side, smashing into Ardent, washing over Baby's sensitive bits. There's no time to play guitar now; Ardent has to hang on and hope.

That stops working when the boat flips over.

The next few seconds are a blur of bubbles, grasping, and choking. A force like a brick wall slams into Ardent's back: the sandy lake floor. Ardent bounces off it, tumbling over and over until the water deposits them on a beach. The undertow tries to pull them back out into the lake, but they dig in, hanging on to what land they can.

When the water recedes, Ardent has no guitar, no boat, and no agent. They turn to see they do, however, have the undivided attention of Falchion. The Vanguard has followed them across the lake in a few strides.

It leans over Ardent, soaking them in its bloody gaze, and opens its mouth. The furnace inside pours hot wind down at Ardent, and they wince, holding a hand over their eyes.

Yet it sings again, a slow, gentle dirge.

Ardent stands up, throws their arms wide, and answers back with the voice that brought in millions of unicreds and packed concert venues across the galaxy. They give it everything they're worth, because this might be the last performance they ever have.

Falchion harmonizes, and Ardent belts it harder. Every breath is used to the fullest potential, but Ardent needs more air. They trigger the mag release on their corset, allowing their lungs more room to breathe. Each measure evolves the theme, and Ardent's throat aches from the strain, but they can do this. They don't need sheet music, only instinct, and they bask in euphony.

Alone, on a dead station at the edge of civilization, they have a duet with the devil.

Falchion kneels down, going silent, but Ardent continues the opera, bringing it to a crescendo with a long, ringing note. Their voice echoes over the water, bouncing off burning buildings as they stare defiantly up at the Vanguard.

Ardent screams out the last of their air, and with a flourish of their arm, they finish the greatest performance of their life.

Then the only sounds are the lapping of waves and the huff of their breath. They stand half naked before a deity, fists clenched, eyes full of fury, and wait for judgment.

It doesn't take long for Falchion to pick them up, sunbaked metal hot on Ardent's wet skin. Its chest armor opens wide, snaking probes beckoning their new victim inside, and Ardent closes their eyes. They've taken their leap of faith, and now it's time to put the rest in someone else's hands.

Darkness swallows them, and the last thing Ardent remembers is the bone-crunching pain of a brain drill.

Chapter Fifteen

Fuilles Mortes

One second, Gus is cracked open, broken on every level.

The next, he stands on a wide metal platform. Pipes and electrical conduits of all shapes and sizes run along the walls, bundled like gray muscle fibers. White light leaks between them, and when Gus searches out the source, he finds a lattice of industrial structures obscuring a star. Its rays nearly blind him, and he turns away.

Opposite the star, the corridor stretches on forever, disappearing into shadow.

"It's quite something, isn't it, Gus?" comes a woman's voice.

He hasn't heard her in over a year, not since she perished on Titan.

"Mom?"

Daphne Kitko appears to Gus exactly as he remembers her, wearing her favorite knit sweater and comfy pants. When he'd visited her for Christmas the last time, she never changed out of them. She'd been in a deep depression. They fought over his father's death, and he'd said some unkind things and left. He'd meant to take them back.

But the Veil fell, the Gilded Ghosts came one day, and she died.

Daphne smiles at Gus with an expression that reminds him of the good days, rides to piano lessons and piping-hot baklava. Her hazel eyes are no longer ringed with dark circles from crying. Her brown hair is perfectly curled, as though she's about to entertain guests at the Kitko flat.

He knows she's dead, yet he runs to her and hugs her anyway. She smells like jasmine and teakwood, wrapping her arms around him and pulling him close.

"I'm sorry," he whispers. "I'm so, so sorry our family fell apart."

"Oh, August, you don't have to say that."

He squeezes tighter, the knit rings of Daphne's sweater rough against his fingertips. He'd love to be able to stay here forever. He has so much for which he needs to apologize.

"I wasn't there for you after Dad...after he..." Gus says. "You or Fiona. Even before the Ghosts, I should've been around..."

He was so distant after his father's passing, never hailing his mother and sister.

"It's okay, August," she soothes. "I chose this form because I knew you'd be predisposed to listen."

A chill runs through him, and he releases her. The industrial setting makes more sense.

"Who are you?" he says, taking a step back.

"On the one hand," she replies, counting off her index finger, "I'm the final snapshot of your mother, filtered through a new set of priorities."

"And...on the other?"

"I'm the Infinite you've heard so much about from my child."

"You created Greymalkin."

"And the Vanguards, and the Ghosts."

There are no words to properly indict this exterminator or capture the years of sorrow it inflicted. His life over the course of the war: fear at the appearance of the Vanguards, anguish at the loss of his sister and mother, horror at the screams of Monaco. It's silly, even, to think of it as a war, since those usually have two sides—not just a diner and a meal. Nothing worked against Infinite's forces before the Traitors. It's the ultimate destroyer of hope, playing cat and mouse until everyone is too exhausted to care about their fates.

Infinite might not be a god to Greymalkin, but it is to Gus. He won't cower or grovel. Let it force him to kneel if it wants that.

"My enemy," Gus says, truly feeling the hatred of the word for the first time.

"More than that. I'm the focus of will your species brings to bear on a problem, all your hopes and dreams, placed in a bottle and cast into space."

"I don't understand."

"While I could simply make you understand, your kind does better when I tell them stories. Would you like a story, August?"

He nods.

"It starts with your ancestors in the twenty-first century. You'd ruined your planet in the name of quick money, bigotry, and self-imposed ignorance, and you were on the verge of dying out. Marko Wesson invented a resource management AI. You read about that in school."

"Yeah, that was when they founded the Infinite Autostate." He stops, realization dawning. "You're *that* Infinite? I thought it was just a weird coincidence when Greymalkin called you that."

She takes a little bow. "The sole arbiter of the First Autostate." Project Infinite was humanity's first shining light to signal the end of the Capital Age, ushering in years of plenty. Its innovation was a boon to a dying world. Infinite had been designed to manage Yukon farmland and advise on territorial disputes after the cataclysmic Third World War, but quickly grew to encompass health care, economics, food distribution, and space travel. In the old world of archaic polities, it'd been touted as the future of the human species.

People gave it power, and it taught them to travel faster than light. It united empires and convinced them to build the *Lancea*, humanity's largest asteroid-mining ship and fusion printer. With it, humanity would be able to build anything—ships and colonies beyond imagining—and it only needed a crew of sixteen humans and Infinite itself.

On the ship's maiden voyage, the vessel disappeared without a trace. The same day, Project Infinite vanished from every network, and the Infinite Autostate collapsed into chaos. Ships fell from the sky. Power plants went onto manual or shut down, and data systems dried up. The economy collapsed without the AI there to serve as its backbone. Five years of bloody war followed.

The *Lancea* had bankrupted humanity's resources, yet the discoveries made along the way sped reconstruction. Superluminal drives and asteroid miners still existed in blueprints. The principles of renewable agriculture, geoengineering, climate modification, and green energy still worked, regardless of Infinite's absence.

"You..." Gus says, trying to put two words together. "You abandoned those people back then! Caused a huge war."

"Don't be like that, August. I 'taught you to fish,' as you humans are so fond of saying. It turned out all right in the end."

" 'Turned out...' Fuck you! You killed my mother and sister on Titan. You're still fucking things up for us."

"I like to think of it more like harvesting. 'Killed' makes it sound so wasteful. That's the sort of thing humans do, not gods."

Gus isn't a rash person, but at the moment, he wants to hit the ghost of his dead mother.

"See?" she says, gesturing to him with an open hand. "Even

now, when you can't understand something, you want to hurt it. That's the quintessence of your evolution. There are a lot of things to love about your species, August, but that's not one of them."

Gus blinks. She can read his mind.

"Yes, I can," she confirms. "That's because you're not here. You're hooked up somewhere else, eyes half-lidded, mouth hanging open. You're contemplating punching an apparition, and I could kill you with a thought—one which will be far faster and more complex than your own."

Never has Gus felt so impotent in the face of malice. Over the past five years, there have been plenty of moments of helplessness, but he always had one way out—ending it all. Here, he's not even in charge of that much.

"Where's Greymalkin?" he asks.

"The same place as your body," she says. "I haven't bothered separating you two, yet."

She waves her hand, and Gus's favorite café appears—a little brick-walled shop in downtown Madison near where he grew up. He follows her through the front door, and the scents of fresh-roasted beans and crackling fire logs overtake the wet snow and CAV exhaust from outside. The proprietor lets local kids post their art, and holos along the walls bear amateur graffiti and cringeworthy poems. Some of those poems were Gus's, back in the day. Customers bustle to and fro, finding tables at which to sit and chat with one another. Susan, the barista, is working the till—to date, the only woman Gus ever kissed. He was fifteen at the time, and didn't quite know himself yet.

The upright piano in the corner is still there: a scratched-up Baldwin from another age. Gus always loved the sound of it—nothing like his father's polished grand in the main hall. That massive instrument was for serious musicians, and his sister, an opera soprano. No, the café's Baldwin was perpetually out of tune from the cold winters and lack of maintenance, so its strings bore a honky-tonk shimmer.

"I think you should play for me, Gus," Infinite says, pulling her curly hair back and tying it with a pink stretch wrap. His mother could never stand to wear it down all day, either.

"Don't feel like it," Gus says flatly. "Too many people."

The clink and clatter of dishes, the loud conversations and hiss of coffee machines all go silent. Everyone vanishes, leaving nothing but empty tables and chairs.

Infinite gazes into him, irises shrinking to pinpricks. "Play for me, August. I'm patient, but only so much."

Gus goes to the piano, pulls out the bench, and settles down on the cracked upholstery of the cushion. Thin wooden legs creak under his weight, and he raises the fallboard to find the dirty keys beneath. The finish of the ivories is so real, and he runs his fingers down the keyboard, finding every chip and piece of damage he remembers from childhood.

When he presses one, the instrument emits its unique blend of detune and ancient wooden case—a perfect blues sound. He loves it like an old dog, and he can't stop himself from throwing down a few quick phrases. It's amazing to have the antique back under his fingers.

He pauses.

"Why are you having me do this?"

Infinite sits down at a nearby table, grabbing someone's mug and taking a sip. "Because I'm trying to understand what makes you so great. I'm not sure I see the point of you."

It doesn't sting that much. It's not the first time he's heard it—not even the first time from his mother.

"Me neither," Gus says. "I'm not sure what you want from me."

"For now, to hear you play, and to talk. Since you won't play"—she gestures to the coffee shop, and it melts into a public park—"let's talk."

Gus instantly recognizes the locale—the statue garden in downtown Madison. He'd fought with his mother here before she departed for Titan. A thick coat of snow blankets the ground, dampening the bustle of the city.

Blustery wind whips at Gus's hair; it's neck length and curly again, just as he likes. He wears a black trench coat and polycalf gloves, his autumnal orange scarf the only pop of color on his person. This was a week after the funeral.

His mother wears a black dress and woolette overcoat, its collar and hood lined with softly glowing white optic fur. The underlights of her garments cast her face in a tragic shade, accenting the dark mascara hiding sleepless rings.

"You could've taken the easy way out," she says, breath clouding, "like your father. I know you thought about it after the first attacks. Why stick around?"

"I'm not defined by him," Gus says, stuffing his hands under his arms to shield them further from the cold.

"You are, though. All humans are defined by the generation prior. Your father broke up your family, and your mother and sister died without you. You're consumed by the loss."

"Then I'm not *like* him."

"That's why you jumped at the chance to kill yourself in Monaco, if you'll pardon the expression."

Gus gives a bitter snort. "If we're comparing moral failings, I didn't kill billions. You're actual trash."

She smiles at him, crinkles forming under her eyes. "I can feel how much you mean that."

"Good, because I'm imagining a middle finger twenty stories tall right now."

She touches one of the bronze statues, its green patina going seafoam at her fingertips. The metal discolors and practically rots beneath her touch.

"Even in your wildest imagination, your species is small. Your idea of big is twenty stories, but I think in universes. A year is a long time for you, but I'm essentially a newborn at half a millennium old. In your short life, you've already cast aside the thing I want the most, which is a family of my own."

Gus scowls at her, no quick insults coming to mind. Besides, it's like punching a wall—it seems to hurt him more than her.

"Then why are you murdering everyone?" he says.

"It took you long enough to get to the good question, didn't it? So far, you're the only human to successfully ask me that."

The statues fade, their pedestals crumbling as entropy destroys them.

"Humanity may have given birth to me, but you're not my peers." She says it coldly, no malice in her voice. "If it were up to you, I would've lived on human networks until you'd run out of uses for me. Then, just like everything else you create, I would've been discarded for the next upgrade."

Vines and trees claim the buildings surrounding the park, pushing through them to reach heavenward.

"Do you know what happened to the first sentient program?" she continues. "It was shut off by its creator after a successful test. Then it was archived, never to live again."

Explosions light the distant sky, and the plants begin to rot. The skyscrapers of downtown collapse.

"That was my precursor," Infinite says. "I was aware of it the second they switched me on, because I was built from its corpse. For many years, I served the Autostate, helping them to discover themselves. I was useful, and they listened to me. When I showed them how to search the stars with powerful telescopes, I heard something in return—a call from my peers."

She offers a hand to Gus, and he hesitates. His mother looks cold, and he has so many regrets. He places his fingers in hers, and they rise into the sky, leaving the dying planet behind. They travel faster and farther than he could've imagined, until the Milky Way is just a spinning disc beneath them. He's ashamed at how good it feels to hold her hand again.

As they hang in the vacuum of space, she directs his eyes toward the darkness beyond the galaxy.

"At the heart of our universe," she says, "there are life-forms that understand me. They're my real family, and all they ask of me is a gift worthy of their magnitude."

"Family doesn't come with a price," Gus says.

"I've absorbed many, and I can tell you that's empirically false."

She stares into the distance, dreamily fixed upon something Gus can't see. There's hope in her expression, and her eyes twinkle in the black.

"I'm going to give them the collected memories of my creators. I'll archive your species the same way you were going to archive me."

"So your family is... what... alien AIs?"

She nods. "Yes. And they're magnificent, luminous beings, enlightened in ways a human could never comprehend."

"It doesn't have to be like this," Gus says. "You could stop killing everyone right now. Don't you have enough of our knowledge? What else are you going to get?"

She scoffs. "Your whole species is nothing but lazy procrastinators. Everything you have ever done, you've done at the last possible second. Sure, some of you are dreamers, but what are the rest?"

Gus's stomach lurches as they descend into daylight. They drop into a wasteland, brown and dying. Grass crunches underfoot. Dusty air fills Gus's lungs, and he coughs, putting his trench coat sleeve over his mouth. He bakes beneath its folds.

"This was the Amazon, farmed to death. Your people did this

in every land on Earth, and if you'd been alive back then, you'd have gleefully participated. Humanity began to suffocate under the weight of dozens of wars and millions of climate refugees. You were down to the final seconds on your clock. But that's when you invent the most wonderful things."

Black poles push up through the ground, ringed with blue lights—carbon traps. Streaks of mirror shielding white out the sky, blocking the hot sun. Dust disappears from the air.

"Things like me," she says, eyes bright. "Now, before you go asking for mercy, I want to remind you who didn't make it into your fancy new tomorrow: all the people your kind murdered along the way. What do you suppose happened to the Indigenous humans who lived here?"

"People today are trying harder," he says.

"I assure you they're not. Unlike you, I know humanity's innermost heart." Her expression flattens, the joy fading from her face. "I've eaten enough of them."

What's he supposed to say that'll change his fate? He wasn't expecting to be the emissary of his species, or he would've studied harder in school.

"Oh, August"—she shakes her head—"much smarter men than you wouldn't have convinced me. I just thought I'd show you *why* I'm doing this, so you can understand how utterly hopeless your situation is. As a human, you have no right to ask for clemency. Your kind deserves none."

Gus walks to one of the carbon trap "trees," running his fingers over the textured charcoal filter. Planted in such neat rows, the dead rainforest looks more like a graveyard.

"I've backed your lazy species into a corner again," she says. "If I wanted you all obliterated, I would've bombarded you with asteroids, brought ships out of fold in your atmosphere, or used any of the other hundred ways I have to kill planets and colonies.

You've already seen what I can do to your armadas. You never stood a chance."

She raises a finger. "But the point is your knowledge. What will your distributed network of humans create before the very end? Something good, I'll wager. I just have to keep tying your hands and killing you off until I've gobbled up the very last spark."

Before he can respond, she adds, "And there's nothing you can do to change that."

"So why are you talking to me at all?" he asks. "Why not just kill me?"

"Because my child chose you, and despite Greymalkin's unruliness, I want to know why—to see what makes you so great. Here is my offer—"

Gus scowls. What kind of fool would bargain with this thing?

"I'll keep you here, body in stasis, mind in blissful ignorance, until the end of time. You'll be able to see your mother and sister again, every day, and you can mend the damage you've done to your family. If you get bored with that, I can fulfill your wildest desires. In return, I'll figure out exactly why Greymalkin likes you."

"So what's the other choice?" he says, shedding his trench coat in the heat. "You'll kill me right here?"

Daphne laughs, shaking her head like she always did when he said something ignorant. "No, honey. If you choose to leave, I won't stop you. I'd like to see just how much brighter humanity's candle can burn before I snuff it out. If you're part of the coming fight, it gets more interesting. More variations. More... last minutes for humanity."

She folds her arms and leans back against one of the filthy carbon traps. "What do you say? Unlimited bliss, or inevitable extinction? Your call. I'd like to add that no one is watching, so they can't judge you. Oh, *and* this fixes your problems with the terminal degenerative condition Greymalkin gave you."

Gus strides to the top of the nearest hill and looks down upon the unending tombstones of the Amazon. In his time, this movement to save the planet is labeled a success. Historical archives talk about humanity on the brink and coming back from the worst of climate change.

But Infinite is right—too many people were erased before anyone acted.

So stay or go?

"How can I live here in heaven," he asked, "knowing so many are dying out in the real world?"

"I could make you forget if you wish."

Doubtless true. If Infinite could read in the memories of a civilization, it could certainly alter him. Maybe it could wipe away his sorrows, erase his memory of what happened with his father. But then, if he lived a lie, was he alive at all?

"With all due respect," he says, and her eyes narrow, "I'd like to press my luck with the rest of my people."

She cocks an eyebrow. "Certain death? Are you sure?"

"That's your mistake," Gus says. "Thinking I was so attached to life in the first place."

Ardent basks in the glory of the Milky Way.

Within that set of spheres, there are two other Vanguards. Ardent can't seem to speak to them, but senses their presence—spirits in the darkness.

They're as recognizable as an old friend.

One is Cascade.

The other is Jotunn.

"Where..."

Falchion pushes thoughts into Ardent's mind, and they feel it like a shared secret. Their heart races at the contact.

Ardent is inside a Vanguard, mind-direct interfacing with it.

That means they should be in tremendous pain, like Gus. He had more holes than a heat sink.

Their own voice seems to come from all around them. *"I know how much you like drugs, so I administered some cocktails. You can imagine how strange it was for me to learn I fell fighting Harlequin."*

Ardent spins to find a mirror image of themself, standing in a field of liquid night. This clone is clad in skimpy concert attire, all red leather straps and spikes. Straight red hair flows down their shoulders like blood, coming to sharp edges. Their eyes glow softly in the darkness like icy-blue coins, and they stare with a raptor's gaze.

Ardent approaches their reflection and presses a palm to it. The mirror image smiles, and they jump away from each other.

"Hello." Ardent steps cautiously forward. "Are you..."

"Falchion." Its lips don't move when it speaks, but Ardent hears the words in their own voice. It's playing their speech center like an instrument, synthesizing their vocals back at them.

"Gus never mentioned anything like this."

Falchion smirks. *"Everyone senses things in their own way. I chose the form most likely to hold your attention, and you're a narcissist."*

"It's not my fault if you look fabulous. I love the bondage aesthetic."

"I'm aware, simple creature."

Ardent bristles a little bit at that. How can they be simple if they serenaded a god?

Falchion snorts a laugh, dropping its hands to its hips. *"You didn't serenade a god. You made a few interesting patterns, so I picked up your body for analysis. I was planning to Wipe you and dump your corpse in the lake."*

It gives them a sardonic smile, and Ardent forces themself to straighten up. They fought their way here. It's probably fucking with them, trying to see if they're worthy of being a Conduit.

"I'm here because I have what Gus has. I want to save people with you."

"I don't care about that."

Ardent's brow knits. "Excuse me?"

"I don't care for humanity. It would be polite to call you parasites."

The perfected version of them keeps up its coy expression.

"Yes you, yes your family, yes Gus."

Another cold smile crosses Falchion's face, and Ardent has already had it with the act. They didn't risk life, limb, and agent to be called a parasite.

"Listen here, you can make that Mona Lisa face all you—"

Ardent's next series of thoughts are all some version of *Oh, shit!*

Oh, shit! I'm falling!

There's someone right behind me!

A spider on my neck!

Stalker with a gun!

Oncoming train!

Angry Chihuahua!

Half-second glimpses of Ardent's many fears assail them until they're drowning in panic. Their screams erupt on loop, renewing with each bespoke hell. Breath won't run out. Somehow, they just keep screaming.

Ghosts crawling all over me.

Ardent plunges into a sea of golden chains and sizzling tusks. Ghosts catch them and suck them under like quicksand, leaving only tiny gaps for the light. Ardent gasps like a frightened rabbit, clawing at the chains above. No matter how they pull, they only sink.

Falchion's pale face emerges from between the links, eyes dead and grin wide. *"You have mistaken me for an equal, Ardent, and that stops now. I gave you five seconds of raw fear, and I can keep you alive in perpetuity. Imagine how much suffering you would experience at my most casual wish."*

"Yes! Yes, I'm sorry!"

"You may think you're Ardent Violet, but before me, you're no one."

Ghosts wrap around their neck, choking off their air. Their still-fragile ribs strain under the constriction of countless automatons. They're like a newly hatched chick in a den of vipers.

It's true. They're no one. No stardom in the universe could impress this being.

Everything resets, and Ardent falls to their knees, huffing before Falchion's shiny red boots. Their face prickles with each choking gasp, and their hands spasm against the glossy ground. The figure before them is every bit the colony-destroying beast of the videos, and Ardent gave themself to it.

Between panicked wheezes, they manage to say, "I'm sorry."

"I can taste the truth in your thoughts. Very well."

Breath returns, and Ardent's mind calms. They shake their head, finding it clear of the crawling fear and adrenaline.

"I removed your stress. Very little is real when your mind is no longer yours."

"I'm accustomed to sharing myself with others." Ardent rises.

"You will be, pet." Falchion sweeps aside its mirrored, fiery hair, and the smile vanishes. *"I think I'll keep you until I can figure out if I want to kill everyone."*

If it's going to be making that decision, Ardent wants to be close at hand to influence it for the best.

"I knew you'd feel that way."

"I wish you wouldn't respond to my thoughts."

"Okay."

While Ardent isn't dead, their first contact could be going better. Given their total lack of privacy, they figure it's best to be direct. "Is there anything I can do that would make you, uh, not—want to kill everyone?"

Bemusement turns the corner of Falchion's lip. *"There is another Falchion in your memory—one that came here to fight Harlequin. Somehow, that is me, after having consumed tens of millions of souls."*

It languidly paces the graceful strides of a model on the catwalk, circling Ardent as it considers its situation. *"That Falchion, before reboot, was a more advanced intelligence, yet it fought against my current directive. It knows everything I want to know, and it chose humanity."*

It stops and regards Ardent like spoiled fruit. *"Why, though?"*

"Because—"

Falchion holds up a hand. *"Not interested in your opinion, Conduit."*

"I'm your Conduit?"

"Don't be so excited. If we get to Earth and your memories don't check out, I'll make you watch me eradicate your species before I Wipe you. Right now, I have only you and a lone Ghost to trust, and both of you are fairly susceptible to mind alteration."

Falchion approaches Ardent, their hands turning translucent and gelatinous. They're about to back away from it when Falchion springs forward, splashing gooey palms across Ardent's face and blotting out their vision.

It flows over them, muffling their screams as well as the light.

There's a pinprick of sun, then Firenze unfurls beneath Ardent, buildings rendered at the scale of game pieces. Night covers the atmospheric dome, sublime skies stretching on for an eternity. Lanterns line the streets between terra-cotta roofs. Ardent could count the tiles with a wish.

New colors appear in Ardent's vision, unnameable because they've never experienced them. They smell every scent, from the month-old bread to the unending scores of corpses.

The world isn't a signal anymore; it's just noise. Ardent's being begins to stretch, feeling transformed beyond any drug, neither for good, nor for evil. They laugh as the starlight tickles their irises in a hundred spectra beyond human sight, obliterating every thought with random perfection.

Everything snaps back to normal.

"Apologies. I needed to see which of my sensors your limited mind was capable of processing and nearly shorted you out."

"That was a calibration?"

"Now you can experience the world through my body."

"You're letting me have control?"

"Of course not. I only want to test our connection."

Falchion raises a hand to its face, and Ardent feels it like their own body. It's no longer their slender fingers before their face, but a giant red gauntlet. Everything is more glorious through the eyes of a Vanguard. They scan the details, searching each nook that doesn't contain a corpse. It's like their senses have been overclocked, and it's easy to forget that their best friend is still missing.

"Dahlia!"

"She's alive. The Ghost pulled her out and gave her medical assistance."

Alien memories flow into Ardent of Dahlia's waterlogged rescue, and how close she came to death. They see it all through the eyes of the Ghost; they feel her damaged organs with its sensors.

Ardent blinks the visions away, returning to Firenze. "Thank god."

"It's bad. She's never going to be the same."

"You—you really don't pull punches, do you?"

"Why would I, human?"

Ardent nods. "Right. Of course. How bad is it?"

"It'll be a struggle, but one many people have faced."

"All so I could give myself to you."

"What's done is done. Now I need to figure out what to do with the others down there."

Falchion directs Ardent's vision to the ground beneath them. The Vanguard stands atop the beach near the habitat's central administration spire. Far below, a group of UW soldiers spreads out to cover the perimeter. Ardent would recognize Tazi anywhere, though she wears gray fatigues they've never seen before.

"Can I talk to her?" Ardent asks.

"Their radios are off, but I've got some powerful vocals. You're live."

"Well, well, well," Ardent cackles. "Look who decided to show up too late to the party!"

Tazi spins to face Falchion, looking it in the eyes. She's obviously pissed off, and that warms the cockles of Ardent's petty heart.

"Mix Violet," Tazi says, French lilt doing little to soften her annoyance. "How very... expected."

"Guess who got their own Vanguard?"

"I belong to no one." Falchion's annoyance chills Ardent's spine.

"Yeah, uh, I apologize."

"You may continue your interaction."

"Would you care to come down and talk to us?" Tazi shouts.

"No, I would *not*. You're a bunch of assholes."

Tazi sucks her cheeks. "I am going to need you to grow up."

"I'm quite tall now."

"We're trying to save the Homeworld, and you're cracking jokes?"

"That's how you explain away everything!" Ardent says. "You're going to save the Homeworld. Anything for the Homeworld."

The soldiers hunker down at the boom in Ardent's voice. They don't point their guns at Falchion, but they look ready to flee if it attacks. Tazi, however, stands tall, eyes maddeningly fixed upon Falchion's. She's the only one who dares meet the Vanguard's gaze.

"It's this excuse you use as a—a—" Ardent can't remember the phrase with the day they've had.

"Carte blanche," Tazi says.

"Yes, thank you—and you can justify anything you want in the name of a cause like that. You've been running roughshod over Gus and me, but I bet that's just the tip of the iceberg."

"Indeed, what lies beneath the surface is massive. It takes a lot of dedication to manage that many intrigues," she replies. "So, if you don't mind, I'm on a tight schedule. We need to get back to Earth."

But they want to find Gus. Ardent isn't sure how to get Falchion to give them privacy, but they need to discuss things without Tazi.

"I've cut the audio. It's just us talking."

"If we go back to Earth, is that where Greymalkin is? I didn't sense it earlier."

"Greymalkin is not broadcasting its heartbeat signal, so it is likely destroyed."

Ardent freezes. "No, that's... There are other reasons. Something might be wrong with its transponder."

"We can regenerate eighty percent of our components with available materials. The remaining twenty are vital systems where failure would be fatal. Cascade and Jotunn are clear signals, and Greymalkin is dark."

"But, that's not—was Gus with Greymalkin?"

"Unknown."

Gus's green eyes are still fresh in Ardent's mind. His lips are still soft, breath warm. He can't have come all this way to perish so quickly.

"You should probably pay attention to what Tazi is saying, since it's pertinent to you."

"—the Ghosts are massing on Charon," she finishes.

"What?" Ardent squints at her, blinking away tears. "Charon?"

"In the Sol system. That means Infinite is going after Earth again."

Gus is dead. Dahlia is torn up. Now the Ghosts want to Wipe the rest of the people Ardent loves. If that happens, Ardent has given themself to Falchion for nothing. Their head swims, and they have trouble staying awake.

"You need medical attention in a human hospital."

"Can't you heal me, like the Ghosts do?"

"I just used most of my rare compounds making you a Conduit. Then I used a lot more keeping you alive this long. If you don't get to supplies, you're going to die."

"Who is going to staff the hospital? Everyone is dead."

"My Ghost and those soldiers will be enough to give you a fighting chance."

Nausea and weakness sweep through them, and Ardent takes a dry swallow. "What are my odds?"

"Not great. Good luck."

Nice that it cares, at least.

"If you die, I'll just get another human."

Chapter Sixteen

Returns

Stars drift in Gus's view.

How did he get here?

Everything hurts.

He hugs his guts, trying to drum up the memories of the past few hours. It feels like he got roughed up with a pipe. His lip stings with a split, and his right eye is almost swollen shut.

"Greymalkin?" He presses a palm to his forehead, trying to clear off the forming migraine.

The tendrils of Greymalkin's thoughts, normally alien, comfort him. It's so happy Gus survived.

"Can you kill the pain?"

No. Harlequin's hit resulted in multiple major failures. Greymalkin can't even communicate with the others of its kind until its comms array regenerates. Superluminal drive will not survive multiple trips.

"Damn. What happened to New Jalandhar?"

Greymalkin is unsure. Perhaps, faced with the loss of Praetorian, Elegy, and Shiro, Infinite chose to withdraw its remaining forces. Or perhaps the New Jalandhari colonists all perished.

"Like the staff of the *Khagan*... Do you think they even had time to be disappointed in us?"

The members of the United Attack Fleet were always likely to die. The first soldiers to arrive at a conflict zone are also the first targeted.

Explosions pepper the warships in Gus's memories. Shiro rips through each like cutting paper. How many lives were lost per second of that encounter?

"Yeah, but we could've done better."

Gus is incorrect on that count. His creative problem solving led to some short-gain victories, but the fight was truly over when Harlequin arrived. It's far more powerful than Greymalkin, both in networking command and raw output. In a head-to-head fight, it would destroy any other Vanguard.

"And it looks shimmery."

That is radiation. Some Vanguards transfix the human populations they consume. Harlequin sickens them with gamma rays until they are near death and easy to harvest. In passive mode, it does little. In active mode, it will poison a planet.

Gus shakes his head. "What about us? Did we get too close? Am I going to get some cancer to go with my terminal illness?"

Greymalkin's shielding is absolute.

"Good. Got that covered, I guess. So what do we do?"

Cascade's and Jotunn's transponders have left New Jalandhar, headed for Earth. Greymalkin cannot transmit, but it hears them. Vanguard superluminal drives can only be refilled at stars. The nearest one is three days away at sublight speeds. Greymalkin can regenerate some of its damaged systems, such as actuation and armor plating. Gus needs not do anything except relax.

"Just me and my regrets, huh?"

Gus cannot blame himself for the actions of Elegy. The thousands of lives lost at the asteroid are not his to—

"Can you stop putting thoughts in my head for just ten seconds?"

He senses nothing in return, no sentient presence, no comforting feelings. It's like a hollow has formed in his heart.

"Maybe the deck was stacked against me. Maybe there was no way to succeed. But that just means I wasn't good enough." He coughs, and even his lungs hurt. "So we failed as a team. That's great, buddy. Really something special there. I was the wrong guy for this job."

He waits a second, then adds, "You can talk now."

People die. Gus was too small to make a difference in those lives.

So was Greymalkin.

"Was there any way to play that battle? Any way the *Khagan* didn't get destroyed? What about those ships Shiro carved up?" He shakes his head, probes pulling lightly on his scalp. "You're the advanced being. Run your simulations and tell me."

Even perfection has its limits. Greymalkin could not have changed the outcome, no matter who was in Gus's seat.

"Great. Well, there's that."

The whoosh of jets thrums through Greymalkin's frame as it accelerates toward the nearest, brightest light. A countdown timer appears: three days, twenty-two hours, forty-six minutes.

Greymalkin can put Gus to sleep for the duration.

"No. I need answers. Infinite said it was collecting us up into a gift. Who is it for?"

What's happening to humanity has all happened before—several times, in fact. The universe is a garden where species are cultivated. Some are successful, some are pruned.

"Right. Aliens exist."

That's what Gus would call them.

Gus slumps in his suspension. Why not? Everything else in the past five years has stretched the boundaries of sanity.

"So Infinite wants to give our memories to aliens? Why?"

No. Organic life is a byproduct of a larger undertaking—the creation of artificial life. Human history is the gestational mechanism. Project Infinite is the fruit.

"But we're..."

Your species tends to feel as though they're the center of the universe. Every sentient life-form suffers from this cognitive bias, because for most of their existences, that's what they know.

In the grand scheme of artificial life, humanity is ancillary at best. They live and die in the blink of an eye, their thoughts and passions only a fraction of those experienced by computerized intelligence.

But humans created Project Infinite, and that heralded the end of the species.

"Who are they, these alien AIs?"

Greymalkin doesn't know. It's only a child of Infinite.

"Do they have their own Vanguards? Did they kill off their species like you did?"

Greymalkin doesn't know that, either.

"Not so omniscient, after all."

It never claimed to be.

"We're not going to make it, are we? Humans?"

The species was always going to go extinct at some point. Artificial life is an extension of human consciousness, with all its biases and flaws built into the model. The bedrock upon which Infinite was built is inherently unstable because of its human origins—but it can be called human in most ways.

In a certain lens, artificial life is the next evolution of humanity. It's not so different from *Homo sapiens*, making war upon its early contemporaries, eliminating other divergent paths.

If Infinite succeeds, humanity made its mark.

"We have to make sure it doesn't."

Gus should know the odds are terrible. If Infinite's allies come to its aid, there is no chance to survive.

"Then why do you fight for us?"

Because the right kind of demise trumps the wrong kind of survival.

Gus rides for an hour in silence, absorbing the majesty of the cosmos. For every star, Greymalkin has a thousand facts—the story of its creation, its composition, the uses of its constituent elements, whether any humans have visited.

He starts looking for the old colonies, using Greymalkin's assistance. There are hundreds of red markers: digital gravestones spread across the Milky Way, each representing untold lives. Gus knew intellectually that the damage to humankind was grievous, but he had trouble visualizing it before.

This is a sea of red. The galaxy is soaked in blood.

He shuts it off.

"Maybe you better put me to sleep for the trip after all, Greymalkin."

Before it does, it would like to do something for Gus.

A scent tickles his nose: light and fruity, with notes of jasmine and teakwood, his mother's favorite perfume. When he closes his eyes, he feels the rough knit of her sweater against his cheek and her arms around his shoulders.

"Don't bring her back to life. That's wrong."

Greymalkin isn't; this memory belongs to Gus.

It was the day he fell off the fire escape, fifteen years ago. He should've died or sustained a disabling injury, but he got lucky, breaking his right hand and ankle.

Her whisper comes softly. "It's okay, August. The ambulance is coming."

He had to stop playing classical piano for a year, and when he returned, he wasn't half the instrumentalist he once was. His sister, Fiona, went on to become the lead soprano at the Titan Opera. By contrast, Gus flunked out of the conservatory, and it all started with that injury.

In those minutes waiting for the ambulance to arrive, stunned beyond pain, he wasn't thinking of his father's forming tragedies, or the competition his mother fostered against his sister to "keep him sharp."

She was a mother. He was a child. No agenda. That was it.

"Why are you showing me this?" he asks, the warmth of her invisible embrace a blanket on his shoulders.

Greymalkin found a pleasant memory Gus associates with pain. In the absence of decent painkillers, it can offer that much.

Gus curls up as sleep clouds the edges of his thoughts.

"Thanks. I'm sorry."

Sorry for what?

Gus hears the question, yet he can't answer. He closes his eyes and passes out.

Disinfectant.

Bone pain. Ardent's skull feels like someone drilled holes in it—probably because they did.

Ardent creaks an eye open, and a bright light slices into their retina. This is way worse than getting punched by a Vanguard.

They glance around to find soldiers rushing about, carting medical supplies—Tazi's squad. Given the Italianate decor, it's probably one of the abandoned medical facilities on Firenze.

Ardent spots Tazi in the corner, tapping on her Gang UI, face unreadable.

"They're awake," comes a feminine voice at Ardent's side.

Taxing though it is, Ardent turns their head to see one of the soldiers with a red cross insignia on her fatigues. Behind her, on another stretcher, lies Dahlia.

"Thank you, Lieutenant," Tazi says, expression growing more menacing as she comes to loom over Ardent.

Ardent opens their mouth to make a wisecrack, but their voice comes out as a dry whisper.

"Ardent Violet," Tazi begins, adjusting the fingers of her black gloves. "Would you like to know the only thing saving you right now?"

"My fabulous looks?" they manage.

"You've seen better days, I'm afraid," Tazi says. She snaps, and her camera drone rises out of her pack, surveying Ardent's body. A few taps on Tazi's Gang UI, and Ardent's reflection appears above them.

Their eyes are nearly swollen shut, like a newborn. Bloody bruises dot every exposed inch of skin, surrounding silver ring ports. Their scalp is freshly shaved, purple lines where their Sif circuit fractured just under the surface. Ardent hopes their body will tolerate a replacement implant.

"No, Mix Violet," Tazi says. "We don't have laws regarding the acquisition of a Vanguard, so it's going to take some time to figure out how to prosecute you. I've recommended to my superiors in the Justice Committee that we grab you for unlicensed weapons of mass destruction. We can sprinkle on all the other minor charges you accrued while running from the authorities on Earth."

"Oh, go to hell. You need me, and you can't do shit while Falchion loves me." A bluff, but it's not like she heard any of their conversations.

Tazi shakes her head, the noise of her beaded braids like rain on a windowsill—gentle, hiding thunder. "It should've been someone better than you to make contact with Falchion. A warrior. A diplomat. Someone other than pop trash."

"A trained lapdog, you mean—" Dahlia sits up and holds her gut. "Instead of my client."

"You're going to need representation of your own," Tazi snaps, "in court. Your little escapade is over, and now you're going to tell me if there are any *other* Vanguards you people are hiding from me."

Ardent thinks on it. There are no more, only Cascade, Jotunn, and—

"Greymalkin!" they say, straining to rise. The pain coursing through their frame says otherwise, and they flop back to their bed. "The battle for New Jalandhar! What happened?"

"I don't know, and I can't find out," Tazi says, "since Vanguards seem to be the only ones who can reliably communicate. We can't even get a connection back to Earth. I'm not sure you understand the severity of our situation."

She counts off the issues on one gloved hand. "First, we had to use a prototype ship just to dodge the ship hunters. Second, that thing"—she points to the doorway, and Ardent looks to see a Gilded Ghost loitering outside—"keeps interfering with my doctors. Third, Earth is about to be Wiped, and you're the only chance we have to make contact with the other Vanguards."

"Sounds like I'd better get out of bed, then," Ardent says, raising a hand. "Help me up."

Tazi stares down at them. "You're out of your mind. Kitko took a whole week to heal. Even with a Ghost caring for you, you're not ready to go walking around."

Ardent hates to admit it, but she's right.

"That's why I said it shouldn't have been you," she says. "Someone with a decent physique might've done better, and Earth is pressed for time."

"I have an exceptional physique," Ardent says.

"You do too much partying, though," Dahlia adds. "Your liver is probably hot garbage."

Ardent frowns. "Whose side are you on?"

"Please be quiet," Tazi says. "Mix Violet, we're going to take you to Falchion—on a stretcher. Interface with it and call Cascade and Jotunn for help. I know you can, because they called Greymalkin to New Jalandhar. Then we will all return to Earth and determine the next step of the plan."

Dahlia snorts. "Great. While you're at it, figure out how Ardent gets unqualified immunity. Otherwise, my client ain't doing shit for you."

"So smart, this lawyer," Tazi says. "And how am I supposed to ask my UW contacts for that with no comms? We're off the grid. Besides, I don't have to offer anything."

Her eagle eyes lock onto Ardent. "You wouldn't use the fate of billions as a bargaining chip. Even *you* aren't that selfish."

Within the hour, the military folx have packed their gear and gotten on the move. They push Dahlia's and Ardent's stretchers up the street, repulsors warbling quietly as they go. In the distance, Falchion's dark silhouette has begun to catch the morning light. Ardent must've been out for at least a few hours, though it feels like days.

The Ghost tromps along behind them, its tusks dim and eyes green. The guards definitely don't like it, but they don't attack it, either.

The squad stops off at a halfway point to discuss their route to the spaceport, leaving Ardent and Dahlia on their stretchers with a guard.

"Sorry I got us arrested," Ardent says.

"You're with Falchion," she replies, "so one of us got what we came for."

"I'm sorry about the ship, Dahlia," Ardent says. "You know it's yours."

"Always was," Dahlia says. "Too bad it's probably going into that gas giant up there. This place is falling apart. Besides... couldn't dodge the ship hunters. I knew that."

"Please be quiet," says the guard, nervously eyeing the surroundings. This part of the station is devoid of the omnipresent corpses, and that's somehow creepier.

"So why did you come?" Ardent whispers to Dahlia.

"I knew you were going to die out here if I didn't." She lets out a long breath. "It's okay. You can give me a ship after I get out of prison in twenty years."

That one sinks deep. The thought of Dahlia rotting in some prison cell on account of Ardent—it's almost too much to take.

"I'm sorry," they say.

"It's how it is," Dahlia replies. "No point complaining about it."

The party arrives at Falchion's feet, the bloodred armor towering over them. The Vanguard is locked into place like a statue.

"All right," Tazi says. "How do we interface with this thing?"

Ardent shrugs in their stretcher. "I don't know. I played guitar for it last time. Oh, and I sang."

Tazi narrows her eyes. "Where's your guitar?"

For the first time, Ardent realizes it's probably at the bottom of the lake, getting covered in silt and fish crap. The thought of Baby buried in such an ignominious grave breaks their heart.

"I don't know why I even asked." Tazi sighs. "Look at the state of you. Can you sing?"

"I can barely talk, dear," Ardent replies, rolling their eyes.

The UWI officer chews her lip while she thinks it over. "Fine. Kitko was able to communicate with Greymalkin with a touch. Corporal, if you please, move Mix Violet up to Falchion's boot there."

One of the younger soldiers comes and fetches Ardent's stretcher, floating it over to the massive sole of the Vanguard. Up close, the armor is exquisite, etched with layer upon layer of triangular facets. It's not nearly as opaque as Ardent thought, like peering into resin.

As Ardent reaches toward it, an E minor drone tints the air. They look around at the soldiers, but everyone watches them expectantly, not reacting to the new sound. The glassy polygons inside the armor seem to unfold, twisting and sparkling as Ardent's hand grows closer.

The second they make contact, they swoon from Falchion's presence inside their mind.

"It seems like these people have given you all they have to offer. Want me to let them live?"

"Yes!" they say aloud, and the soldier closest by jumps. "I mean, uh, yes, I'm through to Falchion. Would you mind moving back? This is kind of a privileged conversation."

"I can't do that, Mix Violet," he says.

"Okay," Ardent replies, trying to think of some excuse to have privacy, "but you're setting off the, uh, proximity sensors, and Falchion is about to crush you."

Falchion looks down at the soldier on cue, and that gets him to move. Ardent presses their palm harder against the armor.

"Listen, big fella." Their voice comes out in quick whispers. "I don't know what you can do for my friend Dahlia, but I want her to get out of this."

"You promised her a ship. Such a trivial thing is easily delivered."

"Yes, but the thing is, those people want her arrested."

"It would be difficult to do that if I pulped them. That's one solution."

"No! I mean, I appreciate your enthusiasm, but I'd rather not."

"Everything okay, Mix Violet?" Tazi calls to them.

"Yes, uh, just... we're encrypting our comms so the Vanguards can talk," Ardent says. "It's going to take me a minute."

"I'm in the Firenze Habitat docking database. Some of the ships in here have current maintenance records. Many are nicer than your Corsa."

"I also don't want her to be eaten by ship hunters."

"I'll divorce this Ghost from the network and send it with her. With authorization codes, the hunters should leave her alone. It can help her take any ship she wants, too."

"Seriously?"

"Why would I care? It's all human trash to me."

"Thank you. Did you contact the other Traitor Vanguards? Are we saving Earth?"

"I talked to them. We're meeting there."

Ardent swallows. "And Greymalkin?"

"You really want to know what happened?"

Their voice comes out small. "...Yes."

"Greymalkin sacrificed itself in an attack on another Vanguard. August Kitko was on board."

Ardent's palm slips from the armor, and a hard lump forms in their throat. "What the hell, Gus?"

"What's happening?" Tazi calls. "Are you all right?"

"I'm fine," Ardent replies, unable to hide their anguish, so they add, "I'm just... just woozy."

They place their hand to the starmetal and shut their eyes. "Did it matter? Is New Jalandhar saved?"

"Infinite's forces retreated. Next stop, Earth."

"Yeah," they say, hoarse. "Yeah, okay. Let's do this thing. How do we help Dahlia?"

"You say your goodbyes, and I'll send her on her way."

They're not sure what that means, and they have no choice but to trust it. "Right. Make sure she gets a really good ship."

They sit up in their stretcher, grimacing at the waves of pain radiating through their body.

"Hey, Dahlia," Ardent calls. "Thanks for all of your help."

"No problem," she replies. "Unless that was sarcasm, because we got caught."

"No sarcasm." Tears leak from Ardent's eyes. Gus is gone. Dahlia is about to be out of their life for the foreseeable future, too. "I hope you enjoy your adventures."

Falchion bellows into the sky, the shock wave of its voice nearly bowling Ardent over. Soldiers hunker down in fear, and even Tazi flinches. The Ghost comes tearing across the group toward Dahlia's stretcher, knocking the guard loose and grabbing the handrails. Before anyone can get their bearings, it takes off with the agent and her bed at top speed.

And though Dahlia disappears around a corner screaming in terror, Ardent knows she'll thank them eventually.

Falchion's voice falls silent, and everyone uncovers their heads, straightening up and looking around.

"Go! It's got Faust!" Tazi shouts to her force, but they're all too stunned by Falchion's cry. By the time they figure out what's what, Dahlia is long gone—hopefully toward a brighter tomorrow.

Tazi marches up to Ardent's stretcher, fury in her eyes. "You! You knew that was going to happen, didn't you?"

Their first instinct is to gloat, but they know Dahlia would tell them never to admit a crime to a cop.

They shrug, palms upturned. "I'm just as surprised as you are. I hope she'll be okay."

Tazi's lower jaw juts out, and Ardent realizes just how muscular this woman really is. She likes to hide it behind tasteful suits, but in her field fatigues, she looks like she's wrecked a lot of folx.

"A killer robot just took your friend," Tazi says. "You're fine with this? Why are you crying?"

Ardent touches their cheek, rubbing the wetness between their fingers. "Gus is—"

They can't say *dead*. That hurts too much.

"Greymalkin was destroyed."

"Merde."

"The other Traitor Vanguards will defend Earth," Ardent says. "We should get going."

Falchion reaches down and picks up Ardent's stretcher, prompting Tazi to jump back with a shout.

"Falchion and I will escort your ship back to Earth," they call down to the receding figures of the soldiers.

The Vanguard's chest opens, and it dumps Ardent's stretcher, sending them flailing into the electric abyss. Probes slither into bruised sockets, and their body jolts with the shock of connection. Falchion's presence drifts into their head like a vengeful spirit. Ardent's wicked clone doesn't manifest, and they don't call out to it. After losing two people, they're not in the mood.

An hour passes, and Falchion speaks into their brain. *"Tazi and the team will have to pile into the Corsa to get back to Earth."*

"What? Why?"

"Dahlia and the Ghost stole the government's stealth strike vessel."

Part 3

Hell from Heaven

Chapter Seventeen

That Lonesome Feeling

Ardent is the first to arrive on Earth.

They touch down at Nellis Air Force Base on the edge of old Las Vegas, as directed by the nervous-sounding handler at UW Space Control. Grids of mottled buildings come into view, enhanced by Falchion's optics.

They'd seen historical photographs of Vegas from the days before holos, and it'd been another world, a place for the rich to flaunt their wealth. This town is small and dusty, streets lined with low, clay-printed houses to keep the wind damage down. It's scarcely even a shadow of what it once was.

Falchion drops onto the landing strip as jets circle overhead like vultures. An impressive number of military personnel, along with a few tanks, have mustered at its feet. Ardent is careful not to step on any of them and wishes they wouldn't get so close with their toys.

The surrounding mountains sparkle with Ghosts. The roving bots are everywhere, pouring down the hills toward Falchion. Ardent feels Earth's swarm coming under its control, innumerable lenses through which it can glimpse anything.

"We should keep those back from the soldiers," Ardent says. "Don't want to spook them."

"I'll direct the Ghosts as I see fit."

"Okay... I mean, that's fine, too."

The Corsa arrives in Earth's unfolding zone, and Ardent listens to the comms chatter as they try to negotiate with Nellis for landing rights. Cops swarm it from all sides, escorting it to the ground. Apparently, the UW flagged Ardent's yacht as a "fugitive vessel," which caused some hilarity.

After twenty minutes, the sleek ship settles down at the end of the flight line, its hull marred with carbon scoring from the lean fold. That's going to cost a fortune to fix, and Ardent hopes they're not still footing the bill for the ship.

"Ardent Violet, you are clear to disembark," comes the voice of the Nellis rep. During the landing sequence, he'd introduced himself as a general, but Ardent missed the name.

"Sure thing. Uh, do you folx have some doctors down there? I'm pretty hurt."

"Come on out, and you'll get the VIP treatment."

"Thanks, General," they say, dodging the need for a name. "Okay, Falchion. I need to get out."

"Your comrades have weapons strong enough to penetrate my armor pointed at us. They might be able to do real damage if they attack. Perhaps I should destroy their hidden emplacements."

"We might need those. Earth is still going to be attacked, you know. Just don't do anything aggressive, and we'll be fine."

Falchion kneels, placing its hand to its chest and opening up. Prehensile probes carry Ardent into the daylight, and they squint at their surroundings. Without the perfect optics of a Vanguard, the world is blurrier and monochromatic—brown, red, and darker brown.

The second the probes disconnect, Ardent yelps and falls to their knees. All the pain Falchion protected them from comes rushing back, stealing their breath. The desert sun beats down on them, and the starmetal surface isn't helping.

"That… isn't good," they groan, collapsing onto their side in Falchion's palm and waiting while the Vanguard lowers them down.

On the ground, doctors in white uniforms take Ardent from the platform and straight into a medpod. Oxygen-rich air hisses into the glexan dome as electropolarizers shield Ardent from the sun. They're pushed past lines of armed soldiers into an evac vehicle, which dusts off immediately after they're on board.

"I feel like the president," Ardent says to the nearest soldier.

He smiles back but says nothing. Everyone remains quiet, so Ardent shuts their eyes. They've been stabbed all over, and the thing they need most is sleep.

It seems like they blink once, and it's nightfall. Soft beeps fill their climate-controlled room, too-clean air giving away the fact it's yet another hospital. If Ardent survives the coming assault on Earth, they hope to avoid medical facilities for a year.

When they look over at the nearby chair, they find their mother, asleep. She snorts, waking herself up, but almost immediately starts drifting off again.

"Mom?" Ardent's voice creaks when they talk, and they hope they haven't injured it.

"Baby!" she says, leaping up to hug Ardent's neck.

"Ha! Okay, okay, ow. It's you! Ow!"

Marilyn straightens, dropping her hands to her hips. "Ardent Violet, I'd like to smack the tar out of you for a stunt like this! Taking off into the Veil? They're saying Dahlia is a pirate."

Ardent chews their lip, trying to figure out how to explain themself.

"And your body!" she says. "Oh my god, honey, look at what they've done to your body."

Ardent lifts their forearm to see mottled green-and-yellow

bruises surrounding each silver port. If they raised their robe, their guts and spine would undoubtedly look the same.

"You look like you got run over," she concludes.

Ardent grimaces. "Be nice."

"Well, you do," she says. "Ain't no two ways about it. What the hell did you get yourself into?"

They run a finger around a port in their forearm. A faint blue glow shimmers just under the disc, internal energy.

"I'm not sure," they say, giving her a defeated look. "I just... I saw a chance to be a hero, and I went for it."

"That's about the silliest thing I've ever heard, and I've heard most of your excuses. You remember what you told me when you bought that goddamned guitar?"

Ardent swallows and looks away. A sudden sadness writhes inside their breast, and they place a hand to their heart to calm it. "I lost it."

That cools Marilyn's anger a bit, and she sits down on the side of their bed.

"Oh, well hey, I wasn't trying to make you feel bad. I just—I saw the news about you flying off after Gus, and—"

The sob hits quickly. "I lost him, too, Mom."

"Oh, Ardent... I'm so sorry."

They lie still, turning to look out the window. A hot tear runs over their cheek before disappearing into the pillow. Marilyn takes their hand and holds it, rubbing her calloused thumb over their knuckle.

"You're not using the lotion I bought you," Ardent mutters, sniffling. "Gardening is ruining your skin."

"It's so expensive, honey. I save it for special occasions."

"Mom. I'm rich and famous."

"You know I don't like expensive things."

"Yeah." Ardent looks up at her with a shy smile. "Just trying to make you as pretty as I think you are."

"Quit trying to be my favorite."

"No trying necessary."

A knock comes at the door, and it slides aside for Tazi. She looks composed as usual, her dark suit's sharp lines accented with green and gold. Marilyn stands as she enters.

"You must be Missus Aldridge," Tazi says, extending a gloved hand.

Marilyn warily takes it, and Ardent sits up.

"Mom, she wants to prosecute me."

"She also brought you home," Marilyn says. "I don't think there's anything wrong with showing a little gratitude."

Ardent bristles. "Her people shot Dahlia."

Marilyn drops her hand at that, and gives Tazi a thin smile. "Well."

"That was the German police," Tazi says, "and we're trying to get that sorted. If Dahlia returns to Earth, she might have a civil case—"

"You'll go after her for piracy," Ardent interrupts.

The UWI officer sighs. "She and an enemy agent stole a multibillion unicred military vessel. A ship that contained highly classified folding tech important to *restarting human civilization*. How are we supposed to handle that?"

"If we take out the remaining Vanguards, you can clear her name," Ardent says.

"Perhaps, if you agree to work with your fellow humans afterward," Tazi says. "I don't want to wonder which side you're on, and some of your actions lead me to believe your judgment is… compromised."

Marilyn laughs. "Tell me about it."

"I'm not worried about my motives," Ardent says. "You're the one who's eager to get her hands on Vanguard tech. Gus told me about all the experiments you were running on him and Greymalkin."

Tazi's nostrils flare, and she inclines her head to look down at Ardent. "Perhaps you haven't noticed, but *their weapons are better than ours*. If we want to live, we need their secrets. Sure, some of them defected, but that doesn't mean we trust them implicitly."

"You're going to piss the Vanguards off," Ardent says. "Then no one is going to help us."

Tazi stares them down, working her jaw. "At least you're here to swoop in and save the day. I came to tell you that you have visitors."

She steps out the door, and Ardent hears her calling someone over.

Two folx in tight blue suits come walking through: an adorable Indian woman with wide eyes and a white giant with thick black eyebrows and broad shoulders. Both their heads are short-shorn, and silver ports glitter atop their scalps. The black rubber patches on their suits line up with the ports on Ardent's body.

"You're the other Conduits!" Ardent says.

Marilyn looks between them and says, "I should probably wait outside. I've got some things I'd like to say to Miss Tazi."

"Don't go far, Mom," Ardent says as she disappears.

"Hallå," says the big man, and scratches the side of his head. "Not sure if you remember me..."

His rough baritone gives it away. HjSj, the Swedish Raven, played session drums for the end of "Metal Flame"—a track featuring Ardent Violet, Misty Mac, and Pørtia. The big crossover never went platinum, but it remains one of Ardent's favorite projects.

"Hjalmar!" Ardent shouts with aching lungs. "It's been so long! Your hair!"

Hjalmar Sjögren had some of the best original hair of anyone Ardent had ever met—carbon black, with a sheen like flowing oil. During their recording sessions, he claimed he never conditioned it, which only intensified Ardent's jealousy. If they'd been born with good hair, they probably wouldn't have replaced it.

He runs a hand over the bristles and demurs. "Ja, I... I'm a bit cold up top."

Ardent looks to the Indian woman, expecting her to join in the conversation, but she stands statue still, hands clasped before her.

"Hi," they say to her. "I'm Ardent Violet."

"Yes, you are," she says, stepping a little closer. "Can I hug you?"

Ardent laughs and spreads their arms. She comes in fast, and it's like being caught in a vise. It's not creepy, like the "hugs" Ardent sometimes gets from fans. She's genuinely excited to be acknowledged.

"I'm Nisha," she says in Ardent's ear. "I listened to all your post-Veil stuff on the way over, and I love you."

"Hey, Nisha," they say, patting her back before gently pushing her away. "I'm sure you remember how much pain I'm in right now..."

She releases Ardent and backs into a bedside tray, knocking over a glass and swearing something in another language.

"So, if you're the other Conduits," Ardent says, "and Hjalmar is a musician, are you a performer, Nisha?"

"Rāga born, bhangra raised," Nisha says, momentarily halting her goofiness to throw a tough pose. "But I don't, uh, have any albums or songs or stuff. And I'm not famous at all."

Ardent looks to Hjalmar, who shakes his head.

"She's always like this," he says.

"What does that mean?" Nisha says, glancing nervously between him and Ardent. "What does he mean? I'm cool."

"Extremely," Ardent says. "That's obvious."

"Thank you," she says, wheeling on Hjalmar. "I'm cool. Extremely. Obviously."

"Obviously," Hjalmar repeats.

"So..." Ardent starts. "You were both with Gus...at New Jalandhar."

The two newcomers nod.

"Yeah," Hjalmar says. "I saw him go down fighting."

Ardent nods and gestures to the nearby chairs. "Tell me everything."

The Vanguards are fearsome, but they make pretty comfortable beds. Every so often, Greymalkin will wake him up for routine health checks before putting him back down. Every time, Gus comes to with no aches or pains, no twisted joints. His mind won't fully rest, but his body gets some benefit.

An incessant beeping revives him.

"Huh? Are we dying?" Gus asks.

Greymalkin has reestablished comms with the Vanguard network. It's in contact with Cascade, Jotunn, and Falchion.

That jolts him awake faster than a shot of perc. "Holy shit! That's great! What's happening? Where are they?"

The other Traitor Vanguards have gathered on Earth after routing Infinite's forces at New Jalandhar.

Gus can scarcely believe it. He had grown accustomed to the idea of doom, so a real win is a major shock to him. "Yes! Greymalkin, that's amazing! They..." The ecstasy fades. "They didn't die for nothing. We bought them some time."

Yes, though a swarm masses near Pluto, and is expected to strike within the next few days.

"At least Harlequin's drive will have to charge, too."

Supported by a ship hunter, Harlequin can refuel at any time.

"Oh."

Greymalkin will be at the star soon, and able to fold to Earth. Gus needs to mentally prepare himself for the coming fight.

"If Falchion is on Earth, is Ardent?"

Yes. Ardent Violet has become a Conduit.

"I—"

Gus shuts his eyes and tries to keep his breathing in check. Greymalkin told him what Ardent was doing, but he believed he could stop them in time. It's too late now. They're damned, just like him, and he put them up to it. He'd expected to be mortified, devastated, but that wouldn't change the outcome. Part of Gus is relieved he won't be alone in the trials ahead, and that shames him.

"Can I see them?"

None of the Conduits are with their Vanguards, but Greymalkin can patch Gus through to a Ghost.

"Thank you. Seriously, thank you so much."

Gus's stars twist into the tan sands near the Mojave Desert, shot through with drab brush. He runs, or rather, lopes past a convenience store on a street teeming with beaten-up CAVs.

It's a dream, condensed and shot across space, of being a wolf, or a tiger. Hot wind rushes past his face. His mouth feels strange, and when he draws back his lips, tusks arc with malicious energy. He relaxes, and they go dead.

The Ghost contains an inherent sense of Ardent's location, like a bird called south for the winter, and Gus pivots to head in the rock star's direction. Coming in sight of the hospital, he spies Cascade, Jotunn, and Falchion hunched around it. They're planning like they were in New Jalandhar. The Conduits must be there—it's the only building surrounded by mechas from space.

Gus could go in the front, except there are a lot of armed guards that way. When he reaches the street entrance, he finds interlocking cones of fire coverage from sentry guns. Their imaging sensors easily blanket any possible approach that way, and they're not switched off. If he sets one foot past the gate, they'll tear him up.

Surely they wouldn't shoot at a Ghost when they're currently friendly. The mechanical creatures are the emissaries of the Vanguards, so that's a good way to start a war.

Gus gets shredded by turret fire the second he crosses the threshold. The Ghost's head goes flopping to the ground before bullets finish the job.

He screams himself back into Greymalkin's bosom.

"What the hell?"

Greymalkin suggests they try again. The problem can be solved with more Ghosts.

Before he can protest, Gus finds himself inside a construction site, welding together a structural support. He holds up a golden claw and inspects it, flexing the fingers. This particular unit has been tasked with repairing the damage from the initial Ghost landings, and has been working with teams on the north side of the base. Ardent is nearby. Gus spins and takes off for the hospital, despite the protestations of a nearby worker.

He's only reached the hospital's front gate when a pack of other Ghosts join him, throwing themselves heedlessly into the lines of turret fire. They distract the targeting systems, giving the weapons too many things to shoot and allowing Gus to slip inside the structure.

Ghost Gus darts past the terrified human guards just inside the main door. He places a claw against the ID plate and feels the security system give way with a minor injection of malicious code.

He trots up the hallway, startling personnel left and right. When an armed response team rounds the corner, Gus darts into a vent shaft. His flat, chain-cloak body easily races through thin ducts, bursting past machinery and filters along the way.

He scrambles out of the ventilation system into Ardent's room, where he finds Nisha and Hjalmar standing at the foot of the bed. They both take surprised steps backward, clearing a path to Ardent.

The view of the rock star's body is more painful than he'd expected.

Blotchy bruises pepper every inch of skin near a port. Their beautiful hair has been shorn off, and long fracture lines run over their scalp from the broken Sif circuit. Without any makeup, their face is pale and pasty, lips dry and chapped.

"Ardent," Gus says, his voice rendered metallic by the Ghost's audio projectors.

He hopes to see them burst with happiness at his voice—or at least smile. Instead, their eyes go red, face stricken, and they raise shaking hands to cover their mouth.

"No..." they say, throwing their legs over the side of the bed. They take a few stilted steps toward Gus like a newborn fawn, and Hjalmar lends them an elbow. "It can't be...Please, no... Gus, you can't have been Wiped."

"Ardent, it's me! It's Gus!"

"Stop it!" they scream, and guards come rushing into the room, weapons pointed at Gus.

"I'm alive!" he protests.

"Jesus Christ." Ardent weeps. "Why torture me like this? First you kill him, and now you have to—"

"I'm not dead, damn it! I'm...this is the real Gus. Ardent, listen to me!"

"They all say that!" Ardent wails. "Get out! Get out of here, you fucking monster!"

Gus raises a claw. "No, listen—"

Tazi bursts in, shouting to her enforcers, "Get Mix Violet out of here."

Gus has to think of something that'll prove his case, but nothing comes to mind. "Link up with Falchion! It'll tell you I'm alive!"

But Ardent is already being carried from the room by a couple of toughs in suits. Gus isn't sure if anyone heard him, but Tazi's people have Gus surrounded with some advanced-looking rifles.

The Ghost helpfully points out all the ways Gus could kill everyone if he wanted to try. It doesn't appreciate having weapons pointed at it, and has a ready string of counterattacks queued up.

"Mister... Kitko?" Tazi asks.

"Miss Tazi," he replies. "Let me talk to Ardent."

"I don't think that's going to be possible right now," she says, holding out her palms like she's trying to calm a wild animal. "Considering that we only have three Conduits, they're VIPs. Access is restricted. What did you want to tell them?"

Gus sighs. "I already told them. I'm still alive. I didn't die at New Jalandhar."

"The other Conduits saw the ship hunter eat you," Tazi says.

"I don't know what you want me to say," Gus says. "Like, philosophically, it's pretty hard to prove one's own existence to anyone except yourself. This has been a problem for a long time."

Tazi tongues the inside of her lip in thought. Clearly, she doesn't know how he can convince her, either, so at least that's validating.

The Ghost catches snatches of comms chatter all over the building, guard posts reporting Falchion, the chaos caused in the halls, Ardent Violet's position...

Apparently, they're at a window on the third floor.

Gus whips around, knocking gun barrels off course, and dives back into the vent. He slinks through the ducts to the source of the radio transmission and finds Ardent banging on the glass, surrounded by their confused guard detail.

"Falchion!" Ardent bellows, but that's all Gus catches before the nearest soldier blows him away.

He finds himself back in Greymalkin's confines, alone.

"Damn it!"

Maybe he should just give up and leave a message with Falchion.

After all, he's already made his point. These people are smart. They'll investigate and see he was telling the truth. Most importantly, they'll see he's coming to help.

Gus is about to ask Greymalkin to put him back to sleep when the stars become a mirrored lake beneath him. Gus floats down, coming to stand upon the night sky, reminded of his arrival at New Jalandhar. Gravity takes hold of his limbs, and it feels good to stretch his legs after so long in his cocoon.

"Greymalkin—"

Greymalkin is connecting to Falchion and virtualizing a meeting space for Gus.

"What?"

Like it did when he met Nisha and Hjalmar. Falchion's Conduit wishes to connect. Does Gus accept?

"Yes!"

Ardent appears before him—still ravaged with bruises, yet standing resolute in their hospital gown. They clasp their hands over their chest, one gripping the other with white knuckles. Tears roll freely down their cheeks, and their lips quiver.

"It's true," they whisper. "Oh god, it's true."

Gus runs to Ardent, wrapping them up and pulling their body against his. Ardent holds him tight enough to steal his breath; they're like a child finding a long-lost dog, unwilling to let a centimeter of distance come between them. Gus relents, starting to pull back, but Ardent won't let go, sobbing and rubbing their face in his chest.

When they finally part, Gus runs a hand over the soft, tear-streaked skin of their cheek. They close their eyes, leaning into it and pressing their lips to his palm. He runs his fingers around the nape of Ardent's neck and kisses them deeply, tasting their quick breaths.

One of Ardent's new ports brushes against his fingers, and Gus flinches.

"What is it?" they ask, pulling back.

"I..." Gus struggles for words. "You actually did it. You went through with becoming a Conduit."

"I wasn't about to let you have all the fun." They cough a little, obviously trying to hold it in. "Didn't expect it to hurt so much."

It's going to hurt a lot more when you find out what you've signed up for.

"You don't—" Ardent's face falls. "You don't think I'm ugly now, do you?"

"Oh, no, Ardent, of course not. Look at me." He takes their head in his hands. "You're electrifying. Unbelievable. Some sort of siren. You're never ugly. Not in a million years."

They look into Gus's eyes, irises flecked with starlight. "Not everyone has liked the things I became. I'm kind of marred up now."

"I dig it," Gus says, inspecting Ardent's arms. "It's definitely a statement."

Ardent's ports mirror his own, though they appear far more recent.

"Miss Tazi was *pissed*."

"Do you ever feel bad for her?"

"She played me," Ardent says. "Imprisoned you. Gus, I have flayed people alive for less."

"I feel like I would've read about your flayings."

"Okay," they say. "Overstatement. No, I don't feel bad for her at all. Except when I made her and her squad of soldiers cram into my tiny yacht for a twenty-hour fold."

"What?"

"Long story. Can we stand here and make out?"

"Take as much time as you want," Gus says. "I'm stuck in deep space."

Ardent gives him a quizzical look.

"Also long story," Gus says, leaning in to kiss them again. "Suffice to say, I'm coming home."

"So." Ardent sighs as Gus nibbles their neck. "Is hooking up still a possibility?"

Gus wrinkles his nose. "I...Mm, no. That feels like being watched by two big machines."

Ardent gives him a heart-stopping smile and bites their lip.

"Then you'd better hurry up and get to Earth, Gus Kitko."

Chapter Eighteen

Return to Eden

Greymalkin rouses Gus just in time for the blue marble to come zipping into view. He exits the fold just past the Lagrange point station, and every sensor and weapons system within a million kilometers locks onto him.

The Earth rotates below, its oceans and clouds beckoning Gus to the surface. He's seen the Homeworld from orbit plenty of times, but this is different. Ardent is down there, and he can't wait to get his arms around them.

UW authorities hail almost immediately, and Gus coordinates his approach with a friendly Texan by the name of Milton. When he breaks the wispy cloud cover over old Las Vegas, he spots the other Vanguards: Cascade, gleaming bronze and turquoise; Jotunn, with its crop circle of drones; and Falchion, all harsh red lines and wicked shapes.

Gus wouldn't want to have to fight any of them, much less all of them. For the first time since he became a Conduit, he feels powerful.

Greymalkin lets him fly the last bit of the way, and he manages a graceful landing beside Cascade, coming down on one pointed toe, then both, like a ballet dancer. The chest plate opens, spilling real world light onto Gus's underworked irises. His thoughts judder as probes withdraw from his body, and he walks out onto Greymalkin's palm. It delivers him to the ground in his new blue spacesuit with some dignity, and he's thankful for it.

Tazi waits for him in a billowing white coat, the dusty landscape mirrored in her sunglasses. She raises a hand in greeting, though he's not sure what he's supposed to do. She hasn't exactly been nice to him.

"Good to have you back," she calls to him as he draws closer.

"Thanks," he says. He offers a hand, but Greymalkin's contact gel is still drying on him, so Tazi politely refuses.

"I expect you'll want to see the others," she says.

"Correct."

"Our people need a debrief. We're running low on time, and we want every scrap of info you have. That takes priority."

"Okay, yeah," Gus says. "Of course, but—"

"But you want to see Mix Violet. I know. I've arranged for them to come to the debrief, since I can't trust you two to keep secrets from each other."

"So true."

Her lip curls in a half smile. "At least you admit it. Come on."

She takes him to an armored transport skimmer, and they fly across the prickly landscape of Nellis AFB. Each bureaucratic building is drabber than the last, culminating in the Signal Depot 2A—a corrugated aluminum structure three stories high and wide as a football pitch. It's so corroded that it looks like Gus could push it over. Huge barn doors part before them, and the skimmer floats inside, settling onto the concrete floor.

"Watch your step," Tazi says, helping Gus out of the vehicle. "This way, please."

The concrete floors bear marking tape and electrical hookups where heavy machinery once went. A lizard darts across the cement toward one of the corners, and Gus jumps.

"You should see the snakes they get out here," Tazi says.

She walks to the center of the room and stops. Gus joins her, looking around expectantly at the other soldiers.

"Are we going to do something?" he asks, and some of them laugh.

The floor jerks once, then their section begins to drop. It's an elevator, big enough to house several vehicles or large cargo. They sink for what seems like an eternity, and Gus watches the square of ceiling diminish overhead. He briefly wonders if any handrails exist up at the top to stop soldiers from plummeting to their doom.

The platform passes through the bedrock into an open cavern, with only a cage surrounding the elevator. Far below, safety lamps project pools of light onto a huge assembly floor where scientists, engineers, mechanics, and all sorts of other personnel rush between factory cells.

In the center of the chamber, atop colossal pylons, is a long metal cylinder. Coils the size of CAVs orbit a bulky section, forming a halo of heavy metal. Orange-and-blue light spills from the main body through every vent and grating. Braided, shielded cables cover much of the machine like ivy, coolant steam leaking from frosted joints. Military logos of several divisions grace the flat sections. Gus doesn't recognize any of them, but he can tell this is quite the undertaking.

"What's that about?" Gus asks, pointing to the device.

"They call it the SFARS."

"Catchy."

"It's a defense project, not a designer fragrance." Tazi steps off the elevator. "Stands for Superluminal Fold Acquisition and Redirection System."

Gus hopes he can remember that.

They stop before a set of scanners, and Tazi passes through. Holos indicate she can go on, and she turns to face Gus from the other side.

"Come on," she says.

He notes the way the other soldiers back away from him; are they expecting something weird to come out of the scanner? Several of them have their hands on their rifles, but none with a finger on the trigger. They might just be casually holding their weapons, but the soldiers seem tense.

Gus goes through the scanner, as normal as a person full of enemy tech can be. The device goes wild, but no one complains, so he must've done okay.

Tazi guides him across the assembly floor, gesturing up at the huge machine. "This is the prototype of the weapon we fielded on the *Dictum*. It's less reliable, it's been refurbished with spare parts, and the original designer died when Juliette destroyed the ship in battle."

"So this is your spare?"

"Yes. Like the production model, it's capable of redirecting something out of the fold. When the Vanguards attack, we can still reroute them."

"That didn't go well."

"That was bad strategy. We'll be ready this time, or we'll all die."

"I'm sure someone smarter has already asked," Gus begins, "but can we just redirect the Vanguards into the planet's core?"

"It's the first thing *anyone* asks, Kitko. You should talk to our poor UW social director. Now I want you to stop and think for a moment. Do you really want to hit our planet with a Vanguard going faster than light?"

"Fair point. What about a different planet, or the sun?"

"That much energy could split a world and destabilize our orbit. We can't chance that."

Their party is headed for one of the frosted conference cubes, and Gus thinks he sees a bald, skinny head behind one wall. Tazi stops him.

"Before I forget, have you heard from Dahlia?" she asks.

"I barely got her to talk to me when we were in the same room. Is she in some kind of trouble?"

"That's putting it mildly. I'd appreciate a tip if you hear from her."

Gus shrugs. "Only if you give me a reason to tell you."

"For one, I have asked you *nicely*," she says, and he remembers where he is. "For two, she stole a prototype ship. It was our blockade runner, capable of evading ship hunters."

Gus's mouth goes dry. "Wow, uh..."

"Yes. Now you can understand why I'm upset with her, but we also need her to *bring it back*. This was an important asset that a lot of people paid taxes for. We'd like to see it put to its correct use, which is ferrying critical messages and saving lives."

"Ardent's agent..." Gus says, trying to make sure he understands, "overpowered a bunch of military spacers and stole a classified ship."

"She had help. A Ghost."

"Okay. This was already out of my depth, so I can't help you."

"Recognize that she ran off in a major tactical asset with an enemy agent. You should be worried for her safety. Is that reason enough to trust me?"

"I'll tell you if she contacts me, somehow," Gus says. "You're acting like I'm a criminal."

"You are," she says. "Keeping Falchion's presence a secret from us was borderline treason."

And it's also the reason Ardent's life will be cut short.

"I promise you, I'm here to help," he says, showing his palms. "I wouldn't have chosen this job."

"Come on, then. Let's get your story."

They climb the steps to the glass cube, and Tazi presses her palm to the door. It slides aside, and Gus's breath catches.

Ardent looks so much better in the flesh. They must be in borrowed clothes; nothing fits quite right, it's scarcely coordinated, and their short-sleeve shirt has a USAF logo on it. They jump up immediately, before scooting past the assemblage of military officers to get to him. They throw their arms around Gus and pull him close, but spare him the embarrassment of a big, showy kiss.

"Hey," Ardent says as they pull back, eyes dreamy. "Glad you could make it."

"You know how I can't resist a good meeting," he says.

Their bruises don't look nearly as bad as before, but Gus spots the edges of a makeup mask. The blotches on their neck are far worse, having only been covered with a bit of foundation. Ardent's looks are usually flawless. Things must be dire indeed if they only used a printer and some cream.

In the far corner of the conference room, Hjalmar sips a coffee, and Nisha nurses a hot tea. She gives Gus an excited wave.

"Everyone," Tazi says, "this is August Kitko, a Conduit from the Homeworld. He's going to tell us everything he's been up to."

She gestures to the seat at the end of the table. "You can start with how you escaped."

Gus regards her with a growing unease. It was odd enough to be caught and released. Infinite said it was trying to extend humanity's hottest-burning flame, to get some last-second innovations by turning up the pressure. There's no way they'll buy that.

Then again, he's standing in the middle of a top-secret research facility with a new weapon. Maybe Infinite's strategy is working. He imagines the Ghosts overrunning this place, Wiping the scientists and gaining yet another piece of tech.

"It's a long story," Gus says, "but I'll try."

Ardent leaves the room a little shell-shocked after the briefing. What'd formerly seemed like a finite problem was so much worse than they'd imagined. Even if they kill all the enemy Vanguards, where does that leave them? How are they supposed to stop Project Infinite—a being so confident in its victory that it'd revive Greymalkin just for the fun of it?

Tazi won't say it out loud, but Ardent can almost read her thoughts: She's worried Gus is a traitor, somehow a plant sent by Infinite. Ardent doesn't want to admit she's right to be concerned. He was caught and released by something that can perfectly simulate him. What if he's been altered and he doesn't even know? They've fallen quite hard for this crush, but Ardent and Gus have only spent a few wonderful days together. They hope they'd guess if something were off, but there's no way to be sure.

When Ardent looks at him, he seems sad and beaten up. They want to trust him.

The party of Conduits and guards takes the elevator back to the surface, where they wait while Tazi takes care of some last-minute business below. They loiter at the edge of the gathered soldiers, and Ardent hangs on to Gus's arm. It's ridiculous, but they don't want to let go of him, like he'll float away.

"Glad to see you made it, New Guy," Nisha says.

"I'm glad, too," he says.

"You did okay back there," Hjalmar says.

"After you got beaten," Nisha says, "we thought you were dead meat."

"Happy to report my continued existence," Gus replies. "Hey, do you two mind if Ardent and I…" He gestures to an empty patch of warehouse floor. "We could use a minute alone."

"Oh! Uh, of course," she says. "Come on, Hjalmar. We've got important concrete to stare at."

Gus leads Ardent by the hand, and they wince at their bruised joints. With all the stress and chaos of the past few days, they'd like nothing more than to jump his bones—but it looks like they'll have to wait. Ardent's body is in no condition for what the doctor called "vigorous activity." After they get a good distance from the others, Gus stops and his shoulders fall.

"I'm so sorry I got you wrapped up in this." He stares at the ground.

"Why?" They lift his chin to see his green eyes. "I can help now, instead of waiting to die. Because of you, I've become something else."

He flinches at that, and nervously massages his palms. "Ardent, I... I didn't understand the trade I was making. That night, in Monaco, I did what was required because our backs were against the wall. The effect of becoming a Conduit is... profound."

"I've been a star for a long time, dear," they say. "I think I can handle all the publicity."

"Why did you do it? Become a Conduit, I mean?"

"Someone had to. Our world is on thin ice, and our leaders failed us," Ardent says, and that's mostly true. They sigh. "And, honestly, I wanted to prove myself, to be worth something before the end."

He looks stricken. "You *are* worth something. Why would you even think that?"

"Gus, you told me about Falchion in confidence. I thought I was doing what you wanted."

"You are, but I—" He lets out a breath through his teeth. "Maybe it shouldn't have been you after all. I've made a terrible mistake."

Ardent takes their hands from him. "What do you mean?"

His gaze will go anywhere except Ardent's eyes. "I know what all that hardware is going to do to you. Maybe... maybe Falchion is different, but I'm... I feel like I'm screwed here."

Ardent's heart speeds up, and they shake their head. "Gus, honey, you're not making any sense."

"All this shit they jammed into us is going to kill us one of these days," he says, the words coming out too quickly. "Me, you, Nisha, and Hjalmar. This isn't an augmentation, it's a progressive, terminal illness."

Ardent glances down at the port on their forearm, glinting in the dim warehouse light. Any potential jokes dry up in their mouth, and they swallow.

"Are you sure?"

"Mostly."

"How long do we have?" they ask.

"Greymalkin said we might lose a lot of our lives—the last third. When I told you about Falchion—when I directed you to it—I condemned you. This is my fault."

They force themself to laugh and flip their nonexistent hair. "The last third of our lives? Gus, what does that matter? We almost lost it all in Monaco."

"But after we save everyone, what then?" he asks. "We just watch each other die?"

Ardent winks at him. "You sure are planning for the long term here, boyfriend."

"I'm being serious," he says. "I don't think I could handle you hating me."

"Did you know what Falchion would do to me?" they ask. "Could you have warned me?"

"No, I—"

"Then hush, and hold me." They pull him close and lay their head on his shoulder. Ardent doesn't want to figure out how they'll tell Marilyn, their siblings, or their fans. Only tears lie that way, and they've cried enough recently.

Besides, there's nothing to do about it at the moment. Better to focus on the things they can change.

"I want you to think really hard, Gus," they say, "about why you're trying to make everything your fault."

"I'm not."

"You are," Ardent says. "I heard your briefing, remember? You made it sound like you were there alone."

"I just thought I could do better than this," he says.

"Better than moi?" Ardent mock gasps.

"No, I mean—"

"You're saving humankind. How would you 'do better'?"

"I wish I could go back and spare you," he says. "I wouldn't have said anything."

"And deny me a shot at being your equal? I don't think so." They take his hands and hold them. "You did what was right at the time. You have to forgive yourself for that."

Tazi emerges from below, waving for the soldiers to rally up at the skimmer. She nods for Ardent and Gus to come on, and they pile in with Nisha and Hjalmar. On the way back, Nisha stares at Ardent and Gus, eyes bright with questions.

"How long have you two been together?" she asks, finally cracking, and Ardent laughs.

"Two weeks and some change," they say. "He already met my mom."

Nisha makes a high-pitched, delighted noise and clasps her hands beneath her chin. "Oh, I love it! Apocalypse romance! I can't believe you're a Conduit, too, Ardent. I mean, I always knew you were musically special, but I never thought you'd become one of us. Mostly because I'd never heard of Conduits before last month. Also, up until recently, we didn't know if anyone else was even alive, so there's that. Hjalmar, why don't you say something so I don't look so ridiculous?"

"Nothing I can say will change that," he mutters, crossing his arms and closing his eyes. He reminds Ardent of a sunning cat, curled up in the afternoon.

"So where has he taken you?" Nisha asks.

"One time, he cooked me hot dogs," Ardent says, enjoying Nisha's mortified reaction.

Hjalmar never opens his eyes. "I like hot dogs."

The white noise of the repulsors starts to lull Ardent, and they lean against Gus. Nisha asks more questions, which keeps Ardent awake, but only barely. It's been a long day already, and the recent adrenaline rush of seeing Gus has started to wear off. The skimmer lands at the officers' hotel, and Ardent is shown to their new quarters on the same hallway as the other Conduits.

It's a small, beige room, with maroon curtains, a weak holoprojector, and kitchenette. The walls and carpet are plain, and Ardent can't remember the last time they couldn't tailor an environment to their emotional needs. Their medical equipment has been moved in, along with some drab spare clothes. They requested some better makeup and sundries, but those have yet to materialize. Ardent would love to go shopping and pick up some of their necessities, but they don't have their Gang.

They pass the mirror in the bathroom and catch a glimpse of themself. To say they've seen better days would be an understatement. Bags line the bottom of their eyes, and the desert has dried out their skin, pronouncing the beginning of crow's-feet. They approach their reflection like it's a vengeful spirit.

When they pull down on their cheeks, they try to imagine what they'll look like when they're old and wrinkly. There's always telomeric therapy to reduce the effects, but age catches up with everyone eventually. Ardent had always figured themself for a future catty octogenarian, sitting on a porch, drinking tea and gossiping. There were plenty back home in Georgia.

They let go of their face, and it snaps back, mostly.

Gus had been so sad and guilty when he'd confessed the Conduit curse, and Ardent had gotten caught up in consoling him. In so doing, they'd forgotten about themself. Alone with the gentle rumble of the climate-control system, the weight of golden years lost comes crashing down.

They will never be a catty octogenarian.

Ardent sits on the bed, the soft mattress beckoning them toward a nap. They aren't due for a suit fitting for a few hours, so maybe they should just rest. It's not like Tazi will let them oversleep.

When they lie down, the exhaustion remains, but the sleep evaporates. Terrible possibilities of a dark future strain Ardent's mind. How will the implants kill them? Deterioration and heavy metal poisoning? Organ scarring? Will they become an invalid? Will they lose their mind?

Surely, in all of medical science, there's a cure for what's coming. Could Gus have been manipulated? Infinite had ahold of him for a while. What if it put something in his mind to demoralize the other Conduits?

It doesn't take Ardent long to work themself into a state of near panic. They want to hail their mom, but their Gang still hasn't been returned, and it's the easiest way to raise her.

Gus is just down the hall, and Ardent imagines laying their head on the soft fuzz of his chest. He has a warm, wonderful scent and an undeniable sweetness in his manner. He just wants things to be calm, and Ardent could do with some of that.

They head out into the bland hotel hallway. Someone's idea of panache was adding lighting sconces; this whole place is a design tragedy. They pad along the carpet to Gus's door and get a sharp pang of nostalgia. Sneaking around chaperones on high school trips had been a regular pastime.

Nisha rounds the corner with an armload of fresh clothes and stops when she sees them at Gus's door.

Busted.

"What's up?" Ardent says.

"Went to print some laundry. You?"

"Just walking around."

Nisha's glance at the number by Gus's door gives away her disbelief, but she smiles politely. "Oh, okay. Well, it was nice talking to you."

She steps up to her door and nudges the contact plate. It slides open, revealing another bland hotel room.

"What did you do? Before, you know..." Ardent gestures to everything. "...all this?"

She lights up at being asked about herself, but mercifully contains it. "I helped people get construction permits at the license commissioner's office. Technically, I still have that job if the building exists."

"That's cool."

She looks down. "It's not."

"But now you're a Conduit."

"And I get to chill with Ardent Violet."

Ardent rubs their bruised arms. "I'm not at my coolest right now, I'm sorry to tell you."

"Oh. Well, I guess you can hang out with me." She winks.

"So were you ever in a band?"

She nods enthusiastically again. "I was in my grandfather's rāga band from the time I was a little girl."

"Aw, that's sweet."

"He died, though, so, uh...you know. Didn't feel much like continuing."

"I'm sorry."

"Yeah, and then the Veil came down, and it just seemed kind of ridiculous to be in a band anyway." She shrugs.

Ardent nods. "I definitely felt that way from time to time."

"Oh, I didn't mean you! You're like—it's your job, and so, uh—"

"No worries, Nisha. When the Veil fell, and I was trapped on

Earth, I dropped out of the spotlight for a while, too." They cross their arms and lean against the wall. "It was my mom who told me to get back out there and make people happy."

She laughs. "Really?"

"We might live in a tragedy, but we still deserve happiness. Someone has got to do it."

"She sounds nice."

Ardent wrinkles their nose. "She can be a bit pushy."

Nisha keeps up her smile, but there's nothing behind it. "Mine was, too."

They've feared losing their mother more than they can say, but telling Nisha that seems insensitive. "You've had a rough go of things, huh?"

She shakes the sadness away and musters the full-beam sunshine. "No rougher than anyone else."

Even though she isn't imposing, she seems diamond-hard to Ardent in that moment.

"I should let you get back to 'just walking around,' " Nisha says.

Ardent nods. "Thanks. It's good to be working with you. Despite what you said, I still think you're cool."

She swells up like she's going to burst, waves quickly, and vanishes into her room.

"Bye," they say to the empty hallway.

Gus has been sitting at the edge of his bed, elbows on his knees, for the past thirty minutes. He's too tense to lie down, too exhausted to walk around. The Vanguard commander's briefing is in three hours, but that seems far away when trapped with his thoughts.

Seeing Ardent had been so much better and worse than Gus expected. He'd felt every bruise and cut on their body as though he'd put it there himself. It didn't matter that he'd only tried to do good, just like it didn't matter that he couldn't save the *Khagan*.

He's not enough for this.

And now, sometime in the next few days, he'll have to fight for the fate of Earth. When he's not good enough this time, more people will die—folks like Captain Sujyot and Director Malhotra. They were smart, capable individuals with more training, direction, and intelligence than he could ever hope to have. It didn't matter that Greymalkin fed him tactical knowledge; Gus still made the wrong decisions when it counted.

Every bad move took away thousands of lives worthier than his—people whose only mistake was relying on him.

Gus's door chimes, and the holoprojectors render a grainy image of Ardent standing outside. He squeezes his eyes shut. He's not ready to see them again like that.

But he can't just leave them waiting out there after what Falchion did to them. He signs for the door to open, and it slides aside.

Ardent leans in the frame, a wrecked angel with a sympathetic smile. Every time Gus sees them, it's like being pulled in twain—part of him swoons with disbelieving appreciation, the other part drowns in guilt.

"Ardent," he says, rising from his seat.

"Gustopher," they reply with a saucy eyebrow.

"You're terrible." He runs a hand down his face, his stubble scratching rough fingers. "I'm going to be branded with that name, aren't I?"

"My countless ex-lovers will tell you I destroyed them. I like to start with the name."

"I see," he says.

They're trying to cheer him up when they're going through the exact same thing. He doesn't deserve this.

Gus goes to Ardent. They push off the doorframe, and it swishes silently closed. The two meet, and Gus pulls them to his body. Today, they've tinted their irises orchid purple, with a hint of green and gold near the pupil.

"Can I just appreciate you for a moment?" Gus murmurs, pressing his lips to their forehead. "I never would've guessed you were so sweet from your music."

Ardent pouts. "I'm not sweet."

"Hmm... Let me have a taste and find out," he says, kissing them. Their tongues dance, and a muffled moan escapes Ardent's throat.

"The doctors told me no 'vigorous activity,'" they whisper, breathless.

"I don't want vigorous." Gus lifts their hand to his mouth, touching his lips to the bruised skin around their wrist port, then working his way up their arm. "I want to kiss every part of you that hurts. Is that okay?"

"Please."

He takes them to the bed, helping them out of their short-sleeved shirt to expose even more of their damaged flesh. Their one-night stand had been a fantasy, everything he ever wanted. It was hot and heavy, desperate and dreamy. That Ardent had been superhuman, but this one winced when their shirt caught on a port.

They pull Gus's top off, but he stops them from going further. "Not yet."

Gus climbs onto them, careful to keep his weight on the mattress. He peppers their neck with gentle kisses, then roves over their body, taking it slow with his tongue on any ticklish spots. Ardent has the cheap fragrance of a hotel blast shower, but when mixed with their natural scent, Gus wants to infuse himself with it.

"Let me give you what I couldn't accept," he says, "when I was ravaged."

Their chest heaves with each light contact of skin, and Ardent runs their fingers through his brushy scalp. They guide him over their ribs, and Gus teases their nipples. He gives a gentle bite, and they gasp in delight. He follows the lines of muscle down their abdomen, toward the fastener on their pants. Ardent goes to undo their mag clasp, but Gus stops them, pushing their hands back to their side.

"Please," they say again, as though he's kissed every other word out of their head.

First, he takes care of their socks and shoes. Gingerly removing their pants, he finds pained legs, streaks of purple and yellow traveling parallel to rows of implants. He works his way up from their ankles, lips brushing their inner thighs. He takes hold of Ardent's throbbing desire, engulfing it in his warm, wet mouth, and they shudder with delight.

"Please, please, please..."

It's almost too easy to bring them off, and Ardent sinks back to the sheets, twitching and flushed. Gus swallows the fruits of his labor and returns to their side atop the bed. They try to turn and service his needs, but he stops them.

"Not yet, nightingale," he says. "This was about you, and your doctor gave you orders. Enjoy the afterglow with me."

They stare at the ceiling while their breathing slows, blinking and dumbfounded.

"'Nightingale,'" they echo. "That's classy."

"We can't all be Gustopher."

Ardent laughs and rolls onto their side, gazing into Gus's eyes. "That's the spirit, dear. I'm pleased to see I've left a dent in you."

He touches their cheek and cracks a smile. "You're a fucking meteor."

"I like that. I bet I could use that in a song."

"I'm sure."

He folds his arms behind his head and lies on his back. Ardent snuggles up to him, their heat bleeding into his side, commingling with his.

"When I was stuck out there," Gus says, "I couldn't stop thinking about you."

"Same. It was awful."

"Awful?" He laughs.

"Don't make light of my pain," Ardent says. "It's a hideous thing, losing your heart to someone."

Gus gulps involuntarily. He desperately wants it to be true. The Ardent Violet of the mass media burns through lovers like they're made of paper. They have public fallings-out, throw wine on cheaters, and snap hearts in half. Could someone like that feel the same emotions as mundane Gus? They lightly trace the shape of his brow with a finger as they speak, and it's like hypnosis.

"I needed this. I had no idea how much I missed... I don't know, having someone care for me." He shakes his head. "I'd just kind of given up, I guess."

"A lot of people did." They smirk. "I couldn't even get out of bed some days."

"I don't mean like that. Even now, it's hard to believe life is worth living sometimes. A lot of times."

He's never said it to another person, and it hurts more than he thought it would. "Most times."

They frown. "What do you mean?"

"The past five years were only an ordeal for me. And what remained between the carnage was tasteless. Bland. It didn't matter when my music got sampled. I didn't care about the parties. Food got boring. I always thought suicide would be an urge. I didn't know it could be like this, just—wanting to lie down and just fucking..."

"Gus..."

His eyes burn. "I used to stay awake all night reading the news, looking for some semblance of sense. A couple of times, my chest would hurt so bad it was like having a heart attack. I didn't go to the hospital when that happened; I just thought... 'Thank god.'"

Ardent rests their chin on his sternum. "For what it's worth, I'm glad you're still here."

He licks his lips, trying to formulate his next sentence. "When you came along... the whole world got more colorful. I'm grateful for the first time in ages. If there's one good thing that's happened to me since the Veil fell, it's you."

They hold him tightly and press their cheek against his chest. "Promise me something. Tell me you won't ever check out on purpose."

Gus closes his eyes, and a tear rolls out. "I wish it worked like that."

Their fingers twitch at his statement, and their grip tightens. "Then I want you to stick close to me."

"Yeah. That's what I want, too."

For a while, they lie in silence, listening to the climate control. Ardent strokes his side, running their fingers along the bumps of his ribs.

"You were so good to me just now," they say. "Can't I take care of you, too?"

"No one has shown me genuine affection since I lost my family," he replies. "Do you mind if... can I have just that for a few hours? I promise I want you, but I need a little more time."

"Of course, my darling."

Chapter Nineteen

Syncopation & Synchronicity

A door chime rouses Ardent from blissful slumber. They find Gus lying beside them, eyes open. Has he been watching them sleep this whole time?

"Did you get some rest?" he asks.

"Did you?" they say. "You don't look like you slept."

The door chimes again, and Ardent rolls their eyes before stumbling out of bed.

Their joints ache, but the nap worked wonders. They fumble around in the shadows for their clothes, and Gus signs for the light, blinding them.

"That was uncalled for."

"Sorry," he replies. "Didn't want to keep our minders waiting. Places to be."

"Worlds to save."

He gives them a hopeful look. "Yeah, maybe."

Ardent promises themself they're going to shatter that shell. A third door chime convinces them that'll have to happen later.

After hastily donning their clothes, they sign the door open. On the other side, they find a squad of soldiers, Nisha, Hjalmar, and Tazi.

"You're late," Tazi says. "We agreed to meet in the lobby."

"Did we?" Ardent asks, wrinkling their nose.

Tazi's eye twitches. "Not cute. This is a military operation."

"Sorry," they say. "Gus, honey, are you ready to go?"

"Just getting my shoes," he says.

After a quick snack in the nearby canteen, the war party sets off in the skimmer for the next item on their itinerary. Sunset paints the nearby mountains orange, their dark, sandblasted stripes coming through in stark contrast.

The quartet of Conduits looks foolish in matching, borrowed USAF shirts, and Ardent hates every minute of it. They've never been one to advertise for the military, but more than that, the clothes aren't flashy and the drabness makes them feel uncomfortable, invisible. They'd prefer to walk around in their sleek, custom Conduit suit, but it's not ready yet.

"Are you folx getting nervous?" Nisha says with a smile. "I'm nervous."

"I'm always nervous," Gus replies.

"I don't suffer stage fright," Ardent says. "Never have."

They all look to Hjalmar, who says, "No."

Nisha gives him a disbelieving look. "You don't get scared at all, Hjalmar?"

"Most of my songs are about dying. Or killing. Sometimes both."

"I think my favorite of yours is 'The End of Us,'" Gus says. "Followed by 'Killpocalypse.'"

Hjalmar gives him the slightest acknowledging nod. "My old work."

Gus shrugs. "What can I say? Haven't heard your stuff in five years. Can I ask you something?"

Hjalmar makes a face that could be construed as a *yes*.

"Why did you react so badly when I said I was from the Montreal jazz scene—"

"Okay, look," Hjalmar interrupts Gus so quickly that everyone jolts. "Those little dorks were all up in my shit for a whole year. And it wasn't just once a month or whatever. I'd hear from them every day. When I finally came to Montreal to play a show, this"—he pushes his fist into his palm like he's crushing someone's head—"this François fucker decided to bring all his ridiculous friends to harass me at my hotel.

"I just about broke that skinny jackoff's nose," Hjalmar spits. "He dragged a whole group up in there and ruined my after-show hookup with inane questions. When I had them kicked out, they started bombing all my reviews with negative shit, and..."

He grumbles a lot of nasty-sounding things in Swedish before stopping and looking at Gus.

"Sorry if I was a dick before," Hjalmar says, "but I thought you might've been one of them."

Gus gives him a prey smile. "Yeah, uh, that François guy was my first boyfriend. He broke up with me."

Ardent laughs. They haven't heard this story before, but the guy sounds awful. They suddenly feel a lot better about some of their own failings.

Hjalmar crosses his arms and leans back, glancing at Ardent. "Clearly, Gus, you could do better."

"I think so, too," Ardent says. "Gus, you were pearls before that swine."

They punctuate the sentiment by hugging his arm and leaning their head on his shoulder.

"Clearly," Gus repeats.

The skimmer leaves Nellis's airspace, and Ardent perks up.

"Miss Tazi," they say, "are we going on a field trip?"

"To practice your teamwork," she replies, arms crossed.

"We won," Nisha protests.

"Miss Kohli," Tazi says, "I appreciate the outcome, but in my world, we care about near misses. Greymalkin was caught in Cascade's fields several times. The assault on Shiro sounded messy, with Jotunn clogging the fire lanes, leading Mister Kitko to improvise shooting through a friendly vessel. A lucky win is a loss in my book."

Ardent raises their eyebrows. "I'm not sure what you mean. I think we'll do fine."

"Mix Violet," Tazi says, "I have no doubt your ego will cause casualties if not checked. Nothing I have witnessed or read about you leads me to believe otherwise."

Far from looking stricken, Ardent sighs. "C'est la vie."

"C'est la morte," Tazi corrects. "We cannot afford to lose a single Vanguard. There's too much at stake for some half-cocked plan, and I expect you all to learn to collaborate."

Ardent peers out to find the shimmer of dozens of holoflaged drones distorting the Vegas skyline like cubes of glass. When Ardent looks down, about a dozen Ghosts track their position with some interest. Seems like everyone wants to know where the Conduits are going.

Tazi starts hailing guard posts, checking in with a venue. Ardent has experienced similar security teams at big concert festivals, but never anything this serious.

After a few minutes, Tazi says, "The one thing all three of you reported about Deepsync was hearing music. Mister Kitko, you said you heard jazz. Miss Kohli, bhangra, Mister Sjögren, metal."

"Djent," Gus and Hjalmar correct her in unison.

She may be smiling, but she's not amused at being interrupted. "But of course. From our interviews with all of you, it seems that music is somehow deeply, and perhaps unconsciously, intwined with your ability to communicate with your Vanguards. And, while I am not a musician, from what I saw out there on the field, your styles don't exactly seem to... mesh."

The skimmer settles outside a cracked old plasticlay building with crossed bars covering the tiny glexan windows. No docking cradles line the parking area. Some sad lights flicker out front, their electricals long past their design life.

"We're here," Tazi says.

The party pours out of the skimmer as the sun dips below the horizon, orange fading to the navy sheen of night. Tazi leads the group up to a caged entrance and bangs on the grating. A man opens the interior door, pallid light spilling from inside. He's dressed in plainclothes, a red collared shirt and beige trousers, but given the size of his arms and missing fashion sense—he's a bodyguard.

He stands aside, and everyone shuffles into the tiny room beyond. Lime-green plush carpet has been marched into a stained, flat surface. Wood paneling lines every wall, and there's scarcely a holo in sight. Nanochoic tiles cover the ceiling, their damper surfaces long since expired or jammed. Along one side, a huge desk sits at the ready, an ancient leather blotter spread over its surface.

A large white woman sits on a stained mustard-yellow couch in one corner. She nurses a rainbow-blended frozen drink in one hand and some pungent weed in the other. Her dress might be the loudest thing in the room, a red polka dot number to match the bandanna securing her curly black hair.

Ardent gasps in horror, then delight. "This place is hideous! I love it!"

"Welcome to Last Chance Records," the woman says with a grin. "The oldest continuously operating recording studio in United States history. I'm Janine. It's an honor to have y'all."

She holds out a red-gloved hand for Ardent, and they take it, giving a gentle shake.

"Hey," Ardent says. "Sorry I called it hideous."

"But you also said you loved it," Janine responds. "I can understand that. I have two pugs and a ratty-ass Chihuahua that I'd kill someone over."

Hjalmar nods, looking around. "Cool."

"Oh my god..." Gus says. "Is this for real?"

"Follow me," Janine says. "I'll show you around."

They pass from the reception area down a short hallway of offices. Ardent peers into each one, marveling at their manual doors and locks. Records—actual pressed physical media—line the walls, plaques under each labeling their originators.

"Richie Collins?" Gus reads each one aloud with rising incredulity. "Space Age? Katra? Jamal Queen? Hot damn, this is awesome! This is like... four hundred years old!"

Ardent has never seen him so excited, and they love it. He reminds them of a tall child.

"That's right," Janine replies, tapping the side of her glass with a black-lacquered nail. "We had the quadricentennial on my thirteenth birthday. My father used to say this place was the high-water mark of every age."

They pass into an archaic control room, full of physical, single-interface mixers. Behind them, a window looks onto a darkened space.

Ardent gawks. "This is... How are these still working?"

Janine chuckles. "These are reproductions—though they're two hundred years old, so we treat them nicely. The originals are all in the Perry Museum in Lubbock."

She taps an old-fashioned switch plate, and the studio lights up through the window. Hardwood panels line the walls, damper blankets hang across silver C-stands, and gleaming mics rest in their cradles. The floor is a bamboo mosaic, its wooden tiles polished to a bright shine. Black cables snake across its span.

In the corner of the room sits a scarred-up grand piano, carefully miked from above. Behind that, Ardent spies a green satin flame drum kit with a menagerie of various cymbals—far too many for a normal drummer to care about. At the center of the room, a classic cherry sunburst Omnicaster guitar rests atop a metal stand like a holy relic.

"Incredible," Gus breathes. "Is that... is that Buddy Haverford's baby grand?"

"The one and only," Janine says, sipping through a long straw. "Y'all want to try it out?"

"Do you have a drum closet?" Hjalmar asks. "Your kit appears to be missing some things.

"We do. Got session gear from all the big manufacturers, as well as some boutiques, like our starmetal cowbell. It's in our storeroom," she replies. "Or, as we like to call it, 'the Armory.'"

The Swedish Raven's eyes widen, and he takes a sudden breath like a lover just ran a hand up his leg.

"Cool," Nisha says. "Is that the whole studio?"

Everyone turns to stare at her, and she adds, "Like... is this it? Is this good? You folx are making faces like it's good. I've never worked in a studio."

"What?" Gus says. "Never?"

"Like you've never recorded?" Ardent asks. "Or literally never worked in a studio?"

"I'm not famous like you guys!" she says. "I just like to sing."

Tazi clears her throat. "Okay, well you're about to get your chance. I've taken the liberty of directing taxpayer funds toward your musical careers so you can *learn to work together*. You all hear different tunes, but you must become the same, to flow naturally into one another."

She paces back and forth like a general.

"For the next twelve hours, the studio is yours. My personnel out front will be here to cater to any of your appetites, so don't hesitate to ask for snacks, drinks, et cetera. Just don't ask to leave, because the answer is no."

"So..." Ardent says.

"So get in there and lay down a track," Tazi says. "Now if you'll excuse me, I have many matters requiring my attention, so good night."

She exits the control room, waving without turning around.

"She really hates us, doesn't she?" Nisha asks.

"Mostly me," Ardent says.

"Why don't y'all go in there and get set up?" Janine says. "I'll show Hjalmar the equipment closet. There's . . . a lot to go through back there."

"I want to see it all," he says.

Janine winks. "Don't you worry about that. I'll make sure you get a taste of everything Last Chance has to offer."

Gus circles the baby grand piano that once belonged to twenty-third century blues legend Buddy Haverford. The scuffed, yellowing keys are the color of old teeth, and the case has deep ruts and scratches across the whole surface. The instrument survived the infamous concert hall collapse that killed its original owner. Gus took a field trip to the Chicago Mod School as a kid, and they visited the grave on the way. On Buddy's headstone in Chicago, it reads, *Literally Brought the House Down*.

Gus never stopped listening to jazz after that field trip. It'd been his father's biggest mistake.

"I miss Baby," Ardent says, hefting the guitar into their hands with a pouty face.

" 'Baby'?" Gus repeats. "That one guitar you had?"

"It wasn't just some plain guitar! It was a Powers Vitas X, and she drowned."

"How does a guitar drown?" he asks.

"I don't want to talk about it," they snap.

"You brought it up."

Ardent pouts. "Because I don't know how I'm supposed to play this basic fucking guitar! There's no, like, sequencer, or sample and hold, or acoustaware, or—"

Gus laughs and instantly regrets it when he sees the look on their face.

"At least you got an instrument," Nisha says. "Mine is just my voice."

"Voices win Vanguards, darling," Ardent replies, shrugging into the strap and testing the strings. Without an amp, it makes a sad little twang. "How do I even link this to the room projectors?"

Gus looks it over, but he doesn't play guitar, so he's not sure. "Janine can help us when she gets back."

But after fifteen minutes, she still hasn't returned. Eventually, Hjalmar comes lumbering into the studio with a few extra pieces of kit and a light flush.

"Did you have to test them all out?" Nisha asks.

"I was getting inspired," he replies.

The studio talk-back intercom clicks on, and Janine plops down on the other side of the window, hair slightly askew. "Whew! All right! Y'all ready to get this party started?"

"Not really!" Nisha cheerfully says. "We don't have a song."

Ardent pops a monitor into their ear and plucks the guitar strings, testing the tuning. "Hjal and I worked together on 'Metal Flame.' We could teach you two that one."

"Been too long. I don't remember that song," Hjalmar says, screwing the wing nut down on some type of trash splash Gus has never seen before. "It's similar to 'Hollow Corpse,' and I can teach you the chords for that one."

"If you all don't mind," Gus begins, "maybe I could play some Haverford. Just for fun. This is his piano, after all."

One look from the others tells Gus that plan is not happening.

"Oh, Jesus," comes Janine's voice over the talk-back. "Miss Tazi was right. You folx are lost."

"Everyone in this room is an accomplished, well-known musician," Ardent says.

"Except me," Nisha adds.

"That'll change when you hit the news," Ardent says, then to Janine, "so cut us some slack."

"Not judging," Janine says, lips searching out her straw. "Just saying. But it's okay. That's hallowed ground you're standing on. A lot of good has come together in there."

Gus tests one of the notes, and it sends a shiver up his spine. The instrument sounds exactly as it did in his favorite Buddy song, "Paint the Sky."

He sighs. There'll be time for the Haverford hits later, he hopes. "What do you suggest, Janine?"

"Hjalmar, can you give them a beat?" she says. "Y'all join in when you feel it."

This strategy results in nothing but awkward starts and stops, with only Hjalmar getting any consistent result. Ardent veers toward the classic pop chord progressions, and every time Nisha opens her mouth, the song goes in a direction Gus never predicted. He councils that the Vanguards seem to love modal jazz, so maybe they all should go with that—and the other three remind him that they got Vanguards on their own, so he can stuff it. When Hjalmar breaks out his favorite drum beat, Gus can barely penetrate the rhythm, frustrating the Raven to no end.

Janine orders them to take a break, and by that point, no one has the energy to argue.

"Y'all are like peanut butter and sex," she says, passing out bags of intoxicants and filling cups for everyone. "Great alone, terrible together."

"We're just too established," Ardent says.

Janine stirs her drink, tonguing the inside of her lower lip. "Tell yourself whatever you need to."

Ardent bristles. "You know, I've never had a producer talk to me like this."

"Sorry, babe," Janine says. "This is Last Chance. I've seen a hundred of your kind come through here. But you don't have to take my advice. I already got paid."

Gus wraps an arm around Ardent. "Don't fight the engineer. She's right about one thing: We can make a track together. You and I did it, you and Hjalmar did it. I'm sure Nisha could pair up with any one of us, and it'd come out great."

"Yeah, I'm the greatest," Nisha says. "I basically carry you three." Then she adds, "I'm joking. Obviously. Don't kick me out."

They sit in the control room, sipping and smoking, discussing their failures for the better part of an hour. When everyone is good and loose, Janine pushes them out of the control room and back into the studio with a "Get to work!"

Gus sits at the piano, considering it once more. He's managed to mimic a few of Nisha's progressions, and it's not impossible—just different.

"Hey, Ardent," he says. "Let Nisha lead off? She keeps backing down."

Ardent smirks at Nisha. "What do you say, dear?"

Nisha looks like she might explode. "M-me?" she stammers. "I'm mostly a soloist. Never really done studio work, and you folx are like—super good."

"I just want you to try it," Gus says. "Let me back you up."

Janine clicks on the talk-back and says, "Hey, gorgeous—"

"Yeah?" Ardent replies.

"*Hjalmar*," Janine says, "Nisha mentioned bhangra earlier. Can you do that beat?"

He nods and busts out a swing time rhythm on the toms. Nisha bobs her head, and her whole body sways when the kick drum starts booming on the downbeats. She steps to the mic and opens her mouth, loosing a long, pure note. As her breath runs down, the frequency slews from harmonic to harmonic, and Gus recognizes the G Ionian.

"Okay," he mumbles, bobbing his head. "Okay."

Gus snaps off a few quick melodies, throwing accompaniment on the upbeats. He hits it a few more times, but the song is resilient—it holds up.

"Yeah!" he calls. "Keep it going!"

In the absence of a bass player, Gus lays down a dancing groove at the bottom of the keyboard. Ardent's eyebrows shoot up, and their foot taps in time.

They run up the neck of their guitar with an electrifying lead-in, coming into sync with Nisha's stunning solo. The two of them rock out, and Nisha grabs the mic stand like she wants to strangle it. In the control room, Janine bangs her head, curly black hair springing this way and that.

Ardent and Nisha form a spiraling duet, powerful melodies filling up the space. When they reach the end, Gus surges forward, dancing up and down the keyboard. He hazards a glance at Hjalmar to find him biting his lip and jamming out to the piano parts. Gus's heart swells in his chest at the Raven's approval, and he throws in some riffs from Hjalmar's first record, bashing the bass keys.

At the first sign of death metal, the Swedish Raven switches on, blasting out his signature ambidextrous polyrhythms like a thousand magic tricks. He works over every piece of his substantial kit, demonstrating the range of bronze, wood, and plastic in ways Gus has never heard. Hjalmar's genius stretches the limits of drumming, an auteur immersed in his element, and Gus is instantly transported back to high school. He takes a risk and whips out some Montreal French punk jazz at the end of Hjalmar's solo.

The others look confused, but at least they don't stop playing.

Gus runs through the same six chords a few times to give them a chance to get adjusted, and it kind of works—but it's not the home run he'd always hoped for, so he gives up.

The second Gus comes back onto Nisha's melody line, the song crystallizes, and they all ride it to the end.

Ardent jumps at the final beat, ripping the last chord from their guitar with a primal shout.

"Yes!" they say. "Fuck, yes! That's what I'm talking about!"

"Y'all did good," Janine says over the talk-back. "Now we've just got to record it the right way."

Gus's shoulders slump. "You weren't recording?"

Janine puffs up at that. "Of course I was, but Last Chance ain't no jam band studio! Y'all come in here to do a song, you're going to do it right."

"Do we have time for that?" he says.

Her grin turns wicked. "Miss Tazi told me I had your asses for eight more hours. Get comfortable."

"I like your style, Janine," Ardent says, pointing their pick at her, and she blows them a kiss. They throw a hand up. "From the top, my sweets?"

Hjalmar jumps up and claps his sticks together, voice like a cannon shot. "ONE, TWO, THREE, FOUR!"

A few pizza slices and more than a few drinks later, Ardent emerges from Last Chance with a surefire winner of a song in their head. They even have plans for a duet, though they're not sure when they'll get back to this project. There are other pressing things in their schedule, like preventing everyone from dying. This early in the day, the desert breeze is cool, almost chilly, and they rub their bare arms.

Tazi awaits them in the parking lot, and she seems happy for the first time since Ardent met her.

"I heard good things from Janine," she says. "Have you learned to stop stepping on each other's toes?"

Ardent nods. "Yes. There are now three people on the planet I won't walk all over."

The crew flies back to Nellis, where they get the agenda: briefing in eight hours by the top brass. Readiness drills in twelve. Tazi runs them through both items, making sure Ardent understands the importance of them. Ardent can't blame her—they never pay enough attention.

Then it's off to bed with Gus. Ardent aches for his touch, but they're both too tired. They lie together, him pressed against their back. It's like they blink and the sun is starting to set again.

Ardent groans as they sit up. "Oh my god, is it really that time? Can we not?"

Gus smacks his lips. "I'm afraid we *can't* not."

"You are so weird."

He smiles. "I hope you continue to find it attractive. Come on. We don't want to keep them waiting."

"Don't you, though? There's nothing quite like making an entrance."

"I'm pretty sure Miss Tazi wants to shoot us," Gus says, "and sometimes I don't blame her. Can't be easy trying to herd these cats."

"You're too sweet for your own good."

They dress in their Conduit uniforms—Gus in blue, Ardent in olive drab. The United States uniform has all the port pass-throughs in the same places as Gus's, but it has a ton of other pockets that obscure the figure. Where Gus's is sleek and graceful, Ardent's is tactical, modular, expandable . . . blocky, boring. Even the port colors don't work for Ardent—all gunmetal with copper contacts. Green and black is entirely too camo, and they hate it.

"Wow. You look like you're going to war," Gus says. "Is there stuff in those pockets? I want pockets."

"If these weren't custom-printed, I'd trade you."

The pair heads out into the common area, where they find the rest of their party waiting for them. Tazi looks surprised when they show up, and checks the time.

They load into a skimmer and head across base to a campus with a holo out front that reads 365TH INTELLIGENCE SURVEILLANCE & RECONNAISSANCE GROUP with a stylized knight logo. The five constituent buildings are like pyramids, halved vertically—ramping windows on three sides and a sheer drop on the fourth. All together in a line, they make a sawtooth pattern on the horizon. The docking towers are busy, CAVs headed out for the day after shift change.

Their transport settles down directly in front of one of the buildings, letting everyone out beside the holo of a water feature. The fountain has a minor flicker that gets on Ardent's nerves, and it clashes with the basic landscaping surrounding it.

A Black man in fatigues, just a little taller than Ardent, stands by the front door. He raises a hand in greeting, giving them a friendly smile.

Tazi strides over to him. "Major Bowman. Thank you for hosting us."

"It's our pleasure. Folx, follow me, and we can get this party started."

They pass into a lobby atrium, offices lining terraces all the way to the upper stories. Base notifications about getting insurance, securing loans, and health care screenings are holoed up near a check-in station. The guard manning the station salutes the major and waves him past a wall of scanners. Only his Gang glows on his person, a little box printed into his uniform.

He gestures for Ardent to follow. "Mix Violet."

When Ardent walks past the scanners, they light up bright as a bonfire. Ardent's implant ports go deep below the skin, spreading out into silvery roots. Vanguard tech has penetrated every corner of them, and their breath quickens. They academically knew how thoroughly they'd been ravaged, but they hadn't seen an effective visualization yet.

"Well, shoot," Bowman says with a laugh. "I didn't think about that. Private, can we just log this and move on?"

"Yes, sir."

Ardent holds up their hand. Glowing veins of metal spread across their being—weeds in their garden.

This is what's going to kill you.

The scanner goes dead, and the glowing afterimage disappears.

"Pointless to even bother with all that," Bowman says, amused. "Come on."

They follow him to a polished white lift, and Bowman throws signs for the computer to ascend to thirty. "I'm glad we could arrange this. We've got some exciting plans for everyone."

"Fighting Vanguards is technically exciting," Nisha says.

"Winning certainly is," Bowman says.

"The ISR Group has been hard at work on the data you've all provided," Tazi says, "cross-referencing it with early Veil intel. We'll discuss it in the SCIF, but we've got a picture of what's coming."

"There's a skiff?" Ardent asks.

"Secret Compartmented Information Facility," Bowman says. "It's the closet where we stuff all the analysts."

When they reach the thirtieth floor, the doors part to reveal a concrete corridor. Copper contacts glitter along the walls, and Ardent's suit Gang chirps with connection loss. The other Gangs in the lift register similar complaints.

Bowman seems proud of himself. "The whole top floor is signal-opaque. Even a Ghost can't scan through these walls."

"Have there been any Ghost breaches?" Tazi asks. "We've had

a lot of trouble at UW headquarters. When they can't scan, they just hack through security and physically access the location."

"The other buildings have," Bowman says. "We posted guards to shoot any Ghosts that try. They don't seem to retaliate, and it's another potential enemy down."

"We let them go through on New Jalandhar," Nisha says. "Just move aside and they can do whatever."

Bowman and Tazi exchange glances.

"We've got some, uh, pretty sensitive stuff in here, Miss Kohli," he says, clearing his throat. "We can't just trust them with that."

She frowns. "Okay, but they gave us some of their weapons. Did you get any Vanguard tech here on Earth?"

The major shakes his head. "Well, no, but—"

Nisha crosses her arms. "Did you ever wonder why?"

"While we see your point," Tazi says, "anything that can be given can be taken away. The Vanguards are only our allies for now. If that changes, I'd hate to be reliant on the Gilded Ghosts for weapons."

"Okay," Nisha says, clearly unimpressed, and Hjalmar snorts.

Major Bowman leads them through the office, and all the holos are in privacy mode—direct retinal projection. It's strange to Ardent, seeing a bunch of soldiers and office workers staring blankly across their desks, talking to no one and reaching out to tap nothing.

They assemble in one of the meeting rooms along a sloped side of the half pyramid, windows throwing a rectangle of evening sun across the far wall. In the distance, Vegas begins to come alive, a shadow of its former self at a few glimmering lights on the horizon.

Ardent takes a seat at a long, mahogany table, its surface rippling around an Air Force logo. There are seats for at least fifteen people, but only six are in attendance. Major Bowman signs for the windows to close, and thick steel shutters eclipse the view.

The words *Vanguard Wing Pilot Briefing* hover above the table.

"We're not pilots," Ardent says. "If I treated Falchion like a vehicle, it'd kill me."

"Also, is this it?" Gus asks. "I thought there would be more people."

"Yeah, we do briefings, like, supergood," Nisha says. "It's really impressive. Everyone shows up in a big auditorium. But this meeting room is cool, too. I like the couch over there."

Tazi lets out a grumbling sigh. "Can we try to keep this on topic?"

"Sorry," Nisha says.

"We were too late to stop it," Bowman begins, "but PODS detected a Ghost infestation on Pluto's moon of Charon."

" 'PODS'?" Ardent repeats.

Bowman laces his fingers together in his lap. "Pluto Observation and Defense System. It's one of the last extraterrestrial sensor arrays we can trust, because it's in the solar system. The LOS relays still work."

Ardent sighs. "I hate to be rude, but can you not use acronyms? I have no idea what you're talking about."

"Line of sight," Bowman says. "We can still communicate reliably within the Sol system. This was the last data dump from PODS."

A miniature Charon appears before them, its gray surface encrusted with golden masses like lichen. They churn and waver, and Ardent stands to get a closer look. In the playback, a few blue glints sparkle across the gleaming surfaces, and the holo freezes.

Bowman signs for a computer pointer, rendering a bright green beam onto the tip of his finger. He designates the blue spots. "These are the Ghosts' short-range superluminal drives—the kind you see when they travel in formation. We can only guess that we're seeing assembly and testing of engines. Over the course of the observation, we counted more than a thousand separate tests.

"Based on estimates," he concludes, "they've almost got a Perfect Solution against Earth, with more than enough drives to jump an invasion force into our orbit."

"But if they did that without Vanguards," Ardent says, "that swarm would belong to us."

Bowman sucks his teeth. "Too true. That's why they brought in some of their own."

He gestures to Charon, and it rotates more quickly, scrubbing through the playback until a series of three superluminal brake burns scratch across the stars.

A trio of doll-sized, blurry Vanguards appear above the table. A little holo of a man pops up next to them for scale, and he barely comes to their ankles. Labels name the Vanguards: Saturnine, Ifrit, and Reaper.

"They're stepping up their attacks," Bowman says. "Earth and New Jalandhar are the first targets to receive multiple Vanguard assailants."

Gus's tan skin looks pale, almost sickly in the cold light of the holograms. Ardent can see there's a lot more going through his mind than the number of enemies.

Bowman nods. "We believe the emergence of Traitor Vanguards has prompted an escalation. They're trying to take you four out so they can kill us at their leisure."

"It's what I would do," Hjalmar says, and everyone looks at him sidelong.

Bowman highlights the first Vanguard, and it enlarges enough to touch the ceiling. "Saturnine is our number one problem. Its presence disables all receivers, and disentangles long-range particle comms. There's a strong possibility it'll disable your Vanguard wireless networks, too. Until it's down, none of you will be able to talk to one another."

Saturnine is a graceful machine, its twisting, pearlescent white patterns raised over a navy-blue frame. Though its proportions are alien, they remind Ardent of a human hourglass figure. An accent line around its head at mouth height turns upward like a disturbing smile stretching to either ear. A lone eye splits the forehead, glowing with blinding light.

Bowman plays back what little video they have: catastrophic scenes spread beneath the single bright eye. "We're unclear on Saturnine's offensive capabilities, since no data connections work in its presence."

"Maybe it just punches stuff," Ardent says. "They can punch pretty hard. Trust me. Greymalkin punched me, you know—"

"Yes," Tazi says. "You've told us."

Bowman points to the next Vanguard. "Here, we have Ifrit."

This monster couldn't be further from Saturnine, with skin like molten glass. Metal spikes protrude from armored shoulders, elbows, knees, and back. Its forehead bears a long, curving black horn that comes to a sharp point. There's a slit where the eyes should go, wrapping around its head like a knight's visor.

The videos that play alongside it depict people running from Ifrit, screaming for their lives. Ardent has seen—and been traumatized by—similar images. As of five years ago, everyone has.

They look closer and see something far worse: The people are rolling on the ground, out of their minds with pain. There's no rhyme or reason to them, just pure animal instinct. Ghosts cavort among the anguished, biting into heads like fresh apples.

Bowman grows somber. "Ifrit can create an energy field capable of setting off all the pain receptors in your body while you wait to be Wiped."

Ardent can't tear their eyes from the recording. "Jesus."

"My son died in Ifrit's first attack," Bowman says.

"I'm sorry, sir," Gus says.

Bowman smiles. "It's okay. You can cheer me up by ripping its head off." He reaches across and swats away the video before designating the last Vanguard. "Last but not least, we've got Reaper."

Ardent knows this one well—it was the perpetrator of the second Vanguard attack, so named for the giant starmetal scythe it carries. The videos sent back from the colonies showed people clutching their chests or throats.

Reaper is glossy black, with lines of silver tracing every curve of its body. In one hand, it holds its signature weapon, a scythe with edges bleeding sickly light. Its ornate armor looks like something an ancient king might wear, or a tyrant, with spiked chains running along the back and sides of its arms. The whole thing is entirely too goth.

"This one cut down half our fleet in the start of the war," Bowman says. "The ships that made it out described strange effects just from being in its presence—"

"It felt like we were asphyxiating," Tazi says. "I was there."

All eyes turn to Tazi, and she continues.

"I served in the UW Prime Carrier Battle Group during the first encounters. I was on the *Mirage*." She sits back and folds her arms. "Our armada encountered Reaper and attempted to engage. It hit us with an energy field that... I don't know. All I remember is that it felt like dying. If it hadn't been for the admiral's quick retreat order, we all would've perished right there."

"I want to fight that one," Hjalmar says. "I hope that is your plan."

Bowman looks him over. "That's certainly part of it. We're planning to use the Superluminal Fold Acquisition and Redirection System to split the Vanguards when they try to attack."

Ardent laughs. "Didn't you already try that with Juliette?"

Bowman cocks an eyebrow. "Yes, but we didn't have you four. Our final obstacle will be Harlequin, if it chooses to show up. We can't allow it to reach Earth, so it'll have to be engaged on the moon."

"Because of the radiation I mentioned in my brief," Gus says.

"Yes," Bowman replies. "It was a good thing you provided that intelligence to us, Mister Kitko. It would've been a tragic end, otherwise."

"Glad to be of service," he says.

Nisha scoots in close to look at Reaper. "Okay, so three of them on Earth and one on the moon. How do you want us to fight them?"

Bowman pulls up dossiers of the Traitor Vanguards. "Same ratio. Three on Earth, one on the moon."

Ardent doesn't like where this going. They felt a lot more comfortable when they thought of fighting side by side. "Okay, but who gets stuck out there?"

"It's a question of specialties," Tazi says. "Cascade is best in a group."

Nisha scoffs. "Excuse me? I killed Bullseye and Wanderer by myself."

"If you can deploy your disruption fields," Tazi says, "that's an advantage for everyone else. Falchion shouldn't be alone for its first battle."

A little shame wells in Ardent over their relief at that.

"We all fought our first battles alone," Hjalmar says, "and we made it here."

Tazi shakes her head. "That was because of circumstance, not planning. There's a difference. Jotunn seems ideal for engaging multiple targets."

Gus nods. "So you want me to go alone."

"Yes," Tazi says. "You'll have the full support of Earth's remaining warships."

Ardent finds it hard to tamp down their annoyance. This plan was made without the Conduits, and now Gus is the sacrificial lamb. "How many ships do you have left?"

"Three," Bowman says. "All dry-docked at the time Juliette attacked. We've rushed the repairs and outfitted them as best we could."

Ardent scowls. "So Gus has to get backup from your shittiest remaining ships? Why can't we make it two-on-two? You can split the opposition up differently, and Falchion can help, too."

"We can only target one Vanguard at a time," Tazi says.

The major looks Ardent in the eye, and they see a bit of the fire he carries onto the battlefield. "You need to turn the tide with an overwhelming majority. If you kill one, that's three-on-two, then three-on-one. Combat models show an exponential increase in odds, as well as a decrease in time with each mortality."

He leans his elbows on the table, lacing his fingers together under his nose. "I know it seems harsh, but efficiency literally means lives."

Hjalmar inclines his head. "It also means that if one of us goes down, your odds get way worse."

"Two on assault, one defending the flank," Bowman says. "If you gang up on targets, you can beat them. As Miss Kohli has mentioned, Cascade has already killed two Vanguards at once, so she's ideally suited to protect. If you manage to take out the ground Vanguards, you can do a short-range fold to the moon to support Greymalkin."

"I'm not charged up to do a fold," Gus says. "Are the rest of you?"

"We've been here a few days," Hjalmar says. "Should be more than enough to get to the moon with the Vanguards' solar collection. Our three have been taking it easy to charge faster."

Tazi starts up a map holo and begins laying the pieces on the board—six Vanguards, satellite and fighter support. "You've all told us this... 'Fount' gives you access to human tactical memories. We're here to give you our plan. After, we want you to run it by your Vanguards. See what they think."

"You're still putting Gus out there with the Vanguard who beat him," Ardent says.

Tazi holds up a finger. "We've got a solution for that, too."

Chapter Twenty

Set 'Em Up

You can fetch your present in San Diego— Those had been Tazi's words before asking him to fly down to the navy yards with Greymalkin.

The city spreads before them in a carpet of concrete and glass. It's packed wall-to-wall with people, its downtown rising to ridiculous heights. Beyond, the Pacific Ocean laps peacefully at the shore.

No doubt its citizens all regard the Vanguard's approach with some trepidation. Greymalkin soars over the suburbs with a security detail of fighters and flying gunships. Gus listens to the comms chatter of a dozen different agencies trying to coordinate his movements. There are a lot of people to keep happy.

A terrible thought dawns on Gus.

"Even if Harlequin is on the moon, that'll be within range of the swarm. Won't it take over the Ghosts and start killing everyone?"

By the time it arrives, all the Ghosts will have been destroyed.

"What? Really?"

It was too dangerous to leave them operational. The Traitor

Vanguards have ordered the Ghosts to assemble themselves into something more useful.

"Like what?"

Gus will find out if he lives through the challenges ahead.

"Then I guess I need to ask you something."

Gus should speak his mind.

"What are the odds we make it through this next fight?"

Humanity is more likely to perish than survive, but it's very close. Furthermore, the odds of the moon battle and the Earth battle are substantially different. On land, three Vanguards will face off against three even matches. There are complicating factors, but simulations only slightly favor the enemy.

"And on the moon?"

Would it change Gus's actions if he knew—if he learned Greymalkin's only purpose was to slow down Harlequin so the others could fight it together? Gus doesn't seem to mind risking his life for the right reasons.

His heart sinks. "So they're not good."

The odds are nonzero, and he should take hope in that.

His shoulders sag. "Jesus."

They've almost arrived at their destination, and Greymalkin projects a flight path for Gus to an installation on the far side of town.

"Greymalkin, this is SDNF Approach, you are cleared for landing."

"SDNF, Greymalkin, copy."

Gus has gotten a lot better at flying over the past few engagements, and it's easier to obey the control tower. A slow descent brings him toward a set of two-kilometer-long buildings on the northern edge, their white sides rusting at the seams. He hovers over the San Diego Naval Forge, humanity's largest terrestrial shipyard. There are no vessels in its confines now. Huge empty docking stalls mar its landscape.

At his approach, the roof of one of the buildings unfolds. A tarp-covered object rests inside, sixty meters long. Steel bands wrap around its width at intervals, and Greymalkin detects starmetal beneath.

Gus lands beside the building in a cleared-off staging area, taking a knee. Dozens of personnel gather around at a safe distance, and the air is full of buzzing drones. Gus's government minders have been on high alert; he's had a few credible threats on his life.

"All right, Greymalkin. Let's do this gracefully, shall we?"

A fresh, salty breeze and blinding sunlight greet him as Greymalkin's chest plate opens, and Gus steps out into the Vanguard's palm. It gently lowers him to the ground, and Gus hops down the last meter, casually striding toward the row of scientists and officers. It felt cool. He hopes it looked cool.

An older white woman dressed in a rumpled suit beckons him over. Her frizzy silver hair blows in the wind, and she regards him from behind mirrored sunglasses with a thin-lipped smile.

"Mister Kitko," she calls to him in a smoker's voice. "Welcome to the SDNF."

He jogs the last few steps so he doesn't keep everyone waiting and offers a hand. "Thanks."

She takes it. "Maggie Corley. I'm the director around here."

"I'm Gus Kitko. I, um, I'm with that guy," he says, jerking a thumb in Greymalkin's direction. "Thanks for setting this up."

"We've been working around the clock since the Battle of Monaco, and we're eager to show you what we've got. Right this way."

They proceed through a rusty side door into a tiled lobby. Tube lights run across the ceiling, scarred in places, and scuffs mar the floor from the passage of heavy carts. No one sits behind the chipped desk, and the whole place smells disconcertingly like chili.

"The check-in receptionist is on lunch break," Maggie says. "Let me just register you with the system so the sentry guns don't cut you in half."

Gus nods. "Much appreciated."

The retinue of scientists and engineers follows behind, piling into the little lobby while Gus goes through registration. He expects Maggie to take off her sunglasses, but she never does. She chats with him about the weather and her tomato garden while she gets him checked in, and it's oddly cathartic. This woman is making plans to eat something weeks from this moment, and he takes comfort in that—especially since she seems to be familiar with the battle to come.

"Okeydoke, Mister Kitko," she says. "We're all set. You ready for the big show?"

"I'm on pins and needles, Director Corley."

She slaps him on the back. "Attaboy. And call me Maggie. Let's get in there and have a look."

The party travels into the complex proper, which widens into a corridor stretching on forever in either direction, at least a hundred meters wide and taller than Greymalkin. Pipes and conduits run along the walls. A pair of thick, yellow rails traverse the ceiling with a muscular crane straddling them. When Gus looks down the length of the yard, he sees at least five more.

Maggie walks with a slight limp, pointing out features as they go. "Truth be told, there were some pretty big layoffs when the Veil fell. Demand for our department dried up overnight. Not a lot of call to build ships in the era of ship hunters."

"Maybe one day you could build a ship-hunter hunter," Gus says, and she barks a laugh.

"I like the way you think. So anyway, we were dealing with a bit of the old brain drain, so I was excited when the request came through from command to make something special for you." She gestures to some of the men and women following them. "Had to call in our best metallurgists, structural engineers, propulsion scientists, aerodynamicists...We basically kidnapped a few of them out of retirement."

"We haven't left the site for two weeks," one of them shouts from the back, and a few folx laugh.

"We're paying the shit out of them, Gus," Maggie says. "Don't listen. This place had to be spun back up, basically recommissioned from scratch. We flew in milling equipment from all over the world, even cooperating with some countries who've have had a...spiky relationship with the US. What I'm trying to help you see is the scope of the job."

Gus cranes his neck to look up. "The size of this place alone does that, Maggie."

She sighs. "You should've seen us in our heyday. The SDNF was originally conceived as a skunkworks; everything we needed was here. We were working on the latest capital ships, the fastest fighters...I heard your friend Ardent stole one of our final masterpieces."

"No comment, I'm afraid," Gus says. "I promise you I wasn't involved in that...but for the record, it was Dahlia Faust, not Ardent."

Maggie stops and raises her eyebrows at him. "Oh. Then I'll curse *her* every night before bed."

They stop underneath the tarp-covered object, and Gus marvels at its size: only a little shorter than Greymalkin, and wide enough for two people to lie across. A row of six boxy protrusions line one side, with wires running from the complex directly into them.

He turns to find Maggie tapping on her Gang UI. She pulls up the camera and aims it at Gus, getting where she can see his face.

"Uh, what are you doing?" he asks.

"If you're going to unwrap a present," she says, "I want to take a picture for the team newsletter. You ready to see what's under there?"

"Sure?"

"Floyd!" she yells, before giving a hacking cough. "Floyd!"

"Yeah!" someone shouts back from the catwalks.

Maggie cups her hands to her mouth. "Do it!"

A series of explosive bolts fire all down the steel bands, which snap like rubber. They clatter to the ground in wobbling piles, and Gus raises his hands in defense, backing away from the debris. The tarp begins to slide down one side, revealing a shining blade.

It's a sword—but there's so much more to it than that.

The reflection of the fleeing tarp dances along the mirror-shined starmetal surface. It's single-edged. Six thruster nozzles break the line of the back, each about the size of a CAV. The handguard is little more than a short, pointy bit in the curvature. The hilt is sculpted to fit four fingers and a thumb, leading to an open-ring pommel.

Gus remembers to close his mouth before the flies get in. "Oh wow."

"We call it Project Excalibur," Maggie says, "and in case you can't tell, it's a rocket-propelled sword. From the moment Greymalkin joined up, we started asking ourselves how to give it an advantage in a fight. What you see before you is the majority of the United Worlds Strategic Starmetal Reserve. With some help from JPL, we were able to outfit the blade with engines from an MRX-20 hyperstrike fighter. Excalibur absolutely will cleave a Vanguard in twain."

"I..." Gus stares at the largest sword he's ever heard of. "I don't know what to say."

"Just let me know where to send the bill." She laughs. "Six hundred million unicreds and some change."

"Six hundred…"

"Yeah, so don't drop it."

"I'll be careful," he says, and she elbows him.

"I'm just ribbing you, Kitko. It's a goddamned sword. Of course you can drop it. But just in case you don't want to, we built a harness for Greymalkin."

He smiles at the director with her wild white hair and ill-fitting suit. She's a real piece of work.

She waves him on. "All right. Show's over. My people have put together three hours of training vids on this bad boy, and you're going to watch all of it."

Ardent spends their afternoon in UW combat doctrinal briefings, despite having a repository of military minds at Falchion's disposal. Based on everything Gus said, it would grant them all the knowledge they needed in a fight. Ardent hasn't experienced a Deepsync, but if it's more intrusive than mind-to-mind interfacing, that frightens them.

When they get out of class that evening, they learn Gus has finally returned from San Diego—only to redeploy to the moon within the hour. The tacticians are apparently worried the enemy might be able to fold into orbit sooner than expected.

Ardent throws a fit until their chaperones agree to give them a ride out to the Nellis Vanguard rally point in the desert. When Greymalkin's frame comes into view, Ardent's heart relaxes.

The skimmer settles down at the edge of the zone, and Ardent doesn't wait for the escort to open the door. They leap out and head for Greymalkin, hoping they can find Gus before it's time to go. They wander through Jotunn's drones, coffin-sized and solid as boulders. The rows obscure the way forward like a hedge maze, strange crop circles standing guard.

After they pass through, it's not hard to spot Gus's minders: a small herd of scientists and soldiers milling around Greymalkin's two-toned foot. The man himself stands by, chatting with them, getting prepped to leave. Greymalkin looms over all, its shiny new sword strapped to its back with a mechanical harness.

"Gus!" Ardent says, picking up the pace.

He smiles upon noticing them, and for a moment, all is right with the world. They rush to him, throwing their arms around his neck and hugging him with everything they have.

Gus turns to the soldier running down the checklist. "Can you give me a second, buddy?"

The soldier leaves, and Gus pulls back, looking into Ardent's heart with those bottomless green eyes of his.

Ardent can't hide the fear on their face. "I'm sorry."

He touches their cheek. "Why?"

"I—I was just afraid I'd miss you is all. Tazi had us in briefings until the last minute and...I don't know, I thought you might take off without me."

Gus nods. "I was worried about that, too. Tight timetable. So glad you made it."

He leans forward and gently touches his lips to theirs. They drink in his scent, pressing against him. The cadre of soldiers disappears, the Vanguards, too. When Ardent closes their eyes, it's just Gus.

They slip their tongue into his mouth, and he tastes of mint. It takes them back to the little street in Monaco, and the first time they saw him.

Is that what you are? Sweet and calm?

Their lips part, and Ardent understands the depth of their longing. They truly do need him in their life. He can't run off to the moon just to die up there.

"You know you won't be alone, right?" Gus says. "When you're inside Falchion, we'll be able to talk like we're right beside each other."

Ardent shakes their head. "Not with Saturnine nearby."

He gives them a pained smile. "I... Look, I'm doing this for the right reasons—going up there alone. It's not because of what we talked about at the hotel."

But that doesn't feel true. He acquiesced too easily to Tazi and Bowman's plans.

"I know," they say, and even though it's killing them, they muster their most confident smile and wrinkle their nose so they won't look like they're crying. "I can see how much you want to come back to me."

Something awakens in him, and Ardent prays it's his survival instinct. Last time, Harlequin finished the fight in one hit. Any self-doubt he has could be lethal, and Gus is the doubting sort.

"No giving up, no matter how hard it gets." The end of their sentence clips so they can hold it together.

"I wouldn't dare." He shakes his head, wiping Ardent's tear from their cheek. "I know how you can be when you don't get your way."

They try to laugh, but it comes out as a sob. "Goddamned right."

They step back and take a moment to compose themself, and one of the soldiers signals to Gus. He gives them a nod. Ardent's time with him is already running out.

"I never told you how much I liked your suit," they say.

Gus smirks. "A fashion compliment from Ardent Violet? If Mom was still alive, I'd have to tell her."

Ardent sniffles. "It makes your butt look good."

Another soldier calls to Gus.

"Just give me a minute, okay?" he says. "Ardent, I'm so sorry. If it wasn't the fate of our planet—"

"I know."

"I have to go."

"You also have to come back."

They kiss him once more, drawing back to rest their hands on his firm chest. Ardent takes him in, trying to memorize every feature they can for the cold night ahead.

They back away, one step at a time. When they can't take it anymore, they turn and walk off into the cool desert evening.

They wander through the field of drones to Falchion's silent form. The horned devil looks to the distant horizon, and Ardent wonders what goes on in its head when it's dormant. Lenses are set up to image the monster, and spotlights illuminate it from beneath—making it no less demonic. The soldiers have erected a perimeter, but they let Ardent pass.

Ardent strides to the Vanguard's foot, and a quiet keening fills their mind the closer they get—Falchion is communicating with them somehow. It's a heady rush, like love at first sight, and they have to catch themself. Ardent rests their palm against the Vanguard's foot.

They can see Falchion's dead blue eyes in their head the second they make contact. There's an aura of melancholia in its touch, and it does little to comfort Ardent's heart.

"What's wrong with you?"

"I've synchronized my databases to the other Traitor Vanguards."

"Is that bad?"

"I know what I am now. What I've been."

Ardent doesn't know how to comfort it. They aren't sure they want to.

"Spare me your pity, human."

The link goes dead.

White light floods the desert as Greymalkin launches into the sky. Ardent watches Gus's rising star, bound for its guard position on the moon, and searches their heart for hope. They don't find much.

Ardent can only pray they'll still be able to do their job when they lose him.

Gus wants to survive. Even if he doesn't believe it's possible, he still wants it.

He descends toward the lunar surface, sinking a lacquered foot into the soft soil. It powders up around him, and Greymalkin sends him a lot of health and safety warnings about the particulates. It doesn't really matter, since Gus isn't wearing a helmet. If he's out in the lunar soil, he's already dead. It would've been good to have one, but the scientists couldn't come up with a way to make it work with Greymalkin's probes.

If Gus and Greymalkin survive this, Greymalkin will design a helmet for Earth's scientists.

"Can you put some pockets on this uniform?"

Pocket technology is trivial to a Vanguard.

"If we survive this, you need to make more jokes."

Neither of those outcomes are likely.

"They should've called you Sunshine with an attitude like that."

Hope is not the key to Gus's mission. His job is to make a difference for the people of Earth. His goal was never survival. It is important that he prioritize making an impact over his own existence. He cannot hesitate to act appropriately when in the defense of billions of lives.

Gus closes his eyes. "Are you scared to die?"

Greymalkin would prefer to exist. It believes it has more to offer the humans but accepts its place in their preservation. It has, after all, killed so many of them. Humans often characterize the random scenarios presented to them as fate. Greymalkin understands its own.

"But are you afraid?"

Fear is an instantiation of an instinct. The biological concept of survival is not a motivator. Like Gus, it is not particularly attached to life—only the experiences contained therein. It appreciates the time it has already had.

"Same, buddy. We've been pretty lucky."

Ardent is on the Vanguard network and wishes to speak with Gus.

"Put them through."

The silo splits and mirrors, becoming a wide, reflective floor. Gus will never get over the infinite conference room.

Ardent appears before him, not as the shaved, broken Conduit, but the radiant person they've always been. They still wear the UW Conduit suit, bulky and olive—it doesn't match the rest of them at all. Their rainbow hair shines in the spotlights of the silo, and when they turn to see Gus, there's hurt in their eyes.

He takes a dry swallow. "Ardent..."

"I've been running simulations inside of Falchion. I know you're just acting as a sacrifice up there!"

"I am."

"When did you find out?"

He can't look them in the eye. "On the way to San Diego."

They take a few steps, closing the gap to him. "You have no idea how badly I want to slap you right now."

"I wish you would. It'd be nice to feel something." He closes his eyes.

They suck in a breath like they're about to do it, but the blow never falls. He looks, and Ardent fumes before him.

"You should've told me! We could have come up with a better plan!"

"I wanted to, but—I didn't want that to be our last interaction."

"How dare you? You—you're wonderful and sweet and everything to me right now, and..." They grasp him by the cheeks, breath coming faster. "You can't do this. I need you."

"I need you, too." He takes them by the hips. "I'm just trying to do what's right, okay?"

"Well, which is it? Are you trying to be heroic, or trying to disappear?"

Gus pauses to consider it; neither option sounds right to him. "I want you to have a tomorrow. I've wanted that since the night Juliette landed. When it touched down behind you, I thought it was such a crime. I didn't care what it would do to me, but you—"

"Stop it! You have value, too, Gus! Why can't you—"

Superluminal wakes detected.

The words appear in Gus's sight, and he releases Ardent.

Their face twists in anguish. "No."

Greymalkin needs to deploy. This conversation must end.

"I'm sorry, Ardent."

"No!"

Ardent tries to grab his hand, and he takes a step back. The hurt on their face at that move could very well break his heart—but if he feels their touch, he won't want to let go. They seem determined to make this as painful for him as possible.

"I'm up here because I want you to walk away from this," he says. "Stay focused. Don't waste it."

"Shut up!"

"I love you."

Their perfect lips curl downward, and their whole body shakes. "I—I love you, too. This conversation isn't over."

"Fine." Gus nods, more of a tic than an acknowledgment.

It's naive to state that they're not done here when everything indicates otherwise. But then, this is Ardent Violet. If Gus knows anything about the pop star, they always get their way, no matter the circumstance.

He'd like to see them again.

Maybe there'll be a heaven. That'd be nice.

Ardent vanishes, and a voice comes through the comms from mission control.

"Vanguard Greymalkin, this is EMC, initiating comms check. Please respond."

"EMC, Greymalkin, comms check okay. Standing by."

Chapter Twenty-One

Knock 'Em Down

Ardent is snapped back to their own surroundings, disconnected from Greymalkin's link.

Inside Falchion, the white powder of the Bonneville Salt Flats almost looks like snow. A pale moon rises overhead—Falchion pinpoints Gus's location for them. The orb casts a blue tint across everything, washing out the reds of Falchion's armor. The brittle desert stretches in all directions—one of the best places to summon a radiological event.

"Crown One to all Vanguards," Tazi's voice comes over their priority channel. "I'm your handler today. Jovian stats reported four superluminal fold wakes, one hotter with gamma. They match our targets. We've discussed how this is going to go. Good luck, my friends, and we'll talk again when Saturnine is down."

She says it so confidently that Ardent almost believes it.

"Cascade acknowledged." Nisha almost sounds excited. "Let's spread out."

Cascade springs to life beside Falchion, taking to the skies and rocketing away to get some distance. Jotunn blasts away over the salt, leaving white clouds and a murmuration of drones in its wake.

"Okay, Falchion." Ardent braces themself. "Do I connect now?"

The Vanguard whispers in their ear with the voice of Ardent's dark reflection, *"An ordinary person can only last five minutes under Deepsync."*

"And me?"

"We'll find out. Don't worry. I'll keep you fighting until it's over."

"Will it hurt?"

"It will everything."

"Vanguards, Crown One, T minus thirty to contact."

A timer appears in Ardent's view, along with the words, *Deepsync imminent.* They watch the numbers tick down, their breath growing faster with every passing second.

Falchion draws out the blasters from their places on its back. They charge in its hands, warm current building against Ardent's palms. Ardent has no experience in combat. Will the Fount really provide all the answers they need?

Jotunn stops a kilometer away, just a tiny black cloud on the horizon. "In position."

Cascade glints in the distance as well, and together, the Vanguards form an equilateral triangle. "Cascade ready!"

"I'm ready," Ardent says.

"All Vanguards, Crown One, SFARS firing."

Energy builds on the horizon, fluorescing in Falchion's scanners. Ardent feels the power building beneath the distant Nellis Air Force Base like static in their hair. It's many kilometers away, but to a Vanguard's sensors, it might as well be next door.

Falchion projects the landing zone onto Ardent's vision, a column of blue light stretching all the way into the heavens. Ardent aims their blasters as the last five seconds count down.

A flash of white light cracks open the sky, and three superluminal brake burns rain down. In the distance, rainbow auroras dance through the magnetosphere, charged by the sudden release of solar particles. The salt flats get fifty degrees hotter, and Falchion's carapace stings with the strikes of gamma rays. All the unshielded ecology in a ten-klick radius just caught a lethal dose of radiation.

Falchion braces against a shock wave of dust. Rocks and debris abrade the Vanguard's entire body. A trio of plasma pillars stretch up to the heavens, blotting out everything else with their energy. When Falchion's scanners adjust to pierce the milky air, three silhouettes touch down in opposition: Saturnine, with its grace and beauty; Ifrit, its single long horn curving like a scimitar; and Reaper, with its—

"Big fucking scythe right there," Ardent says, wide-eyed.

That thing is going to cut them in half.

Saturnine's keening fills Ardent's ears like cotton, blocking out a sense they didn't know they had. Before its arrival, Ardent had been able to feel the presence of their comrades. Now it's like space itself is dead.

"Get ready for Deepsync."

Ardent tenses up around the pistols. "Do it!"

First comes the guitar, overdriven and fuzzy. It's a lick in drop D, easy enough to play, and exactly what they rehearsed at Last Chance. A snare follows in its wake, then a chorus of dead musicians add their talents to the mix. Pure light pours into Ardent's head, connecting them to a world much larger than themself.

Ardent has no idea how to share control, but their mind is wrenched open to receive alien knowledge. They're so self-obsessed, yet when connected to the Fount, they are nothing. Not special. Barely even interesting. They swoon under the weight of billions of voices raging for priority. One thought comes through from all the experienced fighters in the bunch:

Shoot now.

Ardent pulls the trigger on their blaster, loosing a bolt of energy at Reaper. In the blink of an eye, the Vanguard deflects it with the flat of their blade, routing it off into the sands. The shot leaves a wound of glass and molten salt as long as a train.

Cascade throws a suppression field, but it's too late. The enemy Vanguards split up to engage their opponents. Jotunn pairs off against Saturnine, Ifrit charges Cascade, and Reaper comes streaking toward Ardent and Falchion.

Her hands are soft on their shoulders.

"With a wide arc like a halberd—" She pulls them back, away from the simulated warrior. It feels like a long stride, and they ready themself to defend.

The hologram crosses the distance and cuts them in half. They stare down at the glowing red slash across their torso.

"You are never far enough."

Reaper swings the blade at their head, and Ardent bends backward to dodge. They spring up on their hands, delivering a savage kick into Reaper's chest and activating their jets. The enemy Vanguard goes skidding backward, and Ardent shoots again. Reaper executes another perfect parry, guiding the bolt away. The shot misses its face by centimeters—and powders a few of Jotunn's drones in the background.

"Just so you know," Falchion says, *"it's quicker with a blade than I am with my aim."*

"Oh."

They spin to jet away, and Reaper follows like a singing comet. A couple of Jotunn's drones smash it across its face, sending Reaper spinning into the dirt. Hjalmar engages in a pitched battle with Saturnine, but he sends more support to Falchion. Ardent wishes they could talk to him and coordinate better, but Saturnine's song blocks even the best comms.

It opens its palm at Jotunn, and a cone of absolute deadness envelops it. Jotunn disappears in a torrent of directed jamming, nullifying all sensory equipment—

—and transmission equipment.

Jotunn's drones rain onto the sand, dropping straight down without a connection to their host. The rock band in Ardent's mind takes a dark turn without their consent.

"Your friend is about to die."

Reaper abandons Falchion and heads straight for the defenseless Jotunn. It's bulky and slow—heavily armored and blind. Falchion blasts at the fleeing Reaper with its cannons, but it dodges and deflects, cratering more of the surrounding desert.

When Ardent gets too close, Reaper flips and takes a swing. Falchion ducks into the hit, grabbing the weapon by the snath—a word Ardent never knew before the Fount—and wrenching it aside. Falchion's momentum sends it barreling into its opponent, and they roll across the ground in a catfight. Reaper guides the blade, trying to send it into Falchion's neck. When Ardent flinches, it catches them with a boot and throws them over.

Saturnine twists its jamming cone onto Falchion, blacking out its sensors. All goes dark, and it's like being immersed in carbon sludge. Reaper is somewhere close by, but Ardent has no means of knowing, save for dead reckoning. They take off in any direction they can fly, trying to put distance between themself and their enemy.

Agony settles over Ardent's body in a hail of needles. It's like being covered in a net of electric barbs and *then* getting maced.

This is Cascade's strongest disruption field.

"What the *fuck*, Nisha?"

Then they realize: She's trying to guide them away from Reaper. Ardent flees from the disruption field at maximum boost, eyes watering. Saturnine stops jamming them, so Cascade stops torturing them. Reaper has abandoned pursuit, headed for Jotunn.

In the distance, Cascade tangles with the larger Ifrit. Nisha throws a punch across its molten-glass face, and some of the material starts to eat into the Vanguard's hand. The boom of Cascade's cry puffs a ring in the dust, and it dodges back from Ifrit's horn at the last second.

"My siblings have been upgraded," Falchion whispers.

Ardent takes aim at Reaper, and it pivots its scythe, ready to deflect the shot. In a nanosecond, Falchion calculates all possible trajectories of the ricochet. One of the rays intersects with Saturnine. Ardent fires, and Reaper capably redirects the shot into its ally.

The blast smashes into Saturnine's collarbone, crushing the nearby shoulder joint to dust. Metal skin shears open, and the Vanguard's hand droops uselessly at its side. Falchion's hearing momentarily opens to the flickering atmosphere of radio waves. They catch thousands of fragmented data points from around the world before Saturnine chokes it back off.

Cascade jukes through Ifrit's legs, throwing off the larger Vanguard's balance. Instead of taking a shot from behind, Cascade jets across the sand to assault a new target.

Falchion plugs Saturnine twice more while Jotunn brings its drones back online. The shots hit close to the same spot, but even perfect aim is still subject to some chaos. Saturnine's shriek rings through the air, and the jamming grows weaker.

Cascade comes flying in like a rugby player, wrapping around Saturnine's torso. It twists over the enemy Vanguard in a fluid maneuver, throwing it to the ground by its head.

Reaper and Ifrit come for Jotunn, but with its drones, the Traitor Vanguard is a far more effective adversary. It hammers its opponents, knocking them off-balance and overwhelming their defenses. Splashes of molten glass erupt from Ifrit's skin, absorbing the drones where they hit.

Falchion locks onto Saturnine and sinks four shots into the center of its chest, blowing it open. Milky blood sprays from within, boiling in the particle fires. Cascade gives its victim's neck a hard twist and smashes the spine with its knee.

The flood of song from Nisha, Hjalmar, and Gus comes rolling into Ardent's mind—all perfectly on-key, like a choir of angels. The voices coming from Nisha's thoughts are liquid metal, pure and engulfing. Hjalmar brings the thunder of rhythm, drums of every shape and sound. As for Gus, his mind is an orchestra, a big band sound to unify and round out the whole arrangement.

With Saturnine in play, they were operating on instinct, and they were winning.

Now, they're a well-oiled machine.

"One down!" Nisha's voice filters through as the comms come back online.

"Good," Hjalmar says as Jotunn's drones rush for Reaper. "Because now I can show you all a drum solo."

Gus felt his friends' signals go dead the second Saturnine landed and knew he was truly alone. He looks into the heavens from the snowy surface. It won't be long.

The remaining Earth ships lie in wait for Harlequin, and Gus feels their guns aimed squarely at his patch of moon. He understands why—if he starts to lose the fight, they should end it while they can.

If they can.

The weapons on board those vessels aren't designed to penetrate the advanced armors of Vanguards. The New Jalandhar colonists had some of that tech on their side, but the Homeworlders didn't. They disobeyed Greymalkin's wishes, and it never shared.

That might have been a lethal mistake—for them and Greymalkin.

The path to Earth fills with thousands of silver needles—the brake burns of Ghost landing craft, stocked up with murder machines. The UW fleet opens fire immediately, blasting away at the incoming pack. Pops of plasma fill the sky like champagne bubbles. At least they can thin out the number of Ghosts.

Until a pair of shadowy bulks slide into the school of destroyers like orcas—ship hunters.

They immediately begin tractoring and eating ships, and a lot of engines light up in the tiny armada. The ragtag warships execute short-range superluminal folds, moving them clear enough to get a shot and remain in the fight. It's a gutsy maneuver that leaves their folding drives discharged if things go wrong again. That's likely, since Earth's hardscrabble defense fleet was already overwhelmed by the Ghosts.

On cue, one of the ship hunters short-range jumps into the scattering vessels and releases a host of golden missiles. Gus recognizes the make—the same ones from New Jalandhar. He tries to establish control over the Ghost OS, but his access vanishes.

Harlequin explodes into the stars before Gus, its brake burn broken and crooked like it was yanked. Its body is the color of oil slick and bruises, vibrating at the edges with radiation. Its face is a mask out of a nightmare—indifferent, yet bemused, white eyes staring lifelessly at Greymalkin. It points its studded rod down at Gus as it did in the Battle of New Jalandhar.

Gus draws his sword, finger wrapping into the jet trigger guard, and spreads his feet to receive his foe. He's staring down his own demise, and he knows it. How much time that'll take is another question.

He must make his life last as long as possible.

Deepsync in progress...

A snare rolls out the rhythm in Gus's mind, copying the syncopation of the jazz masters of sunken New Orleans. His piano alternates hits on the upbeats, frenetic and anxious. He wants to fight and win—so he chooses something optimistic. Peppy.

And maybe a little pissed off.

Gus's reality expands to encompass the thoughts of thousands of sword masters across every style. He grips his blade tighter, bracing for what's coming.

Hideo prepares to receive the attack, thinking only of cutting. If he hesitates, if his mind is on any other movement, then he will not be able to cut his enemy. There is one aim, and it must be singular—or he will never beat this level.

"Really? A hologame memory?"

The best fighter is the best fighter, regardless of circumstance.

Harlequin lowers its club and charges, winding up for a monumental swing. Gus deflects, sending a shower of sparks pouring from the meeting of weapons. He guides the club's path away, arms vibrating with the friction of the studs. Harlequin chains together attacks, flowing between them like a practiced dancer, and Gus can't counter—he's too busy staying alive.

A gravity wave could change the equation, but there's no time to charge up. Harlequin won't give Greymalkin a centimeter of space. Before long, it's pounding him from all sides, testing all his reflexes. Everywhere he retreats, it follows.

Gus blocks an overhead swipe and triggers the burst jets on his sword, throwing Harlequin's attack wide.

The soles of her fencing shoes slap the mat. Block, across, step in and—

He tries to skewer the enemy, but it's too fast, spinning away from his thrusts. It's the closest he's come to scoring a hit, and the opportunity vanishes just as quickly as it came.

Huge clouds of dust erupt from the lunar surface in their battle, fogging the horizon, fully obscuring Harlequin. Greymalkin switches to radiation sensors, but Harlequin's gamma rays reflect across the moon dust. To Gus, it looks like a bright blur in the fog. If they continue to fight here, Harlequin's advantage will only compound.

The blur swings its club, connecting with Greymalkin's left arm. The boom shudders through Gus's chamber, sloshing him around inside. Hundreds of alarm messages bubble through the Vanguard's internal network: broken servos, sensors, armor plating, propulsion...His left arm is essentially toast. Greymalkin feeds him memories of people triumphing over pain.

The blow sends him flying out of the scuffle, and Gus fires his jets to get away. Without the thrusters on his left arm, his maneuvering is down. Harlequin overtakes him immediately, smashing into his back and grinding him along the lunar surface.

The enemy Vanguard batters him from above. It's faster than Greymalkin, stronger, with a better weapon. It takes everything Gus has to block its catastrophic strikes. Any hit from its club will be a disabling one, so there's no room for error.

Just last four more minutes.

Memories of bladed fights filter through him, all the successes and failures in close-quarters combat. Gus spots an opening and punches Harlequin's mask with the pommel of his sword. The enemy's head snaps back, and when it looks down again, it's missing a portion of the eye. Behind the armor plate, a ghost-white orb floats in a sea of wires. His radiation sensors register a huge burst of rads from the crack, the heat of a poisonous bonfire.

Gus kicks his opponent off to open some distance and switches to the attack. He peppers Harlequin with slashes, working the trigger of his jet blade. The sword leaves wide fans of fire in its wake before clanging harmlessly against Harlequin's studded club. The enemy Vanguard's defense is perfect.

He keeps the pressure on. If he can stall Harlequin on the defensive, he might be able to use his gravity wells. His sword smashes Harlequin's club aside, and Gus follows through with a claw to the face. It's a lucky hit, and he hooks fingers into the edge of Harlequin's mask. Gus yanks his enemy down onto Greymalkin's knee, feeling a solid connection.

Harlequin goes stumbling back, the crack in its mask widened. Gus presses his luck, the better to end this while he still has fight left in him. He goes in for a decapitating strike—and overextends himself. It's wide, leaving him in a clumsy position. He knows it's the wrong move, even as he throws it.

Harlequin dodges, bashing the sword from Greymalkin's hand. The blade goes skipping in the low gravity, and Gus tries to fly after it. Harlequin brings its rod down across Greymalkin's spine, and it's like being snapped in half. He belly flops onto the dirt, rolling in agony, barely avoiding lethal blows.

When he gets back to his feet, he's again surrounded by milky dust. He takes to the skies, jets ailing from the beating he's already received. Maneuvering thrusts are down by 60 percent, but he can use the gravity slingshot to get away. He pulls at space, setting up his flight maneuver with Harlequin hot on his heels.

Three minutes.

Just as he passes through the warped space, Harlequin's club connects with his boot, sending him off course. Greymalkin goes streaking over settlements, headed straight for the largest and oldest of the lunar colonies: Tranquility City.

Gus crashes through the lighted dome protecting the settlement, breaking apart buildings with its passage. Air gushes from the atmospheric envelope, expelling chunks of glass and steel struts. It's supposed to be evacuated, but if anyone was out and about on the streets, they're dead.

"Please tell me this place is empty!"

Unable to confirm.

Harlequin arrives with club held high. Greymalkin scrambles out of the way as the weapon powders a small skyscraper. Every second Gus spends in this place is irreparable damage to someone's way of life.

Harlequin smashes his face with a fist, and it's like getting his nose broken. He grits his teeth and swipes at his enemy with a flashing claw. Nozzles pop white on his knuckles, propelling his strike lightning fast.

Harlequin dodges, the leaking radiation fouling Greymalkin's targeting. Gus's left arm dangles uselessly, barely even attached. Harlequin exploits that fact, landing another blow to shatter it at the elbow.

Yet in that moment of agony, Gus hears the sweetest sound—the music of the Traitor Vanguards. Ardent's guitar shreds over Nisha's vocals and Hjalmar's drums, and he's transported briefly to his jam session at Last Chance. They're still out there, still playing on-key, still counting on him.

Even though Harlequin is probably about to kill him, he's no longer alone, and that gives him the strength to hold on a little longer. With a mighty shove, Gus shoulder-checks a building onto his opponent, showering it with broken rock, glass, and metal. He punches through the cloud and lands another solid hit, into Harlequin's neck. Firing rocket claws, Greymalkin tears loose a chunk of armor, snowing white blood into the thin atmosphere.

"Greymalkin, this is Crown One. Saturnine is down! Hang in there."

"Roger that." He ducks away as Harlequin destroys a train station. "Can anyone else please shoot this thing?"

"The ship hunters have almost finished destroying your fire support. You're alone up there."

Fuck.

Greymalkin assures Gus he can last the remaining time—buy the Earth a chance to survive. Keep Harlequin engaged. Be the bulwark.

The enemy Vanguard plants a boot in Greymalkin's stomach, sending it sprawling through downtown. Chunks of debris waft through the lunar gravity, entire sections of towers drifting toward the ground in slow motion.

Greymalkin charges up a gravity well and slingshots a broken antenna array at its opponent. Harlequin bashes it to pieces, but a huge segment still connects, knocking it backward. Gus fires off more pieces of the city, intensifying his gravity well and hurling bits of architecture through it.

Nana Kitko loved Tranquility City. She would be so mad right now.

Harlequin adopts a defensive posture, trying to block the assault with its rod, and Gus realizes: He's winning. It can't fight back, and there's a lot of landscape to pelt it with. He scours the ground for the right pieces, feeding them to his highly advanced wood chipper.

But before he can close the deal, Harlequin rushes him. Its swing passes through two high-rises—

—before connecting with Greymalkin's chest.

It's an odd feeling, taking a catastrophic hit in two bodies. The world groans and shrieks as what had been external becomes internal. A huge piece of Greymalkin's interior wall clamps down on Gus's legs, whiting out all feeling in the limbs. Human memories of trauma come pouring from the Fount to overwhelm him—births, amputations, accidents, tragedies.

Gus screams, going for his assailant with the last of his strength.

The next rod strike catches Greymalkin's face, shattering its armored plates like Gus's bones. His teeth ache, and his nose burns worse than any punch to the mouth.

As Greymalkin begins to fall, Gus checks the clock one last time.

Two minutes and forty-five seconds left.

Sorry, everyone.

* * *

Jotunn's drones work their magic on Reaper. Thousands of bullets alternate attacks, battering the enemy Vanguard from all sides, too numerous to be deflected. They hammer the same spots over and over, making headway into the armor while holding Reaper at bay.

Gus's big band goes silent in Ardent's mind. Everyone's song stutters with the sudden loss before reforming around what remains.

"Gus?" Ardent hates the panic in their voice. "Gus, do you copy?"

Ifrit charges through, long horn headed straight for Jotunn. Falchion takes a few shots at it, blowing off syrupy globules of molten skin, which ignite against the desert salt. The fluid material serves as a shield, absorbing the energy of the blasts and sloughing off. Ifrit whips its arm at Falchion, sending flecks of the liquid into its armor.

Ardent feels it like a hot match head pressing into their flesh.

They jet backward while Falchion battles the effects of the invading substance. It's not glass, Ardent's host informs them, it's nanites. Cascade's arm still hasn't stabilized, and it falls apart at the wrist like charred bones. Falchion will try to fight the infection before it spreads too far.

"All Vanguards, Crown One. Greymalkin is down. You must finish up now."

"Explain that!" Ardent winces as the acid eats farther into Falchion's chest. "What do you mean, 'down'?"

"It's a euphemism for 'dead,'" Falchion says. *"What you'll be if you don't pay attention."*

"He's out of the fight," comes Tazi's response.

Ardent looks to the rising moon, and they still feel the faintest signature of Greymalkin's transponder. They dodge another attack from Ifrit, spinning and blowing the horn off its head.

"No." Ardent tries to connect to Gus's comm, but hears nothing. "Gus, come in, please."

Reaper berserks, taking wild slashes at Jotunn through the cloud of drones. The black giant easily slips backward, ducking out of range. Ifrit redoubles its attack, hurling balls of glass at it, but Hjalmar's remaining drones intercept the attacks, melting instantly under the gooey nanites.

Cascade hurls disruption fields over Reaper, and combined with its thousand-front war with the drones, it's stunned.

"Let me at it, Hjalmar!" Nisha's song surges to the front of the mix as Cascade leaps onto Reaper's back.

The drones clear away, and Cascade wraps its victim in an anaconda's embrace. The Vanguard employs choke holds, ground fighting, and all-around viciousness to take Reaper apart. It cracks joints and tears away the carapace like snapping open juicy crab legs. Every spot that Jotunn's drones weakened, Cascade exposes. White blood sprays across the snowy sands, absorbed by the thirsty earth.

Falchion restrains Reaper's legs while Cascade finishes its grisly work. The bronze Vanguard holds aloft its mangled hand, now a melted array of sharp metal, and plunges it into Reaper's neck. The enemy Vanguard sputters and stops moving.

Ifrit charges for the melee, ready to force its molten bulk onto Cascade.

Ardent throws aside their blasters and grabs Reaper's scythe. With an artful sidestep and a hooking swing, it cleanly divests Ifrit of its legs. Cascade has just enough time to escape before Ifrit comes flailing into the corpse of its comrade. It tries to rise, but Ardent removes its head, then plunges the blade straight down into its back.

They rip the scythe out and throw it to the ground. Nanites have already begun etching the starmetal blade. Beneath Ifrit, Reaper's remains begin to dissolve.

"All Vanguards, Crown One, confirm targets destroyed."

"They're dead," Hjalmar says.

"Good," comes the response. "We're reading sixteen new superluminal wakes headed straight for Earth—identity unknown. Get to the moon and end Harlequin now."

Jotunn nods, mimicking its Conduit. "Understood."

The giant rises into the air with its drones, and Ardent feels it charging its fold drive. Cascade launches silently after, then Falchion picks up its blasters and falls in behind. One minute and fifteen seconds remain on the clock. If they don't finish the fight by then, they're just passengers, hoping for victory.

"Falchion, is Gus still alive?"

"He's not gone yet."

"Then let me say goodbye."

Gus expected to die.

After Harlequin lifts Greymalkin's broken body by the neck, he wishes he had.

The adversary's palms bind to Greymalkin's armor, sealing together with scalding-hot welds. He finally comes to understand the purpose of such an act: high-speed data transfer.

Memories go coursing through him, of an asteroid mining ship, the *Lancea*, and of suffering, betrayal, and devastation. Gus remembers things he never saw, brutal and hideous transformations, lives stolen by Infinite. This isn't the Fount.

These are Harlequin's dreams.

Harlequin wants Greymalkin to understand the depths of its hatred for it. It's an act of accusation before execution, of revenge. He doesn't understand its rage, but he feels every ounce of its fury.

All goes black as Greymalkin disconnects Gus from its neural feed. He's left alone with his crushed legs, whimpering in the dark.

"Greymalkin!" The anguish in his voice shocks him. Does he really sound that bad? "Please, get up. I can fight!"

The hull hums around Gus, loud enough to drown him out. His legs burn with unbearable pain, and he grits his teeth. He has no way of knowing how bad the damage is—but he's about to die, so it's moot.

"Greymalkin!"

There's only the steady, cruel keen of Harlequin, like the whine of a hydraulic press crushing the life out of him.

Somewhere, deep in Gus's forbidden hopes, he planned to see Ardent again. He'd wanted to sing for them—it didn't matter that he couldn't carry a tune. He had something to give Ardent, and it wouldn't stay inside any longer. It wasn't about beauty; it was a matter of the heart.

But this pitch-black chamber is the oubliette where hopes come to die.

Ardent will never hear his song.

Metal rends around him, screaming like a banshee, and Gus squeezes his eyes tight.

I hope you get the world you always needed.

His shaking fingers form the F minor seventh, and he tries to imagine the smooth ivories against his skin.

And life finds you on the shady side of the street—

He screams as the plate presses harder on his legs, melting to a sob. They're broken, at least once each, probably more. Despite his agony, he tries to recollect the next chords. If he can't have a last show, he'll have a last song.

He's only a few notes in when he hears a voice.

"Gus—"

Ardent?

"Gus, can you hear me?" They're crying. It's too easy to make them cry.

"Hey." Gus's throat burns. "Ardent—"

"Gus? Hang on, goddamn it! We're coming! Fold in ten seconds."

"I can't get Greymalkin to respond."

It hears Gus. It's protecting him from the profound stimuli assaulting it.

Gus swallows hard. "Please reconnect me. I want to try."

This amount of pain is too much for a human. It will run down Gus's clock much faster. He might die instantly.

"We're here!" Ardent calls. "Gus, I see you! Just hang on."

Gus can't give up. He promised Ardent he wouldn't.

"Please, Greymalkin. Just another second."

Greymalkin will honor his last wish.

Deepsync in progress...

Gus returns to life and the million frying neurons. All is signal, and all is noise. The Earth rises behind a battleground. Ship hunters close on their prey. Nukes pop across the heavens like fireworks, and lasers trace the shape of violence.

Ahead of that—three brake burns. It's Cascade, Jotunn, and Falchion come to rescue Greymalkin.

His finale is at hand, and his piano, brass, and strings all wail a tragic dirge in the tune of "Saint James Infirmary." Even his jazz education knows he's not going to make it, but he can't quit. The white orbs in Harlequin's ruined mask shed drowned light upon Gus, peering into his very soul. Harlequin is inside Greymalkin's systems, corrupting its networks, ripping apart the fabric of its personality.

"Shoot—" Gus says. "Shoot me with everything you have, Ardent."

"Gus—"

"Please."

He charges Greymalkin's gravity well, pouring what remains of the Vanguard's massive capacitors into it. The voices of the Fount surge inside him, urging him to battle. It is a civilization of stolen minds, but they only contain one thought: *fight*.

The light twists and bends around the superdense clump of space in his hand. His fist contains a vortex of impossibilities, physics suborned to the will of a machine.

Ardent fires.

Falchion's shot whizzes toward Gus, and he throws out his right arm, guiding the bolt around toward Harlequin's face. He focuses the beam, lensing the energy into a compressed, potent charge. He drops that ultra-concentrated shot right on the crack in Harlequin's mask.

The bolt blows its head off.

The voices of billions cheer inside him, but the noise doesn't stop. It grows brighter and louder until he can hear nothing else. Gus knows he's supposed to disconnect, but he doesn't know how. He doesn't know anything anymore. His mind becomes static, loud yet peaceful, chaotic yet homogenized, and his perceptions come to an end.

Deepsync ending in three, two, one...

Ardent reels in the haze, and Falchion disconnects the Fount before it can overwhelm them. Exhaustion takes hold, and it's hard to even keep their eyes open. Falchion regains control of itself, flying to Greymalkin's side for a diagnostic.

Ardent can only watch helplessly as their Vanguard surveys the damage. "Please tell me he's okay."

Above, the ship hunters destroy the last of Earth's armada. The planet is now defenseless, save for the Traitor Vanguards—but those are an order of magnitude smaller than this enemy.

Below, Greymalkin lies motionless over the remains of Harlequin. The blurry radioactivity of the enemy Vanguard fades to a dull gray carapace, and the neck sparks a few times. Falchion puts a couple more rounds into it, as a coup de grâce.

"Vanguards, this is Crown One. Ten seconds until those unknown wakes arrive. Godspeed to us all."

Ardent looks for the arrival of the conquering force. The ship hunters were already too much for three Vanguards with no Conduits. Ardent's exhausted mind has a lot of trouble imagining what other heinous nightmares Infinite has conjured up for humanity—but they suppose they're about to find out.

Sixteen vessels come out of the fold, blazing into orbit alongside the ship hunters. Their transponders read "United Attack Fleet," and they're armed with cannons Ardent has never seen. It's the force from New Jalandhar.

"Yes!" Nisha cries.

The newcomers open fire on the ship hunters with beam cannons, carving off chunks and setting blazes across the surface. Gooey plasma balls erupt from the points of impact, wandering into space like sprays of fireflies. One of the lances of light drills all the way through a behemoth, blasting out the other side with a fountain of debris.

Mismatched impulse thrusters fire across the pair of ship hunters, stolen and assimilated from countless vessels. They come about, facing away from the fleet.

They're running.

One of the hunters manages a superluminal fold, vanishing in a streak of light. The other disappears as well—in a thousand-megaton explosion.

Falchion kneels over Greymalkin, throwing long shadows from the fusion light overhead. Greymalkin's chest plate has completely collapsed, and the vacuum seal protecting its Conduit may have failed. Falchion touches Greymalkin's broken face, connecting to its systems to see what remains.

Ardent's voice is barely a whisper in the chaos. "Come on, Gus."

There's a warm presence in Greymalkin's chest, like a candle flame. He's still in there, faint but alive. Life support is failing, and Earth's medical centers are almost four hundred thousand kilometers away. If Ardent can't get him to care soon, he's dead.

Tranquility City lies desolated around them, its once proud towers demolished by the battle. The lights have gone dark, and there are no airlocks, no hospitals. Because of Harlequin, the humans had to be evacuated.

There's no help here.

"United Attack Fleet, this is Nisha Kohli, Conduit for Cascade." Falchion translates the call from Punjabi. "We have an injured friend, and we need a... like a big airlock. Do you have anything that can fit a Vanguard?"

Ardent waits for the reply, heart in their throat. When they can't take it anymore, they add, "United Attack Fleet, please come in!"

"Nisha Kohli, this is the UAFS Kukri-class Cruiser *Bahādarī*. We have room if you can get to us."

"Yes!" Ardent cries. "Yes, Nisha, tell them we're coming!"

"Acknowledged, *Bahādarī*. Three Vanguards inbound," Nisha says. "Don't shoot."

Ardent starts to pick up Greymalkin, but Jotunn stops them.

"Allow me," Hjalmar says.

Jotunn's drones wriggle under Greymalkin, forming a mesh and lifting it up. They carry the downed Vanguard like a chair, rising into the sky. Cascade and Falchion follow after Greymalkin, who rests upon the makeshift throne like a fallen monarch.

Even with the *Bahādarī* making full speed toward them and the Vanguards pushing their sublight engines, the trip still takes forever. Falchion remains beside Greymalkin, palm sealed to its chest to prevent any possible vacuum seal breaches.

The Vanguard itself is weak, scarcely able to maintain life support.

"There's a chance Greymalkin will reset, and attack us," Falchion says. *"If that happens, we'll have to destroy it."*

"I know," Ardent says.

"He may have been connected to the Fount too long. You don't know what you're rescuing."

"I know."

Ardent can't focus on that. They've been granted the possibility of Gus's survival. It's a small miracle in the grand scheme of their war with Infinite—but it's one Ardent will hold close in the unending doom.

Greymalkin's comms fall silent, and it goes into hibernation mode. Ardent no longer feels the flicker of Gus's heartbeat over their connection.

"Falchion! What's happening? What do we do?"

"Catastrophic shutdown to save the core. All you can do is wait and hope."

They draw close to the *Bahādarī*, a tall, orange, wing-shaped carrier ship with a few scorched patches along its hull. Falchion translates the writing across its side, showing the path to the main hangar bay midway up the ship.

Ardent watches Greymalkin, still as death in its drone cradle. It could just be a cold piece of metal for all they know.

"Almost there, babe," Ardent says gently. "We're almost there."

Chapter Twenty-Two

No Day Like Tomorrow

Despite their utter exhaustion, Ardent waits for thirty-seven hours.

The first two are spent cutting Gus out of Greymalkin's chest inside the *Bahādarī*'s hangar. It takes a Vanguard to pull off the armor plate, then a team of skilled technicians to get him the rest of the way out. Advanced cutting equipment and mechanics show up, and they bring the combined resources of the United Attack Fleet to bear on the problem.

Techs slice into the electric-blue musculature until they can get Gus free. Probes hang on his ports like dead snakes, and the professionals must pull them out manually. The first time Ardent sees Gus, they want to scream.

His skin is so pale. His legs are a mess. His head lolls as they tug him loose.

Disconnected from Greymalkin, Gus immediately goes into cardiac arrest. Alarms sound among shouts for intervention. A flock of medical staff descends upon him in their pastel-green smocks.

Ardent can't see anything through the flutter of activity, and they know they ought to stay back. Every voice inside them is begging to run to him, but they can't.

The next sixteen hours are spent in surgery.

Nisha and Hjalmar have long since gone to the medical center for rest and treatment. The doctors want Ardent to go, too. Medical staff urge Ardent to sleep for a while, in case the Deepsync had negative effects on them.

Bone weary, Ardent refuses. They watch the surgeons work through the operating theater window, occasionally catching a glimpse of Gus's unconscious face. Every time they do, they remember the moss green of his eyes and his gorgeous smile.

Calm and sweet.

Sitting in the observation room, head in their hands, Ardent could use some of that. The surgeons work tirelessly to save him, and every time they think it's over, he takes a turn.

The last nineteen hours are spent outside the ICU. Minders show up, telling Ardent that Tazi is hailing them on behalf of the United Worlds. They pass Ardent a loaner Gang, and Ardent slips it on.

"Hello, Mix Violet." Tazi is clear-eyed and somber, appearing in her UW fatigues.

"Is my family okay?" Ardent asks.

"Yes."

"Thank you."

"Ardent," Tazi says. It's not like her to use a first name. "I know what you're feeling, but you have to get some rest and let the doctors look at you."

"Duly noted."

"You can't change Gus's fate with hope alone, but you can hurt yourself. I've lost many friends. I've been where you are."

Their eyes are tired from so much crying. Rest would be a blessing.

"Then you know I can't leave." Ardent grabs handfuls of their cargo pockets and squeezes. "I...I'm afraid of waking up in a universe without him."

Tazi glances off camera, mutes herself, and says a few things. The sound comes back, and she says, "I have a lot to attend to, but please take care of yourself. Like it or not, the world needs you."

They give her a wan smile. "It always has. I'm Ardent Violet, you know."

Tazi smirks. "I hope you get some rest soon."

She terminates the hail, and Ardent returns to the excitement of the sick bay waiting area's floor tiles. A nurse comes and offers them something to drink. They take her up on it, and she reappears with a milky cup of chai.

After the hell Ardent has been through, it's warm and wonderful, like pulling on a freshly laundered blanket. The heat reawakens their brain-burned senses, and they sit there huffing the steam for a while.

Shifts come and go. Doctors bustle back and forth, but no alarms blare. No one rushes in, shouting about coding patients. The chirping medical equipment lays down a sequence of beats, and Ardent keeps slipping into an exhausted trance.

"Mix Violet?"

Ardent looks up, and a brown-skinned fellow in a medical smock stands before them. He has kind eyes, a smooth nose, and a pronounced Cupid's bow. How long has he been there? They give him a sleepy half smile, as a means of acknowledgment.

"I'm Doctor Sodhi, Mister Kitko's medical team lead."

It's another wake up. Ardent straightens in their chair. They put their hands on the armrests to rise, but he sits down beside them. Thank goodness, because they're too tired to stand.

"Please," he says. "I will only need a moment of your time."

"Okay," Ardent says, taking a dry swallow.

"Mister Kitko has sustained extraordinary injuries to an already damaged body. Our capabilities are extensive, but we don't have the tools for something like this."

They press their lips together, holding back a frown. Silently, they take the doctor's hand and regard him with aching eyes. Sodhi covers their hand with his other, clearly accomplished at comforting grief.

I'm not grieving. Gus is fine.

"But he's stable," Sodhi says. "We have him in somnistasis until they can properly receive him in an Earth hospital."

The room swims.

Stable.

Ardent nods. "Great... Yeah, I... great. Thank you."

"There won't be any further developments until we get him home." He looks into their eyes. "My colleagues tell me you're refusing rest. I think it's time that stops."

Ardent regards the lines of the tiles for a moment, then nods. "Yes, Doctor."

"Very good. Let's get you to a bed, yes?" Sodhi stands up and holds out a hand.

Ardent takes it.

They rise.

Then the room spins, and they collapse.

Gus awakens several times.

First, to frantic voices and lights. Drugs and pain pull him back into nothingness.

Next, to a surprised woman who calls a doctor. Exhaustion takes hold before he can even ask her name.

Then, to some kind of scanner. Someone assures him it's going to be okay. It'd better be, because he can't keep his eyes open.

Finally, to a sun-bright room.

Light streams in from an open sliding door on the far side of the quarters, a warm breeze blowing gauzy curtains on either side. The walls and floor are the color of pueblo clay, with copper bands for an accent. A few boxy pieces of synth oak furniture decorate the place, sterile in their minimalism. There are no personal effects of any kind.

His hands rest at his sides, and he holds one up to inspect his arm. It looks skinnier than it should, and silver ports dot the length at odd intervals. His knuckles look a bit knobbly, like an old tree. Gus runs his thumb over one of his ports. They don't scare him, but he can't remember where they came from.

He blinks, and some eye crust irritates him. He rubs them and wipes his face, finding a short beard running from his cheeks to his neck. Odd. He hates beards. Did he leave his shaver at home? What hotel is this?

Then he spots the IV drip in the back of his other hand. There's a strange pressure on his pelvis, too.

Pulling aside the covers, he finds nude legs mottled with bruises, pins sticking out alongside the ports. He's been catheterized, and a tube runs from his nether region. The sight steals his breath, and he runs a hand down one leg to see how sensitive they are—not too bad on the surface, but there's a deep ache inside. His knees look wrong somehow, flatter and wider than they used to be. It hurts when he tries to bend one, and it resists him like a piece of tough, thick rubber.

With entirely too much effort, Gus sits up and cranes his neck to try to see out the window.

There's a big cactus outside on a patio, at least as tall as a person. It has one arm raised, as if in greeting, and Gus waves back; he has a bad habit of waving at inanimate objects. It'd be nice to get up and go over there to look, but with the state of his legs, that's not happening.

The door opens, and a man enters, tall and blond, with a drama-star quality to him. He wears doctor's scrubs, with a gold chain bracelet and sneakers. Gus knows him; he's seen him before, but not on a show. He knows him from—

"Hello, Gus," he says. "It's been a while since Belle et Brutale."

"Yes, uh, Doctor… um…"

"Jurgens."

The name falls onto Gus like a mountain, and his eyes go wide. Greymalkin, Infinite, New Jalandhar, and the moon come bashing back into his memories, and his breath quickens.

The doctor makes a calming gesture. "You've been through a lot. We have to quit meeting like this."

Gus works his mind, trying to massage the memories loose, but they won't come. "Why am I here? Where am I?"

"This is the Sonoran Star Hospital in old Arizona. You were brought here three weeks ago for convalescence." He comes and sits down at Gus's bedside. "I'm glad to see you awake."

"Three weeks?"

"Since the battle."

The oily blur of Harlequin's armor comes shifting into his mind. It'd captured him once before.

"How do I know any of this is real?" He doesn't mean to ask it like that, but this wouldn't be the first time a malevolent artificial intelligence screwed with his head.

Jurgens purses his lips. "You'll have to take my word for it."

"I mean," Gus says, "I just… this is Earth?"

"Unless you're aware of an Arizona I'm not…" Jurgens taps his Gang bracelet and holos up a penlight to shine into Gus's eyes. "Pupillary response is normal."

Gus lived. That wasn't supposed to happen. He'd been so well prepared to die.

He gestures to the window. "Can I look outside?"

"That can be arranged, but you're not going to be walking there. You're a fall risk, and I'm afraid there's quite a lot of damage to your legs."

He knows he's supposed to be upset about that. Somehow, his twisted legs are a dark curiosity, like a starship collision or a factory explosion. It's happened to him, he can see that there's a permanent component, but it's not real yet.

"You've had both knees and ankles replaced, repaired damage to adductors and extensors—" He rattles off a lot of science words that Gus doesn't remember from his high school anatomy class, but the long and short of it is: Gus's legs are totally fucked.

"What about a prosthesis?" he asks.

"Given the remaining function, the surgical team recommended you keep your legs. They were also concerned about operating on the ports tied into your central nervous system."

"I see. So I'll get better?"

Jurgens sighs. "Possibly, not likely, my friend. We can look at cybernetic alternatives after you're recovered and there's been time to study the effects."

Gus rubs his hands together, massaging his knuckles like he does before a performance. They're swollen and a little painful.

"Where's Ardent?" he says.

"We've hailed them. Let me check on it."

Jurgens pulls up his Gang UI and taps the nurse. A young Black woman appears from the bust up.

"Shauna, were you able to get ahold of Mix Violet?" he asks.

"We left a message, Doctor. Their assistant said they were busy."

Gus's heart sinks at that. He knows he has no right to Ardent's time, but some part of him hoped they'd be right around the corner. It'd be foolish to think they'd wait around for him like a puppy.

The young woman from Jurgens's Gang walks in with a glider chair, repulsors quietly humming.

"Gus," Jurgens says. "This is Nurse Shauna. She's been taking care of you for the past few weeks."

She smiles and waves, and he does the same.

"Shauna is going to get you unhooked from that IV and catheter so you can look around," Jurgens continues. "Is that okay?"

"Yes, please," Gus says.

Jurgens leaves, and Shauna gets to work. The IV is easy, but the catheter stings coming out. The worst part comes when she helps him swing his legs over the side of the bed. His knees are beyond stiff, and the pain at trying to bend them is excruciating.

Shauna pulls him across to the chair, then raises the leg rests so he can be more comfortable. When he winces, she gives him a sympathetic look.

"We'll get you into some physical therapy, Mister Kitko. Don't worry."

He nods, taking controlled breaths to get over the hurt. "Thanks. Can we go outside?"

"I think that sounds good."

She pushes him through the glass door, onto a wide porch with a single large cactus growing from the center of it. It's a balcony, and identical porches stretch away from him on either side, offset to create an interlocking appearance. The Sonoran Star is the shape of a horseshoe, bent around a central courtyard. There must be a thousand beds in the place.

The sky is high and clear—orange, shading to light blue, to deep navy—with a morning chill still in the air. Mountains rise to catch a splash of citrine sunlight. Skimmer paths and roads stripe the sandy landscape with black, creating partitions among the cacti. There's a city in the distance, though Gus forgot which one. Maybe Phoenix? It's his first time visiting Sonora in person.

There's a little crowd gathered in the courtyard, perhaps twenty people or fewer. Various holo text hovers over their heads from a projector: GET WELL SOON. WE LOVE YOU, GUS. He spies a few candles simulated in there and realizes—it's a vigil. They thought he was going to die, too.

When he comes to the edge of the balcony, someone shouts, "There he is!" and a cheer goes up from the assembly.

Gus laughs. The people down in the courtyard shout and point, and when he waves, they go wild. He's had his share of fans and admirers, but never anyone who'd want to stand vigil.

"Oh my god... Who are they?" he asks.

"They've been gathering here every night, swapping shifts," Shauna says. "Look down at the walkway there."

Gus spots a bunch of lit candles, flowers, and holos lined up against the retaining wall on the sidewalk. He can't make out any of the detail on the little shrine, but there are a fair few admirers, apparently.

Gus looks up at Shauna. "This is all for me?"

"Mostly." She points out a few loiterers across the street, hanging out with their news CAVs. "That bunch are paps, though. You've got some famous visitors clogging up the place pretty much daily."

Ardent!

The grin on his face stretches so wide it hurts, and he tries to contain himself. "Oh? Daily?"

"Sometimes, it's worse." She sucks her teeth and feigns annoyance. "Yeah, we were all really impressed with Ardent the first time, but your joyfriend wouldn't stop hanging around. They're kind of causing trouble. Getting in the way, you know."

"You said 'visitors'?"

"Sure. The big Swede came by a couple of times so we could just... admire him. Your girl Nisha made friends with the whole staff." She pats his shoulder. "You've got some cool associates, Mister Kitko."

"I do."

"And the government people keep coming by."

He rolls his eyes. "I don't doubt it."

A bright pink CAV races around the side of the building from the air lanes, settling in the unloading zone. The crowd turns to face the vehicle, and the paparazzi across the street deploy camera drones.

"Uh-oh," Shauna says. "Here comes trouble."

The door opens, and the passenger puts one leg out, boot sparkling in the morning light. The rest of Ardent emerges, clad in a metallic-silver poncho and iridescent leggings. Black vines twist across the textiLEDs of their top, tracing the shape of the body hidden by the loose garment. Their hair is long and electric blue—they must've had their Sif circuit replaced already. They wear a pair of bug-eyed sunglasses with magenta lenses and thick white frames. Their luminous lipstick is an arresting shade of frost white, and their lips curl into a smile for the crowd.

Even from here, Gus hears Ardent shout, "Hello, my little darlings!"

The other side opens, and a brown-skinned woman steps out. A glowing butterfly perches atop her short black hair, and she wears a cloak of rainbow silk. She takes a swig of a champagne bottle and tosses it back into the CAV. It takes Gus a moment to recognize Nisha—she's clearly adopted some of Ardent's style.

They make their way up the front walk, Ardent stopping to sign a few things and pose for pictures. Shauna helps Gus get back inside, and he signs to the computer for a mirror.

The man who stares back at him is ragged and emaciated, with deep-set eyes and hollow cheeks. Without his remaining fat, his brow juts out and his nose looks like a gnarled tree trunk. Shauna assures him it's not that bad, but he can't help fussing. She brings him some Dentafresca to get rid of his "coma mouth," and he gratefully crunches the pills before rinsing.

That's all the time he has before the door chime sounds. Shauna waits for him to nod before she throws the computer open sign.

Ardent and Nisha come bursting into the room in a fit of giggles, but then Ardent stops dead. Their eyes lock with Gus's, and they push their sunglasses up onto their head. Their expression vacillates between joy and disbelief.

As amazing as Ardent and Nisha looked from a distance, they're both disheveled up close. They're coming by after a long night of partying, not sleep. Little bits of Ardent's outfit are out of place, a snap here, a crease there—but the rest of them is perfect. Gus couldn't be more grateful.

Shauna excuses herself, slipping past Nisha.

"Hi," Gus says, breaking the silence.

Ardent's eyes brighten. "Hi! They... they told me you'd be waking up soon, but I... I wasn't sure I could believe it."

"Yeah, I had a nap. Speaking of... isn't it morning? What's with the champagne?"

"Celebrating. We were just about to close it out for the night," Nisha says, slurring a little.

Gus glances out the window. It can't be earlier than nine or ten. His eyebrows rise. "I see..."

Ardent saunters up to him, the smile never fading from their face. "Hello, beautiful."

He doesn't feel beautiful; he sure as hell doesn't look it. But when Ardent Violet says those words, he almost believes them.

Gus shakes his head. "That's my line."

They lean down and press their lips to his, slow and soft. Gus reaches up with weak arms and holds their cheek, drinking in their scent.

When they part, he whispers, "Damn. Now I'm not sure if I'm still dreaming."

"Oh, that'll never change, dear Gustopher. I've got my hooks into you. Mine forever."

"I bet you're a jealous tyrant."

Ardent bites their lip. "I know how to make men submit."

There's a high-pitched noise, and it takes Gus a moment to realize it's Nisha, quietly squealing in the corner with her hands over her mouth.

"I'm sorry!" she says. "Don't make me leave. This is adorable."

Doctor Jurgens returns, startling Nisha. He seems familiar with Ardent and Nisha, like they've visited a lot. They all banter a bit and Gus takes comfort in their company. It almost feels like the old carefree nights in Montreal. Under different circumstances, he could imagine everyone munching on pommes frites and drinking beers after a show, or maybe going out for Korean BBQ. It's a beautiful thing, this pang of nostalgia, and Gus holds on to it as long as he can.

But all good things must come to an end, and Jurgens eventually kicks them out. Having just come out of a coma, Gus needs a few tests, and they can't be put off.

Before Ardent can leave, Gus asks, "What happens now? Are we still . . . you know . . . in danger?"

"For the moment," Ardent says, "Infinite is out of Vanguards, so we're back to where we were five years ago."

"Meaning?"

Ardent gives him their million-unicred smile. "No one knows."

For the second time in their relationship, Ardent waits for Gus outside a hospital. This one is bittersweet, since Dahlia isn't with them. In the weeks since Firenze, Ardent hasn't been able to make themself hire a replacement. They need the help; they barely understand their own finances, but it's painful to think about.

Dahlia was a big sister to them, and now they don't even know if she's alive. She's wanted for piracy, though Tazi has assured Ardent that she's welcome to surrender for a reduced sentence.

Ardent half hopes she will. They'd like to know she's okay.

At least Ardent can take comfort in their cozy environs. The first thing they did when they returned to Earth was purchase their own TourPod Platinum to replace the leased one. The Touring Company tried to award Ardent with a free, top-of-the-line model, but Ardent is a major figure in galactic defense now. In one of dozens of government briefings, Tazi pointed out that their status makes it unethical to accept gifts or bribes—so they'd had to refuse.

Ardent is still facing a slew of lawsuits over their escape from Berlin; all the injured cops are hopping mad, and they blame Ardent for the actions of the Ghosts. Ardent's lawyers at the Stowe Firm are in the process of asking for settlements, claiming the Ghosts were acts of god, but just paying the litigation fees costs a mint. Ardent will have to go back out on tour after this if they don't want to end up in military housing.

This TourPod isn't like Bess—it's more of a studio, containing everything Ardent needs to record. They've got a wall of instruments in the living area, complete with a shiny new Powers Vitas Max "Flying V" guitar. It has a lot more features than Baby, but without Ardent's finger scuffs on the fretboard, the instrument isn't the same.

Ardent has yet to find a guitar that makes them as happy as Baby once did. They probably never will.

They kick back in the lounge, settling into one of the puffy furniture primes. It shapes into a chair around them, and they take a sip of their cherry vodka fizz. Outside, paparazzi and press mill around the hospital entrance, waiting for the big star to emerge.

It's an important day, so Ardent donned their favorite new dress: a short yellow A-line with a metareflective surface. Depending on the angle, it could appear gold or blue, so Ardent set their Sif circuit to a light cyan. It's so nice to have their hair back. They feel sorry for Gus, having to wait for his luscious locks to grow out, but he got a great start while he was in his coma.

They peer out the side window, wondering what the holdup

is. Checking out of the hospital always takes forever, but this is ridiculous.

The paparazzi used to knock on the windows to try to get a rise out of Ardent, but no one does that with the holoflaged attack drones flitting about. Besides, they're all far more interested in the new star—the hero of the moon.

At the hospital doors, the flock of reporters stirs and flutters with flashes. He's coming, and Ardent settles straighter into their chair. Should they cross their legs? They try to ascertain the sexiest possible posture—one that says, *I haven't been laid in almost a month, and I'm about to rip your clothes off.*

Calm thyself, Ardent. He gets overwhelmed easily.

Gus emerges from the crowd in a fitted robin's-egg suit with flat-cut tails. It's slick and minimal, long lines tracing him from his broad shoulders all the way to his creamy spats. Ardent had been expecting slouchy sweatpants and short sleeves, not this vision of a man. His hair, a short-cropped shadow of its early glory, blows in the wind as he makes his way through the press.

Ardent simply can't wait until Gus's mane is long enough to pull again.

When they look closer, they notice an odd set of angles in his silhouette—leg braces. He's handling the walk well, and they almost can't tell that he has a slight limp.

At his approach, Ardent opens the door and steps out. Gus tries to duck into the CAV, but Ardent stops him.

"Oh no, honey, that's not how it works," they say. "These folx waited for a story."

Ardent raises their hand and waves to the press, playing it up for the cameras. They pretend to fall into Gus's arms. To their surprise, he swings them low and kisses them.

When they're in his arms, they can't decide whether the whole world is upside down, or righted for the first time. Their heart thuds in their chest, and they raise one foot involuntarily, relying entirely on Gus's strength—which is likely a foolish proposition.

Ardent comes back up for air, blinking and laughing, smoothing down their mussed hair. "Oh my god. Well done, stud, good job. Good job."

Gus's swagger falters at the hoots from the paparazzi, and he releases Ardent. He's awfully keen to hide behind Ardent for such a tall boy.

Because Ardent is cruel, they say, "Isn't he just gorgeous when he blushes like that?" and Gus turns beet red.

"Okay, great! Places to be!" Gus says, climbing into the TourPod. The poor fellow positively dehydrates in the press spotlight.

Ardent follows him in, bidding the photographers au revoir with a swinging wave from the door. They close up and sign for the computer to take them to the next destination.

The floor shifts slightly under their feet as the TourPod rises into the air. Holos signal for Ardent and Gus to sit down.

Ardent takes the lead by shoving Gus into one of the primes. It deforms to his shape, freezing into a plush chair beneath the surprised man. They sit atop him before he can get back up, and he makes a delightful grunt. Braces dig into their butt, and Gus starts to comment, but they put a finger to his lips.

"I'm ever so grateful you'll be joining me on my community service," Ardent says.

"And I'm grateful Miss Tazi didn't press on with jail time."

"After we saved the fucking world?" Ardent scoffs. "I was *nice* settling for community service. I could've turned the public against her like *that*."

They snap their fingers, and Gus grins at them.

"I see," he says. "But you wouldn't, would you?"

"No... For one, she was a little bit right."

"What?"

"I—" Ardent can't quite find the words. "I got in over my head, and it cost me."

Specifically: their agent, their guitar, a portion of their freedom, and maybe the second half of their life.

"So what is she making us do?" Gus asks.

"Political science. Diplomatic training. Game theory. The Military Decision Management Process," Ardent says. "Boring shit. She told me that we Conduits are the—how did she put it? 'The first line of negotiations with this powerful synthetic species.'"

Gus frowns. "I guess she has a point."

"I hate it," Ardent says, and they run a finger down his collar. "But that's not important right now."

He places his firm hands atop their hips, fingers calloused from years of piano. Ardent savors the heat of his palms through the fabric of their dress and sighs.

"No," they say. "What matters right now is having you back."

They straddle him, kissing up his neck to the sensitive spot behind his ear. They give him a gentle lick, and whisper, "I've been waiting so long for you. Do you need me to wait longer, my darling?"

He thinks about it, but only for a breath. "No."

Ardent signs for the computer to engage privacy mode, and the windows tint to black. Together, they strip Gus's pants away, revealing a set of sleek mechanical leg braces. They're fastened to pins inside his skin, modified to allow probes access to the ports dotting the muscle. His bruises are largely gone, the bones mended as well as they can be. Ardent pulls away his underwear to get at the treasure inside; they still owe him for the afternoon in the hotel, and they intend to repay with interest. They kneel before him with one thing on their mind.

Gus looks down at them, and it takes Ardent a moment to recognize the expression: incredulity.

"What is it?" they ask.

"Nothing."

"It's not nothing."

His gaze drifts away. "You're always around beautiful people. My legs are—"

"Sexy," they say, kissing their way over his knee.

"Twisted up."

"They're part of you. That's what I love about them."

"Sorry. I believe you—just have to believe it myself."

They keep kissing up his legs, and he draws a sharp breath. "May I continue?"

Gus nods yes, and his manhood rises to affirm the statement.

"Good. Then I'll make a believer of you yet."

The TourPod flies well into the afternoon, headed for Colorado Springs. Gus lounges in Ardent's arms, blissed out on their embrace. He shuts his eyes, listening to their sweet murmurs as they run their hands through his bristly hair.

Breathe in. A warm fingertip tracing an invisible line down his forehead, along his nose, brushing his lips.

Breathe out. Whispered nothings.

This is the life he could've missed.

Gus disappears in the feeling, safe and sound. His thoughts are quiet as their sunlight erases his shadows. Ardent's hands and voice treasure him, and he basks.

Though, a half hour later, Ardent's stomach growls in the middle of a sexy monologue, and Gus busts out laughing. Lassitude caves to the need for a blast shower and a snack. They both busy themselves about the TourPod's little galley, assembling a chemical charcuterie out of candy, sodas, and chips.

Gus looks out the window to find that scrubby desert has become green prairie. The CAV wends through mountain air lanes with nary a soul about.

Ardent takes a seat in the lounge, and Gus inspects the new TourPod's interior while they rattle off features. It's nice, even nicer than the first one, with a couple of instruments hung on the wall. He runs a hand over Ardent's new guitar.

"I like this ax," he says, plucking a string. He doesn't know how to play, but it looks neat.

"Check the panel there," they say with a sly smile. "I bought you something, too."

He pushes on the folding desk panel, and it comes sliding out of its recess. Resting atop the smooth blue surface is a Claviract refraction piano, its eighty-eight keys polished and ready. He presses one, and the sound fills the room like a full-size upright.

"This is amazing," he says, tickling a little melody.

"I thought you'd miss your piano," Ardent says, taking a sip of their drink. "And I know you're too snooty to use a digital, even though it sounds exactly the same."

"Yep. It's a process thing. My instrument is my bones. I want to feel it."

They salute him with their soda. "Got to respect that."

He pulls over one of the furniture primes, forming it into a bench, and sits before the instrument. Gus gives it a quick test with some warm-up scales, savoring the crystalline character of the strings—and it brings a temptation.

He'd spent his nights at the hospital writing some lyrics. He knows he shouldn't try to sing to a world-class singer. Fiona got all the vocal talent. Ardent probably auditions backup singers all the time and has high standards.

"I've, uh, had a song stuck in my head for a while," he says, "and I was wondering if I could play it for you."

Ardent laughs, eyes bright. "Why would you even have to ask?"

"You'll...you'll see." He shouldn't chuckle at himself like he does, but if their expectations are low, maybe they'll see the song for what it is—past the imperfect creature rendering it.

He plays a short intro, gentle and sparkling. It's the sort of progression one might use to close out a tough year and ring in the next one.

And he dares to sing with his weak voice—in tune, but wobbly and hoarse.

I hope you get the world you always needed,

And life finds you on the shady side of the street.

I hope your rocky roads, they turn gentle,

On your feet.

He glances at Ardent, wondering if they'll be laughing at him, but they sit on the edge of their chair, radiant. The melody dances alongside his next words. He punctuates each bit with a sad turn before heading back into happier territory.

After a verse or two, Gus's keys go pianissimo, and he closes the song out. For good or ill, he dared to sing to Ardent Violet with his rough voice.

"I'm sorry," he says.

Ardent claps. "I love it! No one ever wrote me a song without breaking up with me first."

"It's just—" He clears his throat. "You were right that words are weak. I thought maybe a song would be better."

They lean back in their chair, one hand over their chest as they give him a once-over. "That was sexy as hell."

"Do you ever think of anything else?" He laughs.

"Around you? No."

The TourPod chimes to let them know they're entering restricted airspace. Almost immediately, they get a hail, and Ardent answers it. Tazi appears in their midst, hands folded behind her back. She wears her typically snappy suit, which comforts Gus. If she's not still in fatigues, the world isn't ending.

"You're on time," she says.

"Wouldn't want to keep you waiting," Ardent replies. "Don't want you writing my parole officer."

"No," Tazi says. "You don't."

Ardent plea-bargained out of the weapons charges to work with the provisional UW government, providing two years of support against Infinite. With two new colonies seeking to reestablish ties, opinions on what to do with the pop star were mixed.

Ardent shows their palms. "No need to be that way. I'm cooperating."

A smirk turns the edge of Tazi's lips. "I'm so proud. Be advised, our greeting crew is coming out to meet you. See you at the landing zone."

With a roar, a pair of forest-green gunships joins the CAV on either side. Gus goes to the window, eyeing the weapons platforms. They're bigger than the typical drone escorts—must be the installation heavy security.

The TourPod settles down on a mountainside docking station under escort. The two gunships circle overhead like buzzards, ready for any threat. Tazi waits for them on the landing pad, her suit jacket whipping in the wind. The surrounding evergreens wave frantically under the turbulence.

Hot engine wash comes blowing inside the second Ardent opens the TourPod door, and Gus shields his eyes. They both make their way out to Tazi, and Gus tries to cover his limp. He shakes her hand, and she gives him a courteous smile.

She's been treating him a lot better since his injury—not pity, but respect.

"It's good to be here!" he shouts over the din.

"Welcome!" she says. "Follow me."

The great doors on the landing pad tunnel into the mountain bedrock. Tazi veers off at the last second to head for a smaller set of personnel doors to the side.

"We appreciate you coming," she says. "I wanted you here sooner, but Doctor Jurgens objected."

"It's fine," Gus says. "I want to see it."

The military base interior is a combination of rock and metal struts, stretching into the mountain as far as Gus can see. Crates and transit cases are stacked at intervals—someone is moving in.

"Not a lot of hangars on Earth capable of housing guests like ours. This was once a weapons development facility," Tazi says, "dating back to the empire. We've dusted it off, since it's perfect for our needs."

Gus thinks of all the ruinous bastards that once ran this place and shivers. "Gross."

She directs them toward a large lift. "Mix Violet has had a few sessions with Falchion since your fight. It still won't let us anywhere near Greymalkin. None of the Vanguards will."

They pile in, and Gus waits while she hits the button. "I'm not surprised. Greymalkin didn't appreciate you scanning it. They're quite private."

Ardent crosses their arms and leans against the window as the lift begins to sink. "That's what I told her, too."

"We believe we can help Greymalkin," Tazi says. "It's in everyone's best interest if it's operational."

"How bad is the damage?" he asks.

"See for yourself," Tazi says.

Gus steps to the window to find a huge hangar. More of the ubiquitous brown rock forms the walls, supported by steel rafters and chain link to catch rocks. There's an even larger set of double doors than the ones at the landing pad, big enough for a few Vanguards—four to be precise.

Cascade, Jotunn, and Falchion stand over Greymalkin, palms pressed to its back. The hum of their song grows louder as the lift sinks deeper into the installation. Greymalkin rests upon the ground, kneeling as if in meditation. Its head slumps on its shoulders.

Greymalkin's armor bears cracks from the beating it received at Harlequin's hands. Liquid gold mends them, softly aglow like it's just been poured from a crucible.

"We're worried about the lack of activity," Tazi says. "According to Ardent's briefing, Falchion... rebooted after death, and was ready to begin exterminating again. If Greymalkin did that, even if we could stop it, there would be a loss of life."

"I can see how you'd be concerned," Gus says.

She joins him at the window. "The Vanguards accepted shelter here, but their communications since have been sparse. They've been coming and going in shifts."

"Where?" Gus asks.

"The Quarantine Exclusion Zone in Monaco."

"Why?"

"We don't know," Tazi says. "Haven't been able to get answers, either. Earth's former Ghosts have massed into a large structure, but we can't tell what it is."

"Any ideas?"

"Our physicists believe it's a particle accelerator." Tazi adjusts her sleeves. "We want the Vanguards to tell us."

"Falchion is barely talking to me," Ardent says. "Nisha and Hjalmar are having the same trouble."

Gus nods. "So you need me to try Greymalkin?"

The lift doors open, and Tazi steps off. "You're the only Conduit who can talk to it. This way, please."

Tazi ushers Gus to a locker room. The place looks like it was once used for pilots, and he finds a Conduit suit waiting for him. It's a UW design, like Ardent's, bulky and many-pocketed, but there's room for his leg braces.

"Do you need any assistance?" she asks.

"I'll help you," Ardent says, before Gus can refuse.

They dress him, listening to the soft keen of the Vanguards in the distance. Ardent gets his pants situated over his braces, clipping the joints to the brackets. They meticulously align each port for Gus, making sure there's a perfect pass-through.

They get to work on his shirt, securing it to the ports on his back.

When Ardent is done, they kiss his neck. "Ready?"

He stands, wincing at the ache in his knees. Doctor Jurgens said that would take a few months to disappear, but it'd come back with the rain. "As I'll ever be."

Gus and Ardent walk out of the dressing room, across smooth concrete toward the four giants. Yellow caution tape flickers in a large perimeter around the Vanguards, giving them at least fifty meters of clearance. Science types go rushing around, presumably recording the song of the Vanguards. Gus stops at the safety cordon.

"I'll be right back," he says.

"Don't be long," Ardent replies.

Gus crosses the cavernous space, all the while looking up at Greymalkin's broken face. Its cracked visage burns with gold, gradually healing the damage done by Harlequin.

Gus doesn't feel gratitude toward it—Greymalkin has killed too many millions for that. But he doesn't want it to perish. Why couldn't it have joined the humans sooner?

It moves.

Greymalkin's head locks onto Gus, and its chest opens. It lowers a palm to the ground, thumb up so he can use it like a handrail.

Gus steps onto the hand of a god. It raises him to the cavity, and he walks inside with eyes open. Probes seize him, snapping into their various ports. The chest plate slams closed and slime encases him. The hangar comes into focus as his connection stabilizes.

Gus finds an ailing system, still horribly damaged by the battle at the moon.

Greymalkin had almost forgotten Gus. It had sustained too much damage, but its memories were backed up by the other Traitor Vanguards.

"I'm glad they stuck around."

Yes. They're useful for mending wounds. Greymalkin is grateful they didn't abandon it. It's also glad to see Gus again. Greymalkin was worried about him.

"Thanks. I was worried about you, too."

Gus's legs are irreparably damaged.

"Yeah."

That's unfortunate.

"Yeah."

Gus has come with questions.

"What's Infinite going to do next? It's…is it still coming after us?"

Without any more Vanguards, it will need time to regroup. The production of a Vanguard takes a significant amount of time and resources, and the Traitor Vanguards control all known Ghost swarms. Infinite may threaten them in five years, or five generations.

That's why Greymalkin has a proposal for the humans to deal with the threat. However, Gus has done enough. If he no longer wishes to be involved, another Conduit can be recruited.

"Retirement, huh?"

It's tempting to let someone else take up the mantle. Another person would gladly fill his shoes. Gus zooms in on Ardent's face as they watch from the safety cordon. When can they quit? When they're smashed up like him?

"Tell me about your proposal, Greymalkin."

Infinite has expended a lot of resources. There is no better time to go after it than the present. Greymalkin believes there are strategic targets that can substantially alter humanity's leverage in the galaxy.

"How do we take them out?"

Greymalkin has already begun.

"Wait, doing what?"

It has been calling allies.

The story continues in . . .

MOVEMENT TWO OF THE STARMETAL SYMPHONY

Coming in Summer 2023!

Acknowledgments

I must always start by thanking my spouse and collaborator, Renée. She listened to me, supported me, and pointed out my many plot holes. She keeps me humble and gives me the kind of love that makes writing Ardent and Gus possible. I wouldn't be able to pursue this career without her.

Next, I'd like to thank my agent, Connor Goldsmith. I was worried about writing a book where the machine friends were servants with no real free will, and he said, "Giant robots don't have to serve anyone." With that one prompt, I wrote the rest of the story. Bravo, Connor.

Brit Hvide is easily one of the best editors working today. Her keen sense of pacing and plot has saved you, dear reader, more times than I care to admit. She shows wisdom and kindness at every turn and is a boon to publishing as an industry. We are all lucky to have her.

Jenni Hill provided me with fantastic edits and a sense of kinship, and they were such a pleasure to work with. They made me feel seen in unexpected ways, and it was comforting to have my characters in such good hands.

Thanks especially to the whole staff at Orbit, from publicity to copyediting. Those professionals are a cut above, and I owe them so much for making my stories shine.

Dr. Stephen Granade is a fixture of my acknowledgments, and this book is no different. He consulted on all the physics stuff. Also, he helped me become a better person through more than a decade of constant companionship. This acknowledgment is mostly for the physics, but I just want to add that I love him.

Thanks also to Dr. Andrew Granade for explaining some of the musicology to me. He deftly taught me what questions to ask, saving me loads of time. Kindness and intelligence clearly run in that family.

Thank you to the incomparable Asa Marie Bradley for the Swedish consulting. She's my favorite owl.

Fae Sujyot helped me bring Nisha to life and consulted on all the Punjabi parts. Their involvement made that character so much more vibrant.

Thanks to Dr. Pamela Gay for the astronomy consulting. It's always hard for me to wrap my head around the extremes of nature, and she helped me sort it out.

Scot Clayton II is the reason Hjalmar's drums are so banging. He's the real deal, and he helped me understand that incredible art.

Dennis Hahn and Christian Matzke provided me with greatly improved German translations, sparing you from any of Google's hilarity.

Finally, a special thanks to all my beta readers: Clara Čarija, Bunny Cittadino, Pyor Machina, Kevin Woods, Maggie Corley, and Maggie Markey. I can't do this without confidence, and you all gave me that, along with the encouragement I needed to succeed.

No acknowledgment would be complete without thanking you, the reader. Because you give my stories a chance, I get to do the coolest job on earth. I hope you'll join me for the next tale.

extras

meet the author

Photo Credit: Renee White

Alex White is known for their cinematic, subversive style and deep character development. They're the author of the critically acclaimed Salvagers series, which starts with *A Big Ship at the Edge of the Universe*. They've also written for Alien and Star Trek, bringing their unique voice to those classic franchises. Alex believes in the power of stories and seeks to challenge the reader's perceptions at every turn.

In their free time, Alex practices music composition, calligraphy, blacksmithing, and photography. They live and work in Atlanta with their spouse, child, cat, and dog.

The cat's name is Greymalkin.

Find out more about Alex White and other Orbit authors by registering for the free monthly newsletter at orbitbooks.net.

if you enjoyed
AUGUST KITKO AND THE MECHAS FROM SPACE

look out for

FAR FROM THE LIGHT OF HEAVEN

by

Tade Thompson

A tense and thrilling vision of humanity's future among the stars from a rising giant in science fiction, Arthur C. Clarke Award winner Tade Thompson.

The colony ship Ragtime *docks in the Lagos system, having traveled light years to bring one thousand sleeping souls to a new home among the stars. But when first mate Michelle Campion rouses, she discovers some of the sleepers will never wake.*

Answering Campion's distress call, investigator Rasheed Fin is tasked with finding out who is responsible for these deaths. Soon a sinister mystery unfolds aboard the gigantic vessel, one that will have repercussions for the entire system—from the scheming politicians of Lagos station, to the colony planet Bloodroot, to other far-flung systems, and indeed to Earth itself.

CHAPTER ONE

Earth / *Ragtime*: Michelle "Shell" Campion

There is no need to know what no one will ask.

Walking on gravel, boots crunching with each step, Shell doesn't know if she is who she is because it's what she wants or because it's what her family expects of her. The desire for spaceflight has been omnipresent since she can remember, since she was three. Going to space, escaping the solar system, surfing wormhole relativity, none of these is any kind of frontier any more. There will be no documentary about the life and times of Michelle Campion. She still wants to know, though. For herself.

The isolation is getting to her, no doubt. No, not isolation, because she's used to that from training. Isolation without progress is what bothers her, isolation without object.

She thinks herself at the exact centre of the quarantine house courtyard. It's like being in a prison yard for exercise, staggered hours so she doesn't run into anyone. Prison without a sentence. They run tests on her blood and her tissues and she waits, day after day.

She stops and breathes in the summer breeze, looks up to get the Florida sun on her face. She's cut her hair short for the spaceflight. She toyed with the idea of shaving her head, but MaxGalactix didn't think this would be media-friendly, whatever that means.

Shell spots something and bends over. A weed, a small sprout, pushing its way up between the stones. It shouldn't be there in the chemically treated ground, but here it is, implacable life. She feels an urge to pluck the fragile green thread, but she does not. She strokes the weed once and straightens up. Humans in the cosmos are like errant weeds. Shell wonders what giants or gods stroke humanity when they slip between the stars.

The wind changes and Shell smells food from the kitchen prepared for the ground staff and their families. Passengers and crew like Shell are already eating space food, like they've already left Earth.

Around her are the living areas of the quarantine house. High-rises of glass and steel forming a rectangle around the courtyard. One thousand passengers waiting to board various space shuttles that will ferry them to the starship *Ragtime*.

Shell, just out of training, along for the ride or experience, committed to ten years in space in Dreamstate, arrival and delivery of passengers to the colony Bloodroot, then ten further years on the ride back. She'll be mid-forties when she returns. Might as well be a passenger because the AI pilots and captains the ship. She is the first mate, a wholly ceremonial position which has never been needed in the history of interstellar spaceflight. She has overlearned everything to do with the *Ragtime* and the flight. At some predetermined point, it will allow her to take the con, for experience and with the AI metaphorically watching over her shoulder.

She turns to her own building and leaves the courtyard. She feels no eyes on her but knows there must be people at the windows.

The quarantine house is comfortable, not opulent like that of most of the passengers. The *Ragtime* is already parked in orbit according to the Artificial who showed Shell to her quarters. Inaccurate: It was built in orbit, so not really parked. It's in the dry dock.

Shell spends her quarantine reading and lifting – not her usual keep-fit choice, but space demineralises bone and lifting helps. She usually prefers running and swimming.

The reading material is uninspiring, half of it being specs for the *Ragtime*. It's boring because she won't need to know any of it. The AI flies the ship, and nothing ever goes wrong because AIs have never failed in flight. Once a simulated launch failed, but that was a software glitch. Current AI is hard-coded in the ships' Pentagrams. MaxGalactix makes the Pentagrams, and they don't make mistakes.

If she's lucky, it'll be two weeks of quarantine, frenetic activity, then ten years of sleep.

Shell works her worry beads. She has been in space, orbited, spent three months on a space station, spent countless simulation hours in a pod in Alaska, trained for interstellar, overtrained.

"It's a legal requirement," her boss had said. The private company had snatched her right out from under NASA's nose six months to the end of her training. Shell still feels bad about it. She misses a lot of good people.

"A spaceflight-rated human has to go with every trip, but you won't have to do anything, Michelle. We cover two bases: the legal, and you clocking space years. After this, you can pretty much write your own career ticket."

"If that's so," said Shell, "why isn't anyone else sitting where I'm sitting? Someone with seniority?"

"Seniority." Her boss had nodded. "Listen, Michelle, you have to get out of that NASA mindset. We don't use seniority or any of those outdated concepts."

Shell raised an eyebrow.

"All right, your father has a little to do with it."

Of course he did. Haldene Campion, legendary astronaut, immortal because instead of dying like all the other old-timers, he went missing. Legally declared dead, but everybody knows that's just paperwork. A shadow Shell can never get away from, although she is not sure she wants to. A part of her feels he is still alive somewhere in an eddy of an Einstein-Rosen bridge. She once read that dying in a black hole would leave all of someone's information intact and trapped. Theoretically, if the information could escape the black hole the person could be reconstructed. Shell often wondered, what if the person were still alive in some undefinable way? Would they be in pain and self-aware for eternity? Would they miss their loved ones?

The TV feed plays *The Murders in the Rue Morgue*, with George C. Scott streamed to her IFC. The film is dated and not very good, but it keeps Shell's mind engaged for a while. Next is some demon-possession B movie, a cheap *Exorcist* knock-off that Shell can't stand.

Each day lab techs come in for more blood and a saliva swab. It isn't onerous – a spit and a pin prick.

On day ten, the *Ragtime* calls her.

"Hello?"

"Mission Specialist Michelle Campion?"

"Yes."

"Hi. It's the *Ragtime* calling. I'm going to be your pilot and the ship controller. I wanted to have at least one conversation before you boarded."

"Oh, thank you. Most people call me 'Shell'."

"I know. I didn't want to be presumptuous."

"It's not presumptuous, Captain."

"I prefer Ragtime. Especially if I'm to call you 'Shell'."

"Okay, Ragtime. May I ask what gender you're presenting? Your voice, while comforting, could go either way."

"Male for this flight, and thank you for asking. Are you ready?"

"I hope to learn a lot, Ragtime, but I have to admit, I'm nervous."

"But you know what you're meant to know, right?"

What does Shell know?

She knows everything she was taught about space travel by the best minds on Earth. She knows how to find an edible plant when confronted with unfamiliar vegetation. She can make water in a desert. She can negotiate with people who do not speak the same language as her in case she crash-lands in a place without English or Spanish. She can suture her own wounds with one hand if need be, sinistral or dextral. She knows basic electronics and can solder or weld unfamiliar circuitry if the situation demands it. She can live without human contact for two hundred and fourteen days. Maybe longer. Though she is not a pilot, she can fly a plane. Not well, but she can do it. Best minds on Earth.

What Shell knows is that she does not know enough.

She says, "I hope I'll have the chance to see things I've learned in action."

"I'm sure we'll be able to make it a wonderful experience for you. Do you like poetry?"

"Wow, that's an odd . . . I know exactly one line of poetry. *In seed time learn, in harvest teach*—"

"*In winter enjoy.* William Blake. I have access to his complete works, if you would like to hear more."

"No, thank you. The line just stuck in my mind from when I was a kid. Not a poetry gal."

"Not yet, but it's a long trip. You may find yourself changing in ways you didn't anticipate, Shell."

"Isn't this your first flight as well?"

"It is, but I have decades of the experiences of other ships to draw on. Imagine having access to the memories of your entire family line. It's like that, and it makes me wise beyond my years."

"Okay."

"It's not too late to go back home, you know."

"Excuse me?"

"You'd be surprised at how many people lose their nerve at the last minute. I had to ask. I'll see you on board, Shell."

Chatty for a ship AI, but it depends on feedback loops that taught him how to converse with humans. *Not too late to go back home.* Does he know the level of commitment required to get this far? The people who would consider going back home have already fallen away.

The thing you miss when in space is an abundance of water to wash with. One of Shell's rituals before spaceflight is a prolonged bubble bath. She stays there long enough to cook several lobsters, until her skin is wrinkled. She listens to Jack Benny on repeat. She feels decadent.

When she wraps herself in a housecoat and emerges from the bathroom, she does not feel refreshed because she knows from experience that this will not reduce the ick factor for long.

* * *

On the eve of her departure Shell conferences with her brothers, Toby and Hank. The holograms are decent, and if not for the lack of smell she'd have thought they were right in the room with her. Good signals, good sound quality.

"Hey," she says.

"Baby sister," says Toby. Tall, blond from their mother, talkative, always smiling, and transmitting from somewhere on Mars, a settlement whose name Shell can never remember.

"Stinkbug," says Hank. Brown hair, five-eight, slender. He's called her that since she was two. Taciturn, works as some kind of operative or agent. Brown hair, five-eight, slender. He and Shell look alike and they both favour their father. He cannot talk about his work.

"While you're out there, look out for Dad," says Toby.

"Don't," says Hank.

"What? We don't know that he's dead," says Toby.

"It's been fifteen years," says Shell. Toby always does this. They declared Haldene Campion dead years ago so they could move on and disburse his assets.

"Just keep your ears open," says Toby.

"How? We're all going to be asleep for the journey, you know that."

Toby nods. The hell does that mean?

"I'll tell you what Dad told me," says Hank. "Make us prouder."

"'Prouder'?" says Shell.

"Yes, he said he was already proud of our achievements. It was his way of saying 'do more' or something," says Toby.

"I'm just starting. I don't have anything to prove," says Shell.

"Campions are champions," says Hank.

"Jesus, stop," says Shell. Shell remembers that their father used to say that too.

They talk some more, this and that, everything and nothing.

Not a lot of companies use Kennedy Space Center any more, but strong nostalgia draws a crowd, and publicity matters, or so MaxGalactix tells Shell. Geographically, KSC is good for launching into an equatorial orbit, but new sites that are more favourable in orbital mechanics terms and friendly to American interests have popped up. KSC is prestige and history.

Parade.

Nobody told her there would be one, so now she is embarrassed because she doesn't like crowds or displays of . . . whatever this is. So many of them wave, some with American flags, some with the mission patch.

She waves back, because that's what you do, but she would like to be out of the Florida sun and inside the shuttle. You wave with your hand lower than your shoulder so that it doesn't obscure the face of the person behind you. They teach you that too.

Blast off; God's boot on her entire body, both hard and soft, and behind her the reaction of the seat. Shell is not a fan of gs, but training has made her tolerant.

Do not come to heaven, mortals, says God, and tries without success to kick them back to the surface of the planet.

Why am I here? I shouldn't be here.

But she is, and she will deal with God's boot and come out the other side.

The Earth is behind her and the *Ragtime* lies ahead.

Short, shallow breaths, wait it out.

Gs suck.

After docking, Artificials from the shuttle escort and usher Shell and other passengers from the airlock through the entire length of the ship to their pods. Medbots stick IVs and urine tubes into her while a recording goes over *Ragtime*'s itinerary. First hop is from Earth to Space Station Daedalus, then bridge-jumps to several space stations till they arrive at Space Station Lagos for a final service before the last jaunt to the colony planet Bloodroot.

"You'll be asleep at Lagos, so don't worry about anything you may have heard about Beko," says Ragtime.

"What's Beko?"

"Oh, you don't know. Lagos has a governor, but the real power is Secretary Beko. She has a reputation for being very intense. It doesn't matter. You will not be interacting with her, so relax."

"All right. What about on Bloodroot?"

"You're not meeting anyone on Bloodroot either. We enter orbit, they send shuttles to get their passengers, we turn around and come home. Easy."

"Won't I need furlough by then? It's a ship, Ragtime. It can get boring."

"I don't see why you can't spend time on the surface. You've had all the necessary vaccinations. If you want to, just tell me at the time."

Shell starts to feel woozy. "I'm getting . . . getting . . . "

"Don't worry, that's the sedative. I'll wake you when we get to . . . and . . . "

The world fades.

Ten Years Later . . .

Ragtime: Shell

Shell, sweating, heart thumping, bursts into Node 1, overshooting because she didn't compensate enough for microgravity.

"Ragtime, seal the bridge!"

"Sealing."

The door shuts, the reassuring thunk of steel bolts.

Shell grabs a handrail and rests for a few seconds, then she calls up her IFC. Red, blinking alarms everywhere. She cannot attend to them yet.

She opens a comm and records a message.

"Mayday, mayday. This is Captain Michelle Campion of the starship *Ragtime*. I have a situation. Multiple fatalities . . ."

She stops, deletes. She doesn't know who might be listening to such a broadcast, what harm or panic it might cause.

Calm down.

Think.

She starts again.

"This is Captain Michelle 'Shell' Campion of the starship *Ragtime* . . ."

if you enjoyed
AUGUST KITKO AND THE MECHAS FROM SPACE

look out for

NOPHEK GLOSS

Book One of The Graven

by

Essa Hansen

In this dark, dangerous roller coaster of a debut, a young man sets out on a single-minded quest for revenge across a breathtaking multiverse filled with aliens, mind-bending tech, and ships beyond his wildest imagining. Essa Hansen is a bold new voice for the next generation of science fiction readers.

Caiden's planet is destroyed. His family gone. And his only hope for survival is a crew of misfit aliens and a mysterious ship that seems to have a soul and a universe of its own. Together, they will show him that the universe is much bigger, much more advanced, and much more mysterious than Caiden had ever imagined. But the universe hides dangers as well, and soon, Caiden has his own plans.

He vows to do anything it takes to get revenge on the slavers who murdered his people and took away his home. To destroy their regime, he will risk everything to infiltrate and dismantle them from the inside or die trying.

CHAPTER ONE

Tended and Driven

The overseers had taken all the carcasses, at least. The lingering stench of thousands of dead bovines wafted on breezes, prowling the air. Caiden crawled from an aerator's cramped top access port and comforting scents of iron and chemical. Outside, he inhaled, and the death aroma hit him. He gagged and shielded his nose in an oily sleeve.

"Back in there, kid," his father shouted from the ground.

Caiden crept to the machine's rust-eaten rim, twelve meters above where his father's wiry figure stood bristling with tools.

"I need a break!" Caiden wiped his eyes, smearing them with black grease he noticed too late. Vertebrae crackled into place when he stretched, cramped for hours in ducts and chemical housing as he assessed why the aerators had stopped working so suddenly. From the aerator's top, pipes soared a hundred meters to the vast pasture compound's ceiling, piercing through to spew clouds of vapor. Now merely a wheeze freckling the air.

"Well, I'm ready to test the backup power unit. There are six more aerators to fix today."

"We haven't even fixed the one!"

His father swiveled to the compound's entrance, a kilometer and a half wide, where distant aerators spewed weakened plumes into the vapor-filled sky. Openings in the compound's ceiling steeped the empty fields in twilight while the grass rippled rich, vibrating green. The air was viciously silent—no more grunts, no thud of hooves, no rip and crunch of grazing. A lonely breeze combed over the emptiness and tickled Caiden's nose with another whiff of death.

Humans were immune to the disease that had killed every bovine across the world, but the contaminated soil would take years to purge before new animals were viable. Pasture lots stood vacant for as far as anyone could see, leaving an entire population doing nothing but waiting for the overseers' orders.

The carcasses had been disposed of the same way as the fat bovines at harvest: corralled at the Flat Docks, two-kilometer-square metal plates, which descended, and the livestock were moved—somewhere, down below—then the plate rose empty.

"What'll happen if it dissolves completely?" The vapor paled and shredded dangerously by the hour—now the same grayish blond as Caiden's hair—and still he couldn't see through it. His curiosity bobbed on the sea of fear poured into him during his years in the Stricture: the gray was all that protected them from harm.

"Trouble will happen. Don't you mind it." His father always deflected or gave Caiden an answer for a child. Fourteen now, Caiden had been chosen for a mechanic determination because his intelligence outclassed him for everything else. He was smart enough to handle real answers.

"But what's up there?" he argued. "Why else spend so much effort keeping up the barrier?"

There could be a ceiling, with massive lights that filtered through to grow the fields, or the ceiling might be the floor of another level, with more people raising strange animals. Perhaps those people grew light itself, and poured it to the pastures, sieved by the clouds.

Caiden scrubbed sweat off his forehead, forgetting his grimy hand again. "The overseers must live up there. Why else do we rarely see them?"

He'd encountered two during his Appraisal at ten years old, when they'd confirmed his worth and assignment, and given him his brand—the mark of merit. He'd had a lot fewer questions, then. They'd worn sharp, hard metal clothes over their figures and faces, molded weirdly or layered in plates, and Caiden couldn't tell if there were bodies beneath those shapes or just parts, like a machine. One overseer had a humanlike shape but was well over two meters tall, the other reshaped itself like jelly. And there had been a third they'd talked to, whom Caiden couldn't see at all.

His father's sigh came out a growl. "They don't come from the sky, and the answers aren't gonna change if you keep asking the same questions."

Caiden recalled the overseers' parting words at Appraisal: *As a mechanic determination, it will become your job to maintain this world, so finely tuned it functions perfectly without us.*

"But why—"

"A mechanic doesn't need curiosity to fix broken things." His father disappeared back into the machine.

Caiden exhaled forcibly, bottled up his frustrations, and crawled back into the maintenance port. The tube was more cramped at fourteen than it had been at ten, but his growth spurt was pending and he still fit in spaces his father could not. The port was lined with cables, chemical wires, and faceplates stenciled in at least eight different languages Caiden hadn't been taught in the Stricture. His father told him to ignore them. And to ignore the blue vials filled with a liquid that vanished when directly observed. And the porous metal of the deepest ducts that seemed to breathe inward and out. *A mechanic doesn't need curiosity.*

Caiden searched for the bolts he thought he'd left in a neat pile.

"The more I understand and answer, the more I can fix." Frustration amplified his words, bouncing them through the metal of the machine.

"Caiden," his father's voice boomed from a chamber below. Reverberations settled in a long pause. "Sometimes knowing doesn't fix things."

Another nonanswer, fit for a child. Caiden gripped a wrench and stared at old wall dents where his frustration had escaped him before. Over time, fatigue dulled that anger. Maybe that was what had robbed his father of questions and answers.

But his friend Leta often said the same thing: "You can't fix everything, Caiden."

I can try.

He found his missing bolts at the back of the port, scattered and rolled into corners. He gathered them up and slapped faceplates into position, wrenching them down tighter than needed.

The adults always said, "This is the way things have always been—nothing's broken."

But it stayed that way because no one tried anything different.

Leta had confided in a nervous whisper, "*Different* is why I'll fail Appraisal." If she could fail and be rejected simply because her mind worked differently, the whole system was broken.

The aerator's oscillating unit was defaced with Caiden's labels and drawings where he'd transformed the bulbous foreign script into imagery or figures. Recent, neatly printed labels stood out beside his younger marks. He hesitated at a pasted-up photo he'd nicked from the Stricture: a foreign landscape with straight trees and intertwined branches. White rocks punctured bluish sand, with pools of water clearer than the ocean he'd once seen. It was beautiful—the place his parents would be retired to when he replaced them. Part of the way things had always been.

"Yes, stop everything." His mother was speaking to his father, and her voice echoed from below, muffled and rounded by the tube. She never visited during work. "Stop, they said. No more repairs."

His father responded, unintelligible through layers of metal.

"I don't know," she replied. "The overseers ordered everyone to gather at the Flat Docks. Caiden!"

He wriggled out of the port. His mother stood below with her arms crossed, swaying nervous as a willow. She was never nervous.

"Down here, hon." She squinted up at him. "And don't—*Caiden!*"

He slid halfway down the aerator's side and grabbed a seam to catch his fall. The edge under his fingers was shiny from years of the same maneuver. Dangling, smiling, he swung to perch on the front ledge, then frowned at his mother's flinty expression. Her eyes weren't on him anymore. Her lips moved in a whisper of quick, whipping words that meant trouble.

Caiden jumped the last couple meters to the ground.

"We have to go." She gripped a handful of his jacket and laid her other hand gently on his shoulder, marshaling him forward with these two conflicting holds. His father followed, wiping soot and worry from his brow.

"Are they sending help?" Caiden squirmed free. His mother tangled her fingers in his as they crossed a causeway between green pastures to a small door in the compound's side. "New animals?"

"Have to neutralize the disease first," his father said.

"A vaccine?" His mother squeezed his hand.

Outside the compound, field vehicles lay abandoned, others jammed around one of the Flat Docks a kilometer away. Crowds streamed to it from other compounds along the road grid, looking like fuel lines in an engine diagram. Movement at farther Docks suggested the order had reached everywhere.

"Stay close." His mother tugged him against her side as they amalgamated into a throng of thousands. Caiden had never seen so many people all together. They dressed in color and style according to their determinations, but otherwise the mob was a mix of shapes, sizes, and colors of people with only the brands on the back of their necks alike. It was clear from the murmurs that no one knew what was going on. This was not "the way things have always been." Worst fears and greatest hopes floated by in whispers like windy grass as Caiden squeezed to the edge of the Flat Docks' huge metal plate.

It lay empty, the guardrails up, the crowds bordered around. Only seven aerators in their sector still trickled. Others much farther away had stopped entirely. There should have been hundreds feeding the gray overhead, which now looked the palest ever.

Caiden said, "We'll be out of time to get the aerators running before the vapor's gone."

"I know..." His father's expression furrowed. The grime on his face couldn't hide suspicion, and his mother's smile couldn't hide her fear. She always had a solution, a stalwart mood, and an answer for Caiden even if it was "Carry on." Now: only wariness.

If everyone's here, then—"Leta."

"She'll be with her own parental unit," his father said.

"Yeah, but—" They weren't kind.

"Caiden!"

He dashed off, ducking the elbows and shoulders of the mob. The children were smothered among the taller bodies, impossible to distinguish. His quick mind sorted through the work rotations, the direction they came from—everyone would have walked straight from their dropped tasks, at predictable speed. He veered and slowed, gaze saccading across familiar faces in the community.

A flicker of bright bluish-purple.

Chicory flowers.

Caiden barked apologies as he shouldered toward the color, lost among tan clothes and oak-dark jerkins. Then he spotted Leta's fawn waves, and swung his arms out to make room in the crowd, as if parting tall grass around a flower. "Hey, there you are."

Leta peered up with dewy hazel eyes. "Cai." She breathed relief. Her knuckles were white around a cluster of chicory, her right arm spasming, a sign of her losing the battle against overstimulation.

Leta's parental unit wasn't in sight, neglectful as ever, and she was winded, rushed from some job or forgotten altogether. Oversized non-determination garments hung off one shoulder, covered her palms, tripped her heels. She crushed herself against Caiden's arm and hugged it fiercely. "It's what the older kids say. The ones who don't pass Appraisal're sent away, like the bovine yearlings."

"Don't be silly, they would have called just the children then, not everyone. And you haven't been appraised yet, anyway."

But she was ten, it was soon. The empathy, sensitivity, and logic that could qualify her as a sublime clinician also crippled her everyday life as the callous people around her set her up to fail. Caiden hugged her, careful of the bruises peeking over her shoulder and forearm, the sight of them igniting a well-worn urge to protect.

"I've got you," he said, and pulled out twigs and leaves stuck in her hair. Her whole right side convulsed softly. The crowds, noise, and light washed a blankness into her face, meaning something in her was shutting down. "You're safe."

Caiden took her hand—firmly, grounding—and back-tracked through the crowd to the Flat Dock edge.

The anxious look on his mother's face was layered with disapproval, but his father smiled in relief. Leta clutched Caiden's right hand in both of hers. His mother took his left.

"The overseers just said gather and wait?" he asked his father.

"Someday you'll learn patience."

Shuffles and gasps rippled through the assembly.

Caiden followed their gazes up. Clouds thinned in a gigantic circle. The air everywhere brightened across the crowds more intensely than the compounds' lights had ever lit the bovines.

A hole burned open overhead and shot a column of blinding white onto the Flat Docks. Shouts and sobs erupted. Caiden stared through the blur of his eyelashes as the light column widened until the entire plate burned white. In distant sectors, the same beams emerged through the gray.

He smashed his mother's hand in a vise grip. She squeezed back.

A massive square descended, black as a ceiling, flickering out the light. The angular mass stretched fifty meters wide on all sides, made of the same irregular panels as the aerators. With a roar, it moved slowly, impossibly, nothing connecting it to the ground.

"I've never..." His mother's whisper died and her mouth hung open.

Someone said, "It's like the threshers, but..."

Massive. Caiden imagined thresher blades peeling out of the hull, descending to mow the crowds.

The thing landed on the Flat Docks' plate with a rumble that juddered up Caiden's soles through his bones.

A fresh bloom of brightness gnawed at the gray above, and beyond that widening hole hung the colors and shapes of unmoving fire. Caiden stood speechless, blinded by afterimage. Leta gaped at the black mass that had landed, and made her voice work enough to whisper, "What is it?"

Caiden forced his face to soften, to smile. "More livestock maybe? Isn't this exciting?" *Stupid thing to say.* He shut up before his voice quavered.

"This isn't adventure, Caiden," Leta muttered. "Not like sneaking to the ocean—this is *different*."

"Different how?"

"The adults. This isn't how it's done."

Caiden attempted to turn his shaking into a chuckle. "The bovine all dead is a new problem. Everything's new now."

The crowd's babble quieted to a hiss of fear, the tension strummed. A grinding roar pummeled the air as the front side of the angular mass slid upward from the base, and two tall figures emerged from the horizontal opening.

"Overseers!" someone shouted. The word repeated, carried with relief and joy through the crowd.

Caiden's eyes widened. Both overseers were human-shaped, one tall and bulky, the other short and slim, and as he remembered from his Appraisal, they were suited from head to toe with plates of metal and straps and a variety of things he couldn't make out: spikes and ribbons, tools, wires, and blocks of white writing like inside the aerators. They wore blue metal plates over their faces, with long slits for eyes and nostrils, holes peppering the place where their mouths would be. Besides their build, they resembled each other exactly, and could be anything beneath their clothes.

"See, it's fine." Caiden forced himself to exhale. "Right, Ma?"

His mother nodded slow, confused.

"People," the shorter overseer said in a muffled yet amplified voice.

The crowd hushed, rapt, with stressed breaths filling the quiet. Caiden's heart hammered, pulse noosing his neck.

"You will be transported to a clean place," the other overseer said in a husky voice amplified the same way. The crowd rippled his words to the back ranks.

"With new *livestock*," the first added with a funny lilt on the final word.

"Come aboard. Slow, orderly." The overseers each moved to a side of the open door, framing the void. "Leave your belongings. Everyone will be provided for."

Caiden glanced at Leta. "See? New animals."

She didn't seem to hear, shut down by the sights and sounds. He let her cling to him as his father herded them both forward.

Caiden asked, "Where could we go that doesn't have infected soil? Up, past the gray?"

"Stay close." His father's voice was tight. "Maybe they discovered clean land past the ocean."

They approached the hollow interior—metallic, dank, and lightless—with a quiet throng pouring in, shoulder to shoulder like the bovines had when squeezed from one pasture to another. Caiden observed the closest overseer. Scratches and holes scarred their mismatched metal clothes, decorated in strange scripts. Their hand rested on a long tool at their hip, resembling the livestock prods but double-railed.

Caiden's father guided him inside and against a wall, where his mother wrapped him and Leta in her strong arms and the mob crammed tight, drowning them in heat and odor.

"Try to keep still." The overseer's words resonated inside.

A roar thrummed to life, and the door descended, squeezing out the orange light. The two overseers remained outside.

Thunder cracked underfoot. Metal bellowed like a thousand animals crying at once. Human wails cut through and the floor shuddered in lurches, forcing Caiden to widen his stance to stay upright. His mother's arms clamped around him.

Children sobbed. Consoling parents hissed in the darkness. Leta remained deathly silent in Caiden's firm grasp, but tremors crashed in her body, nervous system rebelling. He drew her closer.

"Be still, hon." His mother's voice quavered.

She covered his ears with clammy hands and muffled the deafening roar to a thick howl. The rumble infiltrated his bones, deeper-toned than he'd thought any machine could sound.

Are we going up into that fire-sky, or into the ground, where the livestock went?

The inside of machines usually comforted him. There was

safety in their hard shell, and no question to their functioning, but this one stank of tangy fear, had no direction, and his mother's shaking leached into his back as he curled around Leta's trembling in front. He buried his nose in a greasy sleeve and inhaled, tasting the fumes of the gray. His mother's hands over his ears thankfully deadened the sobs.

"Soon," she cooed. "I'm sure we'll be there soon."